PATHFINDER SQUADRON

PATHFINDER SQUADRON

Harold J. Wright

WILLIAM KIMBER · LONDON

First published in Great Britain in 1987 by
WILLIAM KIMBER & CO. LIMITED
100 Jermyn Street, London SW1Y 6EE

*Pathfinder Squadron was published in Australia
under the title Pathfinders "Light the Way"*

"That Old Black Magic"
Composer: Harold Arlen, Words: Johnny Mercer
Copyright 1942—Famous Music Corp., New York.
Reproduced by permission of Chappell & Co. (Australia)
P.O. Box 250, Kings Cross, N.S.W. 2011

Printed and bound in Great Britain by
Biddles Ltd, Guildford and King's Lynn

FOREWORD

By Air Vice-Marshal D.C.T. Bennett, C.B., C.B.E., D.S.O., Former Commander of Pathfinder Force, R.A.F.

Much has been written about World War II, and published as fact or fiction for the education or mis-education of the present-day reader. Here, in this book, we can rest assured that, although presented as a novel, it has maintained authenticity in detail and in atmosphere. The author was himself a Pathfinder.

To be at the receiving end of thousands of guns and searchlights on a major heavily defended target deep in Germany is an experience guaranteed to bite deeply into mind and heart. To go through such high risk, prolonged danger, scores of times seems almost incredible. Harold Wright survived...and so we are privileged to read this book and thus to share the hopes and fears of a Pathfinder crew—the leaders of Bomber Command, the most powerful and vital force of World War II.

I congratulate him.

Don Bennett

= = � = =::::: = = = =

This novel is dedicated to "Cookie", Squadron Leader A.S. Cook, D.F.C., D.F.M., and the crew who were shot down and killed over Frankfurt on 3rd October, 1943 and to the many other Pathfinders who did not make it "back to base".

CHAPTER I

The target lit up. Searchlights stabbed the sky. The fingers of deadly light weaved, crossed, reached out for the bombers overhead. A golden speck appeared like a moth in a beam. Like vicious snakes other beams darted towards it. They merged to concentrate millions of candle-power into the horrifying blue cone.

A plane was caught. The black puffs of heavy ack-ack bit at it. Multi-coloured hosepipes of light flak poured up in a lethal spray. The golden speck flamed orange for a brief instant, it turned red. Then began the crazy side-slipping plunge to earth. It exploded on impact and burnt.

Mannheim had claimed its first victim.

As the first marker planes began the attack, target indicator flares cascaded like great red bunches of grapes. They hung above the city to act as guides to the other bombers. Illuminating flares lit up the ground for the eyes of the other pathfinder bomb-aimers.

"T.Is. down ahead skipper," a bomb-aimer called.

"Right, I see them," a pilot replied, letting down his seat. If they were coned, then his eyes would not be blinded.

The Visual Markers located the aiming-point, two bunches of yellow T.Is. tumbled down over the centre of the city, falling into one another to form a great yellow cluster. Seconds later, several greens appeared. The target was marked for bombing.

"Pathfinders bang on time skip," Jeff Johnson called from behind his pilot. His eyes were on his watch.

"O.K. Navigator."

"Course in 165 degrees, course out of target 270 degrees for ten minutes."

"Roger, going in," Syd. Berry called to his crew, "keep your eyes peeled gunners, fighters around."

With a sigh, he settled himself more comfortably in the cockpit of the Lancaster Y-Yorker. The throttles moved forward under his hand. Mick Ryan, the flight-engineer, took over. He synchronised the four roaring, powerful engines.

The bomb-aimer, Red Ainsworth, set the bomb-sight with deft, steady fingers. He lined up on the target ahead. He had no thought of danger or fear. Here was the excitement he had always yearned for, the excitement his old pre-war life had never given him.

Al Macintyre, the wireless-operator, leant back in his small cramped position. He glanced over the set. He thought, "I've got to keep this damned thing working." It seemed somehow, terribly important, yet he could not analyse the sudden realisation.

The navigator stood near the starboard blister. He peered into the darkness, now split by the terrifying holocaust of bombing below. The brilliant flares hung over the town. Bombs and incendiaries poured down. He was young. He wanted to be unafraid, but his tongue flicked over dry lips.

The two gunners, Harry Evans and Tich Mulgrave, kept their turrets turning. Scanning the blackness of the night for signs of enemy fighters, their eyes never rested. Each had his thoughts, but they were fleeting, unrelated thoughts. They were so busy, so intent.

The attack was under way, in spite of the defences. Incendiaries spread great waves of fire across the alerted city. Wave met wave to form a sea of twinkling light. Blockbusters tore the hearts out of great buildings in quick blossoming mushrooms of violence. Lighter H.Es. tumbled down to add their punishing destructive power to the inferno.

From the inferno, the searchlights still shone. Though many were destroyed, the numbers seemed not to diminish. Flak still poured up from the batteries. The planes roared over. They dropped their loads, fought their way out through the defences. Several were coned. Most won through, but others, dropping like comets with fiery tails, added to the hell of destruction on the ground. They added their twisted, burnt skeletons to the wreckage.

Y-Yorker approached the outer defences, approached the weaving beams.

"How the hell are we getting in there?" a voice asked over the intercomm.

"Don't talk like a sprog," another voice laughed, "we

always get in, blast it. Its the getting out that worries me."

"Quiet crew," Syd called good-humouredly, but his fears were the same.

A beam flicked over the starboard wing-tip. Pressure on the control column and rudder-bar sent Yorker's nose down and round towards the beam. It passed over them. As it groped its searching finger back, they were past. Other beams clutched at them vainly. They slid behind or dived away.

"Bomb-aimer to pilot."

"Roger, go ahead."

"Target coming up, get on course skipper."

The plane's nose rose and settled on course.

"On now, bomb-aimer."

"We're too damned far over to starboard," Red snarled at no one.

"Left-left a lot," he called.

They yawed over.

"Steady, steady ... left-left ... hold it!"

The slight movement satisfied Red.

"Steady ... steady ...," he murmured at intervals as the target crept slowly along the drift wires of the bomb-sight.

The comforting darkness in the plane was suddenly gone. A master beam had them caught. Its satellites swung over to add light to light until the rivets and dirt on the fuselage floor were as visible as in daylight. Black puffs of smoke appeared in the light around them. The deadly puffs of flak. The smell of cordite stung their nostrils. Pieces of shrapnel peppered the plane with the sound of hail. Yorker bucked nervously away from the bursts.

Syd fought against the powerful urge to hurl the Lancaster down and round to escape. Reflexes were too strong however. His left foot pressed involuntarily against the rudder bar slightly.

"Keep the damned thing straight and level," Red yelled angrily, "we'll miss the T.Is. Right ... right ... steady. Level up skipper."

"Straight and level now," Syd shouted back, "get those bloody bombs off, we're coned."

"Think I don't know, I'm nearly blinded," Red growled. He paused for a moment.

9

"Steady ... Bombs gone and to hell with them."

Yorker leapt with appreciation as her bomb load left her. Syd held her steady over the target until the photo had been taken.

"Shut the bomb-doors Mick," he called at last. Throwing the control column forward, he kicked the rudder bar hard starboard.

"Bomb doors closed skipper."

"Hang on chaps, we'll see if we can lose these lights."

They dropped fifteen hundred feet, the speed building up to over two hundred and fifty miles an hour. Then it was drag back on the stick, hard port rudder into a climbing turn. Up and to the left they flew, their speed slackening off. The sudden force of gravity as the plane rose forced Jeff to his knees as he made his way back to the navigation compartment. He secured his instruments and held on as he wrote the time of bombing in his log.

In spite of all Syd's efforts, the lights still held them. The box barrage of flak still followed. The peppering of the plane continued. Yorker weaved and dodged through the sky, up and down, left and right. The speed built up in dives and died nearly to stalling point as Syd forced the nose up viciously. Then it was hard rudder, full throttle, down into another screaming, turning dive, holding that until the strain on plane and man seemed nearly unbearable, then up once again, hard rudder, throttles back. It seemed interminable.

These corkscrew tactics prevented direct hits but the shrapnel of near misses still bit at them. The beams followed them by virtue of their number, passing Yorker from group to group.

"To hell with this," Syd called angrily to the crew on a climb, "This time I'm going to stuff the nose down and keep it down. We must be somewhere near the outer defences by now."

"We're with you skipper," Red replied for the crew.

At the apex of the climb, Syd kicked hard rudder and swung Yorker down. The nose fell, speed mounted rapidly. He checked the turn and urged the plane to greater speed. The airspeed indicator crept round. The lights, the flak puffs, were still there, but this was to be the gamble.

This was it, one way or the other. Height fell as they screamed down.

Suddenly it was all over. They were out.

It seemed unbelievable as the blessed darkness closed in on them when the last beam flicked away.

"Thank God that's over," Red said in a subdued voice.

"You're telling me," Tich added with a burst of machine-gun fire at the last light. It was only a gesture.

A babble of voices sounded over the intercomm as relief set in on the crew. As the tension eased, their voices loosened.

"Shut up, damn you," Jeff yelled over the babble. "Are we on course 2–7–0 skipper?"

"Listen to old track and ground speed," Harry Evans laughed from the mid-upper turret.

"We have just escaped from the very jaws of death," Red bellowed, "and he worries about his navigation."

"Quiet chaps," Syd said with a smile, "on course now Jeff."

"Where are we setting course from skipper in relation to the target?" Jeff demanded as he wrote time of setting course in his log. "Did we come out on course?"

Laughter sounded through the plane.

"Where you been Jeff," Tich shouted, "hiding behind the blackout curtain? We were coned."

"It's all right for you mugs," Jeff snarled, "but I've got to get this damned flying contraption back to England."

"Get on the hero," Red jeered with a laugh.

"O.K. crew," Syd called, "I haven't the slightest clue where we are Jeff, you'd better come out and have a look."

With a growl, Jeff unhooked his intercomm cord and oxygen tube. He turned·off his light. Pulling back the black-out curtain, he stepped forward once more into the cockpit behind the pilot. The target was astern. The red glow of fires burned below the searchlights which still hunted for other bombers as the attack mounted to its climax.

"We're about six miles south of track now," Jeff said to himself as he estimated their position.

He ducked past the curtain once again and fastened it.

He began calculating the new course. He estimated time of arrival at the turning point.

"Nav. to pilot," he called shortly.

"Go ahead Navigator."

"Alter course 2–8–1 degrees. E.T.A. turning point in 7 minutes, 2058 hours."

Syd set the new course on the compass. The plane's nose turned slightly as he altered course.

"On course now Navigator," he said, "keep your eyes skinned gunners, fighters still around. Mick, you check for any damage."

Mick Ryan, his fear still upon him, made his way through the plane. In the light of his small torch he looked over the full length of the plane. The damage fortunately, was slight.

To the north of them, thin white streaks of tracer bullets from a German fighter hammered at an unfortunate bomber, homeward bound, until it burst into flames and fell, a flaming coffin.

Yorker rose and fell in corkscrew motion under the pressure of Syd's hands and feet. Evasive action was necessary to escape the flak and the fighters still to be encountered.

The turning point, an imaginary spot on the ground where a latitude and a longitude line crossed, was passed. The new course was given by Jeff. The long leg to the Dutch Coast and the North Sea began.

Jeff entered time of setting course in his log. Long fingers worked the computer as he calculated the time for arrival at the coast. The results were also entered.

"E.T.A. Dutch Coast at Overflakkee 2157 hours skipper," he said into the microphone of his oxygen mask.

"It's a bloody insult," Red Ainsworth laughed, "to make us fly over a place with a name like that, after what we've just been through."

"Go bag your head," Tich replied through the laughter.

The long dark minutes dragged by as Yorker sped on. The red glow of the target dimmed as they passed over the sleeping land. It dimmed and finally disappeared. Koblenz lit up her searchlights as a bomber strayed off track over the town. The searchlights failed to make a contact and

12

soon went out.

Jeff came forward once again and plugged in his inter-comm cord beside the flight-engineer's. He rested his hand on Mick's shoulder. The big engineer sat beside the pilot, watching the phosphorescent gauges on the instrument panel.

"We should soon pass between Liege and Aachen Syd," Jeff murmured softly, half to himself, as he worriedly strained his tired eyes for the first glimpse of searchlights or flak ahead. This would be the only indication of the position of the towns. He depended upon a sighting of them as a check on his navigation.

Being a navigator meant not only getting the crew to the target and back to base, it meant also staying on track. To stray away from the set track could, and did, mean trouble if they flew over a defended area, and stragglers were easy prey for the German ground controlled fighters. Changes of wind, if not detected, could cause a plane to be miles off track in a short space of time. With radar-aids jammed by the enemy and astro-navigation hindered by the need for constant evasive action, the navigator's job was difficult.

Returning to the nav table, Jeff once again checked his calculations for the time between turning-point and passing Aachen. The result was the same. With an anxious frown on his face he went forward.

"The damn towns should be in sight soon," he said, peering into the darkness ahead.

"Can you see anything on the ground, bomb-aimer?" he asked Red.

"Not a thing Jeff," came the reply.

"Any chance of a pin-point later?"

"Don't think so, it's too dark. I can't see the ground at all."

"Keep trying will you?"

As Jeff finished, a laugh sounded over the intercomm.

"Lost, Jeff?"

The chuckled question angered him.

"No, I just want a check."

"Searchlights starboard bow," Mick's voice came over the ear-phones.

With a sigh of relief, Jeff gazed at the weaving beams cutting the blackness ahead. How strange it was, he thought, that so few minutes before they had put dread and the coldness of fear into him. Now the sight of lights meant relief.

"Searchlights ahead port, Jeff," Syd called moments later.

Jeff watched a plane coned in the beams of Liego, then rushed back to his table.

"South of track skipper," he called, "alter course to 340°, I'll give you correct course in a while. All that mucking about over the target. Don't know where we started from."

He ruled a new track line on the chart laid out on the table, then calculated a position for five minutes ahead on the new course he had given Syd. Mumbling under his breath he ruled and calculated. Finally he wrote the results in his log. Looking at his watch he switched on his microphone.

"Nav. to pilot, alter course to 334 degrees now."

"Roger, 3-3-4, 334 degrees. On course now navigator."

Jeff sat back with a smile at his chart. He now had something to work from. Slowly he rose and went forward. Each town's searchlights were passed. In the dim shaded light on the side of the fuselage, he noted the time on a pad with an estimate of distance.

On Yorker flew, engines pulsating in a monotonous droning. Antwerp's lights showed to their port and slid behind.

"Water ahead navigator, Red's voice called eventually, "can just see it."

"Thank's bomb-aimer, Jeff replied thankfully, "get a pinpoint if you can."

"Right. I can make out the east end of Overflakkee coming up."

In the bomb-aiming compartment, Red took his map out. In the red glow of his dim torch, he compared his map with what he could see of the ground below.

"Bomb-aimer to nav," he called at last, "we'll pass eastern tip of Overflakkee two and a half miles north of

14

track."

Jeff ruled in the track they had flown then waited.

"Bomb-aimer to nav," Red said, then paused, "crossing now."

"Thanks Red."

With a glance at his watch Jeff finished his calculations. A feeling of exhilarated relief filled him. His body relaxed against the seat back. He never failed to experience this feeling as the enemy coast receded. The trip out from base to the target and back to the enemy coast always worried him. To fail to reach the target was a nightmare to him. He took pride in his navigation and staying on track, away from flak areas, meant more to him than a smooth landing did to a pilot.

Constantly working, finding new winds and position fixes as checks to his work, constantly worrying lest he stray from track, Jeff's nerves were stretched taut as violin strings each operation. Once the enemy coast was passed on the way home to base, he allowed the pleasant tiredness to take control. With the drone of the engines in his ears, he laid his head down on the table. For a few short minutes he dozed.

The trip across the North Sea he always considered easy. Within radar range unjammed by the Germans, he could fix his position at any moment. The intensive nerve-wracking navigation over Germany itself was no longer needed. Every ten to fifteen minutes he worked the Gee-set and plotted the fix. The actual speed over the sea determined, he leisurely calculated the time they should arrive over Orfordness.

"Pass the coffee up, Wireless-op," Syd called when the Dutch coast was far behind. He switched over to the automatic pilot, setting Yorker into a slow, shallow dive. He stretched his legs, weary after fighting the controls for so many long hours. His arms ached, but a smile creased his face. Sixteen done, fourteen to go to finish this tour. He thought back with satisfaction to the target. Had he done everything he should have? Was there anything more he could have done? He went over every moment of the action, analysing his own actions and reactions. He was satisfied, even pleased. It did not pay to become over-

15

confident on operations. An occasional bad trip sharpened the wits, providing they lived through it.

The coffee and sweets came forward and were quickly consumed.

Orfordness appeared and disappeared behind them. The last leg of the trip began. Over sleeping, but alert England, they flew on towards base. Base, tucked away in the wolds of North Lincolnshire. Base and bacon and eggs. The lights of other dromes lit up all round them as bombers from other squadrons arrived home.

"Forty miles from base, skipper," Jeff called lazily at length.

"O.K. Jeff. Tell Al to call them up."

Leaning round the partition between their tables, Jeff touched Al's arm.

Al switched on to the intercomm.

"What?" he asked shortly.

"Call up base," Jeff replied, "we're nearly there. E.T.A. 0022 hours."

"Roger."

Turning back to the set, Al called up and reported, giving the E.T.A.

Another op done, he thought. He felt like a passenger at times. This operation, he had done practically nothing. Nothing except listen out to Group's broadcasts and call up base at the finish. However, there were other ops. Ops. where the wireless-operator was the difference between getting back or being lost. He thought back to cloudy nights with no radar. With a grin, he recalled Jeff's constant call for wireless bearings, then he felt better about this operation.

"Quiet crew," Syd's voice called, "I'm calling up."

In the cockpit, he switched on to R/T. The home beacon flashed out its welcome in red morse code. The runway and its satellite lights lit up.

"Hello April control. This is April Y-Yorker, over," Syd called to the W.A.A.F. Sergeant sitting in the control-tower waiting, waiting and counting.

"April Control answering. Y-Yorker circle at 500 feet. Q.F.E. 1004, you are second to land, over."

"Y-Yorker to April Control, roger out."

Syd switched off the R/T.

"Damn it, someone beat us home," he said irritably.

They circled until the other Lancaster made its approach to land. They watched it as they prepared to follow. From the flight-control van at the end of the runway, their signal to land came. Yorker's great weight settled down as the speed decreased. Throttles back, flaps and wheels down, the engine changed its roar, then with a screech of tortured rubber and a shudder, Yorker landed.

"You beaut, a greaser," Red yelled from beside Syd, "more pots you collect."

"Thank God that's over," Tich drily remarked, "I'm as cold as a maggot."

They were home. The swaying taxi-ing to the dispersal was quickly over. The engines stopped and the silence was eerie. Jeff made the last entries in his log then packed his maps and instruments. He looked for his parachute. Suddenly, he realised that over the target he had not given it a thought. A wry grin crinkled his face. He found it and laden with it, his heavy navigation bag and sextant, he clambered over the main spar and down the fuselage.

In the wireless compartment, Al switched off and gave the set an affectionate pat before he followed Jeff.

The gound crew clustered round in the darkness as the crew took off their parachute harnesses. The plane was just as much theirs as it was the flying crew's. They cared for it. They kept it flying. They loved it.

"Sorry Chiefie," Syd said to the Flight-Sergeant in charge. "We did it up a bit for you tonight."

"Everyone O.K.?" he asked, but his eyes were on the huge shape of the bomber outlined against the sky.

"We're right, but she'll have a few holes in her."

"Any other trouble?" the Flight-sergeant asked.

"She flew like a bird and much faster," Syd knew the reply that was wanted.

"Birds don't fly at night, they're not crazy," Harry Evans said cynically. "Anyway, let's get away for a fag."

The crew wandered off, laughing away some of their tension. They pulled crumpled cigarette packets out and lit up. Inhaling deeply they felt the muscles loosen. The tension finally eased. Each looked round, wondering if all the other planes had returned.

The flight van drew up and the pretty W.A.A.F. driver backed it up towards them.

"Good trip?" she asked, really concerned.

Red went over to her, threw his arms round her and kissed her.

"Peggy my darling," he laughed, "you nearly didn't see your most ardent admirer again. There we were, upside down, nothing on the clock but the maker's name—"

With a laugh she looked up into his eyes—"You always say that. Get in. I've got other crews to pick up."

Syd jumped in beside her and the others clambered noisily into the back.

"Are they all back?" Syd asked seriously.

"L-London hadn't called up when I came out," she replied.

"Maddox's crew. Hope they're O.K."

* * *

The de-briefing room was crowded and noisy. Smoke fogged the air. The crews, discussing the operation, clustered round the stoves drinking coffee, or coffee and rum. W.A.A.Fs. handed out the steaming cups to the tired but elated airmen. Security posters looked down from the walls. Parachutes, harnesses, equipment and belongings were strewn over the floor. The crews, dressed in a motley collection of battle-dress, flying-suits and civilian clothes, all crumpled and dirty, mixed with one another. In retelling their doings of the night they put them further behind them. Another one done—one less to do.

"Is L-London back?"

"Not yet, but she still has petrol left anyway."

The interrogation was soon over. The crew sat together in a small de-briefing room to the side of the main one.

They answered the Intelligence Officer's questions. Jeff had his log and chart out to give time and positions. Finally, with a joke they rose and went out to join the others. They were loath to leave the comradeship too soon. Loath to leave before they had retold their story of what had happened.

"L-London—is she back yet?"

"Still overdue, petrol must be running out by now."

The Commanding Officer of the squadron came into the noisy room. He had stayed out on the drome until the last but one had returned. He had scanned the skies and strained to hear L-London. Now, sadly, he came in to speak to his other crews. He went amongst them.

"Oh Berry," he called, when he caught sight of Syd.

"Yes Sir?"

"Sticky do tonight?"

"We got back Sir."

"Pleased you did Berry," he smiled. He liked this young Australian.

"You've done well here," he continued, "you and all your crew. I've had a request from Pathfinders. Want a crew. You know the rules—must have done fifteen trips or more, good crew with good results and must be volunteer. You'd have to do forty-five ops instead of thirty but they count as two tours."

Syd gazed at the lined face before him. The worry of having to send young men out to possible death, night after night, showed. Before Syd could reply, the C.O. continued.

"Well you've done so well here that I wondered if you would be interested. I'm not trying to influence you."

As Syd once again began to speak, the C.O. stopped him.

"I don't want a reply now," he stated bluntly, "chew it over and let me know."   ⋅

"I will have to see Jeff and the crew Sir," Syd said and his mind was in a whirl as he walked away.

Pathfinders!

He was pleased at the honour, but those extra fifteen operations! With mixed feelings he called Jeff over.

"Don't tell the crew yet," he said to the lean navigator "but the Wing-Co. asked me if we'd like to volunteer for Pathfinders."

"Hell, They're a dicy mob," Jeff gasped, "after tonight I'm wondering how we did sixteen and missed drawing a harp or a pitchfork, now you spring this on me. That means forty-five straight off the bat and then I'd have to swot up my nav. all over again. Hell, no wonder I'm going

19

grey."

He paused, grinned and then spoke again.

"Well, when do we go?"

With a laugh, Syd slapped Jeff's shoulder. He knew this long navigator he flew with and Jeff had eased his own doubts and fears. He wanted to go, he appreciated the honour. However, the ever-present fear was there in both of them. The fear of each and every operational flight. they knew the odds against finishing a Main Force tour of thirty ops were great. Too great, they thought, when their friends were lost. The additional fifteen made the odds disproportionately greater.

"It's not as easy as that Jeff," Syd replied, "we'll tell the crew in the morning and see how they feel. It really depends on the lot, not just the two of us."

Jeff ran his fingers through his untidy dark hair.

"I suppose I'll have to worry all night, or morning I should say."

As they turned, Red Ainsworth rushed over. A mug of coffee and rum spilling in his hand, a wide grin was on his face.

"L-London's safe," he yelled. "She got shot up and landed away. Not a scratch in the whole bloody crew."

*   *   *

From the bed, his arms folded behind his head Syd watched the batman throw aside the blackout curtains. The late morning sun flooded the small, austere, sparsely furnished room.

"Morning, Sir," the fussy little Welshman said, "time to get up. Have a good sleep?"

"Not a wink," Syd smiled wryly, his eyes bloodshot from the lack of it.

"That isn't good you know, Sir."

"I'm all right, I've just got a few things on my mind."

As the batman bustled out for shaving water, Syd stared up at the crossbeams of the hut ceiling. He would soon know how the crew felt about going to Pathfinders. Mixed thoughts ran through his own mind, as they had ever since he had gone to bed in the dark of the early morning. Even though he wanted to go, the fear of the extra operations gnawed at his stomach. He was no coward but fear was

there in him, as it is with all true courage. He neither looked upon himself as brave nor as cowardly. He had a job to
do and hoped he did it well. He and the crew were half-
way through their first tour, and the additional fifteen
operations, after that thirty, made the end seem a long
way off.

The crew would make up his mind for him he decided as
he threw the bed-clothes aside.

In the Sergeants' Mess ante-room, as he waited for
lunch, Jeff watched the other crew members. They lolled
about in the armchairs, joking with one another. He, too,
wondered what their reaction would be. He had lost no
sleep, but a vague feeling of disquiet upset him. He, too,
was pondering over those extra fifteen operations. Fifteen
more nerve-wracking battles with changing winds, bad
weather and staying on track.

He felt that all his life, he had known no other existence
but this one. The old life at home in Australia seemed so
distant. His parents he fondly, lovingly, remembered.
However, they seemed to inhabit another world, a world
he barely recalled. His hunger deserted him, abruptly he
stood up.

"I'm going up to the flights," he told Red Ainsworth.

"No lunch?"

"I don't feel hungry."

"What's up, got a fit of the shakes after last night?"
Red's laugh boomed across the room.

Jeff flushed a little.

"Don't try to be so damned funny", he angrily replied,
"nothing's wrong. I don't feel hungry."

Slowly he walked out, hands clenched into fists and
deep in his pockets. In spite of his anger he grinned. Red
was one of the crew he knew would want to go. Not a
single fear it seemed, ever passed through the bomb-
aimer's huge frame. This life was made for men like Red.
They found zest in the constant danger and showed up best
when trouble was worst. Always efficient, but with a
reserve for the moment it was needed. On the surface, Red
appeared to be an easy-going, lazy, untidy person, but
beneath that exterior was another Red. The Red who
become the serious bomb-aimer up in the nose. He would

21

want to go.

Of the others, Jeff was less certain. The wireless-operator, Al, would probably go if the majority decided for it. Al detested change. He felt himself to be a member of this crew. He liked them and would want to stay with them. The flight-engineer, Mick Ryan, and the mid-upper gunner, Harry Evans would not go. Mick was married with a baby, he would not take the risk. Harry was an enigma but Jeff believed he, too, would not go. Tich would he swayed by the others.

Slowly, he made his way to the flight. His head bent, his face serious, he did not notice Syd approaching until the pilot spoke.

"You worried about it too?" Syd asked.

"A bit," Jeff smiled, "mainly I've been wondering how the others will react."

"Me too. Had lunch?"

"No, what about you?"

"I couldn't."

"Me either."

They laughed and felt easier.

The Squadron assembled before the afternoon parade. As they filed in, Jeff drew the members of the crew aside to a corner of the long crew-room.

"The C.O. asked me if we want to join Pathfinders," Syd spoke bluntly. "I told him it's up to you."

He glanced from one to another as they absorbed his words.

"I'm asking you now, do you want to go?"

After pausing for a long moment he continued.

"There's no compulsion, it's a volunteer show and it means doing forty-five instead of thirty. It's more dangerous too as you'd know."

"Hell, Syd," Red burst out with a chuckle, "they're all chop squadrons."

"What are you trying to do, buy us a Burton?" Mick Ryan's voice was serious, his face clouded.

"Syd's not trying to make anyone go Mick," Jeff said quietly, "if any of you don't want to, you can stay here and finish your tour with other crews if the rest of us go."

After he had spoken, Jeff felt relieved. He had made up

his own mind.

"Well, I'm not going," Mick blustered, "it's bad enough to do thirty."

"What about the rest of you?" Syd asked. "If the majority don't want to go, we stay here."

"Hell, I'll be in it," Red grinned, "might become a bloody hero."

One to one.

"Or die young," Harry Evans spoke for the first time. "I'm against it. We shouldn't stick our necks out any further than we have to in this game."

Two refusals, Syd thought. Two to one.

"Tich, and you Al," he said quietly, turning to them, "what about you two?"

"What do you want to do?" Al countered.

"I'm not saying until you make up your minds."

Al pondered for a moment. Then looking slowly from one to the other he answered through dry lips.

"I'll go."

Two to two.

"Tich?"

"I'll go if you do, might as well stick together." His small face puckered up into a frown as he spoke.

Two to three.

"Jeff?"

"I'm for it Syd. Get them over and done with in one belt."

"I'm for going too," Syd added quietly.

The decision made, he felt happier. He realised at last that he was pleased. Pleased that he was going to Pathfinders. He looked at Jeff. They grinned at one another.

"Hello sucker," Jeff said.

CHAPTER 2

THE MEN

Extract from letter:
Pilot Officer Sydney Berry to Mr. & Mrs. Berry, Perth, Australia.

"We're going off to a new squadron tomorrow. It's a kind of special squadron and I can't say anything about it. We lost two of the crew, they aren't coming with us but there are still five of the originals, including me.

Jeff Johnson, the navigator, is another Aussie as you know and comes from Queensland. He's twenty-two, long, lean and dark, a bit of a grumpy type at times in the air, he thinks navigation is the only thing worth doing in the Air Force. He loves it and worries about it, if things aren't going as well as he thinks they should. He calls me the bus-driver by the way. On the ground he's different. Full of fun, untidy, lazy and likes a bit of a bash at the local pub every now and again. He has a rather biting sense of humour at times but there's no nastiness in him.

Al Macintyre, the wireless-operator is from Scotland. He's a medium-sized bloke about twenty-five, sandy hair and sandy gingerish moustache. He's wizard at the set and often when we want a wireless fix from him, the set is in pieces on his table or on the floor of the plane. He's as happy as a dog with two tails when something goes wrong, because he can fiddle with it and pull it to bits. He's a rather serious type and I think he worries about the ops. and getting through. He's engaged to a girl in Edinburgh and writes a letter to her every day. I'm afraid he doesn't get as many back.

The wag of the crew is Red Ainsworth. He's a New Zealander and is built like an elephant. He's over six feet high and looks like a wrestler. He loves a brawl and will fight at the drop of a hat in town after a few beers. Don't get me wrong about him, he never picks the fights himself. Someone else starts them, Red just happily joins in and, laughing most of the time, he finishes them. He's always happy, hasn't a care in the world, so it would seem, and is great fun. His laugh is like an explosion.

The rear-gunner, Tich Mulgrave, is the other original. He's short, blocky, speaks with a north of England accent and would sleep with his guns if you let him. Every day he's working on them. He's pretty quiet type until you get him going, and then he never stops. All the way home over the North Sea after an op., he sings "You are my sunshine." He knows one verse only, and repeats it over and over until everyone tells him to shut up and then he doesn't. He's a good bloke and only twenty.

Of the two new members first we have the mid-upper, "Happy". His name is Clarrie Kemp, he comes from London and is about twenty-nine. When you first meet him, you think—here is the saddest man in bomber-command. We have hardly seen him smile yet. He has a fetish about being clean and washes his hands every few minutes when he can. He would seem to be pessimism personified. When he volunteered to come down with us to the new squadron, he said, "I'll probably go for a Burton (that means shot down) but I'll be in it. You can't last in this game, it ain't in the statistics." He seems a nice chap all the same.

The last of them, the other newcomer, is the flight-engineer, Doug Fletcher, a Canadian about 23. He is a hot-rod (pepped up cars to you) fancier so he tells us. Talks about cars and engines nearly all day and we think he has oil for blood. He wants us to buy a car for the crew so that he can muck about with it. He's of medium height, fair, good looking and a bit of a lad with the ladies I think...."

CHAPTER 3

The new station was a surprise and a disappointment to them.

Surrounded by their luggage, they watched the plane fade into the northern sky. The plane had flown them from their old squadron and was their last link with it. The control-tower behind them was shabby and in need of paint. The long squadron headquarters buildings nearby were in a similar state. There was an air of nonchalant untidiness about all they could see.

It was a dispersed camp, dispersed over the countryside as a protection from bombing attacks. The flight offices and headquarters were over half a mile from the messes. The sleeping huts were half a mile further out again. Huts and billets had been erected in an apparently haphazard fashion in a setting which was attractively rural. They huddled beside trees and merged their camouflage paint with the trees.

The buildings of the small village of Battleson clustered together at the northern edge of the drome itself. The "White Heron", the large village pub, its only one, edged its bowling-green into the perimeter of the drome. It appeared to be extending an invitation to the airmen to enter its hospitable walls.

"What a dump," Clarrie Kemp exclaimed disgustedly after a long look round.

"No spit and polish anyway," Red grinned, "it mightn't be too bad, you're too fussy. I only hope Syd tees up transport soon, I'm taking root standing here."

As he spoke, Syd and Jeff came out of the control-tower. As they walked towards the crew there was a happy look of anticipation on Syd's face.

"Well, we're here officially now," he said with pride in his voice. The die cast, he felt pleased to be with Pathfinders, pleased and proud.

"And now we're here," Red replied, "when do we move from this concrete?"

"I got transport and it's on the way. We'll go to the billets first and they're arranged for now."

"Thank goodness for that," Al said, pointing to his many kit-bags, "I'd hate to have to hump this load very far."

When the van arrived, a clerk from the orderly room sat beside the W.A.A.F. driver. He immediately took charge. The luggage was quickly stowed into the van and directions barked to the pretty young blonde driver. The crew climbed aboard and sat on their gear. Jeff and Syd sat beside the W.A.A.F.

"Welcome to Battleson," she smiled as the truck lurched forward.

"Thanks," Jeff replied over the clashing gears. "It's good to be here."

"I don't always start like this," she stated between clenched teeth as the gears shrieked once again.

"Oh well", Jeff laughed, "you know the old saying—throw them in today, sort them out tomorrow."

She turned and frowned at him.

"I don't think that funny, Flight-Sergeant."

When Jeff laughed, her face grew red. They approached a corner and as she prepared to change down, he gently removed her hand from the gear lever and her foot from the clutch. Their legs touching, he eased the gears in without a sound.

"It's quite easy " he smiled at her, "now press down on the accelerator unless you want us to stall."

Angrily, she stamped her foot down. The truck bucked forward, throwing them against their seats. Her eyes narrowed, she turned to face Jeff.

"That also was not funny, Flight-Sergeant."

"If you don't watch the road, we'll be in a ditch," Jeff said quietly with a grin.

"Oh!" she snapped.

"Don't say it, I'm too young," Jeff replied.

In tense silence, they drove the remainder of the way. Jeff chuckled to himself. Syd smiled as the van drew up outside his billet. With her eyes still facing ahead, the W.A.A.F. sat taut and tense, her lips tightened to a thin, grim line. Syd was quickly unloaded with his luggage and installed. They drove on, again in silence, a further sixty yards to the N.C.O's. quarters.

"Thanks Miss," Jeff smiled down at the girl, as he reached out to open the cabin door. She turned and glared at him. Her face was still flushed and anger shone from her eyes.

"L.A.C.W. to you Flight-Sergeant," she snapped, "and don't thank me, I have to drive this crate. If I'd had a choice I'd have run you into a ditch."

"And spoil a beautiful friendship just when it was budding!"

27

Furiously, she turned away and went to open her own door. She quivered with rage. Jeff reached over and took her hand. She tried to shake free in vain. As she turned again and faced him he smiled.

"Don't be angry, I was only fooling," he said softly, "I'm sure you drive well normally."

"What are you up to now?" she asked suspiciously and with curiosity.

"Nothing," he replied, "I just want to be friends."

"Friends!" she exploded, "I'd rather make friends with Goebbels or Himmler."

"Hey Casanova!"

Red's voice startled them. The big bomb-aimer leant through the window of the van.

"Are you getting out Jeff," he asked, "or are you setting up camp in here?"

The W.A.A.F. tore her hand from Jeff's grasp and hurriedly jumped out. Her trim figure disappeared from Jeff's sight.

"Red, my boy," Jeff mused, "I'm going to see a lot of that girl."

"From what I saw—and heard," Red replied, "you'll need a telescope at a safe distance."

The orderly took them into the long barracks hut. It was one of several side by side. Trees grew behind it with branches spreading out over it as though in protection. It was long, bare, and unlined. Hard iron stretchers lined two walls, fourteen to each side, beside each stretcher a plain steel locker stood. Two flight-sergeants, sprawled on their beds watching the newcomers, were the only occupants. However, most of the beds had owners, as blankets and belongings testified. There were nine vacant.

"New crew eh?" one of the occupants asked as the six hesitantly sought out places.

"Yes, just got in," Al replied, placing his blankets on an empty bed.

"Wouldn't take that one," the other said casually, "last seven bods in that one haven't lasted five ops."

Al hastily picked them up again and wandered further down the hut to another place.

"Wouldn't try that one either, it's another chop bed."

28

As Al once again moved off, looking for another vacant bed, Red walked over to the flight-sergeant. Belligerently, he leant down over the figure lying on the bed.

"One more crack from you, little man," he said ominously," and I'll wring any ops you have left right out of you."

With a cheeky grin. the other glanced up at the big bomb-aimer.

"No offence Tarzan," he said, "just trying to be helpful to the sprogs. The name's Bill Evans."

Holding out his hand, he languidly rose from the bed. They shook hands, each taking the other's measure as he did.

"That's O.K.," Red replied, "it doesn't worry me, but Al's rather touchy."

With a sweep of his hand, Bill indicated a bed in a corner. On the one beside it, the other stranger still lay sprawled.

"That one will do him. No one has slept there long enough for it to become unlucky. Joe Weldon, that's the bloke lying there, snores like a fog-horn. No one stays next to him for more than one night."

"It's a lie!" Joe Weldon yelled, leaping to his feet.

He was a small man of lean athletic build. His hair was completely gray giving him an aged look, different from the youthful appearance of the normal flyer. Bill saw Red and Jeff gazing at it.

"That hair isn't premature either," he grinned, "he's as old as Methuselah; had to put his age back ten years to get in as thirty-four."

The little man slowly walked over to Bill who towered over him.

"Pull your ugly skull in before I feed it to the pigs," he threatened, then turned to the others.

"I'm Joe Weldon."

"I gathered that," Red replied.

After introducing the crew, he threw his gear onto the bed which Al had rejected first.

* * *

In his billet in the officers' quarters, Syd followed the cockney batman who was in charge of the hut. He opened a door and motioned to Syd to go ahead of him.

It was a small two-bed room. A dressing-table stood against one wall separating the beds. A tin dish on an iron frame occupied one corner and another corner had been curtained off to provide hanging space. As Syd gazed round at its austerity, the batman placed his bags on a bed.

"This is your room Sir."

"Anyone in the other bed?" Syd asked.

"Not now Sir," the batman said sadly, "two nice gents they were that had this room. Went missing night before last."

Momentarily a shudder passed through Syd.

"Hope you don't mind Sir."

Syd laughed drily.

"It wouldn't matter if I did, I'm afraid," he said. "If you worried about beds like that in this game, you'd be sleeping in the fields."

"Quite right Sir."

He turned to leave, then paused.

"My name's Robert, by the way Sir," he said softly, "and would you like a cuppa, I've got the pot boiling now?"

"I'd like one very much," Syd replied, holding out his hand, "thanks, and please to meet you Robert."

Self-consciously, the little cockney wiped his hand on his trousers. He shook hands and hurried out.

Syd looked down at the empty bed for an instant, then began his unpacking. As he stowed away his belongings, he scrupulously left room for whoever would eventually share the room with him. When the unpacking and the cup of tea were finished at last, he wandered down to the crew's barracks. Being the only officer in the crew, he felt alone on this station. The others would enter the sergeant's mess together and he envied them. He would face a crowd of strangers on his own. However, he thought happily, Jeff's commission should go through the various channels quickly. He was pleased that he had forced his navigator to action when he had been recommended for a commission on their old squadron. With a smile he recalled Jeff's objections and how, by constant arguing, he had over-ruled those objections until Jeff had agreed to fill in the initial papers.

The crew were still noisily in the process of settling in as he walked into their hut.

"Hi Skipper," Jeff called, "come and give me a hand."

He pointed to a pile of clothing, books and souvenirs accumulated over the months he had been overseas.

"Dump them into that big kit-bag Syd, I won't want them for ages. Don't know why I keep most of it."

In time, they had their beds made and their belongings stowed.

"Well, let's go," Red said. He stood back and surveyed his new home.

"Wait till I have a wash up," Clarrie called.

"Hell Clarrie," Tich growled, "you just had one."

"Won't be a minute."

"Minute be hanged," Tich continued, "he'll be there for half a friggin hour."

The crew left Syd standing at the entrance to the Officers' Mess. He watched them until they had entered the Sergeants' Mess nearby. Taking a deep breath, he went into the ante-room. The late afternoon sun shone through the wide windows of the brick building. It shone on armchairs and tables, upon both of which airmen sat. There was a pleasant hub-bub of noise. One end of the room was crowded with a large billiard table, at the other end chairs were clustered round a brick fireplace. One long side was broken by the bar and a small lounge. The doors to the dining-room opened behind the billiard table.

Syd stood diffidently surveying the scene when a be-ribboned Squadron-Leader noticed him and walked over.

"You're Berry I suppose?"

"Yes Sir."

"Pleased to meet you. I'm Cannover and you'll be in my flight. Like a beer?"

"Thank you Sir, I would."

Syd's eyes strayed to the other's tunic. The D.F.C. and bar were represented there. The flight-commander took him over to the bar. A short, dark, thickset man about forty, with the three stripes of a Wing-Commander and the ribbon of the D.S.O., was arguing with five other officers.

"That's the C.O., Wing-Co. Bolton-Adams. Hyphenated you know," Sqd. Ldr. Cannover stated. "He's arguing that Christopher Marlowe wrote Shakespeare's plays and that Shakespeare was nothing better than a ham actor. Quite batty about Marlowe he is, good old boy every other way."

He barged into the center of the group.

"This is Berry, the new pilot Sir," he interrupted. He introduced Syd round the group, then ordered four beers and four lemonades.

The Commanding Officer paused in his arguing to greet Syd.

"Nice to have you with us," he said, "you've come with a good record. Press on old boy now you're here. I'll see you officially in the morning. Anything you want, let me know."

With that, he took up his argument exactly where he had broken off, including Syd in it.

Cannover took the drinks from the mess steward.

"These four are on tonight," he laughed as he handed out the lemonades.

They were all young men, young men with old faces. Their faces were lined and tired. Tired from the constant strain. Beneath the tiredness and strain however, there was a boyishness which belied their appearance, and a feverishness which seemed to consume them.

During the evening, Syd watched the operational crews. When they left for their final briefing, the mess was strangely quiet. The C.O., Sqd. Ldr. Cannover, the other flight commanders and section leaders left also. Syd went to the bar to order a beer when a tall figure sauntered up to join him.

"Can't have it old man," the newcomer said firmly, "you can't buy a drink in the mess the first night you arrive. 'Tisn't done you know, against all the traditions of the squadron dear boy."

The newcomer was tall, slightly stooped, and dressed in an untidy uniform of R.A.F. grey. Grey eyes twinkled over a huge sandy .moustache. The pilot's wings on his left breast were sewn over the ribbon of the D.F.M. Flight-lieutenant's rings circled his sleeves.

"I'm Jake Anderson," he said, "you must be Syd Berry,

I heard you were coming."

"That's right," Syd replied.

After ordering two beers, Jake led him over to join a group near the billiard table. As they drank, the operational crews returned for their meals. They ate quickly and nervously, their voices loud. As they finished, they trickled out, once again taking the noise with them. As Syd sat down to his meal, late because of the operations, he heard the first planes start up. As he ate, he heard the roar of the first take-off. As he drank his coffee, the drone of the last plane off faded away.

*   *   *

When the remainder of the crew had entered the sergeant's mess, Red and Doug's eyes had lit up. Scattered throughout the large room were groups playing poker and pontoon.

"This'll do me," Red said, rubbing his hands together.

"Me too," Doug replied, "I can just feel those ivories now."

He looked at Red.

"Play pontoon?" he asked.

"Since I was weaned."

"Well let's just go over and win us some dough, guy," he said, taking Red by the arm. "I see a school over there just ripe for plucking."

"See you later," Red grinned at the other four of the crew.

They were too dumbfounded to reply.

This mess was much larger than the officers' and there were many more airmen congregated here. It was a long plain building with the ante-room occupying half its space and dining-room and kitchen the remainder. The anteroom was cluttered with chairs and tables, two fireplaces warmed it. Round these, groups were clustered, talking loudly. A number were at the bar. Cigarette smoke formed a grey haze over all.

"It's fuggy in here," Clarrie complained, "and the place looks dirty."

"Worry about that after we've had a beer," Jeff laughed.

They went over to the bar and ordered.

33

"Hey Jeff," they heard someone call.

Bill Evans, standing in front of a fireplace, beckoned them over.

"Grab a beer and come here," he shouted.

"These are the new sprogs," Joe Weldon told the group as they came up.

"Thanks for the compliment," Jeff replied.

"Think nothing of it."

Like most of the group, Bill and Joe were not drinking. Jeff knew the reason why without being told. Bill was already dressed for ops in battle-dress with a whistle dangling from the collar catch. Under his jacket he wore a heavy white operational sweater. Wound round his neck like a scarf, was a girl's silk stocking. Joe was in battle-dress also.

"Sorry we can't have one with you," Bill said, thirstily eyeing the mugs of beer. "You know how it is."

"The reaper works tonight," Joe added.

"I'll stoke up the fire in the hut for you, before I go to bed," Al said.

"Thanks, we'll need it by the time we get back," Bill laughed.

As time for final briefing drew near, the airmen drifted out until only a small number remained. Here also a quiet descended. As the groups playing cards broke up, Red and Doug rejoined the others.

"Thirty bob up so far," Red boasted, rattling the coins in his pocket. "This squadron will do me."

"How about you, Doug?" Jeff asked the quiet Canadian.

"It's my thirty bob," he replied.

*   *   *

Before going to bed, Al stoked up the fire for Bill and Joe. He piled coke on until the stove was full.

In the morning four beds were unoccupied. Joe was lying fully clothed on the bed beside Al's. His eyes stared, unseeingly, at the roof above. Glancing over at Bill's bed, Al saw it was empty. As he stirred, Joe heard him and turned.

"Bill O.K.?" Al asked.

"Bought it," Joe quietly answered, "silly bastard.

Doesn't seem the same somehow, without him. On Turin of all places, a blasted milkrun and only one kite missing from group, his."

He got up and went over to Bill's locker. Opening it he took out a carton of American cigarettes and two bars of chocolate. He dropped them on Al's bed.

"You might as well have those, instead of the admin. bludgers."

Al watched him go out into the early morning.

Joe never mentioned Bill's name again.

*   *   *

There were no morning parades on the new squadron. The airmen assembled in the crew-room at 0900 hours. It was an informal gathering. The crews lolled against the walls, in the few chairs, on the tables or sat on the floor. However, when the Commanding Officer entered, all hurriedly leapt to their feet and stood at attention until he stood them at ease. The training schedules for the day were given by the flight-commanders and section leaders. Crews were detailed to perform various duties. After the discipline of the old squadron, this informality amazed Syd and the crew. When finally it was over, the airmen jostled one another good naturedly as they went out.

Squadron-Leader Cannover beckoned Syd.

"Berry," he said, "the C.O. will see you and your crew in ten minutes. Get them together and be outside his office then."

"Yes, Sir," Syd replied.

The Commanding Officer's office occupied a corner of the same building. They felt uneasy as they stood there waiting. Another ten minutes passed before the door was finally opened. The Adjutant, a middle-aged balding man called them in. As they entered in single file, each saluted and stood at attention.

"At ease, at ease," the C.O. snapped. He then smiled as he leant back in his chair.

"Well," he said, "you've come with a hell of a good reputation. We'll see if you live up to it here. Reputations can be broken as they are made—by results."

He paused for a moment and the smile left his face.

"We set standards here which we expect and demand

35

you abide by. This is Pathfinders. I'm sure you will abide by them because of your past efforts. If you don't, we don't want to know why you didn't. You didn't and that is all."

He glanced at the intent, if hurt, faces before him. So young, he thought. Another crew full of youthful enthusiasm. Again he felt the strain of sending these lads out on the dangerous flights they had to fly. He could recall every crew which had stood before him as this one was. Of all those, he recalled sadly, so very few remained.

"Our standards are exacting," he continued harshly, putting emotion aside. "There are reasons for them. This game is navigation plus, piloting plus and bomb-aiming plus. We expect each member of our crews to be superior."

He pointed at Jeff.

"Johnson," he said, "you're the navigator. Our work here is based on navigation. It's the most important aspect of the job. Being on track and getting to the target on time so the marker flares fall exactly on the zero-hour, that's your job. You'd better do it well. Timing, timing, timing, that's what we want."

A stubby finger, stabbing at the blotter on his table, punctuated his words. Jeff uneasily shifted his weight from one foot to the other.

"If met winds are hopeless, as they often are, find your own. That's no excuse. You're a navigator and be proud of that and proud of your work. We allow you two minutes either side of zero hour of the time allotted you. Outside that limit you have questions to answer and your answers had better be good."

Red was grinning at Jeff's discomfiture as the C.O. turned and faced him. He hastily smothered the grin.

"Ainsworth, you're the bomb-aimer. The bundles from heaven we drop are more important than bombs. We drop them too, but the Target Indicator Flares are our main load. You're to drop them exactly where you are told. I want none dropping in fields."

Red gave a sigh of relief as the C.O. turned to Syd.

"Berry, I know you are a good pilot and I want you to be better. If the navigator tells you to fly a certain course, you fly that course. If he tells you to fly at a certain airspeed to arrive on target on time, you fly that airspeed and none other."

From man to man, the C.O. went. Each word, each stabbing glance, each thudding blow of blunt-ended finger on blotting pad punched deeper the impression of the exactitude, of the precision the job required. Even the gunners were not spared. Then having addressed each in turn, he relaxed a little.

"Now that's that," he said flatly, "I'm sure you know what I expect."

They smiled self-consciously.

"I suppose you wonder exactly what we do here," he continued in more even tones.

"First of all, this is a Lancaster Squadron and there are four grades of crews here. Supporters, backers-up, illuminators or blind markers, and lastly, visual markers. Working up, there are the supporters. They are the crews in training for the other jobs. They carry only bombs and go in with the early wave to lend weight of numbers. Backers-up go in throughout the raid, to keep the target marked during the attack. They normally drop green Target Indicator Flares or T.Is. as we call them. Above them come the illuminators or blind markers. They work on radar, find the target area by radar and go in before zero hour. They mark the area with red T.Is. and drop illuminating flares which light up the target for the last group, the visual markers. They go in two to four minutes before zero hour to find an actual aiming-point on the ground, a building, a railway or road junction or something which stands out. Have you got that?"

Feeling rather dazed, Syd replied that he had. He felt as he had in the first days of his training, unsure and worried. The genial, talkative officer in the mess, of the night before, seemed so different from the man before him. He began to have fears that he would never measure up to the standards of this new life.

"Now about the shite-hawk, the Pathfinders emblem," the C.O's. voice broke in on his thoughts. "You wear it on your pocket-flap below your wing or wings, but before you wear it, you earn it. To earn it, we expect you to do six good supporter trips at least. You get a temporary award then, if we think you deserve it. It doesn't become yours permanently until you have finished your two tours of forty-five ops unless you are shot down or wounded and taken off flying."

The telephone interrupted him with loud insistence. Syd and the others started at its strident summons. Sheepishly they looked at one another. The C.O. answered, then after talking quietly for a short time he replaced the receiver.

"Well men," he said, facing them once more, "that is all, unless you have any questions."

"I have Sir," Syd replied diffidently, "we always flew Y-Yorker on our old squadron. I wondered if it was possible to have the same here."

The C.O. smiled.

"I like to see you chaps place interest like that in your planes and fortunately for you no one has Yorker here at the moment, so that's alright. ... Anything else?"

"Well, Sir," Syd went on, again uncertain of himself, "Jeff—I mean, Flight-Sergeant Johnson here Sir, was recommended for a commission on his last squadron, but he hasn't had a board yet."

"I'll see about that to-day."

"Thank you Sir," Syd replied and saluted.

The C.O. stopped him as he turned to leave.

"Not so fast Berry,—are you settled in yet?"

"Yes Sir, except for filling in forms."

"Good show, I hope you like it here and have good luck. I'm pleased to have you all with us."

He stood up and walked round his desk. He shook hands smilingly with each of them. Then, as they were filing out of the room, he spoke once again.

"By the way you men, that 'phone call meant ops tonight and you're on. Your first supporter trip. Good luck chaps."

CHAPTER 4

The huge wall map of Europe faced the crews as they noisily settled down for final briefing. Red strands of wool reached out upon it from base, across Europe, to the target. Each length represented a track to be flown. Each pin upon it represented a turning point. Daubs of violent red ink indicated the defended areas to be avoided. They were numerous and close to one another. The red wool passed near several.

Charts were laid out on the tables round which the crews sat. Tracks for the journey were already drawn in. Navigators, their computers in hand, worked out their flight plans from the meteorological information handed out to them as they entered.

Bomb-aimers ruled in the tracks on the detailed maps covering the route. The other members of the crews sat there noisy and bantering. Cigarette smoke rose over their noise in clouds to hang beneath the roof like a grey pall.

"Punch" Andrews stood upon the raised platform. He motioned for silence, the map at his back. He was verging on middle age, balding, inclined to plumpness and with a profile which gave him his nickname. He took his job of Intelligence Officer seriously and felt his job could help these lads. Any crew member could go to "Punch" for information, and he would dig deep in his volumes of detail for the answers. As he stood at the beginning of each final briefing, he always felt sad. He felt that he was also beginning the final chapter in the lives of some before him.

"The target for tonight is once again Turin," he said gazing round at the crews. "After last night most of you know much more about it than I do."

He appreciated the ripple of mirth from the room.

"The milk run again," a voice sounded behind Syd's crew.

Jeff looked up from his calculations with a frown.

"Some bastards always have to sound off," he growled irritably to Syd.

"The route is as shown on the map." Punch continued from the platform. "The nav leader will go into that. The

39

defended areas you will have to watch are shown in red. I want all navigators to mark them on their charts. The target itself is heavily defended for Italy. The quality of the defence is not as great as with a similar German town but it is still heavy."

He paused to let his words have effect. Telling them about the defences they would encounter was difficult. He could state the number of searchlights, heavy and light ack ack, but they could visualise it. They would encounter it.

"There are 410 planes staging this concert for Musso," he went on. "Our own effort is nineteen. One visual marker, four illuminators, six backers up and eight supporters. Zero hour is 2230. Illuminators and supporters go in at zero hour minus six minutes, visual marker at minus four, first backers-up at minus two."

"That's us at zero minus six," Syd thought. He looked at Al and winked. Al grinned in reply. He had been solemnly listening to each word but his mind had been on the set in the plane.

They hadn't been to Italy before. Syd had always wanted to make the trip. The Alps in moonlight must be beautiful he thought. It was normally an easy trip too, even if they had lost a crew last night.

Red stifled a yawn as Punch's voice continued listing times for succeeding backers-up.

The Nav. Leader, long cane pointer in hand, rose as Punch sat down. Tall, lean, and sandy haired, Squadron Leader Richards walked confidently to the front of the platform. Once again the tracks for the journey were listed, this time with bearing and distance. The navigators checked their computations. The turning points were named and indicated with a stab from the long cane pointer.

His manner was superior, his tone the tone of the school master. He had done less operational flights than many of the navigators listening to him, but he considered this not at all. Supremely confident in his own ability, he was unreasonable to suggestions from the men beneath him. He was disliked, he knew it, he cared not at all.

Each Section Leader rose in turn, gave the information required by his men and returned to his seat. Finally the C.O. stood and came forward.

"Well boys," he began, "Turin again. Look after yourselves and have a good trip. I'm going myself so it can't be too tough."

He smiled at the roar of laughter. Smiled and was pleased. They all knew he flew at every opportunity whatever the target. He liked to share the dangers with his crews.

"Does Group Headquarters know Sir?" a voice called from the rear of the room.

"What they don't know won't hurt them," he replied, hoping that Group wouldn't know until after he was in the air.

"Operational meal at 1645," he concluded. "First plane off at 1820."

As Jeff, Red and the others left the hut to go to the flights they looked at Bill's empty bed. Crossing two large fingers Red smiled wordlessly. He missed Bill as they all did but that was the past.

The late winter afternoon was cold. The sun was already hidden behind the hills. On the drome itself, fitters were testing a plane's engines. The droning rose and fell as they walked silently towards the flights.

"Final winds Jeff," Syd said as they entered the crew room. He handed a folder to the navigator.

"Thanks."

Syd had his chart and computer laid out ready on the table. Jeff smiled his thanks. The minutes sped by as he worked. The room grew dark. The lights went on, blackouts went up. Outside there was still the afterglow of the short winter day.

"Finished yet?" Syd asked at last.

"Just about, I'll finish it in the kite. Hope these met. winds are O.K."

"Me too. By the way, we're in X-Xray for tonight. The C.O. promised me Yorker next op."

"Bang on, Skipper," Jeff replied. He began stowing his equipment away.

The locker room was crowded with men in all stages of dress. Gunners were getting into their bulky heated suits. Suits needed in the cold and loneliness of the turrets. Operational white long-sleeved sweaters rubbed against others knitted by loving hands. Long underwear, fancy

41

pyjamas, women's silk stockings all were in evidence. The mascots, the emergency rations and escape kits were stowed away.

Time for take-off drew closer. The room became less crowded. The crews left in groups. Flight vans were outside to take them to the planes.

A Flight's van skidded uncertainly to a stop in front of Syd and his crew.

"I bet I know who's driving," Jeff laughed.

"I suppose that means I ride in the back," Syd replied.

"Well if you don't mind Skipper."

"Would it matter if I did?" Syd grinned as he picked up his gear. He threw it in the back of the van. Jeff threw his in beside Syd's then got into the front beside the blonde W.A.A.F.

"It's you again," she snapped.

"Correct," Jeff replied with a smile, "I'm glad you remember, Jean."

Her head snapped round.

"How did you find out my name?"

"Jean Walton. I rather like it. You don't know how well known you are here. I only had to ask two bods to find out. Besides you don't know how interested I was."

"Well keep your interest to yourself," she said, turning away.

She felt the colour rising to her cheeks. Without looking at Jeff, she could imagine the smile on his lips. She was annoyed at the effect he had upon her. Annoyed, but pleased he had displayed interest also.

"Anyway, how come you're on ops. so soon?" she asked. "You only arrived yesterday."

"Thanks for feeling concerned."

"I'm not, I just wondered."

"Hey Cas," Red's voice boomed from behind their heads," if we stay here much longer we'll miss the op."

Jean started at the suddenness and nearness of the words. She hurriedly pressed the starter. The starter motor whirred and died.

Reaching over Jeff turned the ignition on.

"That should help," he said, smiling.

"Oh!" Jean snapped in exasperation.

She angrily stabbed the starter again. The motor caught. The crew cheered from the rear. They lurched forward.

"Well, I've done it again," Jeff said to the silent girl. "I meant to be so nice too. I was going to say nice things and ask you to forgive me."

The girl remained hunched over the wheel. Her eyes, tightened in a frown, watching the perimeter track. Her lips were an angry slit.

"I really was," Jeff continued. "I was going to be polite. Ask after your health. I wasn't even going to mention driving."

"Huh," she grunted.

"Really. You see I wanted to ask you to come out with me one night."

With a derisive laugh, she looked at him.

"Just as well you didn't," she said, "the answer would be the same."

"I haven't asked you yet," Jeff reminded her.

"Well don't."

She stopped the van near the plane. It stood like an ominous black bird of prey at its dispersal point. She heard Jeff open the cabin door beside him. Then she felt his lips pressed against her cheek. His hand was on her shoulder.

"In case," he said and was gone.

She was too surprised to speak. She smiled in spite of herself. Her fingers touched her cheek. She realised that the long Australian was interesting her—perhaps too much. She leant out the cabin window. In the dull light, she could see him struggling to the plane with his equipment. The heavy, large green nav. bag hung from one shoulder. Over the other, his parachute harness was draped. Parachute and sextant were held in his hands. He turned as he reached the plane. Seeing her still there, he bowed low. His equipment fell round him.

As Syd and the others talked with the ground crew, Jeff climbed up into the plane. He clambered forward, dragging his gear. At the nav position he laid out his charts, his pencil tin and calculator. He checked the equipment in the plane, then completed his flight plan.

He always liked the quiet of this moment. The knot of fear he always felt before an op was there. He worried about his flight plan and checked it. Over both the fear and worry, however, there was a feeling of contentment and achievement.

The crew clambered in. The clamour of their coming sounded through the long narrow tube of the fuselage. He stood up and pushed his seat under the table on its arm. Red pushed past, digging him in the ribs as he went. Syd stopped beside him.

"Well, here it is Jeff," he said, his face drawn from him own feelings, "first op here, hope it's a good one."

"It'll be O.K." Jeff replied with an assurance he didn't feel. They smiled at one another. Each understood the other too well now to cloak his feelings. Each of them had a responsibility. Flying the plane was Syd's. Getting to the target and back was Jeff's.

The time of take-off drew closer. Syd ran through his cockpit drill. Al checked his set and switched on the inter-comm. The gunners tested the turrets and guns. The flight engineer checked his gauges. Red, in the nose, patted the bombsight and saw to the bomb settings and camera. Jeff worried over his flight plan. Below them on the dispersal, the ground crew plugged in the battery cart. All were keyed to a straining point. The fear of what was to come was felt by all. This was always the bad moment. A moment when voices could become raised and angry. The final few minutes before the great bird left the ground with its lethal load. Their thoughts differed in detail but were allied by fear.

From the control tower a blob of red light rose suddenly. It curved up to hang motionless for a moment. Then it dropped quickly to die in a last spurt of flame upon the grass.

Incredulously, Syd watched it die.

"A bloody scrub," he yelled over the intercomm.

Jeff bounced from his seat and rushed forward.

"The bastards," he angrily shouted.

Cries of anger came from the crew. In the nose Red slammed his hand down on the floor in rage.

The fear of a moment before was forgotten, as anger at having the op cancelled took control. After the tension of preparation, this was anti-climax. Jeff crumpled the flight plan in his hand. The flight plan he had worked on and worried over. Syd sat dejected in the cockpit looking at the control column. He felt drained. Slowly he unhooked his seat harness. He climbed down. As he passed Jeff he put his hand on his friend's shoulder.

"Well we don't buy it on this one Jeff," he said soberly.

"To hell with them," Jeff smiled, throwing his gear into the voluminous bag.

"You work for hours on the lousy flight plan, and this happens."

Listlessly, they waited for the van to pick them up. Silent, except for angry exclamations, the group of ground and air crew sat together. The cold dark settled down on them and the plane behind them.

The van arrived, Jeff got into the front seat beside Jean without a word. Behind, them, the crew was also quiet. Jean started gently. The van eased forward. When Jeff made no comment, she looked over at him for the first time. He sat slumped in the seat. She forgot her anger.

"Disappointed?" she asked.

"Worse than that," he replied quietly.

"It seems strange," she continued, looking forward at the perimeter track.

"What does?"

"Most of you hate ops," she said reflectively, "you hate them but you keep on going. Tonight when there's a scrub, you all look as though the end of the world has come."

Jeff glanced at her.

"You don't understand."

She laughed.

"I've driven round this drome for four months now. I know what you'll do."

"What?"

"Well, most of you will go to the mess or town and get good and drunk. The rest will sit and mope."

Jeff smiled. He felt eased. He felt comfortable sitting beside the girl.

"Know why?" she asked, knowing his eyes were on her.

"Go on."

"Well, you've already done half the op before you the

45

leave the ground."

Her voice became serious.

"You're keyed up. You visualise all the worst things that can happen and you say it could be this time. You see the target, the lights, the guns and the fighters. You see them in your minds, and when the plane leaves the ground you've done most of the operation already. There only remains the real danger and the actual flight. That never seems so bad to a lot of you. You enjoy it to a great extent."

Astonished, Jeff looked at the slim pretty girl beside him. He noticed the mistiness of her eyes. The understanding she had shown surprised him.

"When a scrub happens," she continued "you feel cheated. Cheated because you have done so much and it doesn't count. The actual flight didn't happen so you just have to get it out of your systems somehow."

"How do you know all this?" Jeff asked.

"My brother was killed in Pathfinders." Her voice caught for a moment. "That's why I wanted to come here."

Jeff slipped an arm round her shoulders. She leant back against it.

"I really am sorry now that I got off on a wrong foot with you."

He paused for a moment as she stopped the van at the locker room.

"Change your mind about going out with me?" he asked as she turned to face him.

"I think so."

"To-night?"

"I'm off duty in an hour."

The hut was a bedlam of noise as the crew pushed through the blackout curtain. Joe Waldon was changing into his uniform. His battle dress and white operational sweater lay on the floor in an untidy heap.

"I'm going out to get as full as a goog," he called to them, "anyone join me?" Joe had more than the scrub to get out of his system. The empty bed preyed on his mind.

"You can count on me," Red agreed immediately.

"Me too," Tich said.

Doug and Clarrie readily agreed also.

"How about you Al?" Red asked.

"No, I'll nick over to the mess for a while later."

"Jeff?"

"Sorry Red, got a date."

"You sly devil," Red laughed, "get on him will you. They give me the label of lady-killer and we're only here a day and the women are falling all over him. What you got Jeff?"

Jeff grinned self-consciously.

"Break it down Red," he said.

"Break it down nothing," Red's voice bellowed through the room. Beckoning the others to crowd round, he bowed low then curtsied.

"You can be the witnesses my friends," he laughed, "from here and now, I give up the crown so well earned, if I do say to myself, to our friend here. The crown of pash-artist of the crew."

To the sounds of cheering and laughter Jeff fled to the showers.

*　　*　　*

The White Heron played an important part in the life of the squadron. It served as club, pub and hub of relaxation and forgetfulness. Its large white sprawling bulk squatted down contentedly on the outskirts of the village. Facing onto a main north-south road, in peacetime it catered principally for the motoring trade. In war, the villagers and Air Force personnel gathered under its hospitable roof to forget the moment. It was a happy place where laughter dwelt in the midst of strain and sorrow.

Jean and Jeff pushed through the blackout curtain into the lounge. It was crowded and noisy. The smell of beer and cigarettes filled the room. Airmen and W.A.A.F's. mingled with the villagers at the tables, and in front of the fireplace. At the old upright piano a young W.A.A.F. beat out the tune of "Beer Barrel Polka." A dozen discordant voices followed her. Laughing groups filled the air with noise.

Looking up at Jeff, Jean smiled.

"See any room for two thirsty travellers?"

"Not a stool," he replied.

Placing his hands over his ears, he asked, "Isn't there a quieter spot than this?"

"Well there's out back on the verandah."

"Wait till I get two beers and then lead on sport."

The verandah looked out on the gardens and bowling green. It was wide and clung to the L formed by the rear of the hotel. Seats were placed along its length. On Saturdays and Sundays it served as the grandstand for bowling matches. It was quiet and dark. Only a few other couples sat out there in the cold. Side by side, Jean and Jeff sat, watching the moon shining, nearly full, over the trees.

Jeff stared at the golden circle silently.

"I'll give you tuppence," Jean laughed.

"Sorry Jean," Jeff replied looking down at her. "I was just thinking how lovely it looks and how I hate it."

"Bombers' moon?"

"Fighter's moon now, I'm afraid. Every time the moon gets past half. way full I start to get Messerschmidt trembles."

Jean reached over and placed her hand in his.

"You're a funny chap."

"How?"

"Your mood changes so suddenly and so often. You can be so damned silly at times and next moment you act so dammed serious."

Putting his arm round her shoulders he drew her close to him. Her head rested on his shoulder. He leant over and kissed her hair.

"Smells nice."

"See what I mean?" she replied. She gazed up at him.

"And this is not one of my so damned silly moments either."

He lowered his glass onto the floor. Then took the half empty glass of beer from her and placed it down also.

"Who wants beer at a moment like this?" he smiled down at her as he took her in his arms and kissed her. Her lips clung to his for a moment then gently she pushed him away.

"I think you'd better get two more right now," Jean said breathlessly, "you're having much too much effect on me."

"As you command highness," Jeff smiled picking up the glasses.

From the bar came the sound of a bellowing laugh.

"If that isn't Red," he said, "I'm a green T.I."

In the public bar, four of the crew stood at the bar itself, drinking and yarning with Joe Weldon. They had been drinking for some time. Clarrie was growing more morose, Red, Doug and Joe happier. Tich however was becoming belligerent.

"Cheer up Clarrie," Red called to the sad faced gunner, "Don't cry, we'll soon be dead."

Clarrie's hand shot out. He knocked on the wooden bar twice before replying.

"Don't say that, even in jest. It's bad enough as it is without wishing it on us."

"Don't worry sport. Drink up big," Doug urged, "eat drink and sing filthy songs, for tomorrow we have hangovers."

Emptying his glass in one long gulp, he placed it noisily on the bar.

"Boy, I sure have a thirst tonight."

"You and me both," Red agreed, "whoof them down and I'll get another round."

"Tich," Doug said to the small rear-gunner, "finish that off, you half-pint, and I'll buy you double that."

The five feet one that was Tich, jerked rigidly upright.

"Any time you think you're more man than me," he snarled shaking his fist in Doug's face, "just step outside."

"Keep your shirt on," Red laughed, "your hairy chest is showing."

"Fug youse," Tich snapped. He lapsed into silence, breaking it only to grunt a thanks as a beer was put in his hand.

Joe Weldon stood with them, listening to the chatter. Drinking quickly, he was becoming drunk. Pleasantly and forgetfully drunk. He wanted to.

The noise of the crowd in the bar enveloped them. Elbows jostled them as others tried to order. Instead of decreasing, the numbers grew larger.

"Hey Doug," Red said, "let's get out of here into the lounge. There's not enough room here to spit."

"Be right with you."

"Besides," Red continued, "I saw some crows in there and I feel like a bit."

"Be right with you again."

Before they could move Tich broke his silence.

"Watch who you're bloody-well shoving," the rear gunner snarled behind them, "you knocked me fugging beer."

"Quieten down small change before I spend you," an airman replied. "Let a man in."

Red and Doug turned as Tich put in his glass on a window sill. The other airman was a stranger. Of medium height but big build, he dwarfed the little gunner. Tich went over to the newcomer his eyes narrowing with anger. He thrust his face up to the other's.

"You'd be no trouble to cut down to my size."

The stranger was partly drunk. Lifting his hand he shoved Tich away. The little rear-gunner staggered back a step, but immediately jumped forward. The other drew his right arm back to punch as Tich came in. Stretching casually out, Red grabbed it. He spun the stranger round. Then taking hold of collar and tie he twisted and lifted. Choking, the stranger rose on tip toe.

"Naughty," Red calmly leered down, "you can't touch one of my crew. Now get the hell out of here."

With a mighty heave he threw the stranger against the wall. He fell to the floor. Dazedly he rose, fumbling at his collar. With one backwards look he went to a far corner of the bar.

"Why did you butt in?" Tich demanded angrily, "I'd have done him."

Doug took the rear-gunner's arm.

"Tich, you're precious to us," he said patiently, "think how difficult it would have been for us, if you'd broken a hand on him."

"O.K.," Tich replied, "but I'd still have done him."

"Grab the bastard and let's hit the lounge," Red said, there must be some lovelorn W.A.A.F. in there just pining away for a man like me. In fact maybe we'll get a dame for Tich too."

Syd sat reading the "Daily Mirror" in the Officers' Mess. Legs stretched out in front of him, he relaxed in the low soft arm-chair. The large room was occupied only by Syd and few others. They sat reading, writing or quietly drinking. Taking advantage of the early scrub, most had hurried into the nearby towns. On the small table beside him, amid newspapers and magazines, stood a glass of beer. His mind gave only scant attention to the pages before him. His thoughts were still of ops. The few done, the many to do. As he mused he became aware of an attractive if subtle perfume.

Surprisedly he looked up. He gazed into the face of a young W.A.A.F. Section Officer. She stood at the table, a frown on her face, sorting through the newspapers. About twenty-one or two, Syd thought. She was slim, pretty and dark wavy hair framed her face. Even the severity of the uniform seemed softened by her.

"Looking for a paper Ma'am" Syd asked.

"It's always the same," she pouted, "every time I come off duty and look for it, someone's taken the "Mirror"."

Folding the paper he had been reading Syd held it out to her.

"What do you read," he smiled, "the scandal or the comics?"

Glancing down at it, she reddened.

"Oh, you have it," she said, "I'm sorry, I must have sounded awfully rude."

Syd rose. He handed it to her.

"You might as well take it," he replied, "I wasn't even reading it. I was miles away."

"It doesn't matter," she said, endeavouring to return it.

"No really, take it," he persisted, "then sit down here and let me buy you a drink. Then when you have finished the paper you can talk to me for a while and brighten my lonely life. Then I'll go to bed happy and sleep well and dream nice dreams for a change."

As he spoke a smile radiated from her face. Syd watched her eyes sparkle, tiny humour lines wrinkled the corners. Her lips curved invitingly.

"Thank you Sir," she replied at last," you may buy me a sweet sherry, and by the way my name is Paula, Paula Penton."

"Syd, Syd Berry is my handle Paula."

51

Syd hurried off to buy the sherry as she sat down.

CHAPTER 5

Al, already shaved and dressed threw the blackout curtains aside. The morning sun shone through on the six figures still in bed. The others in the billet were all in various stages of dress.

"Don't any of you want breakfast?" he called to the six recumbent figures.

"Go boil your face in oil," Red's voice came from below the blankets he had drawn up to shut out the sun.

"You'll miss it if you don't get up now," Al insisted.

"Here I am dying," Doug groaned, "and all he can think of is food. It's inhuman."

"I only thought you might want to know the time."

With one hand on his head, Doug sat up. Reaching down beside the bed he took hold of a boot.

"If you don't scram in five seconds," he growled, "you'll get this right at your head."

Smiling, Al walked over to Jeff's bed. The navigator was wide awake. He lay back gazing at the ceiling, his hands clasped under his head.

"You were sober last night Jeff and got in early, aren't you coming?"

Doug's boot flew through the air. Missing Al it smashed into the wall. Doug subsided back with a moan.

"Leave Jeff alone too," Red yelled, "he doesn't need food, he's living on love,—and close those blackouts."

Picking up Doug's boot with a grin, Al walked over to the Flight Engineer's bed. Holding the boot up high he let it drop. It crashed to the floor. Four moans followed his hurried exit.

"What the hell's the use," Doug growled sitting up, "little men with hammers are sure using my skull for my anvil."

Jeff threw his blankets aside. He swung his legs over the side of the bed.

"You know the old saying Doug," he said, "the man

that doesn't drink always feels well."

"But he doesn't know it," Joe Weldon muttered as he slowly lifted his head from his pillow. "You have to be as sick as this to really know how well you are when you are well."

Red let out a low moan.

"Repeat that slowly will you," he said, "so I can work it out."

"Don't bother," Doug said as he slowly rose, "it's much too early to have to think."

Jeff picked up his towel and shaving kit.

"You ought to be cases," he said to the others. "Do you know what time you got in?"

"I have not the slightest idea," Red replied.

"It was after three."

"It was sure worth it," Doug said, "Hey, Red, did you finish with that big blonde?"

"No, Tich did."

"Hell! she'd give him three stone."

"That might have been the idea. She had nothing to fear."

Red laughed.

"He reminded her of a teddy bear she had years ago, so she said."

"Oh shut up," Tich snarled, still curled up in bed, his eyes only half open.

"That's a break," Doug said to Red, "I thought the guy must have been dead."

"How did you go Doug?" Red asked.

"On the beam all the way boy," he replied. "How about you?"

"I did alright, but I'm hanged if I can remember her name. I'm supposed to meet her tonight if we're not on ops."

"Me too!"

"But hell," Red continued, "if I can't remember her name or where, how the hell can I? I'll dip out."

*   *   *

Shortly after morning assembly, they knew ops were listed for the night.

The feverish scramble began once again. Hangovers

53

forgotten or ignored, the crew worked.

Tich and Clarrie stripped their guns with loving care. After cleaning the already shining parts, they re-assembled them. At the aircraft, they mounted and calibrated them.

"Might get one tonight Clarrie," Tich said enthusiastically.

"I don't even want to see one," Clarrie replied.

"No ambition."

"My ambition is no trouble ever."

"You're in the wrong game."

Syd and the others came out and joined them. The large plane looked graceful and lacking in evil in the daylight. It stood at its dispersal point expectantly. It seemed to have life as the sunlight shone on its mottled camouflage.

"There she is Jeff," Syd said with pride as he looked at it, "Y-Yorker,—our own kite."

Jeff laughed.

"You sound like a hen with new chickens," he said.

"You feel the same way and you know it."

Walking over to the sergeant in charge of the ground crew, Syd introduced himself. These were the men he would depend upon. He called Jeff and the others over. The ground and air crew met. They liked one another on sight.

"There she is Sir," Sergeant Mackenzie said looking at the Lancaster, "she's brand spankin' new. Came in two days ago."

"You and the skipper are a pair Mac," Red smiled, "I think you both have fallen in love with her."

"You will too," the Scotsman replied, "when she keeps bringing you back to your eggs and bacon."

"If she keeps on doing that," Red said, "I'll give her my eggs and bacon."

Noting the disappointed look on the ground chief's face, Syd motioned Red to be quiet.

"Don't take any notice of him Mac," Syd said, "he's a moron and born to be hanged. He'll come into line with us."

Yorker was spotless. The ground crew had worked to get every mark, every spot of grease off the plane. The interior shone. A long mat stretched up the fuselage.

"Hope you don't mind the mat Sir," Mac apologised, "it helps a lot to keep her clean."

"Good idea," Syd replied, "I'll look after her, and the others will too."

Syd was as pleased with his ground chief as Mac was with Syd. Each considered himself fortunate in finding that the other was prepared to love this structure of metal.

The take-off for the Night Flying Test was uneventful. Jeff checked his navigation equipment, Al his wireless. Both were working perfectly. The gunners swung their turrets. Red worked on the bomb sight. A feeling of satisfaction ran through the crew. The new plane, that was their's, pleased them. Syd threw it round the sky, revelling in its response to the pressure of his hands and feet. He felt exhilarated at its lightness. As he reluctantly turned for base, the starboard outer engine lost power. A discordant note sounded in the roar of the engines. Decrease in the revolutions of the powerful motor caused desynchronisation. Syd worriedly watched the needles on the instrument panel indicate the loss of power.

"Cut the starboard outer, Doug," he called over the intercomm.

"Cutting starboard outer, Skipper," Doug replied, his hands already at work.

He also anxiously watched the great blades slowly come to a standstill.

"This is lovely," he said.

The huge plane seemed to fly equally as well on three engines. It sped towards base. Syd called up the control tower. He requested immediate permission to land. As they made their approach to land, Syd could see the little knot of men standing at their dispersal. Anxious faces peered up. Syd worried Yorker down. The trees drew nearer and sped by faster. The end of the runway came closer. They crossed the drome boundary fence, the great Lancaster settled down. The tyres screamed as the rubber scorched on the concrete. There was no bounce and Yorker ran on.

Mac himself signalled them into the dispersal. As soon as the engines cut, he jumped in. He rushed forward into the cockpit.

"What happened Sir?" he anxiously asked.

"I don't know Mac," Syd replied, "she was flying like a bird, then the starboard outer lost power. It wouldn't keep the revs up. I had to cut it."

Without answering, Mac threw the cockpit window open.

"Strip the starboard outer right away," he screamed to the men below.

"Think she'll be O.K. tonight?" Syd asked.

"Can't say yet, but I'll soon know."

As though apologising for the plane, he continued. "If she's not too bad, you'll fly her."

As he turned away, tears of disappointment shone in his eyes. Syd watched him as he raced down the fuselage. Syd looked round the cockpit. He too felt the disappointment. He felt Yorker had let them down. Then he remembered how she had responded before the trouble. He recalled how beautifully she had reacted, like a feather in a wind, to his pressure.

Lunch was forgotten as the ground crew worked like demons on the engine. Bared of its covers it looked a maze of metal and wire. Mac appeared to be doing a dozen things at once. His hands were sure and fast. Finally he straightened. He wiped his hands on cotton waste and climbed down. A worried frown knitted his brow.

"There are about ten things wrong with it," he said to Syd.

"Can you do it for tonight?" Syd asked.

"Don't know Sir," he sadly answered, "but we'll do our best."

"You can't do more Mac."

As they left, he was climbing back up to the job again.

"Hey Mac," Red called.

"Yes?"

"I'll drag some tea and tucker out for you."

"Thanks a lot Red." Mac's face lit up. He had reviewed his judgment of Red.

*　　*　　*

The briefing was a repetition of the previous day's. Target, tracks, bomb-loads, all were identical. Syd and the others heard hardly a word. All they could think of was

56

Yorker and the ground crew working on her. Doug was absent. As Flight Engineer he stayed by the plane to help.

As the crews shuffled out after final briefing, the C.O. called Syd.

"I've heard about the trouble with Yorker."

"The ground crew are working on her now," Syd said quickly, worried that they might be taken off the op.

The C.O. smiled at Syd's young anxious face.

"I know that. Normally I'd cancel Yorker and you'd fly the spare. Tonight there is no spare. I'm flying."

"Yes, Sir," Syd answered.

"However, if Yorker isn't ready by ten minutes after last take-off time, you don't go. You understand."

"But Sir—," Syd cried.

"No buts, Berry, that's final," the C.O. interrupted, "I know how you feel. It's better to stay back here if you can't make the target within the thirty minutes the raid is scheduled to take."

"Very well sir."

Syd turned despondently away.

"Good luck Berry," the C.O. called after him, "hope you make it O.K."

"Thank you Sir," Syd muttered as he left.

When they were driven to the plane, Mac and the others were still working. Jean stopped the van nearby. She held her face up to Jeff's to be kissed. Then her eyes held his for a long moment, her face serious.

"Luck Jeff."

"Thanks Jean."

He took his gear from Syd and they walked slowly over to Yorker. Mac, Doug and two others on the high platforms were working on the engine. Doug's and Mac's faces and arms were black with grease.

"How is it Mac?" Syd asked.

"How long to take off?" he replied without looking up, "I've lost all track of time."

"Fifteen minutes to first take off," Syd said looking at his watch, "that means we've got fifty-five minutes in all for ours."

Mac straightened his back and sighed.

"We might make it at that."

57

"Anything we can do?" Syd asked.

"Not a thing Sir, except keep out of the way."

Syd laughed as Mac bent his aching back over the engine again. His strong capable hands were quick and sure.

The minutes sped by too quickly. As the light began to fail Mac called for electric lamps. As Doug held it, Mac and the others worked on.

The drome's quiet was broken as the first planes started. The sound of the warm up reverberated round them. Mac's head jerked up as the engines of the plane in the adjoining dispersal began their song of power. He frowned for a moment, wiped his brow with a greasy wrist, then resumed.

The surge of four Merlins heralded the first take off. In the dusk they saw the navigation lights of the plane speed along the runway. The great black shape lifted and was airborne. One by one the others followed. The later backers up started, left their dispersals, taxied round and took off. Syd grew worried. He glanced at his watch every few minutes. The rest of the crew sat silently and despondently together on the grass beside the dispersal.

The flight commander drove up.

"How are you going Berry?" he asked as he got out, "will you make it?"

"I don't know Sir," Syd replied, "Mac's working like a beaver, but there isn't much time left."

"If you can't it's just bad luck."

As he spoke Mac straightened up. A great grin creased his face. He patted the engine.

"She'll do now Sir," he called out exultantly.

"You beaut Mac," Syd cried, the flight commander forgotten. "Come on mob, pile in, five minutes to go."

The test of the engine went perfectly. Mac and his ground crew hurriedly fitted the engine covers. They clambered down and wheeled the platforms away.

"How will we be for time on target Jeff?" Syd asked as he warmed up the other engines.

"If nothing happens," Jeff replied, "we should hit it with the last wave. I can cut the first corner and save a few minutes."

"O.K. Jeff."

They left the dispersal, to the waves and smiles of the ground crew. Mac sank tiredly onto the concrete to wait for the takeoff. Yorker sped along the dark perimeter track as Syd urged her along to catch up precious seconds. He swung her onto the runway immediately he saw the green from the control wagon. He gunned the engines, held Yorker back for a moment on brakes, then gave her her head. She raced down the runway building up speed, then gently and lightly, she rose into the air.

"That's the girl," Red called joyfully.

"Turin here we come!" Tich added from the rear- turret.

"Shut up will you," Jeff yelled over the other voices. "Nav. to pilot."

"Go ahead Navigator."

"Set course right away skipper. 204 degrees true—214 degrees magnetic. Climb on course and belt the engines a bit will you. I'll want 140 miles an hour on the clock when we reach height. That will give us about 180 to 190 true air speed."

A moment passed as Syd swung Yorker round onto course, setting the courses on the compasses as he turned.

"On course, navigator. 204 degrees true—214 degrees magnetic."

"Roger Skipper," Jeff replied, interrupting his calculations, "we're supposed to go by Reading and Selsey Bill to Cabourg on the French coast. I'm cutting corners. We'll edge close to London and alter course for Cabourg from west of London. That way we save over fifteen miles and a little over five minutes."

"Good work Jeff," Syd said. The five minutes saved by Jeff's work would be valuable later.

London was passed unseen. The new course was given and flown. Yorker was flying perfectly. As in the air test, she responded like a light plane to the controls. The English coast was crossed. The line of it, visible in the moonlight dropped behind and was finally lost in darkness. The channel glistened below as they flew towards the enemy coast.

Le Havre was lit up ahead. Searchlights formed a cone above the city as other late comers flew in. They saw one bomber coned. Flak burst round it, but it eluded the defences and flew on. They crossed over Cabourg on track.

In his blacked out compartment, Jeff worked incessantly. Finding new winds from fixes, he altered course and estimated time of arrival at the turning points and target. When satisfied with his calculations, he called Syd on the intercomm.

"We should be on target ten minutes before the end of the raid if you can keep this pace up."

"It's flogging the engines, but they seem all right so far," Syd replied.

The endless evasive action over France went on for forty minutes.

"Engineer to pilot," Doug called, an anxious tone in his voice.

"Go ahead Doug."

"The port outer is losing power Syd."

"Oh hell!" Syd replied and checked on the gauges.

"We can't keep this pace up," Doug continued. "We'll wreck it properly if we do."

"We'll be late on target if we don't," Jeff said, his mind on navigation.

"We won't get there at all if we don't cut down," Doug replied, "we might be able to nurse it along if we slacken down."

"Well its up to you Skipper," Jeff said.

Syd sighed, a frown crumpling his face.

"I'll have to cut down to 130 knots," he said, "how late will that make us?"

Jeff picked up his calculator and worked out the new time.

"Nav to Pilot," he called at length," we'll miss the main attack completely. We'll be the only silly bastards there. Everyone else will be on their way home."

Syd slowly digested this information.

"Listen crew," he said, "we're in our rights in turning back."

"Fug that," Tich snarled.

"Give it a go Skipper," Al spoke for the first time.

"That's what I think too," Syd smiled. "What about you Clarrie?"

"I'm scared to hell now Syd," the mid-upper gunner replied, "I couldn't be any more so, so it don't matter if we do go on. I won't be any worse."

"Good for you Clarrie," Red laughed, "here we go on our own private raid. I only hope the boys have done a good job and blasted the defences."

The decision made, they flew on at reduced power. The long weary miles were left behind. They flew out of radar range.

"Nav to bomb-aimer."

"Go ahead nav."

"Can you see the ground Red?"

"It's not too bad," Red replied peering through the bombing panel. "Do you want a pinpoint?"

"I will shortly," Jeff said, "I think the winds were beginning to change when we ran out of radar. If you can't I'll use astro."

"Should be right Jeff. Where are we?"

Red got out his maps as Jeff gave him an estimated position. He marked the latitude and longitude position with a cross on his chart. After studying the area round the cross for a minute in the dim shaded light, he scanned the country below.

As his eyes became accustomed to the darkness below, the country appeared in clearer detail. Woods, small lakes and streams became visible in the light of the moon. In the distance ahead the Rhone glistened. Hastily he switched on the lamp. On the map he carefully studied the river on either side of the ruled track. Memorising the features he switched off the light. He waited for the river to come nearer.

"Bomb-aimer to nav," he called when they were still some distance away.

"Go ahead Red."

"We're coming up to the Rhone, get your map ready."

"Right Red," Jeff answered, "I think we might be a little north of track."

There was silence while Yorker struggled on under reduced power. The Rhone drew closer.

"Bomb-aimer to Nav." Red called again.

"Roger, Red."

"See the junction of the two streams right on track?"

"Yes Red."

"We'll pass two miles north of that."

Jeff marked the position on his detailed map. He measured off the latitude and longitude and transferred that to his plotting chart.

"Nav," he heard Red, "we're crossing the bank of the Rhone,—right now."

Jeff noted the time in his log and dashed out of the compartment to check the pin point. He saw the junction of the two streams two miles to the south. Satisfied he returned to the hot compartment.

"Thanks Red," he said as he resumed work.

He measured the distance between this position and the last known one. He calculated the speed over the ground. With the protractor he measured the track they had made since that last position. With that information, he calculated the new wind. Applying that wind to the journey still to be flown, he worked out times for arrival at the turning point at Lake Bourget and at the target.

"Nav to Pilot," he said over the intercomm.

"Shoot Jeff," Syd replied.

"E.T.A. Lake Bourget 2344. E.T.A. Turin 0009 and that means we are 19 minutes late for the raid. "I'll give you an alteration of course shortly."

Syd frowned. Nineteen minutes meant that they definitely would be the only ones over the target.

"That's bad Jeff," he said.

"Well there was nothing I could do," Jeff snapped irritably.

"I know Jeff," Syd replied calmly.

Silence fell upon the crew. Each was thinking of being the only plane there. There was no question of not flying on but the miles seemed to vanish behind too quickly.

Fear was there.

Turin showed up red in the distance. The raid had been successful. The glow of fires led them in. A few searchlights swung madly across the sky. There was no flak.

As they drew nearer, more searchlights lit up, stabbing the sky. All too quickly they reached the outer defences.

"Nav to Skipper," Jeff said. "Course out 294 degrees

true 301 degrees magnetic."

"Roger 294 true—301 magnetic."

Syd set the course on the compass.

"Here we go chaps," he said quietly. Sweat oozed out on his brow.

After turning off his light and securing his instruments, Jeff went forward to stand behind the flight engineer. Doug's eyes were fixed on the instrument panel.

"All on our blinking own," Tich said, his voice raised high, "our own private dollop for Musso."

"Pipe down Tich," Red replied.

Red's eyes were fixed on the inferno below, trying to identify the aiming point.

"All T.I.'s. are out Skipper," he said, "but I think I've got the layout. Open the bomb doors."

"O.K. Red," Syd replied.

"Bomb doors open," Doug said moments later.

Searchlights groped for them. One by one they lit up until they became hundreds. Flak burst round them. The light flak guns threw up their spray of multi-coloured shells haphazardly. There seemed no method in the defence. It was wild but widespread. The lights appeared to be under no control, as they dipped, rose and circled. They were coned by a small number but Syd evaded them quickly.

"No guts the Ities," Red bellowed, "they're working from shelters."

As he spoke, Yorker staggered from two near misses.

"You would open your big mouth Red," Clarrie complained from the mid-upper.

"So what," Red replied, "we're still flying. O.K. Skipper, left, left—left—left." He paused while Syd edged Yorker over. "Steady—steady. Coming up. Steady— bombs gone."

Syd held Yorker on course until the photo was taken. Her nose dipped then, as Syd dived to increase speed. They eluded the lights. They were free.

There was relieved silence for a moment.

It seemed incredible that a single plane could escape so lightly over a city with Turin's defences.

"Hell, that was easy," Doug said surprisedly.

"The raid must have bashed them silly," Tich added.

Jeff took a last look at the city blazing behind them. Rushing past the blackout curtain, he sat down in the darkness of the compartment. He felt sick with relief. He had believed that no one could live alone over the target. They had bombed and were still alive. After fastening the blackout, he turned on the light. He entered the details of their attack in his log.

Bombs gone 0009

Heading 109°. Indicated Air Speed 125 m.p.h.

Height 10,000 feet.

Picking up his calculator, he worked out times of arrival at Lake Bourget on their way back.

Mont Blanc, with its mantle of snow, shone white on their starboard. The Alps, grand and majestic in the moonlight, crept by under them. Lake Bourget was passed. The long flight to Cabourg and home began. They continued to lose time. Doug continued to nurse the port outer engine. It kept turning, but at the decreased speed they were left further and further behind the main stream of bombers.

Bourg was passed, the Rhone also. Yorker struggled on. Orleans lit up her lights as they approached. They flew by to the north of the city. Chartres remained unseen and dark. The French coast appeared. They turned over Cabourg on track and set course for England.

"Bomb-aimer to Pilot," Red said when the French coast line had vanished behind them.

"Go ahead Red."

"We'll probably be given up as lost," Red continued with a laugh. "They'll all think we're dead by the time we get back to base."

"You're probably right the way we're crawling along," Syd laughed.

"Jeff, how late will we be?" he asked.

"Near as I can make it," Jeff said, "forty-nine minutes"

"Cut the speed down a bit," Tich said, "let's really worry them."

"Hey cut it out," Al replied, "I'll have to report to base when we get over England."

"You do and you get out and walk," Red snarled.

"But I have to," Al repeated.

"Bust a valve or something," Tich laughed, "they'll never know."

"Skipper," Al said, "what do you want me to do?"

"Let 'em worry Al," Syd replied, "let 'em worry."

They crossed the coast at Selsey Bill. As they flew over England, they felt they were home. They were tired, but the op. was nearly over. One more done.

Dromes lit up for bombers and training planes dotted the country. Beacons flashed their identity in morse code. Their own beacon finally beckoned. When they flew over base Syd finally called up the control tower, fifty three minutes overdue.

Mac was waiting at the dispersal for them as Syd swung Yorker in and braked her to a stop. He swung the door open.

"My God," he said as they clambered out," I thought you'd bought it."

"Not tonight Mac," Red grinned.

Mac waited for Syd.

"Something wrong?" he asked.

"Sorry Mac," Syd replied, "the port outer went duff on us. We nursed it along, but it's probably had it by now."

Mac looked up at the dark bulk of the plane. Disappointment showed on his face.

"It's not your fault Mac," Syd said, "the starboard outer behaved perfectly."

"I don't know what's wrong," the ground chief replied in a flat tone, "we went over her with a fine tooth comb when she arrived."

"Mac, you must remember she was still new. A kite's like a racehorse. A two year old starting off hits all the trouble you can imagine. Give it a race or two and if it's any good it's a winner."

Mac looked up.

"Yorker, believe me," Syd continued, "is like that. She'll be a winner. She flies like a bird when she's right."

"Thanks Skipper," Mac said, brightness in his voice again, "we'll have her right for you tomorrow night, even if we have to change the whole damn engine. I'll get on it right away."

"What?" Syd said, "aren't you going to sleep?"

65

"Had a doze while you were away."

"Like hell he did Sir," a member of the ground crew interrupted, "he prowled up and down the dispersal all night. When you were overdue I thought he'd wear a track in it."

"Shut up," Mac snarled, "get the platforms out under the port outer and get the light ready."

"O.K. Chief," the other replied with a smile.

"I thought it might have been the starboard outer gone wrong again," Mac said self-consciously.

"I know Mac, but I think you ought to get to bed."

"I'll be all right Sir," he replied. "Good-night and I'm glad you're back."

"By the way Mac, I think you'll find a few flak holes," Syd smiled as he left.

Jeff was waiting as the van drew up. Jean stopped with a jerk. She waited until he got in. Turning to him, tears glistening in her eyes she put a hand on his arm.

"You great goon," she said, "you had me worried to death. I thought you must have gone. They'd already listed you missing."

"Only the good die young," Jeff laughed.

CHAPTER 6

THE MESS

Their home for the present, the present unreal.
Lolling in armchairs a beer at their side.
In front of the fire watching the flames.
Glancing through papers, just skimming through.
Reading the war news they helped to write.

*　　*　　*

Mac:　　Hey Bill, it says here we were out on ops last night.

Bill:　　No!

Mac:　　Here it is in black and white. We started fires.

66

Bill: You don't say.

Mac: One guy counted 30 fires over the target.

Bill: How many did you count Mac?

Mac: Brother I was too busy worrying about yours truly to count even one.

Bill: Me too.

Mac: No wonder our navigator was bang on the target last night. It says here, I quote, "Crossing the Alps, bomber crews saw fires ahead of them." I thought our bloke cheated, he probably told the pilot just to point the nose of the kite at the fires.

*　　*　　*

Ear bash sessions that last till morn.
The talk of women, the talk of leave.
The talk of loving, the talk of grog.
The talk of playing some sport in the past.
The planes they flew, the men they knew still living—
The dead they did not mention.

*　　*　　*

Bunny: You know, these kites remind me of dames.

Rowley: How do you mean?

Bunny: Well just look at them. Some are easy, compliant, do anything you want with them. Another one won't do a damn thing you want. Fight you at every turn. Some are neat and lovely. Others are like slovenly, sloppy, slatterns. You find them mean, hungry, generous, hateful or lovable.

Rowley: Go on dear boy.

Bunny: Just take B-Beer, my kite. It's another type again. She's flying perfectly. You think you have her measure. Everything is going beautifully—for a while. Suddenly, bingo. You don't know what's hit you. She tears out on a rampage. In a moment everything goes haywire and you don't know why.

Rowley: I know what you mean. It's no wonder we call them 'she'.

Letters from home and letters to write.
The future so dim, the present so near.
The past was the past so shaded and lost.

Fear ever present but hidden they thought.
Young faces old, lined and twitching.
Voices raised high, their owners unknowing.
Signs of the nerves drawn taut.

       *   *   *

George: The place gives me the willies.

Arthur: You and me both.

George: Every day you sit around waiting for ops to be on. Then if they are on you get out to the plane and they scrub it. You traipse back to the mess then and the bar's shut. If you do get airborne something goes wrong and you have to turn back. Bar shut again. If you get airborne and nothing goes wrong with the kite, you're on the leg to the target when the navigator gets you off track or something. A Jerry Messerschmidt wanders up, has a go, and you cop the lot.

Arthur: Happy thought.

George: Then if you get airborne, you reach the target on time, you drop your bombs and the flak will probably get you in the belly. If you get there, have no trouble from flak and you get all the way back to England—you find base fog-bound. They divert you to some joint in the middle of nowhere that you've never heard of. You get there, they don't expect you. You get a scratch meal that's lousy, as well as cold. There are no spare beds, you sleep on the floor, cold as a frog, with one blanket, and still no bar open.

Arthur: For heaven's sake shut up, you depress me.

George: Me too.

Arthur: Well let's flog the grog.

       *   *   *

Discussions on home lands, home towns and homes.
Arguments friendly on customs and race.
Jobs rudely dissected, the jobs of prewar.
Insults both thrown and taken in fun.
Religion a topic respected, discussed but little,
    argued never—

       *   *   *

Vince: I don't know how any sensible thinking person

	could be an atheist.
Eric:	Why not?
Vince:	Well just start with the earth itself.
Eric:	O.K. we start there.
Vince:	Where did it come from?
Eric:	If I say thrown off some sun in the dim dark eons long since past, what then?
Vince:	That Sun then, where did it come from? You just can't say it came from some other sun ad infinitum. You can get back if you wish to a gaseous state which some say was the beginning of all things, if you want to.
Eric:	I mightn't want to.
Vince:	The way I look at it, is that there must be a beginning and a prime mover. You can go back and back but you must finally come to that fact. I call the prime mover my God. I'm a navigator and I can navigate by the stars, the moon and sun. Their movements through the universe are so exact that astronomers can calculate their position in the heavens a thousand years from now. That precision just can't happen, it must be planned and who could plan it but a being above the laws of nature. A God.
Eric:	If there is a God, above the laws of nature, why do we have war?
Vince:	I believe God gave man free will. If man wants to make a silly ass of himself he can. Wars are man made. Anyway, how about a game of billiards?

*   *   *

Jokes and horseplay, fun and games.
Mess parties wild, lasting all night.
Quiet some evenings drowsy and pleasant.
Singers and mimics surprisedly good
Might brighten an evening and lighten the mood.
The piano beats out a ribald tune
And voices join in for the chorus.

*   *   *

The war's not over, can they last it?
The ops aren't finished, the last's not done.

To heck with worry, let's make our plans.
The war must end. What then?
The old job waits. So what?
Straight from school. What's there?

*   *   *

Pete: If I ever get through the bloody war I'm going to get me a farm miles past the black stump.

Marty: Where the hell's that?

Pete: Way past back of beyond.

Marty: Oh!

Pete: They'll deliver the mail once every three years if you want it. Then if another war breaks out, I don't want to hear about it till its over. I don't want to see another drome or plane for the rest of my life.

Marty: Me for the South Seas boy. All I want is to get on one of those islands. I'll just sit in the sun sipping gin and bitters. One beautiful dusky Dorothy Lamour will be fanning me if its warm while another, who'll look a bit like Hedy Lamarr, will stroke my hair. And all the time the coconuts will be growing me copra. Boy, that's the life for me.

Pete: First thing you've got to do is finish ops.

*   *   *

CHAPTER 7

The sun was high in the sky next day as the crews began to trickle up to the flight office building. Tiredness, after the long flight to Turin, etched lines on their faces.

As Syd entered C Flight office, Squadron Leader Cannover beckoned to him.

"Berry," he said with a smile, "you appear to have won a reputation for you and your crew after last night's effort. Good show old man, even if I don't entirely approve of bombing a target on your own. We've plotted your photo and it's bang on the aiming-point."

"That's good, Sir," Syd replied self-consciously.

"The C.O. wanted to see you as soon as you came up to the flights. You'd better dash over there right away."

"Do you know why Sir?" Syd asked, wondering why he was being summoned.

"Haven't a clue my boy, but get cracking."

The Adjutant showed Syd into the Commanding Officer's office. The Wing Commander was seated at his desk studying one of the many memos and forms which were piled up in front of him. Syd saluted and stood at attention.

"At ease Berry," Wing Commander Bolton-Adams said, looking up for a moment. "This paper work binds me, but it has to be done."

He wrote for a short time, put the papers into the out tray, then leaned back in his chair making it squeal in protest. Looking up at Syd, his face was non-committal.

"Have to give you a blast Berry," he stated flatly. "Can't have our crews risking their lives and their planes like you did last night without a blast, so Group tells me. So you're blasted. O.K.?"

Syd automatically came slowly to attention, as he replied with reddening face.

"Yes Sir."

The Wing Commander's face lightened into a grin, he leant over and held out his hand to shake Syd's.

"That's the official verdict," he said, "now unofficially I'm bloody pleased with your effort. It was a wizard show, but if you quote me, I'll have you posted."

"I'm glad of that Sir," Syd replied with relief.

"You and your crew showed very commendable press on spirit," the C.O. continued, "that's what we want here. Don't do it again of course. I wouldn't want that, good crews are scarce enough. Can't have you committing suicide."

"Yes Sir."

"Eh?"

"I mean No Sir."

"Wouldn't have got away with it over the Ruhr, you know."

"I realise that Sir."

"Remember it in the future. No more pranks like this one. Very pleased it went so well for you. Ten flak holes too I hear. Must have been a bit hot eh?"

"It wasn't too bad Sir," Syd replied, "actually, I thought we got off lightly. I had expected it to be worse over the target."

"Right spirit my boy, never underestimate the enemy, don't get over confident. Always on your toes. That's the idea. I'm putting you up as backer-up right away."

Syd's face lit up. The Commanding Officer smiled at his keenness.

"Pleases you eh?" he said. "I'm glad. Your navigator was recommended for a commission from your old squadron. I've signed his papers. No need for an interview, he seems to be on the ball. Did a good job last night. Tell him he'll see Air Commodore Bennett within the month. Shouldn't have any trouble there if he knows his gen."

"He does Sir," Syd declared, "he does a fine job, and thank you Sir."

Turning to some forms on his table, the C.O. riffled through them until he found what he sought.

"I see you came here without taking leave first," he said.

"That's right Sir."

"Well you are overdue for some, so you can whizz off for seven days starting three days hence."

"Thank you Sir."

"Well that's all Berry," the C.O. stated, a note of finality in his voice, "keep up the good work."

"We hope to Sir."

Squadron Leader Richards frowned immediately he saw Jeff enter the navigation center. His eyes narrowed as he called him over.

"Johnson!," he barked.

"Yes Sir?"

"I've been going over your log and chart of last night," he snarled. "When I give you tracks to fly at briefing, I expect you to fly them. I don't want you gallivanting all over England on your own say-so."

Jeff felt his blood rise. Tired still from the worry and length of the flight, he was irritated by the Navigation Officer's brusque manner.

"I had to save time," he snapped in return, "we took off twenty minutes late as my log clearly shows."

"Don't be impertinent. I don't care what excuse you

think you have. I insist on you flying the tracks given."

Jeff placed both hands on the table. He leaned over towards the seated Richards. His voice rose slightly.

"I don't suppose the safety of the crew matters a damn to you?"

"Don't adopt that tone with me."

"What tone can you expect?"

"I wouldn't say any more, Johnson."

"I'm just expected to take this stupid attitude then?"

"Johnson, I warned you. As you know, you were recommended for a commission on your last squadron. You can expect it to go no further after this."

The Navigation Leader's voice grew shrill. His face worked angrily. His hand thudded down on the table.

"I'm telling you now that you won't get it."

"That suits me," Jeff shouted back, "if you want to be so damned petty."

"Get out Johnson, get out."

"I'm going—Sir."

As he left the room, Jeff angrily slammed the door. He stalked out of the building into the winter sunlight. Cursing to himself at the small-mindedness of the Navigation Leader, he walked past Syd without seeing him.

"Hey, Jeff," Syd called after him.

"Sorry skipper, I didn't see you. I'm so damned mad at Richards, I could spit red T.I.'s."

"Never mind him, we're little heroes according to the C.O. To quote, 'You showed very commendable press on spirit'."

Jeff smiled cynically.

"According to that honourable officer and gentleman Richards, I'm just one flea jump ahead of a court-martial, for disobeying his precious instructions and flight plan."

"Hell, what's wrong with him" Syd asked incredulously.

Jeff's retelling of the heated exchange lost nothing in detail. As he described the Navigation Leaders's attitude and his threat to block Jeff's commission, Syd also became angry.

"Don't worry about that," Syd said, "the C.O. has already signed your commission papers."

"Well, that's a dollop in his eye anyway, even if the

73

hound stops it from there."

"I don't think he can," Syd replied seriously, "not now. We've got an hour before lunch, feel like ducking out to the kite?"

"Might as well," Jeff said despondently, "ops. on tonight?"

"No, we're stood down so Cannover told us."

"Hell, we'll never get this tour finished at this rate."

Syd turned in surprise.

"You'll get your gutful of ops before we're through with this squadron."

They walked silently together for a moment then Syd propped and laughed.

"I nearly forgot the most important bit of news," he exclaimed, "we go on leave in three days."

"You little beaut," Jeff replied brightening up, "look out London, here I come."

At the dispersal, Mac and the ground crew were still busy on Yorker. The two port engines were bare, stripped of their covers. The fitters swarmed over them.

Mac grinned as the two flying crew walked towards him. His eyes were bloodshot and his face was lined from lack of sleep. He and his uniform were greased strained and tired in appearance, but his florid face was happy.

"How is she Mac?" Syd asked.

"She's right now," came the reply. "The port outer had an oil blockage. We fixed that and luckily there was no damage. We've checked both port engines and the starboard inner. They shouldn't give any trouble now."

"Hell!" Jeff gasped in amazement, "you've been working."

With a wry grin, Mac turned and faced Yorker.

"I don't want you to have any more strife," he replied.

"Thanks Mac," Syd said, "there aren't any ops tonight anyway. You should be able to get some sleep at least."

"I could do with it Sir."

*   *   *

After a lazy morning at the flight office, Syd entered the Mess dining-room. Immediately he saw Paula Penton sitting alone. He went over to her table.

"Eating alone by choice," he smiled down at her, "or

may I sit?"

"Be seated by all means," she replied, "join me in a Welsh rarebit. That's all there is today I'm afraid."

Syd made a grimace.

"I wouldn't mind," he said, "if they made it eatable but when they dish it out, it looks, tastes and is as tough as leather."

The W.A.A.F. waitress put the meal in front of Syd.

"I always see you alone in the Mess," Paula remarked as he took up knife and fork. "Aren't there any other officers in your crew?"

"Not yet," Syd replied between chews, "the navigator should get his through soon and I'm working on getting commissions for some of the others."

"It must be lonely for you in the mess."

"It is at times. I've made some friends here but you get close to a crew. It becomes like your family somehow. You have differences of opinion, fights and squabbles, but there is a bond there, which is hard to describe. You wouldn't swap one of them."

Paula looked at the serious young face opposite. She wanted to reach over and touch it. She began to feel possessive towards this airman who, though older in years, seemed younger than she was.

"I know a little of how you feel," she said quietly. "none of the friends I made in training have commissions. I felt out of it myself when I was first posted here."

"You're in intelligence aren't you?" Syd asked.

"Yes, and no cracks," she laughed in reply.

The meal was soon over. Syd and Paula walked out into the ante-room together.

"Cigarette?" Syd said, offering his packet.

"Thanks."

"Coffee?"

"Please."

Syd was filling the two cups from the steaming urn, when the untidy stooped figure of Jake Anderson sidled up. He sat on the edge of the table while Syd poured.

"Doing a line with Miss Untouchable, I see," he grinned.

"Miss Untouchable?"

75

Jake's long arm swept the room, indicating all the airmen lounging around.

"I don't think that there would be one bod in the room, including myself, who hasn't cast his field service cap at her feet and tried to do a line with her."

"So?" Syd said self-consciously.

"So," Jake replied, "good luck old boy, you'll need it. No one has ever got past 'good afternoon' with her."

"Thanks for nothing," Syd said with a laugh, and turned away with the cups of coffee.

As he returned to where Paula sat, he felt a dozen pairs of eyes watching him.

"Your coffee Paula," he said, handing the small cup and saucer to her.

"Thank you, and what was Jake saying to you?" he smiled.

"Oh nothing."

"That would be a change for Jake."

Syd sat silent as Paula drank her coffee. She slowly put the cup and saucer on a table beside her.

"I'm free this afternoon," she said hesitantly. "I was thinking of going for a cycle ride round the district somewhere."

She paused for a moment, watching Syd.

A pleased, if surprised look appeared on his face.

"Could I go with you?" he asked hurriedly.

"If you want to."

Wondering why she had spoken as she did, Paula also wondered at the shy feeling which had come over her. Her poise was very rarely ruffled, she prided herself upon that. Sitting beside Syd however, as she spoke, she felt the armour of her self-possession becoming dented. She wondered if the fact that she had seen Jake Anderson talking to Syd had made her speak as she did.

"Of course," Syd added, "that is if I can get away from the flight office. I should be able to, there are no ops on."

She smiled at him.

"Well I must be off now. See you at three, outside the mess here."

"I'll be here."

He watched her neat figure wend its way across the room

until it disappeared through the door.

As he sat back, he became aware of Jake Anderson standing beside him. The tall pilot was grinning down at him.

"One word from you," Syd said quickly, "and I'll brain you."

*   *   *

The airmen assembled in the crew-room after lunch. Amid the din Syd collected his crew together. They lounged around with Red and Doug sitting on the floor, their backs against the wall.

"Well chaps," Syd said bluntly, "we go on leave in three days' time."

The group instantly became alert.

"Bang on," Red shouted, springing to his feet, "leave at last. Let me at it."

Doug scrambled up, a wide grin split his face.

"Where are we going?" he asked Red.

"Haven't a clue yet," the big bomb-aimer bellowed. "A few days in London I suppose, to see how many of my old mates have gone for a Burton, then Lady Ryder's scheme for the rest."

"That sounds good to me," Doug replied thoughtfully, "mind if I tag along?"

"The more the merrier," Red laughed. "Any more for a week of hilarity and bash?"

Jeff smiled at them. He could visualise the trouble the two big, wild, good-natured crew mates could get into.

"Not for me," he said, "I'm too young to go to the boob and I'll bet the C.O.'s new car you finish there, I know your form."

Clarrie's sad voice broke in.

"We still have three days to go," he reminded them, "we might buy it before we even get the leave."

Red glanced at the gunner then turned to Doug and winked. Doug quietly opened the window behind him, unnoticed by Clarrie. He opened it wide then the two of them advanced upon Clarrie.

"Mother's little ray of sunshine," Red grinned evilly, "always trying to brighten up the party."

Clarrie backed away. They pounced on him, one on

77

either side. Taking an arm and a leg each they lifted him off the floor and swung him to and fro.

"Put me down," Clarrie yelled.

"Right you are chum."

Clarrie's arms and legs waved about as they threw him through the open window. As he picked himself up, the window slammed shut.

*　　*　　*

Shortly after three, Syd watched Paula ride up to meet him as he waited outside the Officers' Mess. Both wore overcoats. The cold bleak day had brought a rosiness to Paula's cheeks. Her skirt had inched up above her knees, showing her long, slim, grey-stockinged legs.

"You look like a young schoolgirl," Syd laughed, as she slipped off the bike to stand by his side. Her breath came fast.

"Sorry I'm a bit late," she apologised, "the Queen Bee got me to do a job before I could get away."

"I'm glad you could come," Syd said soberly. "Where are we off to?"

"Let's just ride and make no plans."

"Suits me."

Climbing onto their cycles, they rode out onto the main road which passed beside the drome.

"Left or right?" Syd asked.

"Left," Paula replied with a laugh, "the hill isn't so steep that way."

They rode up the incline in silence. Nearing the top, a lane turned to the left off the main road.

"That looks interesting," Syd remarked.

Turning into it, they rode between hedges, hedges which shut out the view on either side of them. Trees, winter-bare, arched gaunt branches making lacework of the blue sky above. The war seemed remote. Syd glanced at Paula and she returned his glance with a smile.

"Cosy and private," she spoke his thoughts.

The lane continued its private way for a mile and a half before the hedges thinned. Fields and farmhouses came into view. The lacy twigs overhead, dropped behind. The feeling of communion with one another continued. Their bikes were side by side, so close, that they could have reached out and touched. The lane slid behind, as their legs pushed upon the pedals. It met another and became a small road. They passed through a village. An old style inn, a few houses and a shop, and they were out among the fields again. When they had been cycling for over an hour, they came to a steep hill.

"This beats me, I'm afraid," Paula laughed breathlessly as she jumped off.

Syd followed suit. Reaching out, he took hold of Paula's handlebars. Then, a cycle on either side of him, they walked to the crest of the hill.

"Let's sit here for a while," Paula remarked, going over to a stile beside the road. She jumped up onto it.

Laying the cycles down on the grassy bank at the verge of the road, Syd went over to her. Taking off her cap, Paula shook her hair out. It fell in a dark shower.

"You look lovely, Paula," Syd said, leaning against the stile and gazing into her face.

She flushed under his gaze. Once again, she felt her self-possession leave her. She smiled down into his eyes. He placed his hand over hers.

"We'd better look at the view I'm afraid," Paula said quickly.

"I am," grinned in reply.

"Well, look at the other view."

They were on the crest. Behind and in front of them, the fields stretched. Broken by clumps of trees and hedgerows, they stretched to further fields and further hills. Farm buildings were dotted here and there. The smoke rose from them, lazily in the still cold air. Above them, the sky's blue was broken by thin white cloud. The sun was low in the sky. A bird's cry broke the silence.

"You wouldn't think there was a war on, sitting here," Syd sighed, as he sat down on the step below Paula. He looked out over the peaceful countryside.

"It is beautiful." Paula replied, "I love this country."

"I do myself now."

Paula glanced down at him.

"Didn't you at first?" she asked.

"It's hard to describe," Syd said, smiling up at the girl, "I did and I didn't. I hated the cold and the rain. I liked the

79

land and the people. They are so different in their own country. In Australia I met a lot of real stinkers who were English. I think I was biased against England before I came over. But after meeting them here, I got to like England and the English people, especially a dark-haired beautiful 'pommy' lass looking down at me right now."

"Don't get personal," Paula laughed. Before she could get down from the stile, Syd had risen. He lifted her down gently. He stood with his hands still around her waist. They stood close to one another for a long moment.

"You delightful person," he breathed softly.

"You're a nice person yourself," Paula replied, "and I'm afraid you are very disturbing."

"I hope so," Syd said firmly. "Let's not go back to the station now. We can have dinner at that pub in the village we passed through. It looked nice."

Gently working free from his hands, Paula ran her hand over her hair. She fixed her cap before replying in a doubtful tone.

"Do you think we should?"

"Why not?"

"Won't they say something at the station?"

"Who cares? I don't. If I want to have dinner in a pub with a girl I like, I damn well will."

Laughing, Paula reached out and took his hand.

"I love that independent way of yours," she said, "but what about the bikes? We don't have lights."

"Miss Knocker, I believe," Syd said, "We'll push them if needs be."

"The Anchor" was tucked away off the road among trees. The few houses of the village snuggled up close to it. It was old. A wooden sign with an ornate anchor painted upon it swung on a chain from above the large oaken door. Darkness was setting in as they entered the inn. The interior was in keeping. They went into a small foyer, to the left was the bar, two small dark wooden alcoves nestled in corners near windows. A large fireplace beckoned them with its warmth. The bar occupied the full length of one wall. Along the remaining wall space, benches were lined up. The only customers were two elderly men playing dominoes at an alcove.

"Good evening, young people," a warm voice hailed them from behind the bar. He was a large dark-haired jolly person, dressed simply in a naval high-necked sweater and dark trousers. "What will you have?"

"Paula?" Syd asked.

"A sweet sherry and then dinner," she replied "I'm famished."

"And you sir?"

"A beer will do me."

They sat on high stools at the bar.

"By the way," the publican said, "the name's Josh Lyons."

Syd introduced Paula and himself.

"We don't have many Air Force people here," Josh remarked, as he placed their drinks in front of them.

"That's strange," Syd replied, "we come from quite close."

"I thought you did but we're off the beaten track a bit. There are closer pubs for those that walk or cycle. If they have a car they push on further down the main road."

Syd turned to Paula. "I must remember that for the next time I can entice you out for an evening."

As they sipped their drinks, the publican left the bar to arrange for their dinner.

They ate in a long combined lounge-dining room. Comfortable cushioned chairs snuggled up to a large fireplace. Attractive original seascapes were hung on the panelled walls. The darkened beamed ceiling was low. The polished wood floor was strewn with thick colourful rugs.

They sat down at an antique oak table. The publican's wife, a slim, still good-looking, middle-aged woman served them. After dinner they drowsily sat in a long settee in front of the fire. After a long silence Paula sighed.

"Why the sigh?" Syd asked lazily.

"I was just thinking," Paula said softly, "about what you said earlier."

"What was that?"

"That the day was so peaceful you wouldn't think that there was a war on."

Turning to look at her, Syd replied, "It's possibly the fact that a war is on that makes us realise how peaceful that land really is. Contrast, you know."

"Contrast or not," Paula smiled, "it has been a wonderful day. I've enjoyed it immensely."

Stretching out luxuriously, she turned and looked up at Syd. He reached out and putting an arm behind her, drew her towards him. Their eyes locked, then he bent his head and kissed her long and tenderly. Paula's hands crept up to his shoulders. For a long moment their lips met. Then, suddenly, she pushed him away, gently but firmly.

"No Syd," she said softly, "we mustn't."

"Why not Paula?" he asked, a hint of astonishment and disappointment in his voice.

"I want no entanglements," she said sadly, "especially with air crew."

"I don't understand."

"I'm afraid Syd. It's easy for you."

She put a finger on his lips as he went to speak.

"Now don't misunderstand me," she continued. "I don't want to become another weeping, sad girl who's had someone she loves listed missing on ops."

Syd watched the flames make patterns against the soot-darkened fireplace. Slowly he took his arm away from her shoulders.

"Unfortunately for me, Paula dear," he said, "I can understand exactly how you feel. I felt the same. Any other time that I began to be serious about a girl or she about me, I'd back off quick."

Turning to look at her, he saw tears in her eyes. He put his hands over hers.

"I should have said until I met you."

He stood up. Reaching down, he took hold of her wrists and gently pulled her to her feet.

"I could fall in love with you so hard it would hurt," he said with a wry grin.

"Let's have a drink at the bar," he said, "and then we'll whiz off to our virtuous couches at the drome."

His mood changed, he went on. "I go on leave in three days."

"I didn't know."

"So you won't have me around for seven days."

She put her hand on his arm.

"Don't be like that, please Syd."

He smiled, looking down into her face.

"I didn't mean it that way, Paula my dear. I'm going to think things over on leave and if I come back with my ideas changed, watch your step young lady. You'll be the target to be attacked and you'd better do some thinking about it yourself."

* * *

When Jeff got out to the dispersal point the following morning, he looked for Syd and found him lying on his back with eyes closed on the grass beside the dispersal.

"What the hell are you moping about?"

Y-Yorker reared up behind them.

"Nothing," Syd murmured.

"Well, off your beam and get mobile," Jeff laughed, nudging Syd with his shoe, "we're on ops and we have an N.F.T. to do."

Slowly Syd got up from the grass.

"Women," he said.

"I thought it might be that. Care to tell Uncle Jeff?"

"It's nothing really."

"I wouldn't call that dark-haired goddess nothing old man."

Turning angrily, Syd snapped at Jeff.

"What do you know about her?"

Jeff jumped back in mock fright, his hands raised defensively.

"Keep your sidcot on sport," he laughed, "we all know you took her out. You can't walk to the latrine here without someone knowing. Jean told me. She saw you coming back."

"Let's forget it Jeff," Syd said. "We'd better get this bloody N.F.T. over."

With a sweeping bow, Jeff motioned the pilot towards the plane.

"Your wish is my command, bus-driver."

With a laugh, Syd joined the remainder of the crew at the plane.

Yorker flew perfectly. Each crew member tested his equipment. No fault was found. After ten minutes Syd turned for base perfectly content with the machine he flew.

He landed and taxied round the perimeter track.

Mac signalled them into the dispersal. He was waiting by the fuselage door as they climbed out.

"Like a bird Mac," Syd said.

"I hope so."

"Bird's right," Clarrie's sad voice broke in, "they fly by day only and then not in the rain."

Red and Doug advanced upon him, threatening grins on their faces.

"Leave me alone you two," Clarrie yelled. "Skipper, stop them."

The two stopped and innocently looked at one another.

"Were you going to hurt Mr. Happiness Incorporated, Red?" Doug asked.

"Wouldn't even consider it Doug," the big bomb-aimer replied. "I wouldn't have it on my conscience. We might get the chop tonight and as I was bailing out, if I was able to, I'd think to myself, I'd struck our lovable mid-upper. Couldn't bear it."

With a suppressed shudder, Clarrie turned away.

"You two can't be serious," he said. "It's bad enough, without you putting the mock on us."

As he walked over to the flight van, Jeff joined him.

"Don't mind them Clarrie," Jeff said. "They're just the same underneath. That's their way of covering up."

"I wish I could be the same," the gunner said sadly.

"You can't be Clarrie. That's their particular individual brand. None of us others could be like those two."

"Thank goodness," Clarrie said fervently.

Jeff seated himself beside Jean in the van. "Hi beautiful," he said, "how's my favourite W.A.A.F.?"

"Not quite sure she is," Jean replied.

"If there weren't so many bods around, I'd soon show you that you were."

"Frightened or shy?" she said with a teasing smile.

As he reached out to take her in his arms, she slipped away. She jumped out of the van and stood looking at his grinning face.

"Don't you dare, not here," she cried.

"Who's frightened now?" Jeff replied. "Come and sit down, I've news for you."

Cautiously, Jean got back behind the steering-wheel. "Well?" she asked suspiciously.

"Have you any leave coming up?" Jeff asked.

"I've a 48-hour pass due now, why?"

Jeff held both her hands as he spoke.

"Now don't get me wrong," he said, "but I'm on leave in three days, if I don't get the chop of course."

The tone of his voice kept her silent. She looked up at him and smiled at his serious expression.

"Could you spend those two days with me?" he continued.

"Where?"

"Anywhere!"

"Well I had intended going home to my parents in Worcester. I've written to them."

A frown clouded his face. She felt a pang of disappointment. For a moment, she thought he was just the same as many of the other men she had met. A few kisses then an invitation to spend a weekend with them in some secluded resort. She had hoped that Jeff was different.

"Do you think they'd mind," he asked pensively, "if I stayed at a pub in town and saw you a few times when you were there?"

She laughed. Her disappointment vanished. He was different, she decided. She felt relief and realised how much he had come to mean to her.

"You had me worried for a moment," she said.

"Why?"

"Don't ask."

"Well, could I come?"

"Of course Jeff, but not to an hotel. Mum and Dad would be only too pleased to have you stay with us. There's plenty of room."

"Are you sure?" I wouldn't want to trouble them."

"You wouldn't. I'll arrange my 48 and write them again."

He slid his arm behind her. He drew her closer and kissed her hair. "I want to meet them," he whispered, his lips close to her hair, "I have designs on their daughter."

* * *

The target was Turin again. The crews stamped noisily

85

into the briefing room.

"Fug it," Tich Mulgrave snarled as he saw the target marked on the large wall map. "Don't they know any other bloody towns?"

"It's an easy stooge," Doug replied.

"Suppose it is," Tich said quietening down, "but it's emptied a few beds here."

The briefing ran its normal course. When it was over, Squadron-Leader Cannover came up to Syd.

"Well Berry," he smiled, "your first T.I. drop."

"Yes Sir."

"Well, you earned it."

"Thank you sir."

"Have a good trip this time. Don't get into any trouble."

"I hope not Sir," Syd replied with a smile, "we seem to be getting more than our share lately."

"Well press on rewardless," the Flight-Commander said as he turned away.

Their role for this operation was to go in with the third wave of backers-up ten minutes after zero hour. At zero hour minus six minutes the raid would begin as usual with supporters and blind-markers. The target would be illuminated with flares for the visual markers, who would drop yellow target indicators at zero hour minus four minutes. At zero minus two, the first wave of backers-up would drop green target indicators on the yellows, to continue the marking of the aiming-point. Each succeeding six minutes throughout the attack, another wave would drop greens to ensure that the aiming-point continued to be pinpointed.

The complete ground crew was gathered at the dispersal point as the van drew up.

"Luck Jeff," Jean whispered as he got out. "You'd better get back now that I have my 48."

"I'd walk back," he laughed, "rather than miss that."

Mac strode over to meet Syd. He took the parachute harness from him and carried it over to the plane.

"If there is any trouble with Yorker this time, you can have me court-martialled."

Syd laughed and slapped the serious Flight-sergeant on the shoulders.

"Everything bang on now Mac?"

"To the last nut."

Yorker ran up beautifully. The four powerful Merlins roared as though straining at leashes. They seemed impatient to be off on the trip. The whole plane quivered with expectancy. The crew settled into their positions. Yorker slipped out of the dispersal to the waves of the ground crew.

The moonlit trip across England and France was uneventful for them. Le Havre claimed a victim which had flown off track over the town. Jeff's navigation was good and they had passed the coast on track and out of trouble. On the long leg across France they saw planes coned and others in combat with enemy fighters. However, they encountered nothing. Lake Bourget slipped behind. The Alps were passed.

"How's our E.T.A. Target, Navigator?" Syd called.

"Should be bang-on Skipper," Jeff replied. "Got a pinpoint a few minutes ago. E.T.A. Target 0010: That's thirty seconds over our zero."

Making quick calculations Jeff switched on his microphone again.

"Nav to Pilot."

"Go ahead Jeff."

"Increase your airspeed to 1–7–0, 170 knots, now."

"Roger," Syd called, "increased airspeed 1–7–0 knots."

Yorker responded immediately. She was flying perfectly.

"Skipper," Jeff continued, "that will give us a true air speed at this height of 202 knots and that makes a ground speed of 237 knots with this wind. That will eat up that 30 seconds."

"Can the double talk Jeff," Doug's voice broke in, "we'll be there on time will we?"

"That's what I said," Jeff snapped back.

Smiling to himself, Syd told the crew to quieten down. Over the intercomm, he could hear Jeff angrily mumbling to himself as he worked on his charts. A suppressed laugh sounded also. He liked his crew like this. They were alert. The barbs they threw at one another in the air were not meant to hurt. They eased the tension felt by all.

The searchlights of Turin suddenly split the sky ahead. Illuminating flares and red T.I.s tumbled down among the lights.

"Pilot to navigator."

"Go ahead Skipper."

"T.I.s down ahead."

Jeff glanced at his watch. "Twenty-five seconds late Syd."

After two minutes, yellow clusters joined the red. Greens cascaded shortly after. The raid was begun. Load after load of heavy explosive spread destruction below the coloured target indicators. Incendiaries splashed through the town with sparkling light. Planes were coned but as the crew approached they saw only one drop from the sky in a flaming mass.

They evaded the groping searchlights and the flak. They dropped their bombs and green target indicators on the clusters of others below.

"Bombs away," Red shouted.

"Ten seconds ahead of time," Jeff said smugly.

"Bang on Jeff," Syd remarked, "good show."

The city below was aflame. Bombs burst in a terrific concentration. The crew saw shock waves ripple out from the bursts. Incendiaries in great swathes of horrible fire, swept through large areas of the city. The defences became haphazard. The searchlights wavered, they circled without design. The flak lessened in intensity. Yorker passed through the outer defences once more without incident. The long trip home began.

"That was easy," Tich's voice spoke over the inter-comm.

"We're not home yet," Clarrie answered.

"Keep it up Happy," Red laughed, "brighten us up."

Italy, the Alps, then France sped by beneath them once again without trouble. The Channel was crossed. Finally, in the distance their beacon flashed out its welcoming morse. The drome's lights were lit up.

As they taxied into the dispersal, they saw the full ground-crew still there. The four engines fell silent. The jubilant crew tumbled out to be surrounded by the ground staff.

"How did she fly?" one asked.

"Like a feather," Syd answered, "perfect."

Mac's deep voice broke in. "She really was Sir?"

"She couldn't be better."

"In fact Mac," Red laughed, "I'll bring her over my eggs and bacon now if you like."

Mac grinned. The long hours of work had borne fruit.

"Well boys," he said with pride, "We'll put her to bed."

CHAPTER 8

LEAVE

"How come you're driving us on leave?" Jeff asked as the crew piled into the van.

"I bribed the transport officer," Jean laughed in reply.

"I wouldn't be surprised if that wasn't the gospel truth."

The van meandered through the station, out the main gates and headed for Huntingdon.

The crew had not operated on the two nights previous to their leave, but the squadron had gone out once for the loss of one crew. Although they had been kept busy during the days, on training, the time had passed slowly.

As the van drew up in front of the railway station, the crew jumped out with their baggage.

"Into the bar men," Doug called, "time for a few quickies before the train comes."

As the others filed after Doug, Jeff stayed in the cabin of the truck with Jean.

"See you on Saturday," he said.

"You'd better," she replied, "after my writing such nice things about you to mum and dad."

"Did you tell them I was an Australian?"

"Yes, why?"

"They will probably think you are going around with a black-fellow."

Jean threw her head back and laughed.

"It's not funny," Jeff said, "a lot do."

"Well, dad doesn't, and he'll explain to my mother. I'll meet you at the railway station."

In the distance, the train sounded. Jeff kissed her, hard and long.

"Well don't go out with any strange men while I'm gone."

"I only know one strange man and you're it. All the others are normal."

"You be careful how you talk about your future husband."

She leaned over and kissed him again.

"You're getting big ideas," she said, then pushed him gently out of the cabin.

She leaned over and kissed him again.

"Get going, or you'll miss your train. I'll wave you goodbye from here."

The train was slowing as Jeff pushed into the bar.

"Come on mob," he yelled, "down your grog. We'll miss the thing."

"Oh boy," Doug shouted back, "be right with you."

They hurriedly finished their beers and dashed out onto the platform.

Tich and Al remained behind as the others piled into a carriage. They watched as the train pulled out. Their's north, went later.

"Feel like another beer Al?" Tich asked at last.

"Might as well," the quiet Scot replied. "We have quite a while to wait."

They wandered back to the bar. Tich ordered two drinks.

"You'll be glad to get back to Edinburgh," he said.

"I will at that," Al replied, "It's a long time since I've laid my eyes on Bess."

Looking into his glass of beer, Tich sighed.

"What's wrong lad?" Al asked.

"Oh nothing," Tich replied, "but it must be nice to have something to go back to, like Bess."

"But ye have your family."

Tich simply smiled in reply.

"Drink that up," he said, "It's your turn to buy."

90

*　　*　　*

Tich stood outside the door of his home for five minutes. He heard his mother's querulous voice rise in anger through the panels. The earliest memory of his twenty years was his mother's voice, lashing and hurting. The lines of strain on his face had prematurely aged him in looks but he felt immature and young. Without knocking, he slowly pushed the door open.

He looked round the parlour. It was as he remembered it, clean, neat and tidy. Every article was in its accustomed place. It still looked unused and unlived in. The kitchen had become the living-room for the family. From it voices rose, his mother's high and shrill, his father's soft and patient.

As he walked through the house, he smiled cynically to himself. The conquering hero returns. He did not consider himself a hero, but the phrase passed through his mind.

"Hullo ma, hullo pa," he said as he entered the kitchen and put his kit-bag down.

Giving a gasp of surprise, Mrs. Mulgrave dropped the cup she was drying up. It fell into the sink and shattered.

"Look what you made me do," she cried, "do you have to creep up on a body?"

"Hullo son," his father said quietly with a smile. He sat in an easy chair by the fire. His left arm was encased in plaster from the elbow down to the wrist.

Going over to his mother, Tich kissed her on the cheek. "How are you, Ma?"

"How do you expect me to be?" she said, looking him up and down. "You've put on weight, but you look much older."

"I'm alright," he replied.

"I wish I could say the same for your father," his mother said. "Just when we need every penny, with you and your brother Perce away in the forces, he falls at the factory and breaks his arm."

Tich looked over at his father who winked and smiled.

"Take that smile off your face Henry," Mrs. Mulgrave snapped. "You've nothing to smile about. Losing overtime and all."

"Ah Mother," he replied, "break it down a bit. The

91

boy's just home."

For a moment her face softened, but immediately the sharp, thin-lipped mask returned.

She was a short, thin woman of middle age. The beauty of her youth had given way to wrinkles. Her eyes had hardened, her lips had thinned, her hair was tied in a severe bun. They all formed the picture of a hard embittered woman. She was dressed austerely and neatly in black.

Her husband was also short, but stocky and powerful. Good humour showed in his face, humour his wife's constant lashing could not erase.

"I suppose you brought home a month's washing too," his mother stated flatly.

"I brought a lot," Tich replied, "but I intended doing it myself tomorrow."

"Leave it," she said with a sigh, "I'll fit it in somehow. Had anything to eat?"

Though Tich insisted that he had eaten, he was forced to sit down and eat a hurriedly prepared meal. The meal was punctuated with complaints. The state of his clothes, why he had not written more often, his brother Perce in the Army in Africa, his father—all were subjects for criticism. As she criticised, his mother was constantly on the move. She was a nervous, restless woman. She bounced from task to task like a ping pong ball in a box. She seemed never to find satisfaction in the completion of anything. Through it all, his father sat, accepting the criticism, ignoring the barbs.

After the meal, Tich helped dry the dishes. He then sat down, trying to make conversation. After an hour of his father's monosyllable and his mother's multi-syllable replies, he fled to the local pub.

As he walked down the blacked-out street, he felt the same disappointment he always felt on returning home after a time away. He always hoped for a miracle to happen while he was away. He always hoped that his mother would have changed to a loving, laughing person. She never had. Tears welled in his eyes. He brushed them away. He felt young and lonely.

A few of his old pre-war friends were in the pub. They were working in industrial plants and were exempt from military service. They treated him like a hero. He went home nearly drunk.

*   *   *

It had been a hectic two days in London for the five crew-mates, Jeff mused, as he nursed his hangover on the train to Worcester.

A constant round of pubs, shows, more pubs; of girls for Red and Doug, and lack of sleep.

Odd happenings brought a smile to his lips in spite of his headache. The doorman at the "Chez Moi" Club who greeted the Australians with verses from "The Bastard from the Bush." Doug's wolf-whistle at the variety show when the showgirl posed in the nude. Clarrie thickly stating that he was sober, then immediately falling through the doorway of the select hotel. Red being the butt of offensive remarks from two large Americans until he could stand it no longer. He had cracked their heads together with a grin and stood aside as they fell unconscious to the filthy bar-room floor. Syd taking them to Covent Garden markets at four in the morning to help unload the morning supplies. Red accosting a prostitute in Regent Street in order to gain admittance to an after-hours club. They went in with her, gave her a pound, bought her a bottle of wine and left her. The lesbians Doug brought over from another table, to show them what lesbians looked like.

His memories of the two days jumbled one on the other. He wondered what trouble Clarrie would have when he returned home, and what further trouble Red and Doug would get into.

As the train pulled into Worcester station he looked for Jean. He could not see her. Disappointed, he stepped down when the train stopped. He looked around once more for her.

"Jeff," he heard.

Turning around, he saw a girl dressed in a gay floral frock with a red cardigan thrown loosely over her shoulders. She was beautiful. Her blonde hair streamed behind her like a banner.

It was Jean.

He stood speechless, looking at her, thinking how lovely she was.

93

"Well, say something," she said breathlessly, "even if it's only hullo. Don't stand there like a mute."

He shook his head.

"You shouldn't spring surprises like this on me," he replied still looking at her.

She flushed slightly, a pleased smile curving her lips.

"I hope you mean what I think you mean."

"Let me get my breath back and I'll tell you," he said, "I feel like kissing you here and now."

"If you do, I'll scream."

He picked up his case, took hold of her arm and led her off the platform.

"Hey, what about yer ticket, soldier?" the ticket-collector's voice sounded behind him.

"See what you do to me?" Jeff grinned down at Jean as he let go of her arm. He rummaged through his pockets for his travel warrant and at last found it. He showed it to the railwayman who grunted in acknowledgment.

"Airman, not soldier, next time please," Jeff said as he took hold of Jean's arm once again.

Jean's home was a large house in the suburbs of the city. Elizabethan in design, it stood surrounded by spacious lawns dotted with evergreen shrubs. A well weeded gravel path led from the gate to the front door.

A pleasant-faced, plump, middle-aged woman greeted them from the door as they opened the gate.

"So this is the Australian that Jean has told us so much about," she smiled as they walked up.

"Oh Mother," Jean said.

"How do you do, Jeff?" Mrs. Walton added, holding out her hand, "I hope you enjoy your stay."

"I'm sure I will, Mrs. Walton," he replied, noting the firm grip as they shook hands. "Thank you for having me."

"We had no alternative," she said, her eyes twinkling, "we received an ultimatum."

"Mother," Jean cried, "for goodness sake don't say any more, just go and make a cup of tea please."

Mrs. Walton laughed and left them. Jean took Jeff into the living room. It was attractively furnished with solid, usable antiques and chintz. On the mantelpiece above the large fireplace Jeff saw the photograph of an airman.

"Your brother Jean?" he asked.

"Yes," she replied softly. "that was Dick. Do me a favour, don't mention that you know about him to Mum or Dad. If they want to, they'll mention it themselves."

"I won't, Jean," he said.

"Come on," she said, her tone changing to a gayer note, "I'll show you your room."

Lunch was a bright meal. Being Saturday, Mr. Walton was home. He was a tall, thin man who shared his wife's good humour. He immediately put Jeff at ease. He had fought beside Australians during the 1914–18 War.

After lunch, he and Jeff returned to the lounge. In front of the fire they exchanged anecdotes over whisky until Jean called from the kitchen.

"You can earn your keep Jeff and dry up with me."

Later, when Jeff and her father resumed their conversation, she left the room for a few minutes. She returned with a heavy coat on, a scarf tied over her hair and Jeff's coat over her arm.

"Break it up," she said. "I only have a 48-hour pass and I'm taking Jeff out for the afternoon. You can talk this evening."

The winter afternoon was cold, but pleasant. They walked until they came to parkland beside the river. He guided her to one of the seats overlooking the stream. They sat down.

"That was a nice manoeuvre," he laughed, "not very subtle, but effective."

"Don't be sarcastic," she smiled back at him, "I was hopping mad. You men."

He put his arm round her shoulders, pulled her to him and kissed her. Her lips clung hungrily to his.

"I've wanted that, ever since you left the squadron," she whispered, "I missed you."

"Me too."

"I'm falling in love with you," he said, gazing into her eyes, his voice serious.

"Me too," she replied.

"I shouldn't, you know."

"Why?" she cried, pushing away from him.

95

"Don't worry," he said, "I'm not married or engaged or what have you, if that's what you were thinking."

"I was," she replied, relieved.

"What I meant was that no one in this flying game should become serious with a girl."

"Fiddle-faddle."

"I mean it."

"Still fiddle-faddle, you can't help it. It's biology or something."

With a laugh, he kissed her again, first on the eyes, then the nose, then lingeringly on the lips.

"Let's walk," he said as their lips parted. "I can't even think straight sitting here so close to you."

After dinner in the evening, they all settled down in the lounge.

"Aren't you two going out?" Mr. Walton asked.

"No," Jean replied, curling up on a rug in front of the fire. "Not unless you and Jeff start anecdoting again."

"I solemnly promise not to," her father smiled down at her. Then, turning to Jeff, with tenderness and sadness in his eyes, he continued, "I'm afraid she's spoiled. She's all we have now. Our son Richard was killed from your squadron. I suppose you know that."

"Yes sir, I do."

As his eyes sought out the photograph on the mantelpiece, Mr. Walton sighed.

"But that is over now. We still have Jean."

The evening passed pleasantly and quietly. Finally, Jean's parents rose and said good-night. Before leaving the room Mrs. Walton leaned over Jean and whispered to her. Jean turned to Jeff.

"You know it never occurred to me before," she said, "but what religion are you?"

"R.C. Why?"

"That's a break," she laughed, "Mum was worried we might have to leave you on your own and didn't like asking you straight out. She'll call you in the morning."

Then rising from the rug, she went to the doorway. "It's alright, Mum," she called after her parents, "he's a mick too."

With a roguish smile she went over to Jeff. He was seated in an armchair. She let herself down onto his lap and curled her arms around his neck.

"Kiss me and mean it, you intrepid airman, you," she whispered, "or do I have to kiss you?"

* * *

Clarrie woke up in the hotel room with a groan. His head ached. For moments, he did not know where he was. Then, as his head cleared, he hazily recalled the events of the previous evening. He smiled, until he sat up. With a grimace, he looked around the room. Doug and Red were still asleep, Doug on a mattress on the floor, Red huddled in blankets like a cocoon on the mattress base of the bed. Vaguely, he remembered refusing, in the early hours of the morning, to go home drunk to his mother. They had insisted that he share their bedroom at the hotel. He had won the toss for one bed. Doug and Red had shared the pieces of the other.

He smiled through his headache. He wondered what his mother would say if she could see him. She would be horrified at the very least.

Two days of his leave were gone. He had hardly given a thought to his home. For the first time in his life, he had let his hair down. He rose out of bed gingerly and sluiced his face with cold water at the wash basin. He gulped down some aspirins, which Red had thoughtfully put out on the dressing table. He put his overcoat on over his pajamas. He had no idea where the bathroom was, but found it without much trouble. After a shower and a shave, he felt much better.

Red and Doug were awake when he returned to the room.

"What time is it?" moaned Red.

"After ten," Clarrie replied, glancing at his watch.

"What's to do today?" Doug asked.

"You two intended to see them at Lady Ryder's Scheme today," Clarrie said, "You were going down for a few days to Somerset, so you said."

"Not today, thank you," Doug said, as he stumbled up off the mattress on the floor.

"Me either," Red added, lying back in the bed, "I

97

couldn't travel today. You must get awfully sick when you die. Hand me some aspirins, Clarrie."

After taking the aspirins, Red sat up. "Hey Doug," he cried, "who'd have thought Clarrie was such a wild fellow?"

"You're telling me," Doug replied. "Remember him with that blonde bombshell? Boy, oh boy, what a line."

Clarrie gave an embarrassed laugh.

"I didn't do anything wrong, did I?" he asked trying to remember details of the evening.

"We wouldn't know," Doug replied, "but you were missing for a long time with her and you don't pick daisies at this time of the year."

As full recollection returned, Clarrie gave a start.

"Oh," he said, "I forgot."

"Forget that blonde?" Red exclaimed. "You're wrong in the head. Where did you go?"

"Her flat was near the party," he replied. "I promised I'd meet her again today."

"You sly dog, you," Red said getting up slowly. He dug Clarrie in the ribs. "I never thought that Mrs. Kemp's boy Clarence was such a wolf. Hi, crew-mate."

The term pleased Clarrie immensely. Until this moment he had felt apart from the others in the crew. He was not very much older in years but in temperament, he felt decades older in many ways. The reserve he had always had, the shyness too. However, with these two members of the crew, for some reason, he had been able to shed both, at least for two days. He smiled to himself.

"Well guys," Doug said, as he shaved at the wash basin, "as I asked, what's to do today?"

"Haven't a clue," Red answered.

"Well, I really should go and see Mother," Clarrie said hesitantly.

As he spoke, he thought of the restricted life he had led with his widowed mother, his aunt and his sister. It seemed that since his father had died when he was still in his early teens, he had been surrounded by women, doting women. That was until he had joined the Air Force. If he went back today, they would fawn on him, pamper him like a child. They would take him to tea parties, church socials and visiting. They would smother him. He loved them all, but a feeling of nausea rose in him.

"Do you have to?" Doug said, rinsing the lather from his face. "Why not stay on the razzle-dazzle. With my good looks, Red's brawn and your manners and charm, we make a swell trio. Be in it."

With scarcely a moment's hesitation Clarrie accepted.

"Well at least for another day," he said, pleased to be accepted at last by these two members of the crew.

"You beaut," Red said, "ring that blonde later and get her to bring along two mates. If you've forgotten her phone number, I'll brain you."

"That part's alright," Clarrie smiled, "I wrote it down."

He did not see his mother that leave.

*   *   *

After leaving Jeff and the others on the second day, Syd caught the train to Windermere. He stayed with friends he had made during his first leave in England. They were homely people with a small daughter. He could do as he pleased there. Although he tried to stop her doing it, Mrs. Headingly brought him breakfast in bed each morning. She was a motherly woman who had that rare ability to put people at ease, no matter whom. Her war effort, she often laughed, was to give airmen from the dominions a taste of home and home cooking to help them relax. She succeeded. Her husband was a perfect partner for her.

Syd hired a cycle and rode through the beautiful countryside. He visited Wordsworth's cottage, cycled round Lake Windermere, through quaint Ambleside, down past Coniston Water. He climbed the Kirkstone Pass to Ullswater and gazed upon its beauty. At Keswick and Derwentwater he spent a full day. The lovely mountainous land, its lakes, small villages with their air of tranquillity and antiquity, were a tonic for the strain he had felt on operations.

As he rode or walked, he constantly thought of Paula. The way she looked, the way she walked, the way she acted, the way she talked. He recalled every incident they had shared. He realised on those walks and rides, how much he had fallen in love with her. He realised also, how selfish he would be if he tried to make her marry him. He knew she was trying, not very successfully, to avoid falling in love with him. He knew also he could probably force back her fears and make her agree—if he wished to.

On the last day of his leave, he climbed to one of the high hills overlooking Lake Windermere. As he sat there, eating the lunch Mrs. Headingly had prepared, he finally agreed with Paula. Previously, he had still had doubts.

As he lay back in the grass, he watched the grey storm clouds gather over the peaceful, beautiful countryside. They gathered in strength, they darkened and put gloom over the land as he gazed at them.

How apt and timely the storm was. The darkness and gloom of the storm of war could so easily settle upon Paula and him. However, with them, if he was shot down on operations, there would be no lightening of the skies after the storm had passed. No sunlight would filter through to bring the day alive again.

As he rose and slowly made his way down the track, the skies opened and the rain fell. If unhappy, he was content.

*   *   *

A light-hearted, expectant Al Macintyre stepped off the train at Edinburgh. Within an hour, he told himself, he would see Bess. It had been six long months, shortly after they had become engaged, since he had seen her. She had cried bitterly as he left on his posting to an operational squadron.

He took a taxi to his home. His mother welcomed him with a kiss. Proud tears welled up in her eyes but did not spill.

"How's my son?" she said happily.

"On top of the world, Mother," Al replied. "How are you and dad?"

"We're well, as if you really want to know about us," Mrs. Macintyre laughed. "If I know you, all you want to do is have a shower and then see Bess."

Al smiled, he put his arm round his Mother. He hugged her.

"You do understand," he said, "have you seen her lately?"

"No, Al," his mother said slowly, "she used to come over often, but lately she seems to be too busy."

He showered and shaved. Then, clad only in his dressing-gown, he sat down at the telephone. He did not see his mother's worried glance.

He dialled the number and waited for Bess to answer.

"Hello, darling," he said, when he heard her voice, "It's me, Al."

"Oh!" came a surprised exclamation. "Where are you?"

"Here in Edinburgh, I'm home on leave. How are you darling?"

"Fine," she replied, "how are you?"

Her tone was not warm. It was hesitant. Al felt disappointed and worried.

"Anything wrong?" he asked.

"No, why should there be?"

"You don't seem very pleased to hear from me."

"I'm just surprised."

"Well I'll be over shortly see you."

There was silence for long moments. Then Bess spoke quietly.

"I'll be awfully busy this afternoon."

"Well, if that's so, I'll be over early this evening."

"All right," she replied.

"Well, I'll be seeing you about seven then Bess."

As he put the phone down, Al stared down at it. He and Bess had written regularly enough since he had left Edinburgh. There had been no indication of a change in her feelings for him in her letters. He felt bewildered. The telephone call had left no doubts in his mind that their relationship was no longer the same.

Bess Crampton was a doll-like creature. She was short, had an attractive figure and a petulant, pretty, if not beautiful, face, framed by a cluster of blonded curls. She had an air of defencelessness about her. She used an invalid mother as an excuse for not being drafted into the forces or into war work.

As he sat by her side in the sitting-room of her home that evening, Al thought once again how beautiful she was. He put his arm round her and kissed her. She cuddled against him for a time.

"Let's go out somewhere," she said suddenly, breaking away.

"Why Bess?" Al asked. "Why can't we just stay here? I haven't seen you for six months."

Her mouth dropped into the childish pout he knew so well. "That's why I want to go out," she said. "Now that you're here, I want to go out with you."

"Very well," he said resignedly, "run up and get a coat."

As she felt the room, he sat back with a sigh. He knew arguing with her would serve no purpose. Beneath her air of helplessness, she had a core of steel.

The days and nights passed in a round of parties and shows. He never seemed to have Bess to himself. She seemed always to be surrounded by crowds of people, all of whom seemed to regard him as an outsider. None of the men were in the forces, they were in reserved occupations for the main part. Their last evening began with a quarrel when he suggested that they spend it alone. It was he who gave ground.

On the train back to Huntingdon the following day, he was uncertain of everything. The engagement was still there but he was bewildered by Bess' attitude.

He felt disappointed and despondent.

CHAPTER 9

"Hell, you were lucky to be on leave," Joe Weldon said when he saw Jeff and Al walk into the mess for breakfast on their return from leave. "We lost four crews," he continued.

"Who were they?" Jeff asked.

As Joe named the missing crews, Jeff and Al looked at one another. All but one were experienced crews with high numbers of operations.

"Well, they told us this was a chop squadron," Jeff said seriously. "I suppose we should expect this, but it still gives you a shock."

"All your crew back?" Joe asked.

"Yes," Al replied. "The others have gone to the hut to sleep off the leave. Syd's back too. Why?"

Joe gave a laugh.

"Can't you guess?" he said. "If ops are on, you're on. By the way, you aren't the sprogs of the squadron now. we have two new crews."

When Syd entered his room, he saw a figure lying asleep in the other bed. A pilot-officer's coat was draped over a chair. He looked like a fresh-faced child. His fair tousled hair lay over a fresh unlined face. Syd tried to be quiet but the other awakened.

"Hello there," Syd said, "a new boy?"

"Got in two days ago."

"I'm Syd Berry."

"Trevor Mason," the other replied as Syd held out his hand.

His handshake was firm. He sat up in bed and drew his knees up. As he sat there, he looked younger than ever.

"Hope I didn't disturb any of your gear."

"Doesn't matter if you did. Sorry I woke you up."

"I have to get up anyway," Trevor said, "it must be getting late."

"Stacks of time for breakfast."

Although he had done fifteen operations on a main force squadron, Trevor still appeared to Syd as shy and inexperienced. He had an air of uncertainty about him. He questioned Syd about the flights with the Pathfinders while they shaved and washed.

During breakfast, while Trevor tentatively asked more questions, Syd looked for Paula. She did not come in.

* * *

Ops were on.

The crew went out to Yorker after morning assembly. They took Mac up with them on the night flying test. Everything went perfectly. The plane responded eagerly to the pressure of Syd's hands and feet. She seemed alive and to enjoy being in the air as much as Syd did.

It was after they had landed that Jeff saw Jean for the first time since he had returned from leave. She drew up in the flight van. Jeff raced over to her. Slipping into the seat beside her, he kissed her.

"Hi, beautiful," he said, "how's my girl?"

"Fine Jeff," she replied, "how's my favourite boy?"

"Better now I've seen you."

"How did you enjoy your stay at home after I left?"

"It was great," Jeff said, "I like your family. Just as well since I intend marrying into it."

She pushed him away with a smile.

"Don't be so cocksure of yourself, young fellow."

At that moment the remainder of the crew noisily tramped up. They began to climb into the van.

"Damn!" Jeff exclaimed.

*　　*　　*

The target was Duisberg in the Ruhr. The crew had only been to Happy Valley twice before. Each time they had had trouble. It was the most heavily defended area in Germany. The concentration of flak and searchlights was intense. The Germans had made the whole area a fortress to protect the heavy industries located there. The bulk of their war materials poured out from the factories there.

Briefing was at 1600 hours, take-off at 1830. After briefing, Syd waited for Paula. She had been on duty. They walked slowly to the mess together.

"On leave I thought over what we talked about," he said.

"I did a lot of thinking myself, Syd."

They walked in silence for a moment. He looked down at the lovely girl at his side.

"You were right you know," he said softly, "much as it hurts me to say it."

"It hurts me too I'm afraid," Paula replied, "but it would be no use going on the way we were."

"Don't worry, Paula, my dear, I won't step out of line again."

Gazing straight ahead of her, she continued in a quiet voice which trembled.

"While you were on leave, I was wondering if I am just a coward."

"Of course you aren't."

"Let me finish Syd," Paula said.

She turned towards him. She put her hand on his arm. They stopped and gazed at one another.

"I've always had an easy life," she continued, "I don't think I could face having someone I loved go missing. I thought it all over and I know I couldn't bear it. I'd go to pieces, I'm a coward at heart."

He took her hand and held it. They walked towards the mess. Her face was white and tense.

"Don't worry about it, Paula," Syd said softly. "We'll just be friends. I won't even hold your hand like this. We'll see an occasional show together and leave it at that."

"Please Syd."

"Later, if I get through this rat race, my dear, you'll have a very different bod to cope with."

He released her hand as they neared the officers' mess.

*   *   *

The crew were backers-up once again, going in with the second wave. It was a bright night. Cloud above and below. Yorker and the other bombers were perfect silhouettes against them. They were visible for miles.

It was an ideal night for the enemy fighters.

They crossed the Dutch coast north of the Hague. Jeff gave Syd the alteration of course.

"The winds have changed," Jeff called over the intercomm. "Bloody met is nowhere near it. We will be late unless you belt the speed up to 155"

"Roger, 155 she is," Syd replied and eased the throttles forward.

Switching off his microphone, he scanned the skies for enemy fighters. Ahead of them he saw Arnhem fighter drome lit up. A burst of tracer bullets from a German fighter split the air to their starboard with streaks of light. The bomber returned the fire until an orange glow appeared in its port wing. Both planes were clearly visible in the eerie brightness between the cloud layers. The fighter closed in and fired further bursts. The orange glow burned more fiercely. Below the bomber there suddenly appeared the glow of red target indicator flares. A Pathfinder was going down. Syd wondered if it could be from their own squadron. It slowly spiralled down until it crashed and burned on the ground. The target indicators it had jettisoned hung above and lit up its pyre.

They flew on. The cloud thinned and broke. Searchlights suddenly probed the sky ahead of them. The target indicator flares went down on time. As they drew nearer, they could see the black puffs as the heavy flak exploded. Light flak hosepiped up its Christmas tree lights. Planes were coned like silver moths. Most won through but several made their last spinning flaming plunge to earth.

Essen and Dusseldorf threw up their searchlights and flak at bombers off track. The whole Ruhr eventually lit up. It was a horrifying spectacle. A sea of waving lights and bursting shells extended for fifty miles in length and breadth.

"God," Clarrie said from the mid-upper turret. "I never thought the Ruhr could be as bad as this."

It was his first trip to Happy Valley.

"You ain't seen nothing yet," Tich replied, "Wait till we get right in."

"How's E.T.A., navigator?" Syd asked.

"Should be smack on or close Syd, near as I can make it," Jeff replied.

They were approaching the main defences. A plane was coned ahead of them.

"Going in behind this poor bastard, crew," Syd called.

"Roger skipper," Red replied from his bomb-aiming compartment in the nose.

He prepared for the bombing run. He lined up his bomb-sight on the T.Is. down ahead and adjusted it.

The coned bomber ahead suddenly burst into a sheet of flame. It had received a direct hit.

"Watch for parachutes," Syd yelled.

They saw none.

"The poor devils," Clarrie whispered.

Immediately the other bomber had been hit and exploded, the searchlights swung towards them. The eerie blue fingers reached for them. One swung over their starboard wing. Syd yawed Yorker away.

"Get the bloody kite steady," Red called, "target coming up. Right-right, right."

He directed the plane over until the T.Is were coming down the drift wires of the bomb sight. Slowly he made the minor corrections. He pressed the bomb release button.

"Bombs gone."

"Roger."

Yorker bucked her relief at the loss of weight. Syd pushed the control column forward. The plane's nose went down, her speed increased. They passed through the searchlight belt without incident. Jeff gave the alteration of course. He noted the position where they had turned, then returned to his charts.

They drew near Arnhem on the way out.

"Hey skipper," Red called suddenly, "bomb-aimer here."

"Go ahead, Red."

"I saved a small H.E. bomb for this damn drome," Red said, "mind if we go off track a little and give them a bit of fun?"

Syd smiled to himself. Red could always be depended upon for the unexpected.

"Well Jeff," Syd said, "what do you think?"

"I'm for it," the navigator replied, "give them something nasty for a change."

"We shouldn't you know," Syd stated flatly.

"Come on skipper," Doug urged him, "be in it."

"O.K. Red, let her go."

As they made their run over the brightly lit drome, they saw a fighter approaching to land silhouetted against the lights. Red lined up the runway. As they dropped the bomb the enemy fighter touched down. The bomb burst on the concrete strip ahead of the plane and blossomed bright as it exploded.

"Hope I got that bod," Red yelled, "I dropped it right on the runway."

"You beaut."

The drome lights were hurriedly switched off. A few searchlights weaved about probing for Yorker. Flak burst far behind them.

"That'll stop them for a while," Al said.

Though combats between fighters and bombers occurred on both sides of them they had no trouble themselves. The Zuider Zee was crossed. The long trip across the North Sea began. The enemy coast receded behind them.

They were in their beds by half-past one.

On Duisberg, Bomber Command had lost nineteen bombers. One was from their own squadron. The bad luck was continuing. Of the twenty-six crews who had been on the squadron when they arrived, six had been shot down besides one of the others who had arrived after them. They had been on the squadron a fortnight.

The crews did not report to the flights until noon. There, they heard that the squadron was operating again that night. Syd scanned the list of operational crews. He saw Trevor Mason's name.

In the mess before lunch, the young pilot-officer walked over to him.

"I'm on tonight," he said.

He appeared strained and a little scared.

"You've operated before," Syd replied.

"Yes, but not with Pathfinders."

Syd laughed. He indicated the airmen sitting around the mess.

"It's not much different. I've only done three here myself."

They sat down close to the fireplace.

"I don't know why," Trevor went on, his face serious, "but it seems different. I don't think I'll be able to live up to the standard."

"I thought the same," Syd replied, "but our crew seems to be doing its job."

Throwing his half-smoked cigarette into the fire, Trevor sat forward. He gazed into the flames.

"The losses here are pretty terrible," he said.

Syd could sense the tension in Trevor. He sat there, looking into the flames as though he saw himself in them or in a plane falling, burning, over Germany. Syd understood his feelings.

"Let's go and have lunch," he said, standing up to break the spell. "We are having a bad session for losses now," he continued, "but it won't last. It never does."

They had lunch together. The strain eased a little in Trevor.

* * *

At the navigator's briefing, prior to the main briefing, he told Jeff of his conversation with Trevor Mason.

"Poor devil," Jeff remarked, glancing over at the young pilot. "I suppose he's scared stiff."

"I can't understand it," Syd said, "he's done fifteen ops."

Jeff put his instruments down. He turned to Syd.

"On main force," he said seriously, "where a tour was thirty, not forty five like here. He probably volunteered for P.F.F. on the spur of the moment. Now he realises that that extra fifteen mean a hell of a lot of extra risks."

Syd nodded slowly. "I suppose the losses here have frightened him too."

"Well they frighten me too," Jeff smiled grimly, "I wouldn't mind if it was only the sprogs like we are, but the bods going down are mainly our best crews. Flight-Lieut. Green was on his forty-second when he bought it last night."

Red looked up from ruling in the tracks on the detailed maps of the route.

"Will you two stop talking yourselves into a panic," he said. "So what if a crew hasn't finished a tour here in nine months. Someone has to eventually, if the war keeps on going. The law of averages you know. Anyway, if you do go for a Burton you won't be worrying about that for long, once old Nick gets hold of you."

They laughed and continued with the flight plan.

The target was Munich, take off time 1740. It was a flight of eight hours duration, mostly over enemy territory. They were routed through the greatest concentration of enemy fighter dromes, deep into the heart of Germany.

Munich, the cradle of Nazism.

Trevor Mason and his crew took off with the first wave of planes as a supporter. Within half an hour he had returned. He reported an unserviceable radio.

Syd warmed up the engines before take-off. He ran them up, waved to Mac and ordered "chocks away". They took off on time and climbed. The French coast was passed on track. They were at 14,000 feet and again forced to fly between two layers of cloud. Looking about them they saw other bombers as visible against the clouds as flies on a tablecloth.

"Look out for fighters everyone," Syd called, as he began evasive action.

109

"Roger skipper," the two gunners answered.

The combats began shortly afterwards. Tracers etched lines in the sky around them.

"The reaper's sure swinging his scythe tonight," Doug remarked laconically. He scanned the skies from his seat beside Syd.

Suddenly—

"Bandit starboard quarter up—800 yards," Tich screamed it over the intercomm.

"Roger," Syd replied quickly, bracing himself for the attack.

"Can you see him mid-upper?" Tich asked anxiously.

"I'm on him Tich," Clarrie's voice whispered.

The fighter edged closer, it was a black mass against the cloud. Tich's keen eyes followed every movement. He waited for the moment when it swung in to attack.

There was silence in the plane except for the breathing of the gunners and Syd over the open microphones. Jeff glanced at his watch and noted the time in his log. Al tuned the wireless to base frequency. If they were shot down, he hoped he would have time to send word back.

"Prepare to turn starboard—starboard—go," Tich yelled the last word as the fighter's wing dipped.

Syd hurled Yorker down and round in a right turn.

The clatter of machine-guns rattled over the intercomm.

"Missed the bastard," they heard Tich say disappointedly as the guns fell silent.

"Can you still see him Rear-gunner?" Syd asked as they levelled out.

"He overshot us," Tich replied, "I followed him down and he broke away to port."

"He kept on going Skipper," Clarrie added, "he must have lost us."

Relieved, Syd settled back. He continued the corkscrewing evasive action.

"You must have scared him off," he said, "he probably wants a sitting duck target. Keep your eyes peeled, however, there are plenty more around."

Jeff made allowances for the time and distance lost during the encounter. He checked his navigation.

"Navigator to Pilot," he called.

"Go ahead Jeff."

"We'll be late if you don't bump up the speed."

"Hell," Syd exclaimed, "not again."

"Don't blame me," Jeff snapped heatedly, "the met winds are hopeless."

"Alright Jeff," Syd said with a smile, "I know. Let's have the airspeed."

"On top of that," Jeff continued, his voice still sharp, "Gee's packed up and with this cloud I can't get a pin-point or astro-fix."

"I know Jeff," Syd repeated, "we'll stooge on and hope your winds are right."

"The one I found was good but there should be a wind-shift soon."

He sat forward on his seat. He estimated a wind from that which he had previously used and the forecasted change. Marking it on the computer he worked out his new course and ground-speed. He applied the ground-speed to the distance still to be flown. They would definitely be late.

Quickly he calculated what speed would be required to enable them to arrive on time.

"Navigator to Pilot," he called once agin.

"Go ahead."

"Alter course to 096 degrees magnetic, 0-9-6 and increase airspeed to 165, 1-6-5, indicated."

Syd set the new course on the compass. Doug pushed the throttles forward until the speed built up to 165 knots. He synchronised the motors until they surged in even rhythm.

"Pilot to navigator," Syd said, his eyes checking course and speed, "On course 0-9-6, 96 degrees, speed 1-6-5 indicated."

"Roger Syd," Jeff replied.

He worked on his log noting the information. Then he pored over his plotting chart. With his dividers he measured distances. He computed the time it would take to fly those distances. Then he switched on his microphone.

"Nav. to crew," he said, "in twelve minutes we should pass close by the south of Saarbrucken. With this cloud you won't see searchlights but watch out for flak bursts."

"Roger, Jeff," Syd replied for the crew.

"For goodness sake, let me know if you see it," Jeff said urgently, "I need that pinpoint if you want to get to the target and on time."

"Track and ground-speed's getting touchy," Red laughed from the nose of the plane.

With a grunt, Jeff returned to his work. After a minute, he reached for the thermos flask of black coffee he carried with him. He gulped down a cup of the scalding brew. Turning off the table light he slipped through the black-out curtain. Standing behind Doug, he peered out trying to pierce the darkness.

The cloud below thinned slightly, but the ground was still not visible. Suddenly on their port bow a few flecks of bright light appeared.

"Flak port bow," Doug shouted, "good on you Jeff."

"Right Doug, I see it," Jeff replied, pleased at the compliment.

"Is it Saarbrucken?" Clarrie asked.

"It can't be any other place," Jeff snapped.

"Keep your hair on Jeff," Red laughed, "don't get excited with the poor lad."

"Ah," Jeff snarled, as he went back to his table. "Let me know when we're nearly level with it."

Jeff estimated the distance from the spasmodic flak bursts over the town as they drew level with them. He used them as a position fix to check on his estimated wind. The new wind differed from the other. There was not a great difference but sufficient to throw them off track and out of timing. He knew it was unorthodox and frowned on by the navigation leader, but he calculated their course on the wind he had found from the flak.

"Richards will probably ground me for this," he told Syd, "but I'm altering course on this wind I've just computed."

He gave the new course and airspeed, them sat back and worried.

Stuttgart was passed as more flecks of flak above and below the cloud. Jeff used this as another check upon his work. The wind he computed compared nearly exactly with the previous one. He gave his Estimated Time of Arrival at the target.

The cloud thinned further as they neared Munich. It disappeared from above them, but below it still partly obscured the ground. The time for the first flares and target indicators went by.

"They're late," Syd said, anxiety in his voice.

The thought passed through his and Jeff's minds that they may have flown in the wrong direction. The wind Jeff had computed and used could have been inaccurate and have caused them to fly miles away from the target.

They weaved on for another two minutes, then the first red T.I. burst like a bunch of brilliant grapes above Munich. It fell directly in front of them. Other T.I.'s swiftly followed. The greens and reds tumbled down but no yellows.

"No visual markers," Red remarked, "There must be mist or cloud over the target. I'll bomb on the concentration of reds."

"Roger, bomb-aimer," Syd replied.

As they neared the city they saw that cloud prevented the searchlights from being effective. They made their run in and out, dropping their bomb load without trouble. Flak burst in a box barrage over the city but none burst near them. They were less than thirty seconds late on target.

The trip home also was uneventful. They saw many combats. Planes were shot down but they sighted no fighters themselves.

Munich was their twentieth trip—nearly halfway.

The squadron lost one more crew, a crew of enthusiastic youngsters with twenty-eight operational trips shown against their names on the flight crew board. Another crew had been shot up by fighters. They had flown their damaged plane back to England and had crash-landed at Manston. The total loss in Bomber Command was fifteen.

The light was still on in his room, when Syd finally returned to it. He was tired from the long trip. His arms and legs ached from the constant evasive action he had had to fly.

Trevor Mason was lying awake, fully clothed on his

bed.

"Thought you'd be asleep," Syd said as he shut the door.

"Did you hear what happened?" Trevor asked turning to face Syd.

"All I heard was that you came back with a duff wireless. It could happen to anyone and the regulations say you should come back."

Trevor laughed cynically.

"The C.O. thinks I didn't have the guts to go on. He thinks I turned yellow."

He got up and sat on the edge of the bed.

"I didn't abort purposely, Syd," he said earnestly. "I really would have done this op."

"Don't worry about it," Syd said, alarmed by the intense look on the other's face.

"Of course you would have gone on," he continued, "everyone has trouble like this at one time or another, even the oldest of crews."

"But don't you see," Trevor cried, his voice becoming shrill, "he thinks we U.S'ed the set deliberately."

"He wouldn't think that," Syd replied.

"He does I tell you, I could tell by the way he spoke to me afterwards. He practically called me a coward to my face."

Going over to the other's bed. Syd took the pajamas from under the pillow. He dropped them onto Trevor's lap.

"Here, get into your pajamas," he said, "and sleep on it. In the morning you'll find everything looks different."

"I doubt it," Trevor replied as he stood up.

They undressed in silence. Syd waited until Trevor was in his bed. He turned off the light and slipped between his own sheets.

"How was the raid?" Trevor asked quietly.

"Bit of a nightmare, but we got through all right. Fighters and flak galore though."

"I would have liked to have been there," Trevor said earnestly.

Perhaps too earnestly, Syd thought.

"Get some sleep," he said. "See you in the morning."

"Thanks Syd, good-night."

As he lay back, trying to sleep, Syd suddenly realised that the youthful face of his room-mate had already appeared older. In a matter of days he had aged in appearance.

*   *   *

Jeff and Joe Weldon walked together into the sergeants' mess for lunch. As they entered the ante-room Marty Coleman, a tall raw-boned Rhodesian, rushed up to them. He waved a newspaper like a flag.

"Get on this bull," he boomed, "the damned Yanks bombed Rouen in daylight yesterday."

"So what?" Joe asked.

"Hell, they get a two column spread," Marty said, stabbing at the item in the paper with his finger. "A two column spread for that undefended dump we wouldn't even send the sprogs to."

Jeff laughed. The long Rhodesian's hatred of anything American was well known.

"Listen to this," Marty continued vehemently, "Lootenant Charles P. Applebury of Wisconsin, is reported as saying that the flak was so thick he could have put his wheels down and taxied in on it to the target. Bull I say, there wouldn't be more than a dozen guns in the whole town. I know, our navigator took us off track over it the other night. They blazed away with everything they had and we didn't even take evasive action."

Joe edged away. "Let them have their fun," he said.

Marty grasped his arm. He shook the paper in Joe's face again.

"That's not the worst," he added savagely, "get on this. After nearly ten inches of double column, the report ends with 'all the bombers returned safely to base.' Then at the bottom of that we get six lines only."

He laid the paper on a table. To emphasise his words he ran a finger under each line as he read it..... "Bomber Command was also out in force last night. Munich was attacked. The target was severely damaged. Returning crews reported explosions and fires. Fifteen of our bombers are missing."

He finished reading then stood back, silent for a mo-

115

ment. "See what happens," he said at last. "The Yanks do a milk-run job, get all the praise and paper space. We do bloody Munich, fly half the night, get shot to ribbons, lose fifteen crews, and then—'Bomber Command was also out last night.' We carry four or five times the fortress bomb load on top of that. It's not fair. The people are beginning to think that only the Yanks are doing anything."

Suddenly, Marty grabbed up the paper. Without another word, he dashed away to join other air-crew as they entered the mess. As they watched, they saw him brandish the paper in front of the newcomers.

Joe laughed. He drew Jeff towards the dining-room.

"He's right you know," Joe said, "You'd be surprised how many people would read that report and think our effort was just a little skirmish and the Yank effort the real thing; instead of it being the other way round."

They went into lunch. The W.A.A.F. waitress put their meal down in front of them.

"Marty's really mad with them," Jeff said.

"So mad, that tonight he'll go into Cambridge and bash up about six of them. He won't mind whether it's one at a time or all together. He'll come back to the squadron battered and happy."

As the crews filed noisily out from the afternoon assembly, Squadron Leader Cannover called Syd over.

"I have a job for you Berry," he said as Syd saluted.

"Yes Sir?"

"As you know probably, Flight Sergeant Ryan landed shot up at Manston."

"Yes Sir."

"Well, I want you to pick him up this afternoon," Squadron Leader Cannover continued. "You should be back here by early evening. However, the met. report is bad, you may be caught and have to stay overnight."

"Very well, Sir."

Syd saluted. He turned away.

"I've informed your ground crew and Manston," the flight commander added as Syd walked away.

He gathered his unhappy crew together.

"Hell, I had a date tonight," Jeff protested strongly.

"Me too," Red added angrily, "I've been working on this dame since we came back from leave. We're on ops two nights and now this."

Grumbling, they tumbled into the flight van.

"Why the heavy frowns?" Jean asked as Jeff glowered beside her.

"It's a damn conspiracy," he said, "just to keep me from taking you out."

"You'll be back tonight won't you?" she asked.

"Not if what the met bod says is right. Within two hours Battleson will be blanketed in low cloud—so he says."

Jean lapsed into subdued silence. She drove the truck furiously round the perimeter track. She pulled up with a jerk beside Yorker to the yells and protests of the other members of the crew.

"Don't take it out on us, Jeannie lass," Al laughed.

"Lover boy will be back in a week or two," Doug quipped.

"Oh, you men," Jean snapped, looking from one to the other.

Jeff drew her aside.

"Anyway Jean," he said, "I'll see you tomorrow night if we aren't on ops."

She gave an angry snort.

"Even if you aren't, I'm on duty roster."

*   *   *

They flew down to Manston. It was a grass drome on the southeastern tip of England. Unaccustomed to landing on grass, Syd bounced badly on touch-down.

"Beers for the crew," Red yelled over the intercomm.

Syd and Jeff went over to the control tower. They arranged for Flight Sergeant Ryan's crew to be picked up from the mess. The duty officer contacted Battleson control for them. He turned from the phone.

"You might as well send Ryan back," he said, "your drome's closed."

"Blast," Jeff snapped.

They slept the night in the sergeants' mess in front of the fire. The following morning they were able to return to the squadron with the other crew. It was three days before Christmas.

The following day they were briefed for a daylight attack on the ball-bearing factory at Schweinfurt. It was in the very heart of Germany. The track they were to fly lay across the main German fighter belt. It would have been a hellish trip. The Lancasters' few 303 Browning machineguns were no match in daylight against the cannons and point 5's carried by the enemy fighters.

The crews were resigned to heavy losses. The usual banter was absent. At briefing they were mainly silent and clearly apprehensive.

To the relief of all, the operation was cancelled in the late morning.

CHAPTER 10

CHRISTMAS

Christmas Eve broke cold and misty. The crews, in overcoats and sweaters, straggled up to the flights after breakfast. They clustered round the pot-bellied stoves in the crew room.

"I bet we're on ops. tonight", Clarrie miserably remarked.

"Cut it out Clarrie," Red said, "Christmas Eve. I can't see all the shiny-bottoms at group giving away their Christmas Eve parties just to make us work."

The C.O. entered with the Flight and Section leaders.

"At ease men," he said as the crews shuffled to attention.

"We are on standby," he said rather sadly, "which means we will probably operate if the weather permits."

"Told you so," Clarrie said smugly to Red.

As annoyed cries rose from the airmen, the C.O. held up his hands for silence.

"I know how you feel," he said, "but you'll do it, so stop bitching."

He held out a typewritten list to the adjutant.

"The adjutant will pin the list of crews on standby on the notice board. The other crews can do as they please for the day."

They stood to attention as he left the room. Then there was a concerted rush to the notice board. Heading the list was W/C. Bolton-Adams. Beside his name as crew was every section leader.

There was silence for a moment.

"Well he's dobbed himself in," an air gunner said.

"I bet old Richards is peeved," a navigator laughed.

"You beaut, we're not on," another voice shouted.

In the pandemonium, Syd and Jeff looked over the list. They were on. Trevor Mason was also.

The young pilot looked at the list. His face was pale. He gathered his crew together and left the crew room.

"I don't know whether that bod is scared stiff or not," Jeff said, watching Trevor leave.

"We'll find out soon enough," Syd replied. "Let's get out to the kite. We'll do our Night Flying Test right away."

Grumblingly, the crew followed them out.

"On again is it?" Jean asked Jeff, as he sat in the truck.

"Even the walls have ears," Jeff replied pompously, "and Hitler listens to every conversation."

Angrily Jean faced him. She stamped her foot on his.

"Ouch", he cried.

"Serves you right," Jean added, "don't get so smug and smart with me."

"Your humble servant Ma'am," Jeff replied with a grin.

A smile curved Jean's lips. Her eyes twinkled.

"I have a bit of a paddy, haven't I?" she said as she started up the truck. "Think you'll be able to put up with it?"

"I'll put up with it or change it," he laughed.

"You've no hope. Mum and Dad tried long enough without success."

Briefing was early at 1400 hours. The target was to be Turin. When the navigators' briefing had finished, the remainder of the crews filed in. They took their places at the tables.

The C.O. was halfway through his preamble when a

signal from group was handed to him.

A grin lit his face.

"No doubt this will make you happy," he said from the platform. "Due to forecasted bad weather on return, the operation has been cancelled."

Shouts and cheers rose from the crowd of airmen. The C.O. motioned for silence and continued.

"If I see one air-crew bod round the flight offices or crew-room in fifteen minutes he's on a charge. There will be three buses for Cambridge outside the guard-room in an hour for air and ground crews."

Cheers rose again.

Jeff gathered up his equipment and maps. He dashed out of the room.

The van was parked as usual near the flight offices. Jean sat back in the passenger's seat with her feet up on the steering wheel. Her eyes were closed.

"Get weaving," Jeff yelled as he neared her.

"What's the excitement?" she replied sleepily.

"Don't ask questions, get mobile," Jeff said, a note of exasperation in his voice.

"What's happened to ops.?"

"Scrubbed," he replied, "now dump this van, get into your best uniform and I'll stake you to a blowout in Cambridge."

Letting her feet fall down onto the seat Jean sighed.

"Just my luck," she said disappointedly, "I'm stuck with this thing."

"You aren't," Jeff snapped, "the C.O. has closed us down."

Jean still sat there unconvinced.

"For goodness sake dash into the flight office and ask Sqd. Leader Cannover."

"I hope you're right," she said, as she slowly got out of the van. She walked over to the flight office. Jeff stood, impatiently shifting weight from one foot to another. He glanced at his watch every few seconds.

Jean skipped out of the flight office. She took his face in both hands and kissed him.

"We're on our way," she said gaily.

"Whip me round to the dispersal first will you?" Jeff

said, hopping into the van, "I want to give Mac a couple of quid for him and the boys from the crew to have a Christmas drink on us."

Jean hurled the van round the perimeter track. She braked to a stop beside Yorker. Jeff dashed over to Mac. Taking his wallet out of his battle-dress tunic he slipped two pound notes out.

"Sorry I can't stay longer Mac," he said breathlessly, "ops. are off, so you and the boys have a drink on us bods. Merry Christmas and see you tomorrow."

Mac looked dazedly after the sprinting figure as it jumped into an already moving van.

*   *   *

After the C.O's announcement in the briefing room, Syd walked up to Paula. She was taking down the lines of red wool which marked the tracks he would no longer fly.

"Paula," he said standing behind her.

"Hello Syd," she said, her eyes finding his.

"Care to come to Cambridge with me?" he asked hesitantly.

"I'd love to Syd, if I can make it in time."

With a smile he began helping her.

"I was hoping you'd ask me," she said shyly, "I wanted to go out with you tonight. Christmas Eve."

He turned towards her and grinned.

"You shouldn't talk like that," he said, "or I might forget my good resolutions."

*   *   *

As he walked out the station gate, Syd saw Jeff anxiously pacing up and down beside the three buses.

"You going in too Jeff?" he asked, as he joined the long navigator.

Jeff gave a start.

"Didn't notice you skipper," he replied with another glance at his watch. "Sorry I didn't see you after briefing but I had to see Jean."

The three buses were filling rapidly as airmen and W.A.A.Fs. piled into them.

"Look at the time will you," Jeff said, pointing a finger at his watch. "They leave in three minutes and where is she?"

Syd laughed. He reached out and took hold of Jeff's arm as he began to pace up and down once more.

"Don't get excited," he said, "we can hold up the last bus for them if we have to."

"Them?"

"Yes," Syd smiled, "I'm waiting too, for Paula."

Settling down, Jeff glanced at his pilot, a quizzical look on his face.

"You two on again?"

"No change in the met. report Jeff."

"Sorry old man."

"It doesn't matter. I think it's for the best."

Before he could say more, Jeff saw the two girls approaching at a leisurely walk.

"Look at them will you," he said, digging Syd in the ribs," sauntering along as though they're going to a funeral. Hey, what are they doing together?"

"I was wondering the same thing."

The two girls smiled as they drew near. They both looked lovely, even in the heavy grey W.A.A.F. overcoats. Jean's eager face was radiant. Her eyes twinkled. Paula's more reserved beauty shone as she looked at Syd.

"Hurry up," Jeff urged.

"There's plenty of time," Jean replied, "half the Waafery has to come yet."

They joined the queue for the third bus. Syd squeezed Paula's arm as they stood behind Jeff and Jean.

"I didn't know you two knew each other," Syd said to Paula.

"Oh we do," Jean spoke up with a smile. "She put me on my first charge."

With a laugh, Paula pushed Jean round gently.

"You'll be on another if you eavesdrop."

With a giggle, Jean faced away. She tucked her arm in Jeff's and whispered in his ear. He turned and laughed down into her mischievous gleaming eyes.

"I've known Jean since before the war," Paula explained to Syd, "we met in London. She's a little imp but perfectly lovable. I didn't put her on a charge either."

Syd looked at the pair in front of them. They seemed oblivious to anything outside them. He felt a tinge of regret. As though Paula read his thoughts, she voiced the same sentiments.

"I wish I could be like her," she said, "she's head over heels in love with your navigator and doesn't care who knows it. She'd marry him tomorrow without any regrets or fear."

Turning, Syd looked down at Paula. He grinned at her serious expression.

"Just be yourself," he said, "I wouldn't change you for an Air Vice Marshal's stripes."

In the bus they found four seats together. Jean snuggled into Jeff. Paula looked at them and nestled closer to Syd.

"You know Syd," she said quietly, "watching those two I could very easily let myself go with you."

Deeming it wise, Syd remained silent.

"Jeff," Jean whispered up into his ear, "what are we going to do?"

"Well I thought we'd walk round the town for an hour or so," he replied, "I haven't been to Cambridge before. Then we'd have a meal at some posh pub. After that a show. How does that sound?"

"Perfect," she replied, "Now don't say another word for a while. I want to nap. You interrupted me earlier in the van."

She nestled her head more comfortably on his shoulder and closed her eyes until the bus pulled up in Cambridge. She sat up yawning as it stopped.

"We're here?" she asked.

"Of course we are," Jeff replied, standing up.

They filed out of the bus. Jeff got down first and handed the two girls out. They stood together uncertainly for a moment.

"Well," Jean said matter-of-factly, "none of us wants gooseberries, so see you on the bus at 11.30."

She made a small curtsy. A roguish smile curved her lips.

"Sir and Ma'am," she added.

"Get going before I spank you", Syd laughed.

He and Paula watched the pair eagerly speed away. Jean was skipping along like a young girl. Taking hold of Paula's arm, he tucked it into his.

"You can't object to this," he said, "you know those

two make me feel awfully old at times."

As they were passing a hotel, Jeff wheeled Jean through the main doors.

"We'll start with a warmer-upper," he said, leading her into the lounge.

They sat down. An elderly waiter shuffled over to them and took their order. As he moved away Jeff felt in his uniform pocket for his wallet.

"Oh no!" he exclaimed.

"What's the matter?" a startled Jean asked.

"I left my wallet in my battle-dress."

"Well we can always wash dishes for a meal," Jean said laconically.

"This isn't funny," Jeff snapped.

"I know," Jean sighed resignedly, "I might know this would happen to me."

Jeff flushed. Irritatedly he stood up.

"I'll look for Syd," he said, "he'll lend me some, I think."

Taking her handbag she placed it on her lap. Under cover of the table she opened it and slipped her wallet out.

"Sit down," she said, "you must have known I got paid yesterday. Here grab this."

She quietly and unobtrusively slid the wallet towards him. No-one saw the manoeuvre. With a hurried gesture Jeff palmed it. He put it in his pocket.

"That's a relief," he said gratefully, "thanks Jean."

"Huh!" she snorted, "the first night you take me out and this happens."

"I'm sorry," he said apologetically, "it's only a loan. I'll give it back tomorrow."

She smiled and put her hand over his.

"I don't care if you don't," she said softly, "let's have a lovely day."

The waiter came. He placed their drinks on the table. They did not see him.

"You know, Jean," Jeff said gazing at her, "when you look at me like that I get prickles up my spine."

"Your drinks, Sir," the waiter said, looking from one to the other with an amused air.

"Did you have to come just now?" Jeff laughed as he

took a note from Jean's wallet.

"Pay the man so he can go away," Jean murmured, her eyes still on Jeff, "then keep on talking."

The day went all too quickly. They did as they had planned. Afterwards, they slowly walked arm in arm through the darkened town to the squadron bus.

"It was a wonderful day," Jean whispered.

"A wonderful day with a wonderful girl," Jeff replied.

"Stop here for a moment," she said quietly, drawing him into the shadows of a doorway. They could see the buses. They could hear the babble of the voices as the airmen and Waafs climbed aboard. Her arms stole up and round his neck. He put his arms round her and drew her closer.

"Kiss me," she murmured, her eyes closed.

As Paula and Syd walked along side by side, their footsteps echoed through the deserted streets. Syd turned up the collar of Paula's overcoat.

"Thanks Syd," she said.

"Have a nice day?" he asked.

"Lovely," she replied quietly. She took his hand. They strolled along hand in hand.

"It seems a shame for it to end," she added. "If we could only keep on walking. If there was no squadron, no ops, or possibly no me."

Syd remained silent for a moment before answering.

"Don't say that. If there was no squadron I'd never have met you."

"It might have been better if you hadn't."

"That's silly and you know it," he said sharply. "It's been a grand day, so don't spoil it with silly statements."

Her laugh brought an answering smile to his face.

"Come on," she said gaily, "or we'll miss the bus."

As they climbed into the bus, Jean's voice called from the rear of the dimly-lit interior.

"Down here, we kept two seats."

They sat down behind the others. Jean turned round. She leant her chin on the back of the seat.

"Have a good day?" she asked.

"A very nice one," Paula smiled at the dreamy-eyed girl.

"Me too," Jean said. She sighed, then sitting up suddenly she nudged Jeff in the side.

"Hey," she said quietly. I just remembered, it was on me. No wonder we went to all the expensive places. Any left?"

Jeff took out the wallet. He looked at the solitary note. He counted the silver in his pocket. He handed both to her.

"About a quid," he smiled.

"Oh well, easy come easy go," she said tiredly, "give me your shoulder."

She leant against it and closed her eyes.

The buses pulled out one by one. Their dim headlamps threw soft beams of yellow light onto the wet roads. As their bus sped out of Cambridge, the singing began. The raucous basses of the drunks blended with the sweet sopranos of the Waafs. They began with "Lindy Loo." When that was finished a baritone began to sing. The others enthusiastically joined in.

They say there's a Lancaster leaving Berlin,
Bound for old blighty's shore
Heavily laden with terrified men,
All lying prone on the floor.
They've been shot up by ack ack and
    Messerschmidts too
And Junkers were there by the score
They shot our hydraulics
They used all their tricks
So cheer up my lads bless 'em all.
Bless 'em all -------

The chorus thundered through the bus.

As the verse was being sung, Jean shivered. She put her arm through Jeff's. Tears welled up in her eyes as she thought of Jeff being the target of enemy action. He bent down and kissed her. Earnestly, she kissed him back. The words sent a chill feeling through Paula also. She had heard it often before but had never connected it with anyone. She also thought of the man beside her as the words thundered on. She could never visualise Syd as a "terrified man" but the thought of him being shot down hurt her. She put her head back. She remained silent. She was frightened to speak.

Immediately the parody ended, a drunken voice began—

126

"Roll me over, roll me over.

Roll me over lay me down ---------"

The song was drowned by the protesting voices of other airmen.

"Cut it out Steve, Waafs aboard."

The bus pulled up eventually outside the squadron guard-room. As they left the bus and walked towards the 'Waafs' quarters together, Jeff looked at his watch.

"Hey it's Christmas," he shouted.

He bent and kissed Jean.

"Happy Christmas darling," he said, then turning to Paula and Syd, "Happy Christmas to you two also."

"Thanks Jeff," Syd replied, "same to you."

Jean came over to them and kissed each lightly on the cheek.

"Happy Christmas to you both," she said seriously, "see it is."

They laughed self-consciously. Syd put his arm through Paula's and drew her away.

"Good night," he called over his shoulder.

They did not hear him. They were locked in each other's arms. As they broke away, Jeff rummaged through his pockets. He drew out a small package done up in tissue paper. It was small and round. He undid it. He fumbled in his pocket for a matchbox. Striking a light he held it over a ring. It was a large blue sapphire flanked on each shoulder of the setting by small diamonds.

"It's beautiful," Jean whispered.

"I got it on leave," Jeff said hesitantly. "It's for your engagement finger, if you want it that way."

"You must have felt sure of yourself," she replied.

Laughingly, she stood up on tip-toes and kissed him on the nose. He threw his arms around her and kissed her hard on the mouth. She clung to him.

"Of course that's how I want it," she said at length, breathlessly, "but you haven't proposed yet."

He dropped to one knee. With a smile he took her hand, kissed it and looked up into her face, lovely still in the half-light.

"Darling will you marry me? I love you with all my heart."

She squatted down on her heels in front of him. There was no mischief in her eyes. There was no laughter. She was all seriousness.

"I love you too my darling," she whispered softly. "All I want is to marry you. The sooner the better."

She slipped the ring on her engagement finger. They stood up.

"Now take me back to the Waafery," she said. "I'll see you at Mass in the morning."

Ahead of them, Syd and Paula walked slowly. They were quiet. Paula drew nearer as they strolled along arm in arm. She slowed her steps as they neared the Waafs' quarters. She finally stopped. She turned towards Syd.

"Kiss me for Christmas," she breathed eagerly.

She put her arms round him, he clasped her in his arms. He kissed her. She clung to him and returned his kiss hungrily. Slowly she eased away. Tears came to her eyes and overflowed down her cheeks.

"I want to," she cried. "I want to love you, but I'm still afraid."

Sobs racked her. Syd drew her into his arms.

"It's alright my sweet," he murmured into her hair. "Don't worry about it. I'll be around, anytime you want me."

She reached for the handkerchief he held out. With her head still against his chest, she wiped her eyes and blew her nose. He tilted her head up. Her eyes were still wet with tears. They glistened in the darkness. He kissed her lightly.

"I won't come any further," he said. "You go on in and get some sleep. Happy Christmas."

"Happy Christmas, Syd," she smiled wryly. "Isn't it?"

He watched as she walked away. She paused as she went through the gates and waved. She could not see him, but she knew he was there. He waved in reply.

* * *

Christmas Day was cold and foggy. As he walked through the clammy mist to 7 a.m. Mass, Jeff huddled in his overcoat. His hands were thrust deep into his pockets. Jean was waiting for him outside the lecture room which had become a church for that morning.

Her cheeks were rosy with the cold. Her eyes shone.

"Hi fiance," she smiled, showing off her ring.

"Hi," he replied still huddled in his coat. "Let's get inside by a fire. Home in Queensland was never like this."

"How romantic you are," Jean said teasingly. "You weren't like this last night."

They went into the hut and Jeff immediately raced over to the stove heating the hut. He warmed his hands, then, raising one foot after the other, he warmed his feet. After a few minutes he stood back.

"Ah, that's better," he said contentedly. "I feel better now. How are you darl?"

"Huh," Jean replied irritably. "We are engaged about seven hours and all you can think of is getting warm."

At the rear of the hall, the priest was preparing for Mass. Altar cloths transformed a table. It became an altar. Over thirty other men and women waited, some kneeling, praying, others sitting or standing near the fire. Jean and Jeff moved forward and knelt together in one of the rows of seats.

They went to Confession, in a corner near the altar. Mass began with an airman acting as altar boy.

They felt in harmony as the Priest's voice carried back to them. They knelt together and received Communion.

After Mass they walked out silently. The fog closed in on them.

"Feel better?" Jeff jokingly asked.

"I do," Jean replied seriously. "I prayed for you. It was nice hearing Christmas Day Mass with you."

*   *   *

Morning assembly was brief. The crews dispersed quickly. The bar opened in the sergeants' mess at eleven. The airmen soon gathered. The homesickness many felt was eased as the party developed. There were men from every dominion and several colonies. French and Belgians mixed with a Pole and a Dutchman. To each, Christmas meant a home in a far country. The British were away from their families also. They were near but unable to join them. They also felt the nostalgia. Sentimental songs were sung at first. However as the hours passed, homesickness was forgotten. The beer and spirits flowed. The songs became more ribald. The strained faces brightened.

129

At one-thirty, the officers and N.C.Os. gathered at the airmen's mess to serve the ground staff and Waafs their Christmas dinner. They dashed from the servery to the tables with the food and drinks, to the sound of jokes and good-natured banter.

After a buffet lunch the parties continued in the officers' and N.C.Os.' messes.

For once during the year the war was forgotten. As the day drew on games were played. Laughter and songs rang through the buildings.

In the evening as the fog darkened with the setting sun they sat down to their Christmas dinners.

The day finished for most with a dance at the Waafery.

*　　*　　*

The bad weather continued into the New Year. The clammy fog and the inactivity strained the nerves of the crews. At night Jeff would lay awake hour after hour trying to sleep. When he eventually dozed off, it was to dream. Nightmares of being shot down, of searchlights, flak, fighters and flames would cause him to wake trembling. The remainder of the crew felt the strain also. They became easily irritated. There was a feeling of tension throughout the whole squadron.

The C.O. recognised the symptoms. He organised diversions to take the minds of the crews off the nerve-wracking waiting. A novelty sports day was held, in which the flights competed against each other. Films were shown on each alternate afternoon. Where they came from, no-one enquired, but good class Hollywood shows were screened with training films in the briefing room. Interesting lectures were given by some of the air crew. Amongst the airmen were many who had led strange and dangerous lives in the remote centres of the world. A former patrol officer from the New Guinea jungles preceded an ex-archaeologist who had excavated sites in the deserts of Egypt. An ex-actor from the London West End entertained with anecdotes and patter. He was followed by a colonial who told of life in his native land.

In the evening, buses took them into the nearby towns.

Through it all, the strain persisted.

Training continued also. If the sky cleared sufficiently,

the Lancasters roared from the runways. Navigators worked at their radar. The gunners checked their guns and
shooting ability in air to sea firing in the Wash. When the
weather prevented flying, the crews practised their dinghy
drill and abandon aircraft procedure. They spent hours
clambering in and out of the planes. It was tedious and
annoying but it occupied them. It could save their lives
should they have to bail out or ditch in the sea.

New Year's Eve passed into New Year's Day to the
raucous noise of parties in the messes.

It was the third of January before they operated once
more.

CHAPTER 11

PRE-OPERATIONS

Briefing—

The long room fills with noise and men.
The smoke haze rises high, thick and dense.
One wall is a map with the target shown,
The target of all entering eyes.
Calm or fear, perhaps relief shows on each face.

*　　*　　*

Will:	"Bloody Essen, that's lovely that is."
Steve:	"Been there before?"
Will:	"Twice and that's three times too many to my way of thinking. The place stinks. Too many guns, too many huns, too many searchlights and too many fighters on the way in and out."
Steve:	"Ah well, you can only buy it once."
Will:	"Well fella here's your chance.
Steve:	"Why do they call the Ruhr, Happy Valley of all names?"
Will:	"Dunno—unless it's because the Jerries are so happy for us to come over there."
Steve:	"Eh?"

Will: "Well, besides all the ack ack they've already got there, they can wheel out all the other guns they made that day in the factories and the whole she-bang poofs up. They can test them out on us. It saves a lot of expense.

*   *   *

The leaders sit on the platform, front of the anxious crews. One by one they stand to say their piece.
The met. man talks of fronts and cloud,
Of wind and ice, of fog on landing.

*   *   *

Mick: As if he'd know. I'd just like to take him on one trip over there and make him navigate on the perishin' winds he gives us.

Jim: Well, I don't suppose they have much to go on with all Europe occupied.

Mick: Much to go on! Hell, at times they don't even give you good winds over base much less over Europe.

Jim: Anyway you can't blame Windy; he only gives out what he gets from Group.

Mick: Even so, Blind Freddie only has to spit to know what way the wind's blowing, yet night after friggin' night I get in the kite with the met. winds and night after friggin' night I scrap them before I hit the English coast and have to use the ones I found myself.

Jim: Now I know how you hit so many defended areas off track.

Mick: Belt it.

*   *   *

Intelligence, nav, bombing and guns.
The leader of each stands, speaks and sits.
The minutes fly by as the details are given until the C.O. rises and says down to the crews "Press on regardless," and briefing is over.

*   *   *

John: "Press on regardless" he says. Bloody "reward-less" would be more like it.

Ian: All for honour and glory, keep the old flag flying high.

John: You can shove that.

Ian: No squadron spirit that's your trouble.

John: The only spirit I'd like right now is a triple whisky.

Ian: Now you're cooking with gas. If we only could, they could de-feather my wing.

John: The very thought of that damn place gives me the belly-flips.

Ian: You and me both, fella. Every time I lay my peepers on the lights in the Ruhr I get sick all over. Still, ours' not to wonder why, our's but to bleedin' well do and bleedin' well die.

John: 'Tis a far far better thing I do that I have ever done if I stay at home in my nice warm Air Force issue bed tonight.

Ian: De-digitate or we'll miss our ops. meal.

Meal—

The Waafs hand out the operational eggs.
The motley crowd sits down and eats.
The meal before them represents
For some the start; for some the end.
To the former the op.; to the latter life itself.

*   *   *

Len: Hey, Johnny, pass the bread and that muck they miscall butter.

Johnny: Coming up. Aren't you having your egg now?

Len: I'm saving my poor lone egg till after the op. I'll feel more like eating it then.

Johnny: Optimist.

Len: I'll have the laugh on you my boy when you're eating Welsh Rarebit and I'm tucking in on hen fruit in the early hours of the morn.

Johnny: If you're here to eat it.

Len: I have my hopes. That's right, wolf into it as though it's your last meal.

Johnny: Jolly well might be.

Len: Your sense of humour appals me.

Johnny: Hey Len, if you don't come back, can I have your egg?

Len: Unfair bargain. You've eaten yours.

Johnny: My fountain pen's on my dressing table.
Len: It's a deal. I have witnesses.

*   *   *

Locker Room—

The long rows of lockers, doors flung wide.
Oddly dressed airmen preparing to fly
Stowing the mascots ready to hand.
All joking and worrying before going out
To the darkness and fear of the night.

*   *   *

Tony: What's that smell?
Ron: Bill's socks. They're on the nose.
Bill: You can peg your nose if you want, but these socks ain't been washed in thirty-two ops. and they stay that way till I finish.
Tony: You'll gas yourself to death with that superstitious smell before you finish your forty-five.
Bill: Belt up.
Ron: You can't talk Tony, with that pair of scanties you tuck away in your battle-dress every op.
Tony: Fond memories of l'amour to keep me warm during the long cold night ahead.
Bill: If yer told the truth, they'd be yer sister's.
Ron: Heaven forbid.

*   *   *

The silent planes stand waiting at dispersal,
Their songs of power still to be sung.
Their loads of destruction cradled safe.
The runway lights, the first engine sounds.
Then one by one the planes give cry.
The operation is begun.

*   *   *

CHAPTER 12

The crews lounging round the stoves at morning assembly sprang swiftly to attention as the C.O. entered the crew room.

"It's on at last," were his first words.

Shouts and cheers rent the air.

"The lists will go up on the board at once," he called loudly, as the noise died down. "We are supplying nine crews only."

He continued with details of training for non-operating crews. He did not name them but listed only the number from each flight for each particular exercise. As the various section leaders outlined their requirements for the day, the crews became impatient. The Adjutant had pinned the operational list to the notice board. The eyes of all the crew watched the slip of paper. It fluttered slightly in the cold breeze from an open window.

As the C.O. and the section leaders left the crew room, there was a stampede towards the notice board. Syd and his crew were listed. Trevor Mason's name was there and so also was Wing Commander Bolton-Adams.

Syd turned round with a smile. His smile faded however, when he saw the expression on Trevor Mason's face. The new pilot was white and strained. Fear showed. When he became conscious of Syd, he gave a weak smile, glanced away, then turned and walked from the room.

"Do you think yon bod is gutless?" Red asked, pointing to the retreating figure of the other pilot. He had seen the short encounter.

"I don't know," Syd replied thoughtfully. "I just haven't a clue. I hope for his sake he isn't."

"I hope so too," Red continued. "I don't think I'd want to live with myself if I couldn't go through with this business, much as I hate and fear every bloody minute I'm over there."

* * *

The vehement tone of Red's words startled Syd. He understood the meaning of the words only too well. However, hearing them come from the seemingly imperturb-

135

able, carefree bomb-aimer still surprised him.

Navigator's briefing was early. Jeff and Red laid out the maps and charts on the long wooden table.

"The Ruhr," Red said slyly, "if these are the only maps we're issued with."

A knot of fear twisted in Jeff's stomach.

"Happy Valley for the winter," he said in reply, driving his fear deeper away from probing eyes.

In front of them, Trevor Mason's navigator and bomb-aimer laid out their charts. The navigator, a small Scotsman named John MacLachan, turned round. He grinned at Jeff.

"Nice quick trip if we get there," he said.

"Can it Jock," the raw-boned Australian bomb-aimer, Andy Neil, said quickly.

The Scot turned slowly round.

"I think what I think," he replied, "we've a jinx."

"I do too," Andy said, "but let's keep it to ourselves."

Red Ainsworth watched the two settle down to wait for the Navigation Leader and the Intelligence Officer. He turned to Jeff with a wry smile.

"Do they mean bad luck or their pilot?" he asked.

"Search me," replied Jeff.

The target was Essen. Punch, the Intelligence Officer, strung the red woollen track lines on the large wall map. Richards, the Navigation Leader, sat and watched him. Punch stood back and checked his work. The red blob of the defended areas of the Ruhr seemed to dominate the map. His throat felt dry as he turned to face the airmen.

"The target tonight is Essen," he said slowly, watching the faces staring up at him.

"The route is as shown on the map," he continued. "Base to Cromer, from where you will immediately set course for position 52 degrees 45 minutes north, 4 degrees 38 minutes east on the Dutch Coast. From there to Enkhuizen on the Zuider-Zee."

He indicated each position on the wall map with a long cane pointer as he named it.

"From Enkhuizen to a point 15 miles north of Essen here, at 51 degrees 40 minutes north and 7 degrees east. The track into the target is 178 degrees. This is important and it must be flown exactly."

Pausing, he gazed round the room. The old young faces looked up as the pause lengthened.

"I repeat," he stressed, "that track must be flown into the target. Now, do you all have the positions of the turning points?"

He answered two navigators who queried latitudes and longitudes then addressed the whole group once again.

"The route home is dicey I'm afraid," he said, "from Essen you fly on a track of 198 degrees for twenty-five miles to position 51 degrees 07 minutes north, 6 degrees 50 minutes east. Good navigation is most essential here because your next leg passes south of Dusseldorf and between Krefeld on the north and Munchen Gladbeck on the south. All of these towns are very heavily defended. Intelligence reports that there are gaps in the defences along the route you will fly if you remain on track. Your next turning point is on leaving enemy territory, the western tip of Overflakkee."

Red dug Jeff gently in the ribs with his elbow.

"That will make Tich happy," he whispered from the side of his mouth, "he'll be able to spring that corny joke of his again."

The Intelligence Officer continued with the remaining details. Then he pointed out the defended areas to be expected along the route. They were many and lethal.

The Navigation Leader rose. He repeated much that Punch had already told them. He gave the individual tracks and distances between the various turning points as worked out at Group Headquarters. When he sat down, the navigators ruled in the tracks on their plotting charts. They measured the angles and distances. The details were entered in the log sheets they would use that night. The bomb-aimers ruled in the tracks on the detailed maps. They searched for prominent landmarks which could be seen from the planes in the darkness.

Jeff completed his calculations, noting them in his log. He indicated the defended areas in red shading on his chart. He was sitting back, smoking a cigarette, when Syd entered with the other captains just prior to main briefing.

"Looks an interesting trip," he said laconically as he sat

beside Jeff.

"I'm glad you think so," Jeff replied. "Personally, I think Group has excelled itself in that leg out of the Ruhr. It's a bang-on leg that, near every defended area possible."

Syd gazed at the wall map. Too much red woollen thread seemed to merge into the red colouring representing the defended areas.

"Hell," he exclaimed eventually. "What bright boy thought that one up?"

"Press on regardless," Red boomed.

In front of them Trevor Mason joined his crew members. He seemed young and inexperienced. The Scot navigator went over the tracks with him. The three of them, Scottish, Australian and English bent their heads over the charts and maps.

* * *

The crews were completely unprepared for the shock Punch dealt them at main briefing. He waited for them to settle down. The Squadron Commander nodded for him to go ahead.

After clearing his throat, he glanced at the sheaf of papers in his hand. Then straightening up, he addressed the crews.

"Tonight the target is Essen," he began, "the objective, to deal a crippling blow to Germany's war effort by destroying or severely damaging the vast Krupps Armament Works -----"

"About time the ruddy place was wiped out," a voice said from the rear of the room.

Punch paused for a moment, then soberly he continued.

"This operation is an experimental raid."

"Bleeding guinea pigs", another voice called out. Laughter resounded through the room.

Wing-Commander Bolton-Adams stood up, a frown on his face.

"This is not a circus," he thundered, "and neither is this operation, as you will find out. Now shut up and let's get cracking with the briefing."

He sat down with a silent apprehensive group facing him.

"As I said," Punch went on, "this is an experimental

138

raid to test a new target marking technique developed by the boffins. In the first place you will be flying higher than usual and because of this new technique you will be carrying no target indicator flares, only H.E. bombs."

He paused again before continuing, he glanced down at his papers then slowly he looked up and spoke.

"There will be only 31 planes making the attack."

There was a stunned, silent moment before the crews erupted. As angry shouts condemning the supposed stupidity of the operation reverberated round the long room, the Squadron Commander jumped up to silence the crews.

"This is it," Clarrie whispered to Syd, as the noise died down, "don't they want us to finish our tours?"

"That's the shot Clarrie, old chap," Red laughed, "bring a ray of brightness into our saddened blighted lives."

"It's just a way of killing off a few crews," Doug added jocularly, "they're getting too many new bods from the Empire Air Training Scheme. Can't find places to put them."

"Put a sock in it," Jeff said calmly. "Give the C.O. a go."

The voices quietened. The airmen settled down. Wing-Commander Bolton-Adams stood erect on the platform. He stared down angrily at the airmen until the last murmur ceased and there was complete silence.

"I don't want any repetition of that outburst." He spat the words out slowly. "If any crew wishes to back out of this op. he can see me after this briefing. This is no easy prang without weight of numbers, I know, but damn it, while you're on this squadron, pathfinders, I expect you to behave like men and do what you are asked—no matter what. Do I make myself clear?"

Heads nodded throughout the room.

"Well, now let the Intelligence Officer finish his gen."

Continuing to stand, he nodded to Punch to go ahead.

Punch adjusted his spectacles. He shuffled the papers in his hand.

"As I said, there is a new marking procedure being used tonight," he went on.

He looked up. The eyes of every airman were on him. He had a sad foreboding that many of these faces would not be present for de-briefing, when the operation was over.

"Red target indicator flares," he said, "will be dropped to burst at 18,000 feet by Mosquitoes using new marking instruments called 'Oboe.' "

A ripple of sound ended nearly as soon as it had begun, as the C.O. took a threatening step forward.

"You will fly on a given track and airspeed from the last turning point north of the city," he paused again before continuing. "You must fly perfectly straight and level and at a given height, 20,000 feet."

Another ripple of angry sound welled up.

"Straight and level for that distance is suicide over the Ruhr," a pilot stated firmly.

"They've put us into the stratosphere," Doug whispered to Syd.

"There goes one of my favourite jokes," Red chuckled quietly, "the Yank commander tells his boys to fly at 30,000 feet. One bright bod asks what will happen if he bombs at 25,000 feet. The C.O. promises him an Air Medal. The bod then asks what about 20,000 feet. The C.O. tells him he'll get a Cluster. At 15,000 he's told he'll get a D.F.C. and at 10,000 a Silver Star. When the bod asks about bombing at 5,000 feet the C.O. tells him not to be bloody silly, he'd run into the R.A.F."

In spite of themselves, the others laughed.

"It's sad it is," Red continued, "especially when we prided ourselves that anyone who bombed above 10,000 feet was a cissy."

"Pipe down will you Red," Jeff laughed. "I want to get this gen down."

The briefing continued to a subdued group of airmen. When Punch finally sat down, there was a strange tension in the air. The Meteorological Officer showed his charts and detailed the conditions to be expected. The other leaders stood for a few moments, spoke their lines then resumed their seats.

Finally, Wing-Commander Bolton-Adams came forward on the platform once more. He looked down at the crews.

"I'm not very pleased with you lot tonight," he said sternly, "but I know you'll press on and do the job regardless."

"Rewardless," a voice spoke up.

A slight twitch of his lips broke the severity of the Commanding Officer's face. Otherwise he ignored the remark.

"Furthermore," he continued, "just so that you won't be lonely up there in the cold, I'm going along too."

"Bang on," another cry sounded.

* * *

"Cromer ahead Navigator," Red called from his position in the nose.

"Thanks Red," Jeff replied.

Yorker was still climbing into the rarified air. The engines growled powerfully as they drew her higher over the darkened countryside. Over Base they had circled up to 10,000 feet, before setting course for Cromer on the English coast. Endless circles they had seemed to the crew, until Base was finally only a red flashing beacon below them.

After unhooking his intercom and oxygen plugs and switching off his table lamp, Jeff went forward. The English coast lay ahead clearly visible. He plugged in behind Doug and stood watching the coast coming slowly towards them. The plane still surged upward. Syd sat silently in his bucket seat. His and Doug's eyes constantly glanced over the luminous dials in front of them on the instrument panel. Needles flickered and the altimeter indicator slowly crept round.

"This is flogging the old girl Skipper," Doug said softly into his oxygen mask, "climbing at this speed."

"I know it Doug," Syd replied, "but we have to do it to get there. So far so good, keep your finger crossed."

Syd called up each member of the crew. After their replies, the only sound in the plane was the roar of the engines. Cromer was passed on track. Jeff gave the new course to fly. The North Sea stretched, a black mass, ahead of them. Jeff returned to his position behind the blackout curtain. He fastened it securely, plugged in, turned on his light and resumed his navigation. Working out a fix from the radar set he calculated a new wind.

"Nav. to Pilot," he said at length. "Mets not too bad to-night for a change Skipper."

"That's good Jeff," Syd replied absently. His attention was given to the green, glowing instruments in front of him.

A bright flash blossomed for an instant on the sea below as a jettisoned 4,000 pound bomb burst.

"Cookie down ahead Skipper," Red called. "Someone's had it and is on his way home."

"Lucky buggar," Tich's voice added from the rear turret, "it's ruddy cold out here."

"I wonder if it's engine trouble, finger trouble or lack of guts," Doug said cynically.

"I wouldn't know," Syd replied, "but they'll be home in bed when we're pranging the Ruhr."

On the long trip across the sea, they saw several more 4,000 pound bombs explode below them as crews jettisoned them before turning back for their home bases. The original small number had been cut down to an even smaller force.

* * *

An hour after the last plane had taken off from Battleson, Trevor Mason returned on three engines. The starboard outer engine was not functioning. He landed competently. The Lancaster touched down gently. It rolled along the runway. He swung off onto the perimeter track and taxied to his dispersal point. A silent, despondent crew climbed down from the plane and hurriedly jumped into the waiting flight van. As the van stopped outside the flight office, another Lancaster thundered overhead.

Trevor and his crew wandered slowly into the de-briefing room. Punch stood waiting for them.

"What happened?" he asked quietly, as they settled down around the table.

"The blasted starboard out packed up on us," the Flight Engineer, a stocky Yorkshireman, said abruptly.

"We were climbing at exactly the rate and revs the Engineering Officer told us to," Trevor added, leaning tiredly upon the table, "then the engine lost power. We

142

stopped climbing and levelled out at that height, but the engine still got worse. We finally had to cut it altogether."

There was not only strain in his voice, there was also relief. Punch's eyes narrowed as he listened. He was a charitable person, but he felt that Trevor Mason was pleased that he had been able to return to base with a valid excuse for not completing the flight.

"Did you jettison your cookie?", he asked, looking down at the sortie report form. He marked it "ABORTIVE" as he listened.

The navigator gave the position where they had jettisoned. Punch noted down the latitude and longitude. He continued through the form asking questions and noted down the replies.

The crew were rising to leave when Wing-Commander Bolton-Adams burst angrily into the debriefing room.

"Well of all the damned luck," he shouted from across the room. "Bloody engine packed up on me over Cromer. Tried to go on but couldn't get any bloody height. Bad show all round."

He stamped up to Punch, his eyes flashing his disappointment.

"What happened to you?" he snapped when he saw Trevor and his crew, standing, unsure of themselves, round the table.

"The same thing as happened to you, Sir," Punch said for Trevor.

"Huh!" the C.O. grunted. "You can think yourself lucky it happened to me too. I might have taken a dim view of it otherwise."

He paused for a moment, looking down at the restless, uncomfortable seven men.

"This is your second abortive," he snapped. "I hope for your sake that your next op. isn't."

"Yes Sir," Trevor answered quietly.

The Commanding Officer turned away from them and faced Punch.

"Well, let's get on with the damned bumph," he said.

After standing self-consciously for a moment, Trevor and his crew saluted and despondently left the room. The C.O. absently returned their salute.

"You were rather hard on them, don't you think?" Punch said.

"What do you mean?"

"Well they had just as much excuse to return to base as you did," he continued looking his Commanding Officer straight in the face. "Is this your way of getting this abortive of your own out of your system?"

The Wing-Commander's head snapped up angrily, his eyes flashed for a moment. Then a sheepish grin softened the hard taut angry lines on his face.

"I'm afraid you know me better than I know myself at times Punch," he said more gravely, putting his hand on the Intelligence Officer's shoulder.

"You're a good man to have around," he continued, "I shouldn't have had that bind at them the way I did, bad show that, but dammit man, he has had two abortives in a row."

Punch waited until the other was seated before replying.

"Both were legitimate, he might just be unlucky. His crew seem very keen and badly disappointed about this one."

"Even if he doesn't," the C.O. added shrewdly, "we'll see about him later anyway. Now, where's my bloody crew, let's get this damned report over."

*　　*　　*

"Navigator to Pilot," Jeff called.

"Go ahead Jeff."

"E.T.A. Enkhuizen 2012, E.T.A. target 2030, bang on time, Skipper, if conditions remain as they are."

"Good show Jeff."

The long leg across the North Sea was behind them. They had crossed the Dutch Coast on track at 20,000 feet. South of them the searchlights of Amsterdam stabbed the sky. As they flew deeper into enemy territory, each felt the tension mount. Knowing the small number of planes which were engaged on the raid, made the crew uneasy. There was safety in numbers.

Ahead of them two brilliant flares rose from the ground, climbed high to Yorker's own altitude, crossed to form an arch then dropped away, their light gradually fading as they descended.

"Bomb-aimer to Navigator," he called. "Enkhuisen dead ahead. You're bang on track."

"Thanks Red."

Suddenly, a mile south of them, tracers spun their fabric of brilliance across the dark sky.

"Fighter flares ahead," Doug shouted excitedly.

"I see them Doug," Syd said calmly. "Keep your eyes open gunners. I'm beginning evasive action now."

"O.K. Skipper," Tich replied.

"Mid-upper O.K., Skipper," Clarrie added.

"Roger."

They all knew the danger of the flares sent up by the Germans on the ground. They were sighted to cross at the height of the attacking planes and their apex marked the track they were flying. They served as guides to the swarms of German fighter planes sent up to repel the British raids.

Below them, Holland slid slowly by. Scattered cloud hid most of it from Red's eyes. He stared down, striving to pierce the mist in his search for landmarks. He looked ahead. Through the clouds, the waters of the Zuider-Zee became visible. The point of Enkhuisen jutted out into the inland sea.

"Combat starboard, three o'clock," Clarrie yelled, "about 1,000 yards."

The combat was short-lived. The enemy fighter's cannon shells poured into the bomber. There was a brief reply from it—too brief. An orange glow appeared. More cannon shells arched across and poured into the glow, until it fell in a tightening, spiral spin to the soil of Holland below. A mushroom of light appeared as it hit, cruelly brilliant for a moment, then subsiding to a dull red as the plane burnt itself out.

Jeff entered a note of the combat and its result in his log.

They set course from Enkhuisen for the last turning point before the target. In what seemed seconds to the tense crew, the searchlights of the Ruhr appeared. Though still miles ahead, they seemed to stretch across the entire southern horizon. From Duisberg to Dortmund the frightening beams emerged and merged to fill the sky.

A feeling of impotence passed through Syd as he watched the lights draw closer and appear to spread wider around the horizon. He felt it was impossible to penetrate the horror ahead. His hands trembled on the control column.

"Skipper!" Jeff's voice sounded unconcerned over the intercomm.

"Go ahead Jeff."

"Four minutes to E.T.A. on the turning point," the navigator said slowly, "then turn onto a course of 199 degrees magnetic, 1–9–9 magnetic."

Syd repeated the course back.

"There's a hell of a drift to port," Jeff added, "the winds are terrific. I've calculated 21 degrees drift."

The calm tone in which Jeff spoke brought a smile to Syd's lips. The Ruhr with all its horrible defences visible lay minutes ahead, he thought, and Jeff spoke of wind strengths.

"Thanks Jeff, for more than you know," he said, feeling the tension of the moment before easing away.

"Eh?" Jeff exclaimed surprisedly.

"Don't worry about it."

They turned on E.T.A. Essen, the target, was fifteen miles away; four and a half minutes. Four and a half minutes in actual time but mentally—an eternity.

The groping lights caught a bomber. They held it like a moth in a candle glow. Flak puffs blackened the sky round it.

"I'm going in behind this poor beggar," Syd called.

"I'm lining up the bomb-sight now, Skipper," Red said, "how are we for time of Target Indicator Flares Navigator?"

"Two minutes dead," Jeff replied, "if it's on time we should be bang on E.T.A."

He gave Syd the course out of the target area. Syd set it on the compass. Red called for the bomb-doors to be opened. As they opened, cold air rushed into the cabin. The engines' roar seemed louder, the slipstream whistled through the plane.

"I'm coming out now," Jeff said, switching off his light. As he drew the blackout curtain aside, the brilliance of the lights startled him. They were in the main defence belt. Searchlights weaved, crossed and re-crossed all round them.

Quickly he plugged in behind Doug.

"Hell," he exclaimed, "what a party!"

"They're no bloody birthday cake candles, Jeff", Tich chuckled dryly.

The bomber ahead suddenly exploded. Debris scattered. A flaming fuselage tumbled down spinning end over end. Immediately the searchlight beams swung away, one job was ended, they sought another. Within moments another bomber was coned on Yorker's port side.

"Where's that flare?" Red snarled to himself. "I don't want to do a dummy run over this joint."

"Heaven forbid," Clarrie agreed.

Within seconds, the red cascade burst. It hung close and slightly to their starboard. Instinctively, Syd jerked at the controls. Yorker skidded across unprotestingly.

"Good show Syd," Red applauded. "Right, a little—right—right—steady."

He paused for a moment, watching the red flare creep along the drift wires of the bomb-sight.

"Steady—steady—steady," he intoned.

The bomb release toggle was in his hand, his thumb on the button—he squeezed it.

"Bombs away—hold her steady for the photo."

When the photo had been taken, Syd pushed the control column forward. Speed mounted swiftly.

"On course navigator," he called.

"Right Syd," Jeff replied, noting the time and speed.

He dashed back to his compartment. This leg of the trip was all important. Again noting the airspeed, he realised it was much higher than he had calculated for. Quickly he worked out a new ground speed on his computer and a new E.T.A. for the next turning point. He passed up the information to Syd with the next course to be flown. Once again he went forward. The target areas had an eerie fascination for him. The pattern of the terrible Ruhr defences was there below him. He compared them mentally with the blobs on his chart. They skirted past Dusseldorf.

They were on track.

On E.T.A. they turned towards England. Once again they flew close by, but outside, the defences of Dusseldorf.

Ahead lay the gap between Munchen—Gladbach and Krefeld. Both towns were pyramids of light. A plane flew over and was coned by Krefeld. It lost height suddenly as flak poured up at it and hit. It flamed as it finally drew away from the lights in a shallow dive.

"He's had it," Syd muttered.

They passed through the gap into welcome darkness. Syd felt the tension ease. He relaxed momentarily, shifting his weight in his seat to a more comfortable position.

"Bandit," Tich screamed, sudden and shrill. "Go port go—Go!"

No longer relaxed but alert and active, Syd hurled the Lancaster over and down to port. Over the intercomm, the machine guns stuttered out their battle cry. Cannon shell tracers ripped the air with light around them. He felt the strikes as the shells hit Yorker. The acrid smell of their bursting filled the plane.

"Anyone hit?" Syd yelled as he continued to hurl the great plane round.

"I've got it in the leg Skipper," Tich's voice declared, shocked and surprised.

"Al and Jeff," Syd screamed, "get down to Tich. Mid-upper can you see the bandit—can you control?"

"Yes, Skipper," Clarrie's voice and the sound of his machine guns mingled over the intercomm.

"Starboard quarter, five o'clock up."

It was a different Clarrie. He was cool and sure. He spoke deliberately.

"Can you take him too Tich?" He asked urgently.

"Think so," the rear-gunner's voice replied faintly.

The guns sounded over the intercomm for long seconds. From both turrets the tracers arched away towards the dark mass which spat tracers back at them.

"Good show Tich, we got him," Clarrie's voice yelled excitedly.

Behind them the fighter flamed, the flames spread, twisted and turned and fell swiftly to earth.

As the battle was fought out, Jeff and Al hurriedly clipped on portable oxygen bottles. They struggled down the fuselage as Syd hurled it round, striving to lose the fighter. They lost their balance and fell against the side as they hurried down. When they reached the rear, Jeff threw himself up onto the catwalk leading to the rear turret. The smell of explosive hung there. Great gaping holes had been punched in the fuselage skin above his head. He hardly noticed them.

Al plugged into the intercomm point near the Elsan. There was no sound.

"Tich, this is Al., can you hear me?" he called anxiously.

"Yeah," a weak voice murmured, "we got him Al."

"Good for you Tich," Al replied with relief, "center your turret, Jeff is behind you. We'll get you out."

There was no reply for a moment. Then Tich replied faintly.

"I'm trying Al."

Between them, Jeff and Al dragged the little rear-gunner out of the damaged turret. Hurriedly they applied a makeshift torniquet. Al unclipped his oxygen bottle and fitted it to the gunner's mask. They carried him to the bed above the bomb bay. They laid him down and switched on the light.

Blood covered the left leg of his flying suit. He was unconscious. Jeff unhooked Al's oxygen bottle from Tich and handed it back to the wireless-operator. Quickly he plugged Tich's mask into the main supply point beside the bed.

"Get into the rear turret Al.," Jeff yelled over the roar of the engines. "There might be more fighters around."

As Al rushed away, Jeff turned to Tich. He drew his knife from his pocket. Opening it, he slit the leg of the flying suit. The leg was badly smashed below the knee. The broken bones protruded through the torn flesh. Blood pumped from severed veins as soon as he released the torniquet. Hastily he ripped off his belt and tied it above the knee as a more effective one. He applied battle dressings to the gaping wound and threw blankets over the rear gunner, tucking them in before he strapped him down.

"Navigator to Skipper," he called up eventually. "Tich looks bad."

"How bad?" Syd asked.

"He'll live, but his left leg looks as if it has had it. Right

149

now he has passed out from loss of blood, so I didn't give him an injection."

"I'll belt Yorker home," Syd exclaimed savagely. "We'll get him back as fast as the old girl will go without falling apart."

While Jeff inspected the plane for damage, Syd pushed Yorker's nose down and slammed the throttles forward. The plane seemed to sense the urgency. Her engines developed a more powerful growl. The airspeed built up to Syd's satisfaction.

"Al and Clarrie," he called, "keep a watchout. I'm not doing any evasive action. It would only waste time."

As they passed Overflakkee, no-one said a word. Tich was still unconscious. Red took Jeff's place as the navigator went back to his table. Jeff sat and stared at blood which he had smeared from his hands onto his chart. Suddenly he shuddered. A spasm of nausea shook him. When it passed, he took up his log and resumed his navigation.

They arrived over base early. Over half an hour passed before the next plane arrived. Red finally took over the rear turret so that Al could return to the wireless. He called up Base to report Tich as a casualty and for an ambulance to be standing by. Tich lay strapped to the bed, moaning softly. Jeff sat beside him.

Syd eased Yorker down onto the runway. The landing wheels squealed for a moment, then ran softly along. There was no bounce, it was a perfect landing. At the dispersal point the ambulance, the C.O's. car and the flight van were already waiting.

After running Yorker onto the concrete apron, Syd turned her and cut the engines. Jeff ran back and opened the rear door. He lowered the ladder. Immediately the doctor sprang on board, racing past Jeff he expertly examined Tich.

"Bad," he murmured to himself as he worked with deft hands. "Have you given him a shot?"

"No, Sir," Jeff replied, "He's been unconscious."

"Good," the doctor said absently. "I will, he'll need it."

In a short time Tich had been placed in the ambulance and it had sped away.

"He's on his way to Ely Hospital," the doctor told the crew. "I don't hold much hope for that leg, but if they get at it right away, he'll have some chance of keeping it."

The despondent crew slowly climbed down from the plane.

"Sticky do, Berry," the C.O. said softly, putting his hands on Syd's shoulders. "Bad luck for your gunner but he's in good hands."

They walked away together silently.

Jean rushed up to Jeff. She threw herself into his arms, tears streamed down her sad-happy face.

"Oh Jeff," she cried clasping him tightly. "It might have been you ----- When you called up for the ambulance ------"

He held her close. He kissed the top of her head.

"You goon," he whispered into her hair. "You should know better than that. I'm doomed to a life of being henpecked by you."

CHAPTER 13

Interrogation over, Jeff and Syd walked away silently, from the operations building together. The wounding of Tich hung over them like a malevolent cloud.

"Tough cake," Jeff broke the silence eventually.

"The first casualty among the crew down here," Syd replied, "and one of the originals. I wonder how the rest of us will get on."

"I wonder myself Syd."

They walked slowly through the darkened camp, huddled up in their battle-dresses against the cold. Their hands were thrust deep in their pockets.

"It was a hell of a do all round," Syd said angrily, "with a small force like that. We get Tich wounded and the squadron loses two crews as well."

"They might have landed away," Jeff replied, knowing in his mind it was a hopeless hope.

"Are you going for a meal?" Syd asked abruptly.

"I couldn't force caviar down," Jeff replied absently, then laughing he said, "I don't know why I use caviar as a criterion. I tried it once and hated the stuff."

"I couldn't eat either," Syd said, "let's go straight to the billets. What happened to the others of the crew?"

"Well I'm pretty sure Red and Doug intend to get good and drunk on operational rum. The others left before us."

The remainder of the long walk to the billets was in silence.

As he quietly opened the door to his room, Syd was surprised to find the light on. Trevor Mason was lying on his bed awake. He was still fully dressed in his operational clothes. He lay back, smoking. A taut, angry, determined expression was on his face. His face had hardened and aged. He no longer looked a lost fearful boy.

"I thought you'd be asleep," Syd said.

"I couldn't sleep," Trevor replied, "the C.O. all but called me a coward in front of my crew and I've been mulling it over and over in my mind until it's boiled."

He looked up at Syd with tired red-rimmed eyes.

"You heard we didn't make the target I suppose?" he asked.

"Yes I heard, but not the way you put it," Syd replied flatly. "I heard one of your engines and one of the C.O.'s. both packed up."

Syd began to undress. The reaction from the trip began to set in. He felt drained of all energy and feeling. All he wanted, was to get into bed and to try to sleep.

"Yes, the C.O. didn't make it either," Trevor continued savagely. "I'll show him whether I'm L.M.F. or not."

"He probably didn't mean it the way you think he did," Syd said patiently and wearily.

Trevor laughed bitterly.

"He meant it all right and said it in front of Punch as well as the crew."

Syd reached for his pyjamas.

"How about getting some shuteye?" he said. "I've had it."

Springing from his bed, Trevor rushed over to apologise.

"Sorry Syd," he said, "I've been so wrapped up in my own troubles I didn't even ask how the op. went. How was it?"

Syd shrugged his shoulders as he began to put his pyjamas on.

"Bloody!"

* * *

That night, after Tich's wounding, Jeff had his first really bad nightmare. He had had dreams and nightmares before but this was terribly worse. It was vivid in its realism and horror. He saw a fighter attacking them, Its cannons flaming. He felt the shells pierce the thin skin of the Lancaster. He saw them explode in great brilliant flashes which wrecked the fuselage. Fire took control of the plane. He saw the tongues of flame enlarge as they licked their way along towards him, engulfing everything in their path. The horrible brilliance of the fire seemed to envelop him and he was petrified, incapable of movement. He heard a scream as he seemed to see and feel his flesh shrivel and sear. The plane dropped, a blazing, stricken wreck, twisting, turning, dropping into a black bottomless void.

He heard another scream. He awoke abruptly, sitting upright in bed. He was wet with perspiration. For moments still, the dream was reality. He looked dazedly round, wondering where he was. Then, sheepishly, he realised the screams had been his. He gazed at the beds close by his but the occupants were still asleep. Some tossed and moaned as they wrestled with their own dark dreams. The hard iron-framed beds creaked in the hut as the airmen moved. Jeff lay back thankfully against the pillow, wide awake.

None of the crew could remain in bed in the morning. They were not expected to report to the flights until noon, but each felt an urgent need for news of Tich. They straggled up to their messes. After a restless night, Syd rose early, shivering with cold. He looked at and pitied Trevor, who lay still asleep, with the turmoil in his mind showing in the contours of his sleeping face. Syd shaved and washed slowly with cold water, then dressed and quietly left the room.

He wandered through the quiet billets area to the mess, too early for breakfast. Still weary, his limbs still aching from the exertion of the operation, he wandered into the ante-room. To his surprise, Paula was seated in front of the dying fire. Her face also was tired from the long night on duty.

"You should still be in bed," she rebuked him as he walked over to her.

"So should you if it comes to that," he smiled down at her.

He sat beside her, pleased with finding her there. He felt at ease again.

"I'm waiting for breakfast, then off I go," Paula said. "You know, I had an idea you would be up here early."

"Why?"

"For news of Tich," she said bluntly. "I rang Ely half an hour ago, just before I left the ops. room."

Leaning over towards him, she gazed reassuringly into his eyes.

"Tich is going to be fine," she continued. "They operated on him as soon as he arrived. It will take a long time, but he will keep his leg even if he does have a limp and otherwise he's doing well."

Syd sighed his relief. The news brightened him. He leaned back in his chair.

"That's great," he said, "you couldn't have given me better news. What about the two other crews, any news of them?"

A sad expression clouded her face.

"No news." she said.

* * *

Of the thirty-one planes engaged in the previous night's operation, only twenty-four reached the target. Of these six were missing.

Morning assembly was quiet and subdued. The Commanding Officer entered the room quietly. His face was drawn. He had not been to bed at all. Through the long night, after the last crew had left the Interrogation Room, he had sat beside the operations phone calling group periodically for news of his two missing crews. After they had officially been posted as missing, he had remained in the Operations Room, silently drinking coffee and smoking, until it was time for him to go to his office to prepare a new day's "battle-order."

"We are on readiness," he told the crews, "which pro-

154

bably means we will be on ops. again tonight."

There was no need for him to tell them that two crews, their friends, were missing. The news had already spread quickly, had been accepted. Now, they pushed all thoughts of these friends back into the recesses of their minds. Only occasionally would their names be mentioned. They were not forgotten, they were the mates who had not come back.

When the assembly broke up, Trevor Mason followed the Commanding Officer out of the room.

"Morning Mason," the C.O. said, conscious of his tirade of the previous night.

"Excuse me, Sir," Trevor said, "but will I be on the battle-order?"

For a moment, Wing-Commander Bolton-Adams thought that Trevor was trying to have himself excused from flying. However, when he saw the hard bitter expression in the pilot's eyes, he knew his surmise was wrong. Realising this, he experienced a feeling of satisfaction and pleasure, tinged however with sadness.

"Why do you want to know?" he asked.

"I want to be on it, Sir," Trevor stated, firmly but respectfully.

"There are other crews on the squadron you know Mason," the C.O. replied, "and a lot of them didn't fly last night."

"They don't have to make up as much as I have either," Trevor spoke with a note of urgency in his voice. "Will you put us on, Sir?"

The C.O. smiled tiredly.

"Well, I might have had you taped wrongly my boy," he said, "be it on your own head but if we go, you go."

A pleased look lit up Trevor Mason's face.

"Thank you, Sir," he said, "I'll tell my crew."

As he turned to go, the C.O. called him back.

"Tell Berry and his crew that I want to see them when you get back to the flights."

"Yes Sir."

*   *   *

"Damn good show you lads bunged on last night."

The C.O. addressed Syd and the crew as they stood self-

155

consciously in front of his paper-littered desk.

"Good show by all of you," he continued, "particularly the gunners. I'm recommending Evans for the C.G.M., he deserves it, belting away and helping to shoot the Jerry down after being wounded the way he was. You Kemp, I'm putting up for a D.F.M."

Clarrie went scarlet, he was unable to say a word. He shyly nodded his head up and down.

"Not every day," the C.O. went on, "that one of my crews bags a fighter. I'm pleased to say that Evans is quite well at Ely; but he damned near lost that leg. He'll be U.S. for quite a while."

"Thank you, Sir," Syd replied for the crew.

They stood for a moment, uncertainly, as the C.O. turned over the papers piled on his desk.

"Here it is," he said at length. "I'm also pleased to give you this news."

Glancing at Syd, he held a slip of paper in his hand.

"They must have thought a lot of you and Johnson at your last squadron," he said, "they recommended both of you for decorations, D.F.C. for you Berry and D.F.M. for you Johnson. They've just come through. After reading your citations I feel even prouder of you. You did a good job on your old squadron and you're doing a good one here."

Syd and Jeff looked at one another in amazement. Grins split their faces. The memory of the bad operations which had merited the decorations had been pushed back in their minds.

"Good show lads," the C.O. added, standing up. "See the Adj. He will have some ribbon for you."

Coming round his desk, he shook the hands of all the crew.

"You'll be a well decorated crew if you keep this up. You won't be on ops. tonight so you can celebrate."

"Thank you Sir," Syd said, saluting as he spoke.

"You little beauties," Red said when they were outside once again.

He threw his great arms around Jeff and Syd.

"Don't forget our bashful Clarrie," Doug added, taking hold of the gunner by the shoulders.

"Forget him!" Red shouted. "I'm going to take him out tonight and get him so plastered, he won't be able to scratch himself."

"Where will it be?" Al asked.

"I suggest," Doug replied, "that we honour the White Heron with our presence tonight, heaven help it."

"And no women," Red said sternly, prodding both Syd and Jeff with a hard finger.

With a laugh, Syd side-stepped the bomb-aimer.

"No women. Roger!" he said, "but I know a better pub. It's a fair way to go but we all have bikes or can borrow them."

"Name it," Doug demanded, "if it's round here I must know it."

"It's called the Anchor and it's run by an ex-naval type."

Doug shook his head surprisedly.

"Never heard of it," he said, "it's a newie on me. Anyway, don't bother about bikes, I can borrow a car."

"You rosiner," Red shouted. "I hate exercise."

* * *

It was five o'clock in the afternoon before Jean came on duty at the flight office. When she drove up, Jeff was waiting for her, dressed in his best uniform.

"This is a pleasant surprise," she exclaimed. "Why do I deserve such an honour? I thought you would be miles away by now."

Jeff leant over the door of the van near Jean.

"You can do a small job for me," he said nonchalantly.

"I might know it wasn't my fatal attraction alone that brought you here."

"Don't be flippant miss," he replied with a laugh, "or I'll get that good-looking blonde in parachutes to do it for me."

"See if I care," Jean shrugged.

"You do care, so cut the capers."

Jean's eyes flashed for a moment, then she smiled. She opened the van door and moved over. Jeff slid onto the seat beside her. He took off his tunic and dropped it onto her lap. Reaching into a trouser pocket, he drew out a small piece of D.F.M. ribbon and an issue sewing kit. He handed both to her.

Her eyes opened wide with surprise.

"Is it yours?" she asked.

"Of course."

"When, how and why?" Jean stammered out the words.

"Today, from my old squadron and if I told you how and why you'd say I was shooting a line and besides, even if you don't appreciate me, others do."

Jean jabbed his hand with a needle.

"Ouch!" Jeff yelled. "That hurt."

"Don't be so off-handed," she said quietly. "I really am pleased and proud of you. I'll find out what you did if it kills me."

As she began sewing the ribbon on, below the observer's wing on his tunic, he put his arm round her.

"I'll tell you later," he whispered, his lips against her ear, "but at the moment I'm still too surprised to believe it."

Jean turned her head and kissed him.

"If you want it sewn on, young fellow," she said as they drew apart, "you'd better let me concentrate."

She sewed the ribbon on neatly, broke the cotton on her teeth, patted her work and then handed the tunic to Jeff.

"Put it on Jeff," she asked, "so I can see it."

Getting out of the van, he slipped the tunic on. He did up the buttons then stood rigidly at attention while Jean inspected him.

"It looks grand," she murmured, tears rising to her eyes, "now I suppose you'll be off for a celebration with the crew."

Glancing at his watch, Jeff gave a cry.

"Hell," he said, "I told them I'd meet them by ten past five. Sorry I have to duck off, honey, but it's after twenty past now."

He kissed her hurriedly and dashed away. Jean watched his tall, thin, running figure with a smile.

*   *   *

The crew were clustered impatiently around an old sedan car, in front of the billets, when Jeff ran up breathing hard.

"Well Romeo, what kept you?" Red asked, "as if we

didn't know."

"Hey, get on the hero will you," Doug exclaimed. Taking out his handkerchief, he dusted the spotless ribbon on Jeff's tunic.

"Lay off," Jeff said self-consciously, edging away, "everyone here?"

With laughs, Red and Doug took hold of him and threw him bodily into the front seat.

"Everyone has been here for about half an hour," Syd replied as he hopped into the car beside Jeff. Syd's ribbon was also sewn on.

The rest of the crew piled into the old car. Doug slid into the driver's seat.

When they arrived at "The Anchor", there were only a dozen local farm workers and villagers in the pub.

"Hello there," Josh Lyons called out to Syd from behind the bar. "Nice to see you again. How's your young lady?"

"What young lady, Skipper?" Red asked with an innocent look.

"Paula, and only once," Syd replied, red-faced.

"Hello Josh," he said to the publican. "I've brought my no-good crew along for a celebration."

When they had explained, Josh called to the locals. After loudly telling them of the decorations, he gave drinks all round on the house.

"It's a pity it isn't Saturday night," he said, leaning on the bar after serving everyone. "We always have a singsong and a party here every Saturday night. After ten when I shut the bar, we get rid of strangers, shut the doors and hoe in."

"Sounds great," Syd remarked.

"Come along any Saturday night," Josh said, "you and your crew and their girl-friends are all invited."

They had been drinking for an hour when the first planes passed overhead. They thundered across the darkening sky. The crew became silent; their faces were solemn and instinctively their eyes looked upwards. It seemed strange to be sitting in the pub drinking while the others were flying overhead on their way to bomb Germany.

*   *   *

In Ely Hospital, Tich also heard the planes fly over. He too, instinctively, looked up and wondered whether the rest of the crew were up there. He lay propped up with pillows, his leg, encased in bandages, was held rigid and raised in traction by weighted ropes passing over pulleys in the metal frame above his bed. Pain still wracked him, in spite of the drugs he had been given.

His eyes were closed, his teeth were clenched against the searing agony, when he heard a nurse's voice.

"Visitors for you sergeant."

Slowly he opened his eyes and glanced towards the door.

His mother and father stood there.

Standing in the doorway of the ward, they seemed smaller. They stood there, uncertain and frightened. Tears ran down both their faces as they walked over to him and looked down. His father's arm was still in plaster. His mother bent over him and kissed his cheek. As she looked into his face, her expression was kind and gentle. She smiled down at him.

"Hello son," she said softly.

"Hello Ma," Tich murmured, gazing from one to the other. "How are you pa?"

"Fine, son," Mr. Mulgrave said. Drawing a handkerchief from his pocket, he noisily blew his nose and wiped his eyes.

"Your Commanding Officer rang us," he continued, "we came as soon as we could."

They were silent for a moment.

"Looks like it runs in the family," Mr. Mulgrave said with a short laugh, "both of us wrapped up. How do you feel son, much pain?"

His mother sat down beside the bed. As she took his hand, he squeezed her hard, work-worn one.

"It's not bad pa," Tich said, "I'm lucky to be here at all."

"We're proud of you son," his mother whispered, "your Commanding Officer told us all about what you did."

Tich smiled wryly. Vividly the previous night's operation came back to him. He shuddered as a stab of pain brought perspiration to his brow. His parents watched him, feeling impotent, unable to help. They felt the pain themselves. When the spasm passed, Tich looked at them.

"Sorry," he said with a strained smile.

They were allowed to remain for only a quarter of an hour. After that time, a nurse came over and gently asked them to leave. They rose immediately. His mother nervously fidgetted with her gloves and purse.

"We're staying in town son," she said softly as she bent over to kiss him.

"We'll see you every time we can," his father said, proudly shaking his hand. "You're all man, son."

Tich lay back, watching the two small middle-aged people shyly walk out of the ward. They turned at the door and waved, then were out of sight.

He felt happy in spite of the pain. At last he felt the miracle had happened. Tenderly he thought of them. He felt they were all closer to each other than they had ever been. Tears stung his eyes. Even if later, home became the place it had been, the place of complaint and criticism, he would never forget the loving tenderness of his mother and the proud concern of his father.

He was content.

*　　*　　*

The operation was a repetition in planning of the previous night. Essen was again the target. The number of planes was again small and the route was identical.

Trevor Mason nursed the engines as he gained height. In spite of the fear he felt, he was determined to finish this operation. The determination to make good over-rode the fear. He watched the luminous dials on the instrument panel glowing blue-green. He strained his ears to detect any discordant note in the smooth surging song of the motors. He fretted over Jock's navigation, realising how slim was the margin of error allowed. He had implicit faith in the Scottish navigator but still he worried.

Their trip was uneventful until they were forty miles from Essen. The Messerschmidt 109 attacked them from the starboard quarter from above. The German drove home his attack against the concentrated fire from the two turrets of the Lancaster as Trevor threw the plane round in a steep diving turn. Tracers flashed as they poured from each aircraft. The Messerschmidt 109 finally broke away after the first attack and was lost in the darkness. It did not make a second attack.

Cannon shells had ripped into the starboard wing. The starboard outer engine was on fire. Trevor and the flight engineer both reached for the fire extinguisher buttons. The engine was cut, the airscrew feather and the extinguisher poured out its foam onto the flames. Anxiously, they watched until there was no further sign of fire. Only a few minutes had passed from the beginning of the attack until the fire was out.

Quickly, Trevor swung the plane back on course.

"On course Jock," he called, "about five miles starboard of track."

"Right you are, skipper," Jock's Scottish burr quietly sounded.

There was stunned silence from the remainder of th. crew for a moment. Then five voices mingled simultaneously over the intercomm in a shouting babble of sound.

"Will ye all shut up," Jock thundered. "I've navigation to do."

The babble of noise stopped, then the flight engineer spoke.

"Hell, skipper, are we going into Essen on three engines?" he asked, a tremor of nervousness in his voice.

"We're over 22,000 feet now," Trevor replied firmly. "Will be able to maintain enough height to bomb above 18,000 feet and we didn't lose too much time so we'll make it by E.T.A."

There was no further argument.

Although still frightened, Trevor felt exhilarated. They had been blooded and had come through. In the moment of danger, there had been no panic, everyone had done his job and had done it well. During the attack his fear had not stopped him from acting correctly. They lost height slowly. Essen was lit up with all its horrible intensity. The Ruhr was a blaze of waving beams from end to end. The crew saw the red target indicators cascade when they were still nine miles from the target. Trevor dropped the nose slightly and opened the throttles more to build up their speed.

The bomb-aimer made a time adjustment as he dropped the bombs towards the dying target indicator. Immediately they were coned in searchlights. Although it was only for seconds, it seemed like hours. Black puffs of flak shells burst round them. Trevor swung the Lancaster to port in a steep diving turn.

The lights lost them.

The remainder of the trip seemed an anti-climax. The wonder of getting away unscathed, kept them quiet until the enemy coast lay behind them and the dark sea was below.

"Mon," Jock's voice murmured at last, "have we got a crew or have we?"

"I'll say we have," another voice replied.

Trevor smiled to himself as he remembered the indecision and fear of the previous day.

When Syd unsteadily returned from the crew's celebration at "The Anchor," Trevor was asleep, a smile curling his lips.

*　　*　　*

The following morning, the Station was carpeted with snow. The white flakes were still falling as the great-coated airmen straggled up to morning assembly. The drome was a wide white sheet. Sweeper trucks plied up and down the runways clearing them of snow.

The squadron was stood down from operations after flying for two successive nights. The training schedule was listed and the crews filed out.

"Damned cold," Jeff stated emphatically.

"Still it's better than rain," Syd replied as the crew walked out together, "besides this is good for hangovers."

"You guys don't know what cold is," Doug laughed, "in Canada now, that's where it does get cold."

Syd and Jeff both bent and scooped up handfuls of snow. They hurled it at Doug.

"O.K. fellows," Doug said, spitting out snow. "I give in."

They drove over to the hangar to inspect the work done on Yorker, before separating to go to the various sections. The plane was nearly ready to air test.

The morning dragged as the tasks were completed. The messes gradually filled as the airmen entered in ones and twos. The fireplaces glowed, poker schools started up in the Sergeants' Mess.

Al walked over to the mail rack. He gathered the letters for the crew. There was one for himself in an unfamiliar hand. Joining the crew round the fireplace he handed out the letters.

Slowly, he opened his own and began to read it. It was from Bess' mother. His face blanched as he read. An incredulous hurt look appeared. He read and re-read it, then angrily crumpled it in his hand. Red looked up from his own letter.

"What's wrong?" he asked.

"Everything," Al said bitterly, "that's what's wrong."

He wandered slowly away and sat at a table. The crew followed him.

"Spill it Al," Jeff said, seating himself beside the wireless-operator.

"It's a letter from Bess' mother," Al said slowly, his hands smoothing out the letter on the table.

"Well?"

"It's a straightforward one anyway," Al continued, "it says in one page that Bess can't marry me because she's having a baby by a chap who works in the factory in an exempt occupation. She says it is probably for the best as I might get killed anyway. Then she hopes that I am well."

Once again he crumpled the letter in his hand. He looked at it for a moment then hurled it into the fire.

"Damn it, damn it," he exclaimed, "why couldn't she wait."

Uncomfortably, the others glanced at one another.

"Well man," Jeff said quietly, "I'd say you're lucky to be rid of her."

"That's not much consolation," Al murmured, "when you've planned on something for years and then find your plans tumbling down round your ears."

His face hardened. He stared straight ahead at nothing. His hands clenched into fists.

"She could have told me she didn't want me when I saw her on leave. She seemed different, but I thought it was just because we hadn't seen each other for so long. She must have known about the baby then."

"Nice doll," Doug said sarcastically, "brother, are you

164

better off without her."

Red drew a small silver flask from the inside pocket of his battle-dress tunic. He unscrewed the stopper.

"Get this into you," he urged, handing the flask to Al. "That's the best Scotch and fella, if ever a Scotsman needed a Scotch you do now."

Al went to push it aside.

"Sink it," Red said firmly, "while I tell you what to do."

He waited until the wireless-operator had tilted the flask and gulped down a mouthful.

"Another one before I tell you," Red said.

Al drank again. Red sat down on the edge of the table.

"We'll probably operate tomorrow night again," he said with a grin creasing his face. "So, Al., you gather up all her damn letters and photos and we'll present the whole lot to Hitler."

Al looked up puzzled.

"What do you mean?" he asked.

"We'll tie the lot onto a bomb," Red laughed, "and right smack bang over the centre of the target we'll drop her billets doux or not so doux."

As the crew roared with laughter, Al's face brightened slightly.

Clarrie entered the conversation for the first time.

"Good idea Red," he said, "that will show her."

"It's a great idea," Doug chuckled, "consign her to the flames and consider yourself purged if that's the right word."

"I think it will do old man," Jeff remarked.

As he spoke, the bar opened. The shutters were thrown open and the steward called for business.

"Come on Al," Red said, "there's nothing to do up at the flights this afternoon, so we'll drown your sorrows in foaming tankards or in demon rum, name your poison."

Slowly, Al got to his feet. He still seemed hurt and perplexed, but the crew gathered round him and led him to the bar.

* * *

The following night they operated with a spare gunner. The letters and photos plunged down into the inferno of flame and bursting bombs that was Essen.

The attacks on the heavy industries in the Ruhr rose to a crescendo. Night after night the heavy bombers of the R.A.F. left their bases in England and thundered across the night skies to bomb the heart out of Essen. In good weather and bad, they dropped their loads of destruction onto the factories which had kept the German armies ploughing ahead in Russia. Essen never fully recovered and Bomber Command had contributed a major part in the ultimate defeat of Germany.

The losses in planes and crews were heavy. The squadron lost seven crews, some new, some experienced. In the period of constant operating, the crews' morale rose in spite of the losses. Though they brought sadness they failed to subdue the crews.

When the month ended, Syd and his crew had twenty-seven operations marked against their names on the flight crew board. Trevor Mason's crew had twenty-two.

Both crews wore the golden albatross, the "shitehawk", on their pocket flaps beneath their wings.

CHAPTER 14

"Hey you guys, I've just bought a bomb." Doug shouted as he dashed into the billets.

"A what?" Clarrie enquired in an amazed tone.

"Don't be a clot," Doug snapped, "not one of those, a car."

Airmen were stretched out or seated on their beds along both sides of the long hut. The Saturday afternoon sun shone weakly through the windows. Some were occupied, writing, reading or mending their clothing. Others just slept. Clarrie was darning socks. Al was reading and the remainder of the crew lay back on their beds relaxing.

Jeff stirred sufficiently to rise on one elbow.

"What's it like?" he asked.

"It's an old Austin sedan." Doug replied eagerly. "It's a big job so we can fit the whole crew in it."

He sat down beside Jeff.

"It's a real bargain," he continued, "only fifty-five

quid."

Red sat up slowly with a wide smile on his face.

"Dawn breaks at last," he said, "how much do we have to dob in?"

"Well," Doug said slowly, "I had a fiver, I used that as a deposit."

"The plot unfolds," Red said, "you want us to come good with the other fifty quid."

"Well if you guys put up the rest, we can clinch the deal."

"Fifty quid!" Jeff exclaimed, "Unless the others can do better than me, we're still not mobile."

"How much do you have?" Doug asked anxiously.

"Well I've got about six pounds to spare," Jeff replied.

"What about you Red?" Doug asked, turning to the bomb-aimer.

"Oh, seven at the most," Red replied, counting the notes in his wallet. "I have to have some left for grog."

"I can let you have four or five," Al said hopefully as he counted out five pounds and put them on the bed beside Doug.

Doug cast his hands in the air disgustedly.

"What are you," he cried, "a bunch of paupers? That only makes twenty-two."

Without a change of expression, Clarrie rose slowly from his bed. He reached into his uniform and drew out a wallet. He threw it onto the bed.

"You'll find what extra you need in there," Clarrie said to Doug.

The crew looked at him with open-mouthed amazement.

Doug grabbed up the wallet. He opened it and looked inside, then he gave a wild yell. A boot, thrown from the other end of the hut shot past his ear and crashed into Al's bed.

"Let an intrepid airman get some rest," they heard the thrower of the boot call out.

Picking up the boot, Doug hurled it in the direction of the voice. Heads ducked along the length of the hut.

"Pipe down you guys," Doug snarled, "we have business to transact here."

Then turning to the crew once more, he continued,

"We're mobile fellas."

Getting up from Jeff's bed, he bowed to Clarrie.

"Rockefeller," he said, "I salute thee. O.K. you others, shell out."

He collected the money and counted it. Then carefully he counted out notes from Clarrie's wallet until the total amounted to fifty pounds. He returned the wallet to Clarrie.

"Hold your horses while I get the bomb." As he spoke, he was moving away towards the door.

Within minutes he had returned.

The car was an ancient, black, battered sedan. It was large and roomy, seating three comfortably back and front with two additional seats folded into the back of the front seat. It looked like the pensioned-off mourning coach it was.

"O.K. you bods," Doug called from the driver's seat after the crew had inspected and criticised the car.

"Pile in and we'll pick up Syd."

"What about making it a night at The Anchor," Red said as he settled in beside Doug.

"I'm game," Doug replied.

"Heck," said Jeff, "I can't. I've a date with Jean."

"Bring her along," Doug said, "there's stacks of room. Syd's bringing Paula anyway, I saw him on the way back."

The crew clambered in. At the Officers' Mess, Syd and Paula got in. Then Doug drove noisily up to the Waafery guard-room. Jeff jumped out and asked the Waaf on duty to call Jean on the Tannoy. Only a few minutes elapsed before she came running up from her hut.

"What's the score?" she asked when she saw Jeff. "I thought I still had half an hour."

"So you had," Jeff replied, "but the crew have bought a car and we are all set for a night at The Anchor."

"I can't go like this," Jean said hurriedly. "I look a fright."

Taking a mirror from her purse, she looked into it. She patted at her hair, then pouted her lips as she inspected her make-up. Jeff took hold of her arm.

"Don't be batty," he said, "you look bang-on, good enough to eat. Anyway, you can doll up in the car if you

168

want to."

"I know I shouldn't go," Jean said, "but I will, against my better judgment."

They walked out together hand in hand. Jean stopped suddenly when she saw the car.

"Is that the bus," she laughed, "or are we going to a funeral?"

"No cheek from you," Jeff replied, "or you don't go."

"Just try to stop me young fellow, if you dare," Jean said, taking his hand again. She drew him towards the car.

When they arrived, "The Anchor" was crowded mainly with local people. However, there were several outsiders including four airmen from another nearby squadron.

Josh greeted them loudly from behind the bar.

"Glad you could make it," he yelled above the din, "what's your poison?"

They ordered and when served, they took their drinks into the lounge. It also was crowded. Groups clustered round the tables. Two village men whom Syd had met, stood up to give their chairs to Paula and Jean. The crew stood round merging into the group of villagers.

At ten o'clock, Josh called, "Time." As he entered the lounge, he motioned to the crew to remain. Gradually the visitors and strangers left. Josh locked the large front door.

"O.K.," he called, "now we can start."

A labourer from the village opened up a violin case. An accordion opened up with a breezy tune. Others wheeled the piano from the lounge into the bar.

There were nearly thirty people, men and women, assembled in the bar room. The crew was quickly introduced to the villagers they had not already met. The majority of them were middle-aged or elderly. The youths of the village had nearly all been called up. A few farm workers, sons of farmers, and two girls in their early twenties were the only young people present. Doug quickly started a conversation with the prettier of the two girls. She was small, dark-haired and had a shy manner. She was pretty without being beautiful.

Doug stayed by her side all evening.

During the evening, they sang and danced, mainly old

music-hall songs and ballads. Josh kept the bar open, passing the drinks out in between songs. At midnight a supper prepared by the women was served.

It was after one o'clock in the morning before they left. The evening had passed all too quickly.

* * *

The following morning, Col Nichols, the crew's new rear-gunner arrived. They took an immediate dislike to him.

He was a short, good-looking, blonde Welshman, who had never flown on operations. He came direct from gunnery school. About twenty-two years old, he was self-assured and loud spoken. His talk was mainly of sex and his conquests. His wavy hair was heavily oiled. Even in the dull grey sergeant's uniform, he appeared flashily dressed.

As they spoke to him, each of the crew thought of unassuming Tich lying wounded at Ely. Finally, he left them to report to the gunnery leader. The crew watched his cocky stride in silence until he was out of sight.

"Who are the bloody sprogs?" Red asked, amazement in his voice, "him or us?"

"I don't think I like that cove," Clarrie said vehemently.

Syd smiled at the expressions on their faces.

"Judging by your looks," he said, "I think that's unanimous. Anyway, let's give him a chance."

They slowly wandered out of the crew-room together.

"Well I shall erase all thoughts of the guy from my mind," Doug solemnly said. "I shall sit down and ponder over the charms of the fair Colleen Graham."

"The dark one at The Anchor?" Jeff asked.

"You're so right," Doug replied.

"Sex rears its ugly head," Red said jokingly.

With a short laugh, Doug tripped the bomb-aimer. Red fell full length on the ground. Doug prodded him in the ribs with his shoe.

"After our session with our high and mighty new gunner," Doug said as he reached down to help Red up, "you should be ashamed to even mention the word sex. Anyway, she's a nice kid."

"You certainly seemed to think so," Jeff remarked. "You spent the whole evening with her. I was surprised you even came home with us in the car."

"She's a fine girl," Doug said. "I'm going to see her again next time we have a night off."

"Well that's not tonight," Al said quietly, "if that hurry-scurry over at the operations block means what I think it means."

* * *

The target was Cologne.

During the night flying test, Clarrie attempted to help Col Nicholls. His help was brusquely refused.

"I know me job," the rear-gunner boasted.

"You'd better if we get a Jerry fighter on our tail," Red stated quietly.

"You worry about your bombs," Nicholls snapped, "I'll look after my end of this flying cigar."

Angrily, Red snapped off his microphone, swearing to himself as he did so. The remainder of the crew were uncomfortably silent.

Over the intercomm., suddenly sounded a shrill whistling. The tune was that of a vulgar song.

"Switch your blasted microphone off Nicholls," Syd snarled angrily.

The whistling ceased.

"O.K. pilot," the rear-gunner replied cheekily.

Over the Wash they descended to test the guns. All worked perfectly. Nicholls proved that he had learned well. His shooting was good. Syd felt easier.

Take-off was at 18.45.

There was less joking than usual amongst the crew. The presence of the new gunner dampened their normally exuberant spirits.

In the crew-room, Nicholls had ostentatiously tied a silk stocking round his neck for a scarf. As he did so, he had made a crude remark of how he had obtained it. He had spoken sufficiently loudly for all round him to hear.

In the plane before take-off, he had kept up a continuous chatter until Jeff irritably told him to "shut up."

The operation was another high level attack.

Over the North Sea, the radar set ceased to function.

"Radar's packed up Skipper," Jeff called over the intercomm., "we will have to go in as a supporter, marking is out for us."

"Any worries?" Syd asked.

"Not yet," Jeff replied, "but let me know when you see any searchlights on the coast."

Jeff checked his navigation. He calculated his estimated time of arrival at the Dutch coast. After a short time, he took up his sextant and went back to the astro-dome. He motioned to Al to turn his lights off and unclipped the dome cover. Standing on the step beside the wireless-operator he eased his head up into the astro-dome. Quickly he scanned the sky, identified the stars he wanted to take sights of. As he took each of the three sights he warned Syd. The pilot brought the plane level to obtain the best results.

Quickly, Jeff completed each sighting and clipped back the astro-dome cover. Back at his table he calculated and plotted until he had the small triangle of lines on his chart. This was his "fix"—the calculated position of the plane at the time of the last star "shot." He calculated the new ground speed and wind from this position, then on his computer he worked out the time they should arrive at the enemy coast. He passed the time up to Syd, then sat back and worried.

Yorker droned on over the North Sea.

"Searchlights ahead Navigator," Doug called eventually.

Hurriedly, Jeff turned off his table lamp. Drawing back the black-out curtain, he went forward. To the north, the searchlights of Rotterdam stabbed the sky. To the south Antwerp lit up. Smaller concentrations marked other defended areas.

He was on track.

The trip over enemy territory was quiet. They experienced no trouble. They saw combats around them but none near.

Soon Cologne showed up in front of them. As the first planes drew near, searchlights pierced the night to form a huge cone over the city. To the north, the huge defended area of the Ruhr was also a blaze of lights. Two planes which had strayed off course were coned. Within minutes, they had plummeted to earth in flames.

Yorker evaded the searchlights on the run in on Cologne. The bombs were dropped. Then Syd forced the nose down, he pushed the throttles forward, Yorker's speed increased. Shortly, they were away from the searchlights and flak. They were in the darkness again, with Cologne blazing behind them.

The trip home was equally uneventful. They were first back.

The new rear-gunner had not said a word during the whole operation, except to reply to Syd's queries. Then his replies came in a quiet subdued voice.

However, as the crew jumped down out of the Lancaster at the dispersal point, he became his usual cocky self.

"Hell," he said, "if that's all there is to ops., I don't know why you make such a fuss about them."

Angrily, Doug took hold of him by his parachute harness.

"Listen bud," he snarled, his face only inches away from the gunner's, "can that talk right now. If you think they're easy, just take a look at our casualty list over the last few months."

He released his hold suddenly. Nicholls stumbled slightly. Then he shrugged, a sneer on his face.

"If that doesn't convince you," Doug added, "whiz over to Ely Hospital and see Tich Mulgrave our old rear-gunner. He's lucky to be alive and will walk with a limp for the rest of his life."

Without a word, Nicholls turned away. He strutted over to the flight van.

"That guy makes me so mad," Doug growled. "I could wring his damned neck."

"Oh leave him be," Jeff said, "he'll learn soon enough."

"I hope he does," Clarrie said thoughtfully. "I always felt comfortable with Tich in the rear turret, but with this chap, I'm not so sure."

*　　*　　*

The next night, the squadron was stood down from operations. Buses were provided to take the airmen and Waafs to Cambridge.

Jean and Paula were on duty, so Jeff and Syd went in together. Col Nicholls was the only other crew member to go.

Doug and Red had left earlier in the car to go to "The Anchor." The others remained back at the squadron.

When the bus stopped in the parking lot in Cambridge, Jeff and Syd thankfully watched Nicholls hurriedly jump off the bus and dash away. They slowly followed the same way and saw him go into the first hotel.

They walked past. At another hotel, they had a few drinks and a meal. Then they went to a picture show.

After the show, they left the theatre and wandered slowly towards the bus stop. It was still early.

"I wonder if our boy wonder is still in here," Jeff said as they drew near to the hotel which Nicholls had entered.

"Let's go in and have a drink anyway," Syd replied.

They pushed through the black-out curtains and stood in a long bar-room. Half the room, nearest the door, was the bar. The remaining near half was composed of booths. The place was nearly full. It was noisy and dirty.

There was room for them at the end of the bar farthest from the door. Jeff walked over and leant against the counter. He ordered two beers. As they stood sipping their beers, Jeff became aware of a loud, rather drunken voice in the booth behind him. The back of the booth was too high to look over.

"There I was," the voice boasted thickly, "and these three German planes, Messerschmidts, you know, were coming in at me, their cannons shooting great slugs at me."

"Go on," a feminine voice urged, "I'm all goose-pimply."

Jeff nudged Syd and indicated the booth from which the voices came.

"I know that voice Syd," he said, "listen for a while and let me know if I am right."

As the voices continued Syd listened.

"What do you think I did then, you lovely thing?" the male voice asked.

"I dunno," the girl giggled. "I'd have been too scared to do anything."

Angrily, Syd turned to Jeff.

"The little bastard," he snapped, "he's done one easy

op. and here he is shooting his mouth off."

"Come on, Skipper," Jeff said, "follow me."

Syd followed Jeff round to the booth. They stood looking down at the four seated there. Col Nicholls was with two girls and a male civilian. The rear-gunner held one girl's hand as he spoke. His back was to Syd and Jeff. The girls first became conscious of the two airmen. They looked up, silent. The civilian followed their glance.

Nicholls noticed their glances. He became silent. Slowly he turned and faced the two crew men. His face flushed guiltily.

Neither the pilot nor the navigator said a word. They stared down at him for a long moment. Then Jeff turned his head away and spat on the already dirty floor.

The two of them then turned and went back to the bar.

"Rather vulgar," Syd smiled, "but awfully effective."

"I hope so Skipper."

Nicholls avoided them on the bus back to the squadron.

* * *

"A fine couple of shits you two were last night," Nicholls complained at the morning assembly. "The girls knew I was shooting a line when you stood there and spat."

He was his usual cocky self. Instead of apologising for his behaviour, he tried to brazen it out. He stood in front of Syd and Jeff, his face flushed and angry.

"I had my dame all set up for the night," he said, "then you two cruelled it for me."

Jeff took a step forward.

"Listen here Nicholls," he snarled.

Taking hold of the navigator's sleeve, Syd drew Jeff back.

"Leave this to me," he said quietly.

He turned to the rear-gunner once again.

"We don't shoot lines here Nicholls," he said slowly, "even when you have ops. on the board. If ever I hear you bunging it on like that again you'll go out on your ear so fast it will make your head spin."

The small Welshman's eyes narrowed. He began to reply.

"When you've been here a while," Syd interrupted him,

175

"you'll know why. This is not an easy life and a hell of a lot of good chaps have bought it from here. So, we don't like sprogs coming along, shooting their bloody big mouths off when they haven't done a damn thing. Get me?"

A surly look appeared on Nicholls' face.

"All right," he snapped. "I was only trying to make the dame, I couldn't tell her I'd done only one op."

"Listen Nicholls," Jeff said sharply, "one op. or fifty, there's not much difference if the luck's with you. If it isn't, it still makes no difference, you go for a Burton anyway."

"Ah hell," the rear-gunner whined, "I don't seem to be able to say anything right."

"No you don't," Jeff replied.

Nicholls looked angrily at the tall navigator for a moment, then turned and walked quickly away.

"I'm getting to dislike him even more," Jeff said.

"When he gets a few ops. in," Syd replied, "he might grow out of this attitude."

Jeff laughed bitterly.

"If he was only half as good as he thinks he is, he'd be a wizard gunner."

* * *

Their next operation was to Milan two days later. Take-off was at 1800 hours.

When the flight van drew up beside Yorker in the evening, the crew tumbled out quickly and gathered their gear round them.

"Well here's another one coming up Jean," Jeff said as he sat beside her, "one more after this and we've finished our first tour."

Turning to face him, Jean's face was solemn.

"It still seems a long way to go to the finish," she said quietly.

"It will pass darling," he whispered as he leant over and kissed her, "then my love, wedding bells if you still want me by that time."

She squeezed his hand.

"I'll always want you, you ass," she replied, "now get going before I bawl."

He kissed her once again, then slowly got out of the van.

"Luck Jeff," Jean called softly after him. "God be with you."

As he walked to the plane in the cold wind, he felt the pangs of fear tighten his stomach. He felt that he hated the great plane looming up above him on the dispersal point. He turned and waved to Jean, when he heard the flight van's engine start up. She waved back then drove away. Slowly he walked over to the ladder. He climbed up into the fuselage, his gear slapping against him. In the navigation compartment, he laid out his charts and maps. He drew out his navigation bag. He placed each object neatly, convenient to his hands. Looking through his flight log, he checked his original calculations. Satisfied at length, he sat back.

Closing his eyes, he made the Sign of the Cross and prayed. When he prayed at the beginning of the operation, Jeff always brought to his mind the image of Christ on the Cross. The sufferings of Jesus made his fears more bearable.

When he had finished, he looked down at his chart, smoothed out on the table. The pencilled track lines stretched across it. The reddened defended areas which had to be avoided, stood out boldly. As he looked at them, his fear dried his mouth. He licked his lips.

Noisily the crew climbed aboard.

The minutes passed slowly. The powerful engines started up. Syd eased Yorker out of the dispersal. They trundled along the perimeter track to the end of the runway. Syd ran up the engines. A green light flashed from the flight-control van. Yorker began her run along the runway. The roar of the engines rose, the tail lifted with the increasing speed. Then slowly like a great eagle, Yorker rose from the concrete. Fences flashed by underneath.

"Wheels up," Syd called, fighting the controls.

Turning from the throttles, Doug manipulated the undercarriage lever.

"Wheels coming up," he said.

They set course immediately and gained height slowly on course. Jeff worked at the radar. He turned the knobs and noted down his results. On the chart he worked out his fix then calculated his first wind. His fear had disappeared. The knot in his stomach had vanished. He was quick and sure. He loved this work. The job was there and he did it.

The long hours passed. England, the Channel and the French coast slid behind them, clearly visible in the bright moonlight. As they flew across France, other bombers, also Milan bound, were clearly visible beside them. Le Creusot's defences claimed one plane which plummeted to earth and burned itself out. Jeff noted the details in his log and used the searchlights as a check on his navigation.

Their role for the raid was track marker and backer up. Navigation was vitally important on this raid to escape flying over Switzerland and to find the target. The last turning point, before the long leg into Italy, was the northern tip of Lake Annecy. Here Pathfinders dropped red flares to guide Main Force and to concentrate the planes once more.

Red dropped his track marker flare amongst the others gleaming over the tip of the lake. As they flew along the last long leg, more flares dropped behind them to act as guides for the later bombers. This marking continued throughout the time estimated for the passage of the entire force.

The Alps gleamed in the moonlight. Peaks thrust up menacingly, clad in mantles of snow.

At last, the lights of Milan lit up ahead of them. The beams waved. The flak burst haphazardly. The first target indicator and illuminating flares dropped above the city. In the light of these, the visual markers sought out their aiming point. They covered it with yellow T.Is. Greens dropped into the yellows and Milan was marked for attack. Sticks of incendiaries cut swathes of fire across the city, crossing and merging, until the city seemed to be drowning in the flames. Block-busters and heavy explosives added to the devastation as they ripped and tore.

As Yorker drew closer, the fires had taken hold. The brilliant gleaming silver began to turn red. The defences became weaker and more ineffective. The searchlights wavered in circles, without method. The heavy flak lessened and the light flak hosepiped up in brightly coloured but futile spirals.

Yorker passed through the outer defences. Red released his bombs and green T.Is. Within minutes, they were once more in the darkness outside the city. It seemed miraculous to escape so easily.

Milan's fires were still visible from a hundred miles away, as they flew towards the Alps on their way home. They crossed the Alps and were over France once again.

"Mid-upper to Pilot," Clarrie's voice broke the silence which had settled on the crew.

"Go ahead Mid-upper," Syd replied.

"Bandit starboard, four o'clock about six hundred yards," Clarrie continued, "seems to be sneaking up on another Lanc. Wouldn't be surprised if the rear-gunner's asleep."

The eyes of the crew peered out into the darkness, trying to locate the enemy fighter.

"Can you see it rear-gunner?" Syd asked.

"Yes," Nicholls replied shortly.

"Keep your eyes on it," Syd added, annoyed by the tone of the rear-gunner's reply.

As he spoke, tracers poured in bright streams from both planes. The bomber's tracers split the dark sky first, hitting the fighter with the first burst.

"Sorry fellow," Clarrie murmured.

"He wasn't asleep," Syd added grimly.

The battle lasted only moments. When it ended the enemy fighter was a twisted burning wreck on the French soil. The Lancaster's port outer engine was on fire.

"I'm going over," Syd called to the crew, as he swung Yorker over in flat turn towards the other bomber.

"Right Skipper," Doug replied quietly.

"Hell there might be other Jerries around," Nicholls' voice sounded harsh and strained.

"That's why we're going over," Jeff said.

"But they might get us," the rear-gunner added weakly.

"They might," Jeff replied, "end of conversation."

A mumbled reply came from the rear turret.

Syd flew up close to the other bomber. As they drew near, the fire had been extinguished. They could see the feathered, motionless airscrew, impotent in its immobility. One landing wheel dangled down like the broken leg of a bird. Easing back the throttles, Syd slowed Yorker back to the speed of the other plane. Quickly, Jeff calculated new courses, ground speeds and E.T.As. for the reduced speed. In the bright moonlight, each plane was clearly visible to the other. They flew side by side over the long miles.

Jeff took over the navigation for both. Each time the other veered off the course Jeff had calculated, Syd banked Yorker sharply away then returned to the previous position in formation but on the correct course. The other pilot soon realised Syd's intention and was content to be led. Shortly before repassing Le Creusot, a third Lancaster joined them, adding a further six Browning machine guns to their united fire power.

At their slower speed, they were soon left far behind by the main force of bombers. The three Lancasters made their solitary journey back across France. The miles seemed longer, knowing that they were three alone in the hostile skies.

Ahead to starboard eventually, Paris threw her search-lights up into a cone. The lights waved and flak poured up for twenty minutes, then gradually the lights died down and the flak ceased. The last bombers of the main stream had passed by.

The three still had many miles to fly over, before Paris lit up a small group of searchlights as a precaution against them. They passed by, on track, north of the city.

At last, in the distance, they saw the English Channel gleaming.

"You beaut," Red shouted from the nose position, "French Coast ahead and I think bang-on track."

"Good show Jeff," Syd said.

Cayeux was passed, England lay ahead. They crossed the English coast at Dungeness. When London had slipped by them, the stricken bomber's wings waggled.

"I think he wants to talk to you Skipper," Doug remarked, watching the other plane.

Syd switched on the R.T.

"Lancasters port and starboard," they heard over their intercomm. "Do you hear me?"

"I hear you starboard," Syd replied briefly.

"Me too port," the third pilot said.

"Thanks sports," they heard, "really appreciate what you did. Thanks a million."

"Think nothing of it," Syd added, "hope you're all O.K. Good luck fellow."

"We got that now, only a few scratches among the crew. Thanks again."

They heard the third pilot speak, then the three planes separated.

"We don't even know his name," Red said dryly, when Syd had switched off the R.T.

"Bloody silly thing to do anyway," Nicholls snarled from the rear-turret.

"Dry up," Doug replied.

"If you didn't like the company," Red added, "you could have got out and walked."

CHAPTER 15

"Flight-Sergeants Johnson, Lodder and Woodley, report to Squadron Headquarters immediately."

The tannoy's harsh call pierced the thin billet walls and roused Jeff. He lay back for a moment, recalling the nightmare which had been interupted. He wiped the perspiration from his forehead with a trembling hand.

They were getting worse he told himself.

"Rise and shine Jeff," Joe Weldon called from his bed opposite.

"I heard it Joe," Jeff replied, slowly rising his mind still fuzzy, "I wonder what I've done wrong now."

"That shows up your bad conscience," Joe laughed, burying his head once more under the bed clothes.

Sleepily, Jeff wandered out to the ablutions. He washed and shaved. As he dressed afterwards, he gloomily looked down the long hut. Most of the beds were occupied. Some of the bodies stirred restlessly. Here and there, a muttered curse and a creaking bed indicated sleeplessness. The mid-morning sun filtered weakly, in narrow rays, through the blacked-out windows. The hut was darkened but not dark. The tired bodies stretched out on the hard beds along both long walls, were endeavouring to sleep away the strain of the long trip to Turin.

How many of the beds had been emptied, since he and the crew had been on the squadron, Jeff thought sadly. The beds emptied as crews went missing. They were filled again, as new crews arrived to bring the squadron up to strength and many were quickly emptied once again. Not one bed in the hut had been emptied by the posting away of a tour-completed occupant.

He left the hut tired and despondent.

"Ah there you are Johnson," the Adjutant said with a smile, when Jeff reported to him.

"I can't be in trouble," Jeff thought, "he's too friendly."

"You'd better spruce up," the Adjutant continued.

"Why Sir?" Jeff asked, puzzled.

"This afternoon you go over to Wyton for an interview with Air Commodore Bennett, about your commission."

Jeff grinned wearily.

"Heck, is that all?" he said.

"What did you say?" the Adjutant snapped, jerking forwards in his chair.

Jeff laughed abruptly.

"Don't get me wrong Sir," he explained, "I thought I must have been in some bother I didn't know about. I didn't expect this. I hadn't given it even a thought."

"That's all right Flight-Sergeant," the Adjutant said, relaxing back in his chair.

"Be ready at the guard-room at 1345 hours," he added. "You, Lodder and Woodley are the only three to go over."

"Thank you Sir," Jeff replied.

He saluted and left the room.

Jeff felt mixed feelings at the news. Whilst pleased with the thought of having a commission, it would mean leaving his present billet and going over to the officers' quarters. He would see less of the crew but more of Syd. He thought of the rowdy Sergeants' Mess and the parties they had had. He thought of the billets and the noisy bedlam in the mornings and nights. As he walked round the perimeter track to see the ground crew, he wondered how it would be to be an officer.

"Ah hell," he mused, "Bennett might knock me back anyway, so why worry?"

He quickened his step and dismissed all thoughts of commissions from his mind.

*　　*　　*

Jeff was last of the three to be interviewed. Harry Lodder, another navigator, was first. He was a young English lad who had done seventeen operations. He wanted his commission mainly to impress his family. He came out of the interview rather crestfallen.

The second airman, George Woodley, was called. A short, tubby, Canadian wireless air-gunner, he had nearly completed his two tours.

"How did you go?" Jeff asked Harry Lodder.

"I have to come back in a month," he replied bitterly, as he sat down beside Jeff.

"He asked me a damned nav. problem I couldn't solve with six slide rules, a dozen computers and all the books ever written. I just looked at him. He gave me a pep talk and then told me to come back in a month's time when I had more operations on the board."

Resignedly, without confidence, Jeff awaited his call. He thought of the books he had not studied.

Woodley came out smiling.

"I'm in," he said.

"Good show," Jeff replied.

When his name was called, he rose and was shown into a large room. Behind a neat desk sat the leader of Pathfinders, Air-Commodore D.C.T. Bennett, D.S.O.

A still young, shortish, slim man, with his straight black hair neatly brushed back from a high intelligent forehead. His eyes were bright and humourous. His uniform was spotless and well tailored. A legend amongst the Pathfinder crews who flew under his command, he had won the D.S.O. after being shot down in Norway, early in the war. He had led his crew across that harsh, cold, mountainous land to the safety and refuge of Sweden.

The tales of his ability were told and retold. He was an excellent pilot in any one of a dozen types of aircraft. Blindfolded, he could strip a Browning machine gun and put it together again as well as any gunner. He could send and receive Morse Code as well as a telegraph operator. He had written a book on Air Navigation which was a standard work. Legend had it, that either it or another book had been written on his honeymoon.

He took a personal interest in all the personnel under him, both aircrew and ground staff. He was like an idol to both.

Jeff stood at attention before the desk. He saluted sharply. His hand struck his forage cap and knocked it askew.

"At ease Johnson," Air-Commodore Bennett smiled kindly at the red-faced navigator.

The interview was brief. He had Jeff's personal papers in front of him. He skimmed through schooling, the sports played and the training undergone. He asked searching questions which tested the long navigator's reaction to operations and to the Air Force in general. They talked companionably of Queensland, the home State of both in far-away Australia.

Finally, the Air Commodore stood up. He walked round his desk, then leant against it.

"Well Johnson," he said, "I noted a couple of black marks, reprimands, in your papers there, but I think your record on operations and your D.F.M. cancel them out."

As he paused, Jeff felt elated. He had expected to share Lodder's experience at best. He knew now that he had been accepted by the legendary man before him.

"We'll put it this way Johnson," Air Commodore Bennett continued with a beaming grin, "whilst possibly not an outstanding example of officer and gentleman, I think you'll do."

Jeff smiled happily.

"Thank you Sir," he said.

"That's all Johnson and good luck."

Putting out his hand he shook Jeff's. Then saluting smartly, Jeff turned and went out. The other two had already left the ante-room and had gone out to the van. He hurried out of the building.

"Well?" an impatient Jean asked as he got into the van beside her.

"On the beam honey," he replied.

"Well if you expect me to call you Sir," Jean smiled up at him, "you can have another jolly good think."

Waggling a finger in front of her nose, he said, "Be careful miss or I'll slap you on a charge."

"You do," Jean snorted, " and you'll eat nothing but burnt toast for breakfast after we're married."

Then, she leaned over and kissed him.

"Seriously," she whispered, "I am pleased."

"Thanks."

She started up the engine and threw it into gear.

*　　*　　*

All the crew, including Syd, raced over to him when Jean stopped the van at the Sergeants' Mess.

"Did you get through?" Al asked.

"I think so," Jeff replied self-consicously, "Bennett said O.K. but Australian Headquarters have the last say."

Syd laughed.

"You pessimist," he said, "if Bennet said O.K. you've got it."

Slowly Jeff climbed out of the van. He turned to Jean.

"Thanks Jean," he said, "see you tonight."

"As you wish—Sir," Jean replied gaily.

"Get going before I tan your hide," he grinned at her.

"Don't try it, I tan too easily," Jean replied as she started up the motor.

Letting in the clutch, she drove away. As Jeff stood, watching the van speed off, Red came up behind him and slapped him on the back.

"Another damned pig in the crew," he boomed, "we'll have to have a grog to celebrate."

As they turned towards the Sergeants' Mess, Syd hung back.

"Don't be an ass Syd," Doug said, taking him by the arm, "be our guest for a short snort."

They all went into the Mess together.

*　　*　　*

They did not operate again for several days. Cold winds blew across the airfield chilling the bone. The airmen huddled in their great-coats or around the fires in the messes and huts. To the crew, even the inactivity of a few days seemed nerve-wracking. They wanted to finish their first

185

tour of thirty operations. It was a milestone, an important milestone, which had to be passed. The Squadron operated once on L'Orient, but they were not on the battle order. Syd complained bitterly, without result, to the Wing-Commander.

They drove over to Ely Hospital to see Tich. The little gunner was still confined to bed. However, he seemed more mature and happy. Pain had etched more lines on his face, but the leg was mending. His family visited him as often as they were able. Instead of dreading to see them, as he had in the past, he looked forward to their coming.

After the visit, the crew became more dissatisfied with Nicholls. He refused to join with them in outings or in the Mess. He became friendly with two sergeant gunners from other crews. They hardly saw him, apart from Squadron assemblies and training flights. Bored and restless from the enforced operational inactivity, they flew on training flights as often as they could.

Eventually, they were once again on the battle order. The target was to be Wilhelmshaven. Jeff prepared his charts and flight plan. The tension was eased. Eased, only to tighten once again, when the operation was cancelled before final briefing, due to bad weather.

The crew angrily piled into the battered car. They drove to The Anchor to get drunk.

The following two days were similar. The battle order was posted on the notice board in the morning. The target each time was the same, Wilhelmshaven. Navigation briefing was held in the early afternoon. Jeff and the other navigators worked on their charts and maps preparing for the operation. The bad weather held however. The biting winds and rain swept across the drome. The heavy grey clouds brought a pall of gloom. Each night the operation was cancelled. On the third night, it was cancelled as the first planes were taxi-ing along the perimeter track to the runway.

The crews became even more tense. Nerves were strained like violin strings. Quarrels between friends became frequent. On the fourth day the weather cleared.

The target was still Wilhelmshaven—naval base and port.

First take-off was at 1800. The crew was in the second wave acting as re-centerers, to ensure the aiming point was correctly marked throughout the attack. They were due on the target at zero-hour plus four minutes at 2032.

Still climbing, they crossed the English coast at Cromer. The long flight across the North Sea began.

Shortly after the English coast had been left behind, they entered cloud at 6000 feet. Syd urged Yorker up through the grey gloomy darkness of it. Ice formed on the wings and air-screws. Pieces thrown off the tips of the whirling blades struck the fuselage like exploding flak shells. The tightly strung nerves of the crew made them shudder at each onslaught of ice.

At 14,000 feet, they were above the cloud. It stretched below them in a seemingly endless mass. The moon was still bright. It lit the cloud eerily, giving it substance and strange form. The time dragged slowly by. Jeff worked at the "Gee" box, getting fix after fix. He found wind after wind until satisfied that the predicted winds were wrong. Applying the wind he had calculated, he worked out ground speed, position and alteration of course and called up the alteration to Syd.

The wind was a tail-wind, stronger than anticipated. Unless time was wasted they would arrive at the target earlier than the detailed time. Before they left "Gee" range, Jeff worked out a dog-leg track to lose time. They turned 45 degrees off their course to port. After ten minutes, they turned 90 degrees to starboard for another ten minutes. When that was completed, they turned 45 degrees to port. They were on their original course once again.

They had wasted nearly ten minutes with this manoeuvre. Shortly afterwards they passed beyond the range of "Gee". Immediately, Jeff got out his sextant and adjusted the astrograph above his table. The last turning point before the enemy coast was a point over the North Sea, where a latitude and longitude crossed. On the flight to this point, Jeff navigated by the stars, constantly taking star shots with his sextant and calculating his position by applying these on the astrograph. From the results he checked on their track, ground speed and on the winds. He enjoyed this work.

On his estimated time of arrival at the turning point, they turned and flew towards the enemy coast. Jeff began to worry, fearing that his calculations were wrong. Switching off his light, he unhooked his intercomm. and oxygen plugs. Then, map in hand, he went forward and plugged in behind Doug. He peered into the darkness ahead trying to pierce the thinning cloud.

"Cloud's breaking at last," Doug said dryly.

"About time," Red replied, "I want to at least see the target. I hate dropping my bombs on cloud."

Syd gazed ahead. He saw searchlights break through, waving their long fingers in futile clawing at the bombers passing overhead.

"Enemy coast ahead," he called, "if those searchlights mean anything."

Leaning into the starboard blister, Jeff watched the pattern of the lights for long moments.

"That will be the islands off the coast," he said deliberately, "we seem to be a little west of track."

He hurried back to his position and plugged in. After drawing the black-out curtain, he switched on the table lamp. Ruling in the new track line, he quickly calculated the new course and passed the alteration to Syd.

"Let me know when we get near, Red," he called. "I'll want a pin-point if possible. We should pass over the western tip of Wangerooge, north of Schilling."

"O.K. Jeff," Red replied, reaching for his detailed map of the area.

Switching on the dim-shaded torch he carried, Red glanced briefly at the map. He memorised the detail, then switched off the torch. He gazed down into the darkness ahead of them. The cloud was thinning further. The waving searchlights drew closer.

The minutes passed silently.

Through the cloud, Red saw the outline of the island.

"Navigator," he called, "Wangerooge coming up."

"Where?" Jeff asked anxiously.

"You're five miles west of track."

"That's O.K.," Jeff said, pleased with the result after the long sea flight. He glanced at his watch.

"How long before we pass over it, Red?" he asked, "I worked it out in about another three and a half minutes."

"Hell!" Red exclaimed, "I'd say in one minute."

"Blast!" Jeff cried, "Slow down, Skipper."

Immediately Syd throttled back slightly. As he did, Wilhelmshaven's defences began their fight against the bombers. The searchlights lit up in hundreds. The multi-coloured light flak sprayed up in parabolae, gaining maximum height. The heavy flak flashed in the box barrage. It seemed a veritable hell and impenetrable.

"I'll waste a minute on the way in Navigator," Syd said. "I can see the target area. Gunners keep your eyes open."

"Over the island now," Red called.

"Thanks Red," Jeff replied, noting the time in his log. He compared it with his E.T.A.

"Skipper," he called, "we are two minutes ahead of time."

Syd looked at the target before him. The first Red T.Is. and illuminating flares fell.

"T.Is. down," he said, watching them cascade over the city.

"Bang on time," Jeff said fretfully. "Can you waste that two minutes? I don't want to be two minutes out."

With a smile Syd eased Yorked over to port off course. "I'll lose a minute at least," he said.

"That's something anyway."

Syd turned Yorker in a flat, wide, semi-circle, wasting the unwanted seconds. On the target, Yellow T.Is. and the first greens tumbled down.

Suddenly, the rear-gunner's voice yelled over the inter-comm.

"We can't go in there."

*   *   *

As Yorker had turned, Nicholls had seen the target and its intense defences for the first time.

"Don't be stupid," Red replied shortly. "What the hell do you think we flew all this way for—to go window-shopping?"

"It's suicide," Nicholls cried, his voice trembling.

"Quiet rear-gunner," Syd said firmly, once again flying on course to the target. "We're going in now, so shut up."

There was silence in the plane, until Red began the bombing run. Low cloud shrouded part of the city.

Flak bit at them. The black puffs appeared like evil apparitions beside them. They felt pieces of shrapnel hit Yorker. Searchlights slid past without touching. The light flak was beneath them.

Red guided Syd towards the fading visual markers' yellow flares which were falling onto the city. He pinpointed their position on the run in and estimated the position of the aiming point. They had drifted east with the wind. Red lined up carefully and dropped their green T.Is. west of the yellows, where he estimated the aiming point to be. They were one minute ahead of time.

As usual, Syd pushed Yorker's nose down. They sped through the defences. Suddenly behind them, a terrific explosion lit the sky. It seemed to spread as if the whole city had exploded. The cloud over the target turned red for an instant.

"Wow!" Red yelled excitedly, "did you get onto that prang? Someone hit the jackpot."

"I wonder what went up," Clarrie said thoughtfully.

"I haven't a clue," Red replied, "but whatever it was, it made a wizard bang."

As they flew back towards the enemy coast, the red glow was still visible below the searchlights, flak and cloud for a considerable time.

Calling up each member of the crew, Syd ensured that none had been injured by the bursting shells over the target.

"Think I'll duck back Skipper," Doug said. "I want to make sure there is no damage."

"O.K. Doug," Syd replied, his eyes scanning the sky for fighters.

With a glance at the instrument panel, Doug slipped out of his seat and clipped his portable oxygen bottle on. He nudged Jeff through the black-out curtain. The light was switched off and he passed through the curtain. As he passed Al, he playfully dug him in the ribs. Al growled an unintelligible remark and turned back to his radio. Doug climbed over the main spar, opened the cabin door and went through into the dark body of the plane. The fuselage looked like a huge black tunnel. He walked down it, flashing his torch carefully along each side.

As they crossed the enemy coast, the fighter struck.

Clarrie's voice screamed over the intercomm.

"Bandit! Go port go."

Instinctively, Syd hurled Yorker down hard to port. Tracer shells flashed past their starboard wing tip with horrifying brightness.

"Nicholls, what are you doing?" Syd yelled.

The only reply was a sob, then silence.

"I see him again," Clarrie spoke slowly and calmly, "starboard quarter up, about six hundred yards."

Suddenly, Doug's voice broke in over the intercomm.

"What the hell's up?" he asked, "you just threw me all over the goddamned kite."

"Fighter, Doug" Syd replied quickly, "see what's up with Nicholls, he's not replying or firing. He must be hit."

"Turn port, turn port—GO!" Clarrie cried, his eyes on the fighter, waiting for the dip of the wing which heralded the attack. His two guns stuttered fiercely as he spoke.

Doug staggered along the heaving, twisting, dark fuselage to the rear. He stumbled against the raised cat-walk which led to the rear turret. He switched on his torch.

In the dim light of its shaded beam, he saw the fear contorted face of the rear-gunner. Nicholls had left his turret. In his panic at the sudden attack, he had thrown open the turret doors and scrambled out onto the cat-walk. In his flight, his parachute harness had become entangled. He was held fast. He sobbed with fright. When the beam of the torch shone on his face, he screamed. He screamed to Doug to release him.

Doug stood there for moments, bewildered. He saw the sobbing face shout. At first, he believed that Nicholls had been wounded. He leant over him and released the entangled harness.

"Are you hit?" he yelled into the rear-gunner's ear.

"Get me out," Nicholls cried, clinging to the engineer's jacket.

"You little bastard," Doug yelled angrily, when he realised that the gunner was unhurt.

Holding Nicholls up with his left hand, he savagely

swung his right fist into the sobbing, fear-stricken face in front of him. The rear-gunner slumped unconscious to the fuselage floor.

Without a glance at him, Doug quickly scrambled along the cat-walk. He clambered into the turret and plugged into the intercom.

"Engineer in rear-turret Skipper," he called. "Where's that damned fighter?"

"How's Nicholls?"

"He's all right now," Doug replied laconically.

"Port, down seven o'clock about three hundred yards," Clarrie interrupted authoritively.

Staring into the gloom, Doug searched for the fighter. Suddenly he saw it, a darker smudge in the darkness.

"Got it," he said, " You direct Clarrie. I'll belt away at him when I can."

"Roger."

As Clarrie gave the combat directions to Syd, Doug familiarised himself with the turret details and lined up the fighter in his gun sight.

"Deflection," he murmured to himself, "must use deflection."

The fighter turned in for another attack Yorker screamed in a sharp turn as Syd obeyed Clarrie's instructions.

The tracer streams from the six guns of the two turrets seemed to merge with the brilliant stream from the fighter. The enemy's cannon shells once again whipped past their starboard wing. The Lancaster was able to turn inside the wide circle the fighter needed. The tracer streams from the bomber seemed to pour into the dark smudge that was their enemy.

They saw no fire or evident damage, but the fighter broke off its attack. It slid away and turned back towards Germany.

"Thank God!" Doug breathed.

"You did it Doug," Clarrie yelled excitedly. "when he saw the rear turret open up at him, he blew through. I hope we got him."

The crew settled back thankfully. Tension eased and their breathing over the intercom became smoother.

"Now," Syd demanded, "what about Nicholls?"

In the excitement of the attack and the combat, Doug had forgotten the rear-gunner.

"You'd better send Al or Jeff back here," he said angrily, "they'll find the little rat near the elsan where I dropped him."

"Where you what?" Syd asked in puzzled tone.

Doug slowly told what he had found on making his way to the rear of the plane. He was still angry. The crew listened in silence until he had finished.

"Stay in the turret for a while Doug," Syd said, "later I'll send Al down to relieve you. Jeff can look after Nicholls."

"Let him lie there for mine," Jeff snapped.

"That goes for me too," Red added.

"Cut it out Jeff," Syd said, ignoring Red.

"Cut it out you say," Jeff shouted, "if Doug hadn't been down the back at the time and able to hop into the turret, we'd be down in the bloody drink now with the fishes."

Wearily, Syd closed his eyes for a moment. To a great extent, he felt as Jeff did, however, as captain of the aircraft he knew that someone had to see to the gunner.

"Jeff, give me the course for the English coast," he said tiredly, "and then look after Nicholls."

"O.K. Syd," Jeff replied, anger still in his voice, "you're the skipper."

"Cut his throat while you're down there," Red added vehemently.

No-one spoke while Jeff revised his navigation. He roughly estimated their position from the searchlights behind them, then he calculated the new course and called it through to Syd.

"I'm going back now," he said, as he changed over to the portable oxygen bottle.

"Right Jeff," Syd replied.

He climbed over the main spar. Then, torch in hand, he pushed the door open and went out into the dark fuselage. He shut the door carefully behind him and inched his way along towards the rear of the plane.

He flashed his torch's light ahead of him.

Nicholls was sitting propped against the side of the

plane. He was breathing heavily from lack of oxygen. His eyes stared vacantly into the beam of the torch.

Gone was the cockiness. Fear still showed, but with the fear, there was a look of terrible failure. He looked to Jeff like a whipped dog. As his anger subsided, Jeff bent and grasped the gunner by the arm and dragged him to his feet. Staggering with the motion of the plane, Jeff helped Nicholls forward into the cabin. He eased the unresisting figure into his seat at the navigation table. Al watched from his own position, his face an emotionless mask.

After plugging Nicholls into the oxygen supply Jeff went forward and called Syd on the intercomm.

"Nav. to Pilot," he said.

"Right Jeff," Syd replied, "how is he?'

"He's in my seat," Jeff said, "he's plugged in so you ask him what the score is."

"There's no need, I can hear you," the rear-gunner's voice sounded dull and lifeless.

"Well?" Syd demanded.

"I lost my guts and blew through," Nicholls replied slowly and deliberately, without any attempt to excuse himself.

"You're telling me," Red exclaimed.

"I couldn't take it," the rear-gunner continued, "in spite of all my talk, I just didn't make the grade."

This attitude from Nicholls was so unexpected, that the crew was stunned. No-one spoke for minutes.

"Well say something and get it over and done with," the rear-gunner cried.

"Will you do the same thing again?" Syd asked deliberately.

Nicholls did not reply immediately..

"I don't know," he said eventually.

"Well at least he's honest," Doug remarked from the rear turret.

Syd decided suddenly. In spite of the gunner's show of cowardice, he was still one of the crew. Syd decided to take a chance.

"We'll see," he said sharply, "now get the hell back to the rear-turret if you can walk that far and let Doug come forward."

"I'll make it," Nicholls replied flatly.

His microphone went dead as he unplugged.

"Are you letting him get away with what he did?" Jeff demanded.

"Have you gone crazy Syd?" Red shouted.

"We won't condemn him on one op.", Syd replied.

"Even if we might have bought it?" Jeff added angrily.

"Well at least Doug got a smack at the little skunk," Red said smugly.

"He's still one of the crew," Syd said the words slowly and deliberately, "we'll give him a chance."

"I get you Skipper," Jeff replied. "I'll get back to the nav. table."

"You're the boss Syd," Red said. "I only hope I don't have to go for a Burton because of him."

"Rear-gunner in position Skipper," Nicholls' voice cut in.

Uncomfortably, Red wondered how much he had heard.

At the interrogation, the crew reported the combat and all details except Nicholls' behaviour.

The rear-gunner, a subdued, different person, looked thankfully round at the crew beside him.

The others in the crew had completed their first tour.

CHAPTER 16

Syd glanced at his watch and cursed.

It was only a quarter past ten. Sleep had deserted him. Restlessly he edged back and leant against the wall behind him. The weak light of the dull, cloudy day filtered through the blackout curtain. He glanced over at the other bed.

Trevor Mason was still sleeping. In his sleep, his body twitched and turned as he flew the previous night's operation once again in nightmare.

With a sigh, Syd threw the bedclothes aside. Shivering with the cold, he slipped into his dressing gown and slippers. Picking up his toilet case, he quietly left the room and walked down to the ablutions.

When he returned, Trevor was still asleep. Syd dressed quickly and went out into the chill, drizzling day.

The mess ante-room was quiet and deserted, except for one lone figure reclining in a chair. Syd went over to him.

"Ops on?" he asked Jake Anderson.

"Nope", Jake answered shortly, looking up, "tonight there shall be wassail and wenching".

The lean, untidy flyer was now the senior pilot of the squadron. He and his crew had completed forty trips. They needed only five more operations to end their two tours. Syd gazed down at the lined, tired face.

"Couldn't sleep either?" he asked.

"Never can", Jake replied, serious for once. He rubbed a hand over his red-rimmed eyes.

"Unless of course", he added, jocular once again, "I have a skinful of the amber fluid. Ah, beer, thou delightful sedative".

With a laugh, Syd sat down beside the other pilot.

"The only trouble with that" he said, "is the headache the next morning".

"Then you are too sick to worry about anything extraneous", Jake replied with a wide sweep of his arm, "you are much too busy coddling the addled, pounding brain".

As he spoke, two Waafs entered the ante-room with the morning tea wagon.

"Oh Milly," Jake called across the room, "would you please bring me mine over here like a good girl?"

The pretty blonde Waaf giggled, hero-worship showing in her eyes.

"Oh Sir," she said, "I shouldn't, it's against orders".

"Be a dear and fetch it over", Jake said, "I simply couldn't make the trip over to there".

The girl began to pour.

"Well only this once, Sir", she replied.

"Thank you sweet girl", he said thankfully, "you'll save my life. Two sugar please."

She brought his tea and a cake over and set it down on the table at his side as Syd got up to fetch his own.

As he moved away, he heard the girl giggle once again.

"Oh, Sir", she cried, "you shouldn't pinch me, someone might see".

"Let all the world watch, my comely wench", Syd heard Jake reply.

While he was pouring his tea out, others entered the mess.

Paula came and stood by his side.

"Hello, Syd", she said, "tired?"

"I am rather", he replied.

He poured another cup for her, and carried both over to a secluded corner. Paula followed him.

"I missed you last night when I got back", he said as they sat down.

"I missed being there", she replied. "That was the end of your first tour wasn't it?"

"It was".

"How does it feel?"

"Hard to tell," Syd said thoughtfully, "that's thirty behind me and only fifteen ahead, but somehow that fifteen seems to be many more than the thirty I've done".

Paula looked anxiously at him. She had never heard him speak so despondently. As she looked at him, she realised how changed he was from when she had first met him. It came as a shock. Seeing him, as she did, every day, she had not noticed the gradual alteration of his features. The lines about his eyes, on his forehead and cheeks had deepened and lengthened. He had aged years in appearance since she had first seen him in the mess. Glancing round the room, she saw Jake Anderson's untidy figure slumped in his chair. She realised that he also had changed in appearance. Suddenly, she fully realised what a terrible strain on nerves and bodies the constant operating had upon these youths.

Turning to Syd, she said soberly, "You could finish ops now if you wanted to."

"Don't be silly", Syd laughed humourlessly.

"Why is it silly?"

Solemnly, Syd gazed back at her.

"Do you really think I should or would, Paula?" he asked, a frown deepening the lines on his forehead.

"No, I don't suppose I do", she replied, "I know you'll go on flying, whether you yourself really want to or not".

To stop tears from running down her cheeks, she closed her eyes tightly.

"Hell we're serious", Syd said, suddenly breaking away from the mood. "Let's change the subject".

"Yes let's", Paula smiled.

"Are you on duty tonight?" he asked.

"No, why?"

"Well, the crew are celebrating at the Anchor and you are invited".

"As one of the crew?"

"You could be", Syd replied gravely looking into her eyes.

She gazed back into his, tired but tender.

"I could be Syd", she whispered, placing her hand over his, "I'd like to be".

* * *

"Hey Nicholls", Red called, "over here".

The rear-gunner was entering the Sergeants' Mess for lunch. He started violently when he heard Red's voice. Self-consciously, he walked over to the crew, who were lounging in easy chairs beside the fireplace.

Each of them had pondered over Syd's words of the previous night. In spite of what he had done, Nicholls was still one of the crew. Joining a crew in Bomber Command was a little like getting married—you were tied together for the duration of your tour for better or worse.

"Pull up a chair and make your miserable life happy", Doug said, without moving.

Nicholls pulled a chair forward and joined them. He sat forward on the edge of the chair, unsure of his reception.

"How do you feel?" Clarrie asked.

"Lousy," he replied.

Red's head jerked back in a ponderous laugh.

"So you bloody well should", he said.

Anxiously, Nicholls leant forward towards Jeff, who sat back quiet.

"What's going to happen?" he asked. "Am I going to be scrubbed on lack of moral fibre? I haven't been able to sleep worrying about it".

Jeff sat up. He felt sorry for the rear-gunner, but the failure was still too vivid in Jeff's mind for him to be friendly.

"No one outside the crew will ever know", he replied,

his voice cold and harsh. "As the skipper said, you are one of us. Not a word will be said about it by us or anyone else from now on, unless it happens again".

With a flushed face, Nicholls sat back. He felt relieved, but he still wondered himself how he would react if they were attacked on some future operation. For the first time, he felt affection for the band of men he had teamed up with. He realised that his boasting and cockiness had been a shell he had constructed about himself. Constructed, because he had been unsure and jealous of the calm efficiency of the crew.

"By the way", Red boomed, "We're celebrating tonight at the "Anchor", our pub. Want to come along?"

"I'd like to", he said eagerly.

"Well we are leaving after supper", Doug said, "so plaster down your hair and be at our hut then".

* * *

As they stamped noisily into the bar of the "Anchor", Josh greeted them with a friendly grin.

"Pop into the lounge", he called in his loud voice, "there's a fire in there just begging for your company".

As the others tramped through to the lounge, Syd and Jeff went over to the bar.

"What's it to be?" Josh asked, drying his hands on a cloth.

"Bitter for nine", Jeff said, placing a pound note on the bar counter.

"Who's the new chap?" Josh asked, nodding his head towards the lounge.

"The new rear-gunner, Col. Nicholls", Syd replied.

"One of the mob?" Josh enquired.

"I think he is now", Syd said seriously, "but it was touch and go".

"Like that, eh?" Josh said with a knowing look, "so long as he is now, that'll do".

He placed the glasses of beer on a tray.

"How about coming in for a drink with us, Josh?" Syd said as he picked up the tray.

"I will in a minute," he replied, "it's rather quiet tonight."

In the lounge, the two girls were seated in comfortable,

low, cushioned chairs in front of the fire. The crew were clustered round them. Clarrie and Al stood leaning against the mantlepiece. Doug and Red sat beside the girls. Nicholls stood slightly apart, still uncertain of himself. Syd felt sorry for him.

"Nick", he called, using the gunner's new nickname, "grab some of these and hand them round will you?"

"Sure thing skipper", Nicholls replied, dashing forward eagerly.

He handed glasses to the girls and to Red and Doug, as Jeff handed out the others. He took his own and drew closer to the group.

"Sit here, Jeff", Jean said, patting the arm of her chair.

"Listen to the hobbles rattle", Red laughed.

"Hobbles would do you a lot of good", Jean snapped back good naturedly.

"Just one big happy family", Clarrie observed from the fireside.

Doug gulped down the first beer and excused himself. Without a further word, he hurried out of the hotel.

"Where the hell has he gone?" Red asked.

"Haven't a clue", Al said, also mystified.

As they finished their drinks, Nicholls collected the glasses, placing them on the tray. As he left to order another round, Red called to him.

"Hey, Nick, this is my round."

"I'll get it", the gunner replied.

"Suit yourself."

As he re-entered with the tray of beers, Doug also returned, arm-in-arm with Colleen Graham.

"Well what do you know," Red exclaimed, "The old bushy-tail".

Doug drew up another chair for the girl.

"I think you know everyone here", he said smugly, as she sat down.

"I do Doug", she replied, smiling at the astonished faces around her.

"Don't be too surprised", she said to Paula and Jean, "we've seen quite a lot of one another since I met you last".

"Poor silly girl", Red said in a psuedo-concerned tone as

he patted her hand, "hasn't anyone warned you about men like him?"

"He'll do", Colleen replied, dimpling her cheeks, "he warned me about men like you, if you must know".

Hastily Red drew his hand away.

"My friend", he moaned.

Paula leant over towards the girl.

"It's nice to have you with us Colleen", she said with a friendly smile.

The evening passed quietly and restfully. Without them realising it, the tension lessened. The taut nerves eased under the influence of the fire, the pleasant company and the beer. Josh and his wife wandered in frequently with trays of glasses. They would stay to talk for a few minutes, have a drink, then return to the bar. Gradually, Nicholls became more a part of the group. Diffidently at first, he joined in the conversation and the laughter. As time passed, he became more at ease and felt that he belonged. The girls did not know what had happened on the operation. The crew did not mention it.

In spite of having Jean beside him, Jeff drank quickly. It seemed that he strove to become speedily drunk. Between rounds in the lounge, he wandered into the bar and drank there also. There was an air of nervousness about him. It eased only slightly during the evening. He laughed and joked, but underlying the banter, there was a tightness which was visible to Jean. His eyes did not smile with his lips. Jean's eyes followed him, as he moved restlessly round the room when he left the arm of her chair. Anxiously, she watched for him each time he went into the bar. Shortly after nine o'clock, Jeff was once again seated beside her. She put her hand over his as it rested lightly on her shoulder.

"How about ducking out for some fresh air?" she suggested, looking up at him. "I could do with some".

"Okey-doke", he replied, tipping his glass to his lips and emptying it.

"Do not trust him, gentle maiden", Doug sang as they walked across the room.

Jean turned with a smile and poked her tongue out.

Outside the hotel, it was cold. The stars were obscured

by low cloud. Behind them loomed the great darkened bulk of the hotel. As Jean drew close to him, Jeff put his arm round her and squeezed her. Silently, they walked the short distance to a seat under a large tree which spread its dark branches above them protectively. As they sat down, Jean turned, threw her arms around his neck and drew his face down to hers. He kissed her hard and long.

"I love you Jean", he whispered.

"Me too, you long, lean, navigator you".

They sat clasped in one another's arms, gazing at one another in the darkness.

"What's wrong with you lately, Jeff?" Jean asked softly and hesitantly.

"What do you mean?"

Jean's brows puckered as she tried to put her thoughts into words.

"It's hard to put a finger on it", she said, "but you seem to be on edge all the time, even with me".

"I'm all right", Jeff replied shortly.

"I suppose you are fundamentally, but there is something wrong". She paused for a moment before continuing. "Is it ops Jeff?"

He did not reply immediately. Taking his arm away from her shoulders, he sat forward, stiffly, with a frown on his face.

"I said there was nothing the matter", he snapped harshly.

"Don't snarl at me Jeff", Jean said, taking his hand, "I love you, I was only concerned for you".

"Well don't be", he replied unbendingly.

"You're finished one tour, darling", she said, endeavouring to put a bright tone in her voice, "only fifteen more to go now".

As she spoke she felt the chills of fear. Every time he took off on operations, she feared for him. Each time he flew, she was frightened that she would not see him return. The memories of her brother's death increased her dread.

Although he knew he was being unreasonable, Jeff was unable to relax or to pass off the mood of depression which had enveloped him. He knew he was scared, scared of the next fifteen operations. They loomed in front of him, like fifteen menacing, ghostly figures. On each of the previous thirty, he had experienced fear. He felt now, however, that their luck had been too good to continue. The operation on Wilhelmshaven had taken a toll upon him. He felt kinder towards the rear-gunner, but the memory of how close they had been to death, made him shudder. He felt he had lost all confidence in his navigation and in himself.

As these morbid thoughts passed through his mind, his body quivered against Jean.

"Are you really all right?" she asked anxiously.

"I told you I was", he replied abruptly, feeling ashamed of the thoughts.

"Don't snap", Jean retorted.

"Well don't pester me".

He loved Jean, but the fear and the effects of the beer he had drunk, prevented him from avoiding the quarrel which now loomed between them. Standing up abruptly, Jean looked down at him. Tears welled up into her eyes.

"I don't intend to pester you", she said, hurt by his words. "Let's go in".

He only had to take her into his arms for the quarrel to be over. Jean was waiting. He simply stood up, took her arm and walked silently towards the hotel with her. As he opened the outer door, Jean broke away and fled sobbing down the passage. Jeff stood watching her, impotent to help. He wanted to, but he felt as though someone or something had control of his body and his mind.

Standing at the lounge doorway, a tray of empty glasses in his hand, Syd witnessed Jean's flight. He went back and asked Paula to go to help Jean. When Paula hurried out, Syd went into the bar. Placing the tray on the counter, he turned to Jeff who sat on a stool gazing moodily at the glass of whiskey in front of him.

"What the hell got into you two?" he asked.

"Nothing Syd", Jeff replied without facing the pilot, "we had a barney outside".

"It must have been a beaut", Syd added, "judging by the way Jean bolted in".

"It was", Jeff murmured, "now let me brood, will you mate?"

Exasperated, Syd picked up the tray and paid for the re-filled glasses.

"See you inside soon", he said as he left.

"Yeah".

The gay mood deserted the group. When Paula returned with Jean, it was evident to the others that Jean had been crying. Her reddened eyes could not be hidden by make-up. She tried to be bright, but continually she glanced towards the door of the bar watching for Jeff to appear.

When he did return, it was clear that he had been drinking heavily. He was unsteady on his feet. He sat down heavily. Red frowned then looked at Jean. When he opened his mouth to speak, Jean motioned him to be silent.

They had one more round, then left.

*　　*　　*

"You got a load on board last night", Red said to Jeff as they dressed in the hut the following day.

"You sure did", Doug added.

With a grimace, Jeff bent to tie his shoe laces.

"I know I did" he said, "but lay off".

"What the hell did you say to Jean?" Doug probed, "boy was she upset".

As the memory of his quarrel with Jean returned, Jeff winced. He felt he could not face Jean but knew he had to.

"Let me be, Doug", he said, "I've the devil of a headache".

"Hangover old boy". Clarrie laughed, "to give it its real name".

During the morning, Jeff made several attempts to see Jean to apologise. However, each time she saw him, Jean avoided him, until Jeff became annoyed and gave up. In the early afternoon, he walked angrily down to the mess.

The squadron operated that evening to L'Orient. The crew was not on the battle order and they stayed in the messes after dinner. The operational crews came and went one by one. The first wave of Lancasters started up on the 'drome. The engines surged as they were run up. As they took off, the full-throated roar of each plane seemed to shake the mess building. With intervals of ten minutes, the succeeding waves of backers-up took off until the last plane's drone was lost in the distance.

"Bloody quiet now", Doug remarked as the sound of the bombers faded away.

"Sure is" Al replied, "like a morgue".

"That's a happy thought", Red said and glanced around the ante-room. Besides the six of them, there were only two other Sergeants in the long room.

"Feels bloody strange not being on ops", he added, "when all the other bods are on".

They were clustered together in front of the fire, settled down in large padded armchairs with tankards of beer in their hands. Doug drained his and placed it on the floor beside him.

"I guess I'll hit the sack", he said yawning.

"Me too", Al replied.

Red sipped his beer for a moment, then turned to the rear-gunner.

"Hey, Nick", he said, "I was just thinking'.

"Oh, the strain of it," Doug laughed.

Leaning over, Red tipped Doug's chair over. The engineer sprawled onto the floor.

"To continue", Red said, "I was thinking, there's a spare bed over in our hut now near the crew. Why don't you shift over and bunk there".

"Good idea", Clarrie added.

Col Nicholls looked up. A pleased smile lit up his face.

"I'll change over right away", he said, and drank his beer down quickly.

As the others finished their beers and stood up, Jeff watched them moodily.

"I think I'll stay here for a while," he said.

"Suit yourself Jeff," Red replied, ruffling the navigator's hair affectionately. "Why don't you whiz up and see Jean, she's on duty".

Angrily, Jeff pulled out his cigarettes and lit one.

"It was perfectly obvious today", he said bitterly, "from the way she ducked every time I came in sight, that she doesn't want to see me".

"Don't be a bloody goat fella", Red said seriously.

Jeff watched the others leave the ante-room, then turned to look at the fire. He sat there drowsily thinking of Jean. With a sigh, he got up, walked over to the bar and ordered another beer.

They operated the following night.

With this trip, Jeff's confidence in himself began to return.

The target was Milan. It was a long trip.

After they had dressed for the flight, in the locker room, the crew slowly walked out to the flight-van. Jean sat behind the wheel. Her lips were pressed tightly together. The crew watched as Jeff threw his navigation gear and parachute into the van and then got in beside her. They clambered into the back.

Jean remained silent, facing ahead.

As he looked at her, Jeff wanted to speak, but when she would not look at him, he did not. They sat there, each wishing to erase the hostility between them, but too proud and angry to do so.

Slowly, Jean started the motor and drove them to Yorker.

Jeff climbed out of the van, collected his gear and walked stiffly to the plane. He looked back over his shoulder, with a hurt look on his face. Jean watched him, tears in her eyes. Her hands tightened on the steering-wheel.

"Good luck, Jeff", she whispered to his departing figure. She was frightened for him.

They took off with the second wave as backers-up once more.

Jeff worked at his navigation, trying to forget both his fear and his quarrel with Jean.

They passed over Dungeness on track and at height. In the moonlight, as they crossed the channel, they could see other Lancasters around them. The long leg across France was quiet. When "Gee" failed, Jeff began astro-navigation. His fixes from the stars pleased him. With the good results from his astro-navigation, his confidence in himself became stronger, as turning-point after turning-point was passed on track and on time.

Green track marker flares dropped directly ahead of them at Lake Aix-Le-Bains. They added their own to the others, to guide the later bombers.

The Alps were clear of cloud. Mt. Blanc rose majestically, its dark rocky ridges making more brilliant, by contrast, the snow glistening in the moonlight.

In the rear turret, Nick scanned the sky for fighters with mixed feelings. The turret turned constantly, guided by his hands. As much as he now wanted to prove himself not to be a coward in an actual attack, he was still afraid. His mouth felt dry every time he saw a speck in the sky. Each time the speck became another Lancaster, he was relieved.

The track markers went down on the edge of Lake Maggiore, the leg into the target began.

They flew in through the outer defences of Milan without trouble and dropped their target indicator flares and bombs on the yellows already down. The defences were evaded once again and the long trip back to base was begun. It was uneventful.

The quietness of the trip helped Nick. The quality of his navigation had pleased Jeff.

One crew was lost by the Squadron on the operation.

On the evening after Milan, Syd and Paula strolled out from dinner together into the mess ante-room. Syd poured coffees for both. They sat down side by side. As they quietly relaxed drinking their coffee, Jake Anderson wandered in. In his arms, he precariously balanced a portable gramaphone and a bundle of records.

"How about a session of music?" he called across the room.

Syd glanced at Paula. She smiled and nodded her head.

"So long as it is soothing, quiet and relaxing", Syd said.

Walking over to them, Jake placed the gramaphone and records down on a nearby table.

"I'm in that frame of mind myself", he said as he wound the handle. Carefully selecting a record, he set it on the turntable.

Through the mess sounded the soft, mellow strains of Debussy's "Clair-de-Lune". Syd leant forward in his Chair. Paula smiled up at Jake.

"That was an excellent choice", she said, her eyes bright.

As the last notes softly died away, Jake switched off the machine.

"That was really beautiful," Paula sighed.

A group of eight or nine clustered round. Three were W.A.A.F. Officers, and the others young flying men.

"Let's take it into the billiards room", one said, "otherwise the peasants here, and the old and staid, will fill the air with lamentation".

"Let's go", Jake answered, picking up the gramophone, "someone bring the records".

In the large billiards room, Jake set up the machine on a table.

"How about a spot of dancing?" he asked the girls as he put a record on.

"Yes, let's", Paula replied eagerly.

Rugs were quickly thrown aside. The girls were claimed as partners as the music of a waltz sounded. Syd sat on a settee and watched Paula. As she and a young Wireless-operator ended the dance, he rose and walked over to them.

"Next dance, Paula?" he asked.

"Yes, please", she replied, smiling up at him.

As the first bars of music came from the gramophone, he took her in his arms.

The tune was, "That Old Black Magic".

As the vocalist's words sounded, Syd tightened his arm round Paula. She pressed closer to him. Their steps blended as they slowly danced round the room. Each fitted the words to their thoughts of one another.

"That old black magic has me in its spell,
That old black magic that you weave so well,
Those icy fingers up and down my spine,
The same old witchcraft when your eyes meet mine."

The words, the music, the presence of Syd so close, Paula felt them and reacted to them. When the song was finally over, she stood close to Syd. With a sigh she opened her eyes and looked up. She quivered as his hand gently caressed her back through the uniform.

"How lovely that was", she whispered.

"Beyond that my dear", he replied.

Their mood was broken by a pilot-officer asking to dance with Paula. She smiled tantalisingly at Syd as she danced away.

Gradually, the group became smaller. In ones and twos the others left, until by ten o'clock only Jake, Syd and Paula and one other couple remained.

"Well I must leave right now", the other W.A.A.F. officer said firmly, "thanks for the music Jake"

"What about you two?" Jake asked, winding up the machine once more.

Paula glanced at Syd before answering.

"We'll stay for a little while if you don't mind," she answered.

"Hell, you can stay here till dawn", Jake laughed, "but don't expect me to stay too".

He placed another record on. The music's sentimental, slow rythm filled the room. Syd and Paula began to dance. Jake watched them for a moment. A soft smile creased his tired face.

"You two make me feel like a gooseberry", he remarked, as they passed close to him.

"I'm going for a grog", he continued.

When he returned, Syd was putting another record on.

"The damned bar's closed", Jake said, "and we're the only three around the place".

Syd glanced at his watch.

"It's well after ten", he exclaimed with surprise.

"I'm off to my virtuous couch," Jake said, "you can dump the noise-box and records in your room for the time being".

As he walked away, he knocked two light switches off, leaving only the light over the billiard table still glowing.

"That's much cosier", he said, then he left and closed the door behind him.

The shaded light lit the table brightly, but away from the table the room was in semi-darkness.

Syd switched the gramophone on. He held his arms out. Paula slowly went to him. As they slowly danced, Syd drew her closer to him. He pressed his lips against her hair. She quivered as he nuzzled her ear. They danced through three more numbers. Paula stood beside him as he changed records. Once again the strains of "That Old Black Magic" wafted gently through the room. Her face was flushed and happy as she gazed up at him.

"Kiss me darling", she whispered.

As he looked down at her, his face was solemn. Gently he placed his hands on her shoulders. Bending his head down he kissed her. His arms crept round her. He pressed her closer to him. He kissed her hungrily, feeling her teeth against his lips. She responded eagerly.

"Syd, Syd", she whispered as they drew apart.

Her hands crept up, lightly touching his face.

"My darling, I love you", she continued.

"I adore you, Paula" Syd's voice was tender.

As he kissed her again, the record grated to its conclusion.

"We had better go right now, my dear", he said switching off the machine.

Paula went over to the settee and sat down.

"Play it once more please, Syd", she said, her eyes lustrous even in the dim lighting.

As the music began once again, he sat beside her. He took her into his arms and kissed her. His fingers dug into her back. Her arms went round his neck and pressed his lips harder against her own.

"I should stay away, but what can I do,
I hear your name,
And I'm aflame,
Aflame with such a burning desire,
That only your kiss—can put out the fire".

Paula's breathing quickened, her eyes half-closed. Clumsily Syd undid the button of her tunic. His hand caressed her breasts through the thin material of her shirt.

"For you're the lover I have waited for,
The mate that fate had me created for—
And every time your lips meet mine—"

Clasping his hand with hers, she pressed it hard against her body.

"Darling, down and down I go—
Round and round I go—in a spin,
Loving the spin I'm in—
Under that Old Black Magic called love".
"Loving the spin I'm in—
"Under that Old Black Magic called love".

As the record ended, Syd reached over and turned off the gramophone. He stood up abruptly and turned off the one remaining light.

When he returned to the settee, he eagerly drew Paula

close to him. His hand came up and undid the buttons of her shirt. As Paula's breath quickened, he kissed her hungrily.

CHAPTER 17

Outside the Officers' Mess before breakfast, Syd waited anxiously for Paula. Worriedly he paced up and down, watching for her trim figure to appear. He had no appetite for food.

He blamed himself for the previous nights happenings. He expected Paula to be remorseful and unforgiving. However, even as he worried, the memory of her beautiful body pressed against his, brought pleasure to him.

When Paula did arrive, she looked beautiful. She smiled self-consciously and blushed.

"Hello, Syd", she said quietly.

"Let's get away from here", Syd said, touching her hand tenderly.

"I'm sorry about last night my dear", he exclaimed, as they walked away from the mess.

Paula walked beside him in silence for a moment.

"Why exactly, Syd?" she asked at length, gazing ahead of her, not looking at him.

"What must you think of me?" Syd cried.

Turning to face him, she took his hand.

"I love you very much", she replied softly.

"Thank God", he said, "I thought you might be hating me".

"I couldn't ever" Paula said.

She gazed about her. They were in the woods, out of sight of the mess. The cloud was overhead still, making the day grey. The chill bit through her uniform but she felt warm.

"I'm sorry it happened so soon", she whispered, "but it's helped me make up my mind".

Syd stopped abruptly. He turned towards her, taking her hands. He looked down eagerly at her.

"Do you mean you've changed your mind?" he asked.

"Yes, Syd."

"You'll marry me willingly?"

"Yes, Syd".

"No reservations?"

"No, Syd."

He stood looking down at her. His eyes shone then clouded.

"It's still not fair on you."

Paula drew closer to him. She stood on tip-toe and kissed him.

"I'm afraid no longer," she said, "I realise the dangers you face."

He put his hands on her shoulders, loving her.

"I may get killed."

"I know that, Syd," she said, "but I pray you won't." She smiled tremulously up at him.

"I want to marry you now, even if it is only for a short while, I love you so much Syd that that is all I can think of."

She took his hands from her shoulders and placed them round her. She nestled in to him.

"I feel strong now," she whispered.

He kissed her hair.

"Thanks Paula," he said, "you've made me very happy."

Then eagerly he held her away.

"I get leave on the twenty-fifth," he cried, "we'll get married then. You must have leave due."

"Oh yes, darling," Paula responded enthusiastically, "but we can't tell anyone on the squadron."

"Why not?" Syd asked in a puzzled tone.

"They'd post me away," she explained. "When we're married I couldn't stay here."

"Oh hell," Syd said annoyed, "Anyway, I'll have to let the crew know."

"I'd like them to know," Paula said.

He looked down at her, then drew her to him and kissed her.

"Let's get back to the mess," he said as they drew apart. "I feel hungry now."

"How romantic," Paula laughed.

"You'll soon find out how romantic I can be," Syd said, taking her hand.

"I have," Paula replied smugly.

* * *

After morning assembly, Syd and Jeff were told to report to the Commanding Officer's Office.

"Hello there, Berry, Johnson," the Wing-Commander said as they entered and saluted. "At ease."

"I've been studying your debriefing reports," he continued, indicating a bundle of forms on the desk.

"Yes, Sir," Syd said, self-consciously.

"Very good," the C.O. smiled, then turning to Jeff he added, "on time most of the time, that's what I want if I can't get all the time."

He paused to light a pipe. He inhaled the acrid smoke and puffed it out in great clouds.

"I'm putting you up to blind marking," he said at length. "You start training today."

Syd and Jeff looked at one another and grinned.

"You'll get another plane of course fitted with H2S," the C.O. added.

"A new one arrived late yesterday, and it's serviceable."

He glanced at Syd as he spoke.

"Can I alter— ?" Syd began uncertainly.

"—It's letter to Y," the C.O. finished the sentence with a smile, "I wondered if you'd ask that."

"Well, Sir?" Syd added.

"You may."

"What about the ground crew Sir?"

"You'll have the same ground crew too," the Wing-Commander sighed, "now get out before you want anything else."

"Yes Sir," Syd replied quickly.

He and Jeff saluted and turned away.

* * * .

The crew began intensive training in the new method. In the blacked out navigation compartment Jeff and Red worked at the radar set. An instructor, another navigator, flew with them for two short flights. Operations were not on in the evening, so they asked for permission to fly on training.

Remembering the teething troubles they had had with the original Yorker, Syd and Mac watched over the new plane like a baby.

Mac flew on each of the flights with the crew. He listened to the song of the engine like a critic at a symphony concert.

They flew three hours, returning before midnight to base, tired but satisfied with their progress and the new plane.

The following night they were once again on the battle order.

The target was L'Orient. They flew once again as backer-up in the second wave.

Take off was at dusk.

They flew in the new plane. A new crew flew in the original Yorker.

They experienced no trouble. The new radar, coupled with Gee, made navigation easier for Jeff. They dropped their bombs only fifteen seconds early. Over the target the flak seemed weak and the searchlights few, after the targets of the Ruhr and Southern Germany.

At debriefing after the operation, Syd sought out Paula.

"Another one done Paula," Syd said, tiredness showing on his face which was still smudged and marked from the oxygen mask.

"Thirty-two down now, thirteen to go," he added.

She handed him a cup of steaming cocoa.

"How was this one?" she asked.

"A piece of cake," he stated, with a wave of a hand, "nothing to it."

Raising the cup of cocoa up to his lips, Syd still gazed over its rim at Paula as he sipped slowly.

"I asked for leave on the twenty-fifth," she said.

"How did you go?" Syd asked lowering his cup.

She smiled tantalisingly before answering.

"I got it."

"Wizard," Syd exclaimed. "How long do you have to wait to get married with a Special License?"

"I haven't a clue," Paula laughed, blushing. "I think three days."

"Come along the twenty-fifth," he said, "I'll have the

214

license all ready."

Paula reddened again. She placed her hand under the cup and raised it to his lips.

"Drink up your cocoa," she said firmly, "and get your crew together so I can interrogate you."

Hurriedly, Syd drank the remainder. He bowed with a smile.

"You honour us my dear."

The squadron had lost one more crew. It was Joe Weldon's crew. Joe however, escaped. He was in hospital with a bout of influenza.

The weather remained fine, but cold. The intensive training in the new equipment continued for the crew.

Each day, they took off from the runway, setting course on a long cross country flight. Jeff and Red sat behind the blackout curtain in the navigation compartment. Without looking out for visual pinpoints on the ground, they navigated round on Gee and the new radar set, the H2S.

Each turning point was a medium sized town. They simulated bombing runs on each. As the towns reflection appeared on the radar screen, Red took over. He made the bombing run without seeing the ground below him.

As he called "bombs gone", Syd and Doug assessed the results.

Jeff then called the alteration of course on the new leg. He navigated until once again Red took over for the bombing run of the next town.

Each night the procedure was the same.

The crew were tired from the constant flying, but they did not complain.

They were pleased with the promotion. They wanted to become proficient as quickly as possible.

After cutting the engines as he guided the new Yorker into position on the dispersal, for the third night in succession, Syd relaxed thankfully. The quietness settled down upon him like a dark cloak. After the constant drone of the powerful motors for three hours, it was pleasant to be still and to hear nothing, except the wind sighing across the plane. The exercise had gone very well. Jeff and Red had hit each town exactly on time and on track. The plane had responded perfectly.

"Hey skipper," Doug's voice broke in upon his thoughts.

"Go ahead Doug," he replied tiredly, stretching his legs.

"Same programme tomorrow?" Doug added.

"No Doug," Syd said, "I think we'll give it a rest for a bit. I think Jeff and Red have the gen and we could all do with a bit of a break."

"You beaut, tomorrow night too?"

Syd eased himself wearily out of his cockpit.

"We'll have a break," he said. "Nothing tomorrow, day or night."

"Good," Doug exclaimed. "This damned night flying is cutting into my love life."

"The fair Colleen?" Jeff's voice asked.

"The one and only," Doug answered quickly.

"Well don't count your chickens before the hens cackle old boy," Jeff laughed. "We'll probably be on ops."

"Belt up," Doug snarled. "I'm too tired to think of a better reply."

Wearily, the crew gathered their equipment together. Slowly they made their way through the long fuselage, thankful to be finished for the night.

They jumped down and strolled away, easing their cramped muscles. When they were away from the plane, they lit cigarettes and inhaled deeply.

"Plane O.K. Sir?" Mac asked, going up to Syd.

"Like a bird, Mac," Syd replied with a smile, "you can wrap her up, sorry we've had you working so much the last three days."

The flight Sergeant glanced back at the dark bulk of the plane behind him.

"We know there are no bugs or gremlins with her now anyway," he said with pride in his voice.

"We won't be going up tomorrow Mac," Syd said, offering a cigarette from his crumpled packet, "unless ops are on of course."

The flight van skidded to a stop on the edge of the dispersal. The crew noisily bade the ground-crew goodnight and walked to it.

"How are you and Jean getting on?" Syd asked Jeff, as they walked over together.

"Well she still has my ring on her finger," Jeff replied flatly. "Apart from that, I might as well be a two-headed toad."

Syd glance at Jeff. The cigarette end glowed brightly as Jeff drew the smoke down deep into his lungs.

"I'm sorry Jeff," he said, "it seems funny you know."

"What does Skipper?"

They were nearing the van. Syd stopped, placing his hand on Jeff's arm. Jeff turned to face Syd.

"What does Skipper?" he repeated.

"Well I always thought you two were set for wedding bells soon," Syd said quietly.

Jeff looked towards the van. He drew on his cigarette, then threw the it away, half smoked.

"I did too, Syd."

"I though there was no chance for me with Paula," he said, pausing for a moment. Then he continued, "Now you and Jean are at loggerheads and Paula and I are getting married when we go on leave in a weeks time."

Jeff was speechless for a moment. Then with a pleased laugh, he took hold of Syd's hand and pumped it enthusiastically.

"Well blow me down," he cried, "you old fox, how did you do it?"

"Never mind how," Syd replied. "But will you be my best man?"

"Will I!" Jeff exclaimed, as they walked to the van. "Can a duck have ducklings?"

"Hello Jean," Jeff said, as he opened the cab door and sat beside her.

"Hello Jeff," she replied flatly, glancing at him for a moment then turning to face ahead.

Her face was sad, as was Jeff's. She wanted to throw her arms around him. She wanted to be happy as they had been such a short time before. However, she wanted him to make the first overtures. She was not sulking, she was simply proud and hurt.

Jeff looked at her. When she turned away, he became angry, believing she was sulking.

"All right," he snapped, "let's get going."

Silently, Jean started the engine, threw it into gear and

drove away. Jeff did not tell her of Paula and Syd.

From the rear of the van came shouts and laugther, as the rest of the crew congratulated Syd. Jeff sat staring ahead.

*　*　*

The following night they flew to Wilhelmshaven on their last backer-up trip.

"I can't win," Doug snarled despondently, as they climbed into the plane before take-off.

"I even rang Colleen last night," he continued bitterly to Red as they walked through the plane. "I told her I'd see her tonight unless we operated. So what bloody well happens, we're going to warm our bottoms over Wilhelmshaven. Here's Syd getting married and his girl in on the squadron. I can't even get to see mine to become properly acquainted."

With a laugh, Red bumped the engineer against the side of the fuselage.

"Quit griping as you would say," he said, "there's always another night."

"Heck," Doug growled, "this makes the fourth night in a row, and there's a damned brown job home on leave who's playing a line for her".

"Surely an Army type is no opposition," Red joked, as he bent to climb down into the bomb-aimers compartment.

"Go boil your fat head," Doug replied, pushing Red with his foot.

The big bomb-aimer stumbled forward onto the bombing panel. He sat up laughing, his equipment strewn around him.

As Nick clambered into the rear-turret, he trembled. His hands felt clammy with perspiration. He looked round the turret. The expanse of perspex gave him a feeling of nakedness.

His memories of the previous trip to Wilhelshaven were still too vivid and humiliating. He felt he could cope, had it been any other target. He was frightened of this town which had made him a coward once. The town had become personalised to him.

They took-off once again at dusk.

The first wave had taken off ten minutes before them.

The sky was clear of cloud, the moon was full.

On the long trip across the North Sea, they could see many of the two hundred bombers on all sides of them. They were lit up like moths in a room by the brightness of the night.

Low cloud had been predicted over the target and the enemy coast. Bomber Command had hoped it would blanket the searchlights without preventing the accurate marking of the target by H_2S.

The route was identical with that of the previous raid on the city.

As Yorker sped along the last leg into the target, there was still no cloud.

"Looks like a met boob Skipper," Red called over the intercom.

"Bags of searchlights as usual," Syd replied bitterly.

In the navigation compartment, Jeff calculated his timing for arrival over the target. It matched their scheduled time.

The islands north of Wilhemshaven appeared yellowish green on the H_2S screen. He took a bearing and distance on the western tip of Wangerooge. It plotted on track. Once again he checked his ground speed and E.T.A.

"Nav to Pilot," he called.

"Go ahead Jeff," Syd replied, watching the first searchlights stab the air over the target area.

"E.T.A. 2032, bang on Skipper," Jeff said smugly.

"Good show, Jeff," Syd said, smiling at the satisfied tone of the navigator's voice.

"Searchlights ahead," he called.

Noting the time in his log, Jeff said, "how about a practice run in on H_2S? I'll make the run in, then Red can take over for the last bit and drop the eggs from up front."

"Suit you, Red?" Syd asked.

"I'm game," the big bomb-aimer replied, "so long as we have no dummy runs."

"You won't," Jeff snapped.

Anxiously, he waited for the smudge of light which would be Wilhelmshaven to appear on the screen.

In the rear-turret, Col Nicholls turned his turret. His eyes smarted from staring into the night sky. Each time a speck appeared, he felt cold perspiration break out on his body. Each time he identified the plane as friendly, or if it veered away out of his range of vision, he felt thankful and relieved. He hated and feared the target ahead of them.

"Pilot to rear-gunner," Syd's voice broke in upon his thoughts.

"Gunner here," he answered quickly.

"Everything O.K.?" Syd asked.

"O.K. Skipper."

As he switched off his microphone switch, he felt better. It was lonely in the turret at the rear of the plane. He felt isolated and apart from the rest of the crew. He listened as Syd called up each member of the crew. Each fifteen to twenty minutes throughout the entire trip, this was the procedure. It brought the gunners closer to the crew up front. They felt part of it again for a brief while. It also ensured that all were well.

The smudge of brightness appeared on the screen. Leaning forward, Jeff worked the black knobs of the set. He ascertained the distance and direction. he set up his track marker on its centre as it crept slowly down the screen. He called the small alteration of course required. Then setting up the bombing marker trace he sat back. He watched the blips of light which were Wilhelmshaven creep closer to the bombing position represented on the glass in front of him.

Suddenly, he realised that they must be over the outer defences.

"Nav. to bomb-aimer," he called, hurriedly switching on his microphone. "You can take over now."

Red's deep voice boomed back.

"There's no need Jeff, by the looks of things. You'll hit the yellows plumb centre."

"Thanks Red," Jeff said, pleased with the remark. Then he added. "Course out of target 280 degrees, 2–8–0."

"Roger, 2–8–0 degrees," Syd replied, immediately setting it on the compass.

In the bright cloudless night, the city was visible below them. The docks, their target, stood out, nearly smothered by the yellow, red and green target indicator flares dropping down upon them.

Incendiaries seared across the docks and the town to

burn and destroy. The heavy explosives and block-busters mushroomed amongst them, hurling them further to add chaos to chaos.

Red lined up on the aiming point. The corrections were few. He pressed the bomb-release button.

"Bombs away," he called.

Yorker rose appreciatively as the load dropped from her bomb-bay.

With satisfaction, Jeff saw the moment of release coincided with that indicated on the screen. He noted the time of release in his log with height, speed and course. Then he dashed forward to look down on the target.

Over the target, the sky seemed filled by the bombers concentrating for the attack. There were many near collisions as bomber closed in on bomber to attack the aiming point. The searchlights and flak were intense, but they passed through uneventfully. They saw one plane shot down by flak, a twisting flaming orange mass. It fell into the town like a bomb.

As they crossed over the enemy coast, multicoloured light flak poured up venemously from a flak ship north of them. A bomber was hit. A glow appeared in the sky which grew brighter and brighter as it dropped closer to the sea. It hit the water and burned dully for a few minutes, then the sea was black once again.

As the fire died, drowned under the waters, the flak ship opened up once more. The lethal spray of tracers arched up but the second plane flew on.

"Think they ditched?" Doug asked in a subdued voice.

"Hope so the poor beggars," Syd replied sadly, knowing the hope was slim.

From the rear-turret, Nick had watched the awful scene with terrible fascination. As the glow grew brighter he seemed to feel the flames on his own flesh. He shuddered. When the flame was extinguished, he cried, thinking of the men in it.

Jake Anderson did not return from the operation. When Paula told Syd in the interrogation room that Jake was overdue, he was stunned. He had regarded Jake, the stooped untidy Jake, as indestructible.

It was the third last trip before he was to have been

screened from operations. When hope had been abandoned, Syd and the crew walked away to the messes, saddened and apprehensive. Still no crew had finished their two tours since they had arrived on the squadron.

* * *

The Commanding Officer sat slumped in his chair when the Adjutant entered his office on the following morning. He stared down at the raid report on his table without seeing it.

"I thought I'd find you here, Sir," the Adjutant said, "when you weren't early for breakfast."

Uncorking the thermos flask he carried, he poured hot black coffee into the cup.

"Drink this," he commanded, holding out the cup until the C.O. took it.

"Thanks Adj," the Wing-Commander said, setting it down on the desk.

"I don't suppose you've had any sleep at all," the adjutant added sternly.

"Afraid not."

Looking down at the tired, troubled man in front of him the adjutant felt sorry for him and worried about him. His eyes were red-rimmed and hard. His forehead and cheeks were heavily lined. His lips flicked with a nervous tic. On his unshaven chin, the stubble showed heavily and dark. His uniform was crumpled.

"It's a blow losing Jake, I know," the adjutant said quietly, "but the squadron is still here. If any of the crews see you like this, how do you think their morale will be?"

The C.O. stirred himself from his lethargy. He grinned ruefully. He reached for the cup of coffee and drank it down in gulps.

"You're right as usual Adj," he said, thoughtfully running a hand across his eyes, "but Jake's was the one crew I thought would beat this jinx that's on the squadron."

Tiredly, he rose from his chair.

"Well the show must go on," he said, "I'll dash off and clean up before morning assembly."

The adjutant watched sadly, as he slowly walked out of the room.

* * *

222

As Jeff lay back sleeplessly against the propped up pillow, he thought of Jake Anderson and his crew. He wondered if the plane which they had seen hit the sea, could have been theirs.

He felt thankful that he and Jean had had their difference. As he lay back, he felt all hope of ever finishing his two tours vanish. He reconciled himself to being shot down, perhaps killed. He no longer expected to come through or to marry Jean. He looked down the long room at the other airmen. Some still slept after the operation. He thought what a waste, as he realised that only a few, if any, of these young men would live more than a few days, weeks or months.

Throwing the bedclothes aside, he got up, shivering as the cold bit into his flesh.

All day he avoided Jean.

After lunch in the Officer's Mess, Syd sought out Paula. He was pale and quiet.

"Something on your mind, Syd?" Paula asked.

"I suppose so," he replied, taking out a cigarette and lighting it.

"Jake?" she asked, looking away.

"Partly."

"And us also?"

"Yes, Paula."

She sat down, Syd sat by her side. She did not speak for long moments. Then, still not looking at him directly, she spoke in a quiet flat voice.

"It still doesn't make any difference."

Syd drew on his cigarette.

"It does Paula."

Angrily she turned to face him at last.

"Now listen to me Syd," she said, "I thought I was the weak one of the two, I looked to you for the strength to make up my mind. Well it is made up and nothing can change it now."

Syd looked at her in amazement. The vehemence in her voice startled him. Finally he smiled.

"Jake was a good friend of mine also, remember," she continued, her calm voice lost in a harsh tone, "and I'm sure he would agree with me."

Ruefully, Syd sat back. He stubbed out his cigarette.

"Very well my dear," he said, "you win. If I get through ops till then, we'll get married as soon as we go on leave."

Paula angrily turned to him.

"Don't ever talk like that," she snapped, "and for goodness sake show a little enthusiam about the wedding. It's not a funeral."

With a laugh, Syd stood up.

"I'm sorry Paula," he said, shamefacedly. "I suppose it did sound rather unflattering. I really am pleased you feel this way, and I feel better about things already. There's nothing I want more, you know that."

"That's better," Paula smiled.

*　　*　　*

Jean came on duty after lunch. She sat quietly in the flight van waiting for orders. As she sat, staring into space, she thought of Jeff. She felt for the ring on her left hand, turning it absently.

She too was shocked at Jake's being missing. Sadly, she visualised him, as she had last seen him, climbing up into the plane the night before. He had been as nonchalant, pleasant and untidy as always.

She waited to see Jeff during the day. Jake's possible or probable death had made her afraid for him. She wanted to see him. She wanted their love to be as it had been before.

Disappointedly, she drove other crews out to their planes. When Jeff's crew climbed into the van during the afternoon, she anxiously waited for him to come out of the crew-room.

Syd slid into the seat beside her.

"Jeff's out at the plane Jean," he said when she glanced enquiringly at him.

"Oh!" Jean answered, hurt evident in her tone.

She switched on the ignition and started the engine.

"You and Jeff both act like Macbeth in his darkest moments lately," Syd said, as they moved away, "what's really wrong"

Jean was silent for a moment.

"You'd better ask Jeff," she said bitterly.

"Well don't blame me," Syd laughed, "but it's a shame

224

to see you two carrying on like no-hopers."

Jean guided the van around the perimeter track.

"I'm sorry I snapped at you, Syd," she said, "but I don't know what to do."

"Do you want me to talk to him?"

"No, don't, please," Jean replied quickly, "it will sort itself out one way or the other, I suppose."

"Roger," Syd replied as the van drew to a stop beside the dispersal, "you're the doctor."

Jean looked for Jeff, but he was not to be seen.

Syd stood till Jean drove away. When he turned he saw Jeff climb out of the plane and walk towards him.

"Jean?" the navigator asked briefly as he came up.

"Yes," Syd replied, "and you're a damned fool."

"Maybe," Jeff replied, his eyes watching the van speeding away, "but what bloody right has a man got to love a girl in this game? It's better to leave things as they are."

CHAPTER 18

The weather had improved. The cold winds had vanished, the sky was clear of cloud, the sun was warm. It was a foretaste of spring.

However, with the warmer weather came fog. The days were perfect, but as daylight faded, the tendrils of mist rose eerily from the low land and crept across the countryside like evil ghostly beings. From the hollows they rose, spread and met, to form the blanket of fog which shut out the night stars. Flying was impossible except during the day.

Each day, the crews took off on training flights. Gunnery practice, bombing practice, radar experience, the crews flew them day by day. Each night, most left the station in groups to descend on the neighbouring towns. Those who remained in camp thronged to the messes. They spent the evening drinking and singing around the pianos.

Shortly after Syd had told the crew that he was marrying Paula, they landed at Pottingborough, an American drome, to pick up a passenger, an American Padre. Syd eased Yorker up onto a dispersal near the control tower. The Flying Fortresses were lined up beside them.

As the crew jumped down, air and ground crews clustered round the Lancaster.

"Say guys," one said, his jaws working rhythmically on his chewing gum, "is this a training ship?"

"Hell no," Red laughed, "she's our operational kite."

"With them pop-guns?" the other asked, pointing to the .303 Browning machine-guns poking from the turrets.

"They do us at night," Clarrie remarked, annoyed by the question, "we don't carry cannons and we wait till we see the whites of their eyes."

"Well fella," another American said, "You can have them for mine. Give me the point fives we carry."

He swept his hand round, indicating the fortress in the next dispersal.

Syd grinned at Jeff and beckoned him. They walked away to the control tower to enquire about their passenger.

The group of Americans slowly melted away.

"How about looking over one of these flying arsenals?" Red said to Doug.

"O.K. be right with you."

They strolled over to the plane nearest to them. It seemed to bristle with guns. The much larger point fives stuck out from all sides.

"Our 303s seem bloody puny against these, Red remarked as he looked up at them.

"But don't forget they fly by day," Doug replied, "if we did daylights our guns wouldn't be worth a cracker, but at night the fighter has to get in close to down us. Then we stand just as good a chance of downing him at the range."

"Quite a speech mate," Red said, "but I'd still like to see these in the rear turret."

Doug snorted as he clambered up into the plane.

"Don't forget we carry five times the bomb load these things carry", he said, "you can't have it all ways."

They walked about the plane inspecting it interestedly.

"Give me the lanc," Doug said at last, "all these dials and notices give me the willies."

They climbed out of the plane and walked proudly

towards Yorker.

"Hey Red," Doug said pointing excitedly, "look over there."

Red looked where Doug indicated. A parachute lay on the concrete dispersal.

"Don't belt your blood-pressure," he replied, "its only a chute."

"Don't you get it?" Doug said taking hold of Red's arm "a wedding dress for Paula."

With a booming laugh, Red pulled his arm away.

"Who are you kidding?", he said, "first we have to pinch it, then we have to get it onto our kite and get it away, then there's only about ten days for the dress to be made up. How the hell could Paula get it made in that time?"

"Colleen," Doug replied briefly, "she'd make it up in less than a week. She's a wizard dressmaker."

Red glanced at the engineer, then at the parachute, then at the plane. There were still four Americans talking to the Clarrie, Al and Nick near the Lancaster's door.

"I'm with you sport," he said, his eyes lighting up excitedly, "I'll make a diversion while you grab the doings."

While Doug walked over towards the parachute, Red strolled over and put his large hands on the shoulders of two Americans.

"How about a game of dice," he said, winking at Al as he spoke.

The four Americans eagerly accepted.

"Let's get away from the kite a bit," he said, leading them to the far side of the dispersal away from Doug. He drew two dice from his pocket and thew them on the concrete. Al and Nick joined them, as they squatted down to play. Clarrie stood watching.

Presently Doug walked over to the group.

"Room for one more?" he asked, grinning at Red.

"If everything is under control."

"Everything under control and battened down Admiral," Doug replied.

When Syd and Jeff returned with their passenger, they had won three pounds.

Early that evening, Red and Doug drove over to see Colleen.

She lived with an elderly aunt in a small thatched cottage on the outskirts of the village. Evergreen shrubs formed a hedge in front. Behind the hedge was a garden. In spite of the season it was well tended. The cottage was painted white with pink trimming. It looked pleasant and homely.

Colleen came to the door eagerly when she heard the car stop. She ran down the path.

"Hi beautiful," Doug called loudly as he got out of the car.

"Hello Doug," she said, her eyes bright.

"Pucker up and give me a kiss," he said as she came up. He kissed her lightly on the lips.

Colleen blushed when she saw Red.

"Don't mind me," the bomb-aimer laughed, "nobody else does, so you needn't."

Doug reached into the back of the car and pulled out the parachute.

"That's a parachute," Colleen said surprised.

"I know it is," Doug replied, taking her arm and leading her through the gateway. Red followed them.

"You didn't steal it from the Squadron, did you?" she asked, her eyes wide and questioning.

"Of course not," Doug replied, "an American presented it to us when we landed on their drome this afternoon."

"That was nice of him," the girl remarked, opening the door, "What do you want me to do?"

They went through the passage into the large living room. When Doug explained, Colleen readily agreed to make the wedding-dress.

"It doesn't give me much time," she said thoughtfully, "but I think I'll be able to do it."

Doug pulled the rip-cord. He laid the silk out on the carpet. It seemed to fill the room. Colleen knelt and ran her hands over it.

"It's beautiful," she whispered.

"I'll see if I can get another when we get hitched," he said looking down at her.

"Stop it Doug," she laughed, reddening, then quickly added, "I'll have to get on it right away. When can Paula come down for a fitting?"

The two men looked at one another.

"Do we have to have her down right away?" Doug asked.

"Of course," Colleen replied, "how do I know what size to make the dress?"

"Hell," Doug exclaimed, "she doesn't know about it yet."

He picked up his cap and hurriedly kissed Colleen.

"We'll go and get her now," he said as he dashed out of the room. With a smile to Colleen, Red followed him.

They enquired for Syd at the Officer's Mess.

"Is Paula inside, Skipper?" Doug asked when Syd came to the mess door.

"Yes, why?" Syd replied.

"Could you get her to come down to Colleen's right away?"

"I suppose so, she's not on duty," Syd said doubtfully, "why?"

"Do me a favour," Doug asked. "Don't ask till we get there."

"All right," Syd replied, turning to re-enter the mess, "but I think something stinks here."

"How do you think he'll take us sending off the chute?" Doug asked anxiously.

"He won't like it," Red laughed, "not one little bit, but if I know women, as soon as Paula sees that silk, he won't have a leg to stand on."

That evening Paula was measured for the dress, to the noise of Syd's protests. Afterwards, as she and Colleen began to unpick the silk, Red walked over to the "Anchor" and returned with bottles of beer.

"Here Skipper," he said, handing a glass to Syd, "calm your guilty conscience with a grog."

Jeff continued to avoid Jean. He was unhappy doing it, but had made up his mind it was for the best. His nights were sleepless, except for nightmare filled moments. He began to drink heavily in an endeavour to find rest. On leaving the mess of a night after drinking, he could look forward thankfully to at least some dreamless sleep.

The strain of not operating was showing on the others in the crew also. There was an air of feverishness about them

229

in everything they did. Their laughter was shrill and forced. Their life seemed bound up with operations. When they did not fly, they complained and sought pleasure with terrible earnestness.

Doug only was thankful for the ease-off in operations. Each evening he drove Paula, sometimes Syd also, over to Colleen's for a fitting and to help with the frock. Each day saw more and more done. Colleen worked at it constantly, in a race to get it finished in time. Doug was contented to sit in the living-room, talking to Colleen as she worked. Occasionally, he wandered over to the Anchor and yarned to Josh.

Syd spent some nights with Paula, other nights he remained in the mess, brooding, because they were not operating.

The remainder of the crew either went by bus to the nearby towns or remained in the mess a compact body. They drank together, making unwelcome all outsiders, with the exception of Joe Weldon.

Joe still had no crew of his own. When gunners went sick, he would fly in their place. He had flown nearly forty operations, but it was only occasionally when he could add to his total. He was happy being on the squadron instead of at a training station, even though he had no choice of the crews he flew with.

When the fog finally lifted sufficiently for them to operate, they went to Bremen. They flew for the first time as blind markers.

Thankfully, if fearfully, they took off into the dusk in the first wave of bombers.

The route to the target was similar to the route they had flown to Wilhelmshaven.

As they flew over England, Red anxiously tested the H2S. When satisfied, he went forward once again into the bomb-aimers compartment.

Jeff worried out his navigation on the long leg across the North Sea. When he could no longer get results from the Gee, he used astro-navigation. Even as he plotted the fixes, he still worried until the search lights and flak burst into life north-east of them.

"Search lights port bow Jeff," Syd called.

"Heligoland Skipper," he replied thankfully, "We alter course when we're south of it."

"Well some silly blighter's off course," Red's voice chuckled over the intercomm.

Jeff checked his navigation with an estimate of the distance from Heligoland. His winds were satisfactory and his E.T.A. good.

They turned south of the island, onto the leg which would take them into Germany. The last before the run into the target. Thin cloud lay below them. It thickened gradually as they neared the coast.

They were routed between, and close to, Cuxhaven and Bremerhaven.

Although the total force was only one hundred and fifty, many flew over each town. The searchlights caught bomber after bomber in their grasp. The flak burst lethally round the bright specks in the beams. Each town claimed victims, broken Lancasters which twisted and spun down in flames until they exploded with their bomb-load.

As they drew level with Bremerhaven, Red came back into the navigation compartment.

"It looks like a blind marker raid Jeff," he said as he sat down.

"Cloud?" Jeff asked briefly.

"Ten-tenths ahead of us," Red replied, "no chance of a visual. I'm not dropping any illumination flares."

"You'd better be good," Jeff added, pointing to the radar set.

Jeff handed a slip of paper to the bomb aimer. On it he had written down the course, speed and wind velocity. Red studied it for a moment, then clipped it to the notes given him by the bombing leader at briefing.

They turned onto the short leg to the target over thick cloud. Flak was visible ahead of them, but the searchlights could not break through the low cloud.

The blips of light appeared at the top of the radar screen. Red took a bearing and distance on the edge of the brightness. He wrote down the result, with the time, on a slip of paper.

"Check E.T.A. Jeff," he said as he handed the note to Jeff.

Swiftly Jeff transferred the information to his chart. On his calculation he worked out the E.T.A.

"Bang on time," he said proudly, "a little south of track. Not enough to worry about now you can see the target."

"Right Jeff," Red replied, turning his attention to the H2S. Unhurriedly, he set it up for bombing.

They seemed to come up to the target all too quickly.

The flak was intense below them, the cloud was lit up by the search lights. They did not break through, but formed a background of light against which the bombers were silhouetted like beetles on a table-cloth. The enemy fighters flashed in, amongst their own flak, cannons stuttering their deadly shells.

Red called for bomb-doors open. His eyes never left the radar screen as he directed Syd towards the aiming point.

"Red T.I. down ahead bomb-aimer, Syd called as the first red target indicator cascaded.

"Right skipper," Red mumbled, his eyes still on the screen.

Another red fell into the first.

"Steady, steady, steady," Red intoned as the aiming point drew closer.

He paused for a moment, then pressed the bomb-release button.

"Bombs gone," he shouted exultantly.

Flak burst round them. Close by, a bomber fought for life against an enemy fighter and won the fight, as the fighter broke away.

Their red T.Is. fell on time, into the cluster of red, partly obscured by the low cloud. Beneath the colour, beneath the cloud, the quick flashing bursts of bombs could be seen as they tore the heart out of the invisible city.

Syd threw Yorker onto the new course out of the target area.

The return flight was uneventful, but fog was thickening as they approached base. The lights of the drome seemed misty as the fog thickened. They were second back of the crews from the squadron. Syd called up for permission to land, as he headed Yorker into the funnel on the approach to the runway. The runway lights were dim as Yorker sank lower. The speed fell away, Syd eased her down gradually, until the wheels screeched protestingly as they made contact with the concrete.

They were the last to land. All other crews were diverted to dromes clear of fog.

The squadron had lost one more crew. A new crew, which had only been on the station two weeks.

Next day, once again there were no operations. One by one, like strays, when the fog cleared, the diverted planes straggled in and landed. The crews noisily tramped into the locker room and stowed their gear away before reporting.

In the evening, once again Doug drove Paula to the village. The wedding frock was nearly finished. While the girls worked, he went over to the 'Anchor'.

The rest of the crew went by bus to Huntingdon and spent the night drinking.

The days passed slowly for Syd and Paula. Each looked forward eagerly to their wedding day.

Paula had written to her people, immediately she and Syd had decided upon getting married. She asked them to arrange for the wedding at their local church on the second day of their leave. Although Paula had written often of Syd in her letters, they had never met him. They had realised that she was in love with the pilot but they had been surprised by the suddeness of their decision. Paula was their only daughter and they were worried.

In spite of their fears, they followed Paula's instructions and made plans to make the day one of happy memories for Paula and Syd.

The weather remained fine, but the fog persisted. It became a period of cancelled operations. Each morning, operations were scheduled. The crews prepared. The navigators worked out their flight plans. Then, in the late afternoon or early evening, Group signalled through the cancellation order.

As day followed day, with the squadron alerted for operations, Syd began to worry. Unless he could slip away for a full day, he would not be able to get the special marriage licence.

Four days before their leave was due to begin, Syd and the crew mingled with the other airmen at morning assembly.

As the commanding officer entered, the crews sprang to attention.

"At ease men," the Wing Commander said, " well at least we know where we stand today, we're on stand-down from now."

Syd glanced up and smiled. He quickly sought out Doug, as the training schedule for the day was read out.

"Hey Doug," he whispered anxiously, "how's the petrol for the Bus?"

"We're Jake," Doug grinned, "we could go to John-o-Groats and back the way I'm in with the local garages and here on the drome."

"You beaut," Syd said.

"Why?" Doug asked.

Syd motioned him away to a corner where they could not be overheard.

"I want to take Paula down to London for the licence," he said.

"Hell haven't you got that yet?" Doug exclaimed.

"Haven't had a chance," Syd replied, "if I did anything about it from the station, everyone would know and they'd post Paula away."

Doug pondered for a moment.

"What if we're on a training stooge?" he asked.

"I'll get out of that."

"Well look," Doug said, "after assembly, you duck off and tie everything up with Paula and I'll make sure the bus is filled up and that you have enough coupons to get you back."

As the C.O. and leaders left the room Syd dashed out. He sped over to the intelligence room and asked the Waaf on duty for Paula.

"What's wrong Syd?" Paula asked.

"Nothing," he replied quickly, "but what time do you come off duty this morning?"

"Ten o'clock," she replied, "I've been on since midnight."

"Good we're going to London for the licence."

"What?" Paula cried, her eyes opening wide with surprise.

"Look," Syd said, "don't ask questions and don't worry, we're on stand-down and I can get the car. So as soon as you get off, I'll meet you in the lane at the back of the mess."

Paula appeared worried. Syd tried to reassure her.

"We can slip out the back way," he urged, "no one will see us."

"But what about getting back on time?" she asked.

"We're only eighty miles from London," Syd replied, "we'll be there by one in the afternoon and we can get back easily in tons of time."

Suddenly Paula smiled. She put her hand on Syd's arm. He smiled in return, thinking how lovely she was.

"You'll come?" he asked.

"Of course," she replied, "as soon as I leave here, I'll go straight down to the lane."

"I'll be parked out of sight of the mess."

Syd hurried back to the crew room. Doug and the others waited for him.

"Everything's O.K. Skipper," Doug called, "Jeff talked Mac into making the kite U.S., so training flights are out."

"Thanks Jeff," Syd said, "how about the car?"

Doug pointed to it, standing out front of the building.

"She's full," he said, "and there are cans in the boot. Mac came good with a bit and a Waaf pal of Red's helped with a bit more."

Drawing his wallet out, he extracted several petrol coupons.

"There are more here than you'll need," he said "but you'd better take the lot."

Syd put them in his battle-dress. Then looked round at the crew.

"Thanks fellows," he said, "see you when I get back."

He drove to his billet and changed into his uniform. He placed the petrol coupons in his wallet with a smile. Even petrol seemed to be no trouble to the engineer. He looked to see if he had sufficient money, then returned to the car.

He drove down to the lane and waited for Paula. When she came, she was breathless.

"I hope it will be all right," she said as she got in beside Syd.

He put his arms round her and kissed her.

"Don't worry," he said, as he started up the car, "No one will even miss us."

The drive down to London was pleasant in the sunny weather. As they approached the outskirts, Syd turned to Paula.

"Why don't we drive to your people's place?" he said "we can see your mother, park the car and get the tube into the city."

"Mother would be awfully pleased," Paula replied eagerly, "if she doesn't die of fright when she sees us."

As they drove up to the house in Hendon, Mrs. Penton was in the garden. They got out of the car as she hurried over.

"Paula," she exclaimed, "this is a surprise."

"Hullo mother," Paula said throwing her arms round her, "it's wonderful seeing you again."

Mrs. Penton was a slight, still attractive woman in her early forties. She was an older edition of Paula.

"I suppose this rather presentable gentleman is Syd," she said, her eyes twinkling.

Shyly, Syd held out his hand.

"I am, Mrs. Penton," he said a little embarrassed, "I'm pleased to meet you and I'm sorry that I haven't before this."

"I'm pleased to meet you at last," Mrs. Penton smiled, "We heard so much about you in Paula's letters, we feel we know you."

Taking each by the arm, she led them through the gate into the spacious garden of the large home.

"Come in and have lunch now you're here," she said, looking from one to the other, "I can manage some spam with our own vegetables."

"Don't bother mother," Paula said, "we won't be able to stay long."

"Don't be silly girl, of course, you'll have lunch."

They walked up the path to the house. As they entered, Syd stood back to allow them to pass.

"Well, how and why did you manage to get down so soon before leave?" Mrs. Penton asked, as they walked into the lounge-room.

"We're A.W.L. I'm afraid," Syd smiled, "we're getting the licence today."

"Good gracious," she said "haven't you done that yet?"

As Paula and Syd explained, they went through to the kitchen where Mrs. Penton quickly prepared lunch for them. They talked over the meal. When Syd and Paula finally got up to leave, he and Mrs. Penton felt they knew one another.

She squeezed his arm affectionately, as she saw them out.

"You had me worried, marrying Paula like this," she said solemnly, "but the war makes young people like that I suppose. There seems so little future, only present. Believe me Syd, I know, I married Paula's father during the last one."

She smiled at them, as they stood upon the steps looking up at her.

"All I hope is, that I can make Paula happy," Syd replied.

"I'm sure you do Syd and I'm sure you will."

As they walked away arm in arm, Mrs. Penton watched them proudly and lovingly, if sadly, with tears in her eyes. They looked so young she thought, so sure of themselves.

They went by tube to the city. It took them some time to get a special licence, but finally Syd had paid the fee and had the document. When they returned to Hendon they saw the Minister who was to marry them. When they hurried back to Paula's home, it was late in the afternoon.

"What time does your father get home Paula?" Syd asked, as they neared the house.

"Shortly after five, why?" she replied.

"Let's wait for him," Syd smiled, "I should ask his permission to marry you."

"It's a little late now," Paula laughed, "I have you in my power now and with witnesses."

As they waited, her mother made them eat another meal. When Mr. Penton arrived, he kissed Paula, then put his arm round her shoulders. He shook hands with Syd.

"Well son," he said, "I'm pleased to meet you at last."

"Thank you Sir," Syd replied, "I hope you're not hurt by the way Paula and I have done this."

"I can't really complain," he said with a wry smile at his wife, "I did pretty much the same thing."

He went to a cocktail cabinet and opened it. He poured whiskies for himself and Syd and sherries for Paula and his wife.

"Let's have a drink to your future happiness," he said, handing the glasses round.

When Paula and Syd left later, he stood on the footpath with his arm round his wife.

"It's strange you know," he said, as they watched the car drive off.

"What is?"

"Well I had things planned to say when I met Syd but I hardly said one of them."

"What were they dear?"

"Oh things like, why they couldn't wait until the war was over, or until he had finished operations."

"I know dear," Mrs. Penton said, as she gave a final wave. "I meant to ask what plans they had made for after the war, where they were going to live, what they were going to do."

"I didn't even ask him if he could support her."

They walked slowly back to the warmth of the house.

"They're a lovely couple dear," Mrs. Penton said, as she poured another whisky for her husband.

"He seems a nice chap, I like him."

CHAPTER 19

The organ sounded through the small, ancient, ivy-clad church, heralding Paula. The notes swelled richly, as her father handed her out to the car. Syd and Jeff, clad in their best, freshly pressed uniforms, stood nervously waiting before the altar.

They had not operated again after Bremen. The days of fog had crawled slowly by until the day of their leave had arrived. With the exception of Syd and Doug, the crew had left together by train for London. The two had remained behind with the car to drive Paula down to her home. Syd and Paula were to have the car for their honeymoon.

Jeff had tried to see Jean before leaving but had missed her. Syd and Doug joined the others in the late afternoon at the hotel they had all booked into.

"Well, here we are," Doug shouted breezily across the large hotel lounge, "let the party begin."

"What party?" Syd asked in a surprised tone.

"Don't be a drongo," Jeff replied, "your buck's party of course."

"You have to go off with a bang Skipper," Red laughed, "it's not every day one of the crew gets married."

The evening became a riotous pub-crawl through the hotels and clubs of the West End and Soho. In the early hours of the morning, singing "Here comes the Bride", they laughingly staggered back to their hotel.

In the morning, Jeff woke with a splitting headache. He lay back, cautiously opening his eyes slowly. With a groan, he sat up.

"Oh hell," he cried, holding his head, "what a beaut."

He glanced over at Syd who lay sprawled across the other bed in the room, clad only in his underwear.

Gingerly, he threw the bed-clothes aside and got up. He looked at his watch. It was after ten o'clock. He stumbled to the wash-basin in the corner of the room. With a shudder, he put his head under the cold water. As he dried his hair and face, he felt slightly better.

"Hey, Syd," he called loudly, "time to get up."

With a moan, Syd stirred. He sat up for a moment, then sank back onto the bed.

"No one can suffer like this and live," he mumbled thickly, his eyes still closed.

"You'd better get up," Jeff insisted firmly, "unless you want to play the part of the missing bridegroom."

Abruptly, Syd sat upright. As he did, pain shot through his head. He groaned.

"I'd forgotten" he cried anxiously, "what's the time?"

With a wry smile, Jeff looked at his watch.

"Ten twenty two," he announced, "but with the wedding at three-thirty, we don't have any time to waste."

Relieved, Syd slowly got off the bed.

"OK best man," he said, as he reached for the aspirin

bottle on the dressing-table, "what's the gen? Brief me."

"First of all, a long cold shower for both of us," Jeff replied, "then pack and downtown for a shave, head and face massage, have our good uniforms pressed, a small pick-me-up and lunch. By that time, I hope we feel human again."

While Syd showered, Jeff woke the others and by the time they arrived at the church, they had recovered.

As the music sounded, Paula made her way down the aisle, her arm tucked into her father's. She looked beautiful. The dress Colleen and she had made billowed round her. Her mother's veil, resurrected from the attic, foamed gently over her head and face. In her free hand, she clutched a bouquet of roses. Nervously, she glanced up at Syd.

Jeff turned slightly to gaze at her as she walked down. While he was thinking how lovely she looked, he became aware of the bridesmaid behind Paula. He had not given a thought to the fact that Paula would be attended and was surprised.

As they drew closer, he realised with a shock that the bridesmaid was Jean. He stared in amazement, as she followed Paula up to the altar. She smiled impishly at him as she took up her position.

She was also dressed in white, a full-length, bridesmaid's frock which accentuated the lights in her blonde hair which cascaded down from under the small coronet of flowers she wore.

"Brethren," the minister solemnly began the marriage service, " we are gathered here together..."

Jeff continued to stare at Jean, his thoughts in turmoil. The smile still played roguishly on her lips. The love he felt for her welled up in Jeff. He was hardly conscious of the words the minister spoke, but he fumbled for the ring and handed it to Syd at the appropriate moment.

Syd gazed down into Paula's face as the service ended. She smiled up at him, her eyes shining with happiness.

They slowly moved towards the vestry. Jeff and Jean came towards one another as they followed.

"You could have warned me," Jeff whispered, as he placed his hand under her arm.

"And ruin everything," she smiled.

"What do you mean?"

"Paula and Syd arranged this," Jean said. Then she asked anxiously, "you don't mind, do you Jeff?"

"Of course not," he replied, "I tried to see you before we came on leave."

Jean looked up at him, her eyes twinkled. She squeezed his hand.

"I know," she said, "I dodged you. I was frightened I'd let it slip that I would be bridesmaid."

"It wouldn't have mattered," Jeff said.

"I thought it might," Jean replied, "I was beginning to think you didn't love me any more."

Jeff looked down into the solemn face beside him.

"That could never happen,' he said.

"I stopped worrying when I saw the your face at the altar."

"It's a wonder I didn't drop from shock."

They entered the vestry, Jean slowly freed her arm.

"I was frightened all the way up the aisle," she said, before joining Paula, "you great goon."

Jeff slowly moved behind her.

The small reception was held at the Penton's home, where the large lounge room had been transformed into a bower of flowers. The gardens of the neighbourhood had been stripped of blooms. Mrs Penton, her relatives and friends had used precious coupons and worked hard for days, to provide the wedding breakfast laid out upon the tables. A bar, laden with bottles and glasses, occupied one corner.

"Welcome into the family," Mr. Penton greeted Syd, as he and Paula got out of their wedding car at the gateway to the house.

"Thank you Sir," Syd replied happily.

"Isn't 'Sir' a little formal now son?" Mr. Penton smiled, as they walked up the path.

Laughingly, the three entered the house. Syd gazed round in amazement at the room. Friends of Paula and the crew thronged towards them. Jean and Jeff hurried up. Jean immediately fussed over Paula's dress, straightening the veil and adjusting her frock. The crew, headed by

Nick, lined up to kiss the bride. Syd felt inundated by people, as men shook his hand and women pecked at his cheek. Paula gazed proudly at him as her friends were obviously impressed by the unassuming young flyer. They clustered round, until the master of ceremonies, an uncle of Paula, called for the couple to take their positions at the place of honour.

After the informal, buffet wedding-breakfast, the speeches and the cutting of the cake, Syd caught hold of Jeff's arm and dragged him aside.

"You can call me all the clots you can lay your tongue to," he said anxiously, "but we've got nowhere to sleep tonight."

"What?" Jeff exclaimed loudly.

"For God's sake don't let Paula know."

"How the hell did you forget that," Jeff asked.

"I booked into the hotel at Bournemouth from today," Syd explained, "but I completely forgot about not getting there till tomorrow."

Jeff threw his head back and laughed. He gazed over at Paula talking gaily to her friends and oblivious of their conversation.

"Well you're a drongo skipper," Jeff said, "can you imagine it, wedding night under the stars in Hyde Park."

"It's not a laughing matter," Syd snarled angrily, "I thought you'd be able to think of something."

"Keep the hair on your chest," Jeff smiled in reply, "we'll get the crew in on this."

Looking round the room, he saw Doug, Al and Red at the bar, glasses in their hands. He turned to Syd.

"You get back to Paula," he said, "leave this to us, we'll get something for you somewhere."

He hurried over to the bar and after a quick drink, he bustled the three crew-mates out of the house.

"What the hell, Jeff?" Red growled. "I was just getting myself around some good scotch."

"Yeah, what goes?" Doug asked, his eyes looking back to the house.

"Something more important than you three getting a skinful of grog."

As he explained the situation the three burst out laughing, Red doubled up as he bellowed his mirth.

"Pipe down Red," Al said, "Or they'll think we're telling dirty jokes."

"Heck", Doug said, tears running down his cheeks. "I could think of some wizard ones to fit this set-up."

"What do you want us to do?" Al asked seriously.

"Whiz down to the nearest phone," Jeff said, "then ring every damned hotel in the West End and try to book them in for tonight somewhere. Don't say they're just married, just ask for a room for Mr. and Mrs. Berry. Start with the Savoy and work down."

"Roger," Red said, "we go to do your bidding, sire."

The three dashed away, jumped into the crew car and roared off down the street. Anxiously, Jeff watched them speed off, then he went back into the house. Jean walked up to him as he entered. Her face lit up when she saw him.

"I haven't seen much of you since we got here," she whispered tenderly.

"That's not my fault my dear," Jeff replied, taking her by the hand and leading her away from the crowd.

"I don't know how I could ever have thought that I'd be able to put you out of my mind," he murmured, his lips against her cheek.

"That's more like my old Jeff," Jean replied a smile on her lips, "it was worth all the subterfuge."

She turned her head, her lips were close to Jeff's, but as he bent his head to kiss her, she drew away.

"Slow down young fellow," she said, "You have to grovel a bit before I'm satisfied."

"How much leave do you have? Jeff asked.

"I go back tonight, worse luck," Jean replied.

"It might be just as well, the way you look right now and the way I feel."

With a laugh, she disentangled herself and went back to the other guests. Jeff followed her.

After half an hour, Doug, Al and Red returned. Jeff knew from the despondent looks on their faces, that they had been unsuccessful. He went over to them. Once again, they went into the garden.

"Well, let me have it," Jeff said.

"We tried every damned one," Doug said, "no dice, It's

the week-end they tell us."

"We got three phones," Red explained, "and went through them in batches and every blasted one gave us the same answer, no room."

"Anyone would think there was a damned convention on," Doug added.

"Well that's that," Jeff said, "We'll have to think of something else"

They sat down on the steps of the house. Behind them, the babble of voices sounded, gay and happy as the guests circulated. They heard Syd's voice and Paula's laughter.

"Get cracking someone," Red said at length.

"I've got it I think," Jeff exclaimed suddenly.

"Well?" Al asked anxiously.

"I still have my room booked," he said, "they can have it and I'll bunk with you two."

"That's great," Doug growled, "you mumble and growl in your sleep and besides, your room only has two twin beds."

"It will have to do them," Jeff replied, "and you'll have to put up with me for tonight."

"Tis a far, far better thing we do, and so on, Doug," Red grinned.

"Well that's settled," Doug replied, "but I know this much, if noise-bag here is sleeping in our room, I'm going to get myself good and plastered before I go to bed."

As they stood up to go into the house, Jeff stopped them.

"Don't be so quick, I haven't finished," he said, "the room will have to be cleaned up and my gear shifted over to your room."

"OK, I get it," Doug grumbled, "you're the best man, so you can't leave. That means us again."

"Roger, and you will have to be back here before they leave."

"Well they won't be leaving for hours yet," Doug added, "so let's get to the bar and start the process of inebriation. Give me the tic-tac when zero-hour approaches. We'll grab the car, dash to the pub, fix things up and be back in time for them to leave."

Jeff immediately sought out Syd when they re-entered

the house. He was surrounded by people with Paula's arm tucked proudly into his when Jeff attracted his attention.

He eased himself away from the crowd.

"Well?" he asked.

"Not good, not bad," Jeff replied.

"Don't keep me in suspense."

"You'll have to take the room we had last night," Jeff said, then told Syd what the others had done.

"We'll clean it out," Jeff added, "shift my stuff and transfer the room over to you. You'd better have the marriage licence handy, in case they don't believe your're married, otherwise everything should go off all right."

Syd sighed his relief. "What about you?" he asked.

"I'm bunking with Red and Doug," Jeff replied. "In spite of their protests I might add."

"Now, do you mind if I concentrate on a bit of work for myself?" he continued.

"Go right ahead," Syd said with a smile, as Jeff walked away towards Jean.

As the evening progressed, Jeff eased Doug and Red away from the bar. They left regretfully when an hour had passed. Jeff and Syd became anxious when Paula had gone to change. The bomb-aimer and engineer had not returned. Syd suggested ringing for a cab.

"Calm down, they'll be here," Jeff said, not believing his own words.

"They won't be," Syd replied, worried and fretful, "then what will we do tomorrow? We're supposed to be driving down in the car to Bournemouth."

"For goodness sake, stop worrying."

Minutes before Paula came down the stairs from her room, Doug and Red returned, their arms laden with bottles of whisky and gin.

"Where the blazes have you been?" Syd demanded.

"We fixed everything at the pub, here's your hotel key and the car key," Doug replied thickly, "then we thought the party might be getting a bit dry, so we bought some supplies."

As they staggered over and placed the bottles on the bar, Jeff turned to Syd."

"Well they were right," he said, "your father-in-law has

opened the last bottle."

"I never thought my wedding day would be like this," Syd said, wiping his hand across his brow.

As he spoke Paula was coming down the stairs. She paused half-way down and threw the bouquet of roses. A primmish, middle-aged neighbour caught it to the banter of her friends. Paula walked down the remainder of the stairs to Syd. He took her hand and they slowly made their way through the guests, until eventually they were at the car. Paula kissed her mother and father.

"I'll look after her," Syd said as he kissed Mrs.Penton and shook Mr. Penton's hand.

"I'm sure you will son," Mrs. Penton replied.

They entered the car in a cloud of confetti and sped away.

As the others went back to the house, Jeff detained Jean and led her to a dark spot of the garden. He put his arms round her and kissed her, hard and eagerly.

"I've wanted to do that for so long Jean," he said, as he held her.

"Well, you could have, you know," she replied.

"Don't growl at me," he whispered, his mouth against her cheek. "I know I was a fool, but I still wonder if it's the right thing until we finish ops."

Angrily, Jean pushed him away. Her eyes blazed, reflecting the moon-light.

"If you talk like that again," she answered, "I dashed well won't make it up with you. You didn't deserve it this time."

"I give in," Jeff said with a smile, "come here, and thanks for being you, and doing what you did."

"Goon," Jean murmured as his lips closed on hers once again.

* * *

Syd and Paula shyly entered the hotel. An aged porter took their bags and led them to the lift, after they had registered. From the smile on the attractive red-headed receptionist's face, Syd knew that Doug and Red had had no trouble in altering the booking of the room.

The room was immaculate. Flowers which Doug had bought, stood in a crimson sheaf on the dressing table.

With a smile, Syd recalled the disorder of the morning. He shuddered with the memory of the hangover as he tipped the porter.

"Well, Mrs. Berry," he said, when the door closed.

"Nothing to report sir," Paula said, coming into his arms, "except that I'm an honest woman now." Then gazing round the room she remarked with a smile, "twin beds?"

Syd grinned in reply, "There's room enough for both of us in one."

Paula turned away. Self-consciously, she opened her suitcase. She took out her night-dress and dressing gown and laid them on the bed. Slowly she began to undress before going to the bathroom. She took off her frock and hung it up. She took her stockings off, then slowly drew the slip over her head. Syd's pulses quickened as her long lean legs became visible. Turning her back to him she clumsily fumbled for the clips of her brassiere.

"Undo me darling," she murmured softly, after trying unsuccessfully for some minutes.

*   *   *

Jean went to change out of her bridesmaid's frock back into her uniform immediately after Paula had left. She and Jeff went back into the house after seeing Syd and Paula drive off. Jeff stood watching her as she walked up the stairs, then went to the bar. The crew were clustered round it. Nick, glassy-eyed and grinning, stood with a drink in his hand. Doug and Al were helping Mr. Penton pour drinks for the few guests who remained. Clarrie and Red were arguing heatedly as they leant against the wall. Jeff smiled as he joined them.

"How about a drink for the best man," he said, leaning on the improvised bar.

"Coming up," Al replied, pouring a liberal amount of scotch into a glass, "get that into you."

"I certainly need it."

"You do?" Doug retorted, "what about us, all you did was give orders. We did all the work."

Jeff drank down the whisky and Al immediately refilled his glass. While the crew stayed near the bar, more guests gradually left. When Jean finally came down, Doug and

Red were the center of a small group of men, singing ribald forces songs. From the kitchen came the noisy clatter of dishes being washed as Mrs. Penton and her friends tried to drown out the sound of raucous singing.

Jeff phoned for a taxi, then he and Jean said their good-byes to the Pentons. Jean snuggled up against him in the taxi, as they drove up to London. He slid his arm round her.

"Bit extravagant with the taxi aren't we?" she whispered.

"Nothing but the best for you today," Jeff replied with a shrug, "even if I have to eat at canteens and doss in the park for the rest of my leave."

"You won't have to, will you?" Jean asked earnestly.

Jeff laughed, "Of course not, but you looked so lovely, I wanted to have you all to myself in the back of a cab."

"Flatterer."

"Pucker up."

They had supper in the West End, then, unwillingly, they went to the station. Hand in hand they went through the barrier. The platform was crowded. They walked beside the train until they found a nearly empty compartment. Jeff placed Jean's suitcase up in the rack then sat beside her. He took hold of her hand and squeezed it.

"I'm glad you were there today," he said softly, gazing into her eyes, "it's been hell since we quarrelled."

"It was for me too, Jeff dear," Jean replied.

"I feel like going back with you. I don't want to go on leave now."

"Don't be a goof," Jean replied, "I'll keep."

"You'd better my dear."

As a whistle sounded, signalling departure, Jean leant towards him and said, "Kiss me Jeff and then you'd better hop off."

He took her in his arms and kissed her. The train was lurching into motion as they broke apart. Hurriedly Jeff opened the door and stumbled out of the moving carriage. Jean leant out of the window, with a smile and waved. Jeff watched the train out of sight.

When he returned to the hotel, Jeff walked past the desk to the lift. He went up to the floor where Doug and Red had their room. As he walked down the corridor, he could hear loud laughter and voices singing. He pushed the door open and found the five members of the crew. Empty bottles were on the floor and on the dressing-table stood full ones.

"Come in and join the party," Red bellowed from the floor. He sat there, with his back against the wall. Nick lay asleep on one bed. Doug, Al and Clarrie sat on the other, passing a bottle of beer from one to the other as they sang.

"We'll be thrown out if you keep this up," Jeff said, looking round at them.

"Couldn't care less," Doug replied thickly.

"Me either," Al added.

When they had returned to the hotel, they had bought more to drink and taken it up to the room. They were all half-drunk. With a laugh, Jeff walked out to the dressing-table. He opened a bottle of beer and tipping it up, he drank in large gulps.

"I might as well be bombed too," he said, "if we're going to be chucked out of here."

They drank, without interruption, into the early morning. Nick was still unconscious when they finally decided to go to sleep. As Clarrie and Al staggered out to find their own room, Jeff and Doug pulled the mattress off one bed and threw it on the floor. They seized Nick, dropped him onto it and drew sheets and a blanket over him. They picked up Red, who had also passed out, and laid him on the spring mattress base of the stripped bed. They placed a blanket over him. Then they took the other mattress and made two more beds up. They tossed a penny to determine who would sleep on the mattress on the floor. Jeff lost.

Later in the morning, nursing their hangovers, they met in the bar, before dispersing for the remaining five days of their leave. Nick, Clarrie and Al were going to their homes.

"Did you two make any arrangements?" Jeff asked Red and Doug.

"I didn't bother," Doug replied, "I thought I might stay in London and hit the high spots."

"After last night I'm for the quiet life," Red moaned, as he drank his beer.

"We can go on the Lady Ryder scheme," Jeff suggested.

249

"Would they have a place on their list, miles from a pub?" Red asked.

"You'd be bored and irritable in an hour," Doug laughed.

"Well, will we seè them?" Jeff asked.

"OK." Red replied, "I'm game,"

"Give them a ring now and find out if the three of us can get a place together," Doug said.

Jeff rang and arrangements were made for them to go to a farmhouse in Somerset. They had a few more drinks before separating and going their different ways.

While the crew were once again discussing the remainder of their leave, Syd and Paula were driving down to Bournemouth. The sun was shining, they were happy. The miles sped by. They took their time and arrived in the early evening at the hotel Syd had booked them into.

The days passed quickly. Pleasant sunny days spent sightseeing or lazing in the sun. However, underlying the happiness was fear of the future. They tried to put the thought of their return to the squadron away, but it continually crept into their minds. They sought enjoyment feverishly as the days flew swiftly by. Content with one another's company only, they avoided contact with the other guests in the hotel.

When the time came for them to leave, they regretfully climbed into the car and drove off.

CHAPTER 20

Once again while the crew had been absent on leave, the losses of the squadron had been heavy. It had operated on three targets, Nuremburg, Hamburg and Essen. On each, one or more had been shot down and five crews in all had been posted missing. Of the five, three had been experienced and well into their second tour. Of the other two, one had arrived and gone missing in the short seven days of their leave.

As Jeff listened to the news in the mess, a feeling of depression settled upon him, a premonition of a similar fate filled his mind. He glanced round the ante-room at the airmen gathered there. He saw in his mind, the many faces which had been, but were no longer there. A shudder passed through him. Without a word, he walked out into the weak mid-morning sunlight. Slowly, his mind in turmoil, he walked up to the flight-office. The van, Jean at the wheel, was parked outside. He climbed silently into the seat beside her.

"Hi loquacious," Jean said, bending her head towards his to be kissed, "what's the trouble?"

"Nothing really," he replied as he kissed her cheek.

"Like heck," Jean laughed, "here we are, haven't seen one another for nearly a week and you meet me with a face a mile long".

Brightening slightly, Jeff leaned over and kissed her again. He slid his arm round her shoulders and drew her towards him.

"That's enough young sir," Jean laughed, pushing him away, "remember it's broad daylight and I'm on duty. Tell me about the rest of your leave."

As Jeff related the incidents which had taken place, Jean watched his face. Some of the harsh bitter look slipped away, as he recalled the bright sunny Somerset days on the small farm. The memory of the peaceful countryside he had enjoyed, brought a measure of ease to his mind. Jean tenderly raised her hand to soften out some of the wrinkles on his brow. He smiled down at her.

"Break it up," Syd's voice broke in abruptly from the flight office doorway, "and come in here, your commission's through".

"Ah hell," Jeff snarled, turning away from Jean.

"Well that's nice," she laughed, "I thought you'd be pleased to hear that news."

"I am really," Jeff replied with a wry grin, "but I was enjoying myself, talking to you just now, everything about the war seemed remote and not to matter, then, bingo, I'm back in the middle of the stink again."

With a hard push, Jean propelled him from the van.

"Be off with you," she said, "and sign any papers that have to be signed—Sir."

"Be careful" Jeff replied, "I can slap you on a charge

251

now L.A.C.W. Walton."

Syd waited for him at the doorway. With a beaming smile he shook him by the hand.

"I'm as pleased as punch," he said, "Cannover just told me, he wants to see you to congratulate you."

The remainder of the morning passed quickly. After seeing S/Cdr. Cannover, Jeff was called in to see the Commanding Officer. The Wing Commander also congratulated him. Eventually, he made his way to the navigation centre. He felt pleased at last, that he had received his commission. The reaction of the crew and the others he had spoken to was such, that he went whistling into the centre, happy and unworried. As he became aware of the other navigators seated around in bored attitudes he propped, his whistle died on his lips. Richards, the navigation leader, was standing beside his table, evidently in the middle of a lecture.

"Johnson," he yelled, his face reddened with anger, "where have you been? What do you mean barging in like this?"

With an effort, Jeff maintained control of himself, "I've been with Squadron Leader Cannover and the C.O., Sir", he replied with an edge in his voice.

"Talking about your commission I suppose," Richards sneered.

"As a matter of fact, yes," Jeff said, "it came through just now."

The nav's leader's angry reply was lost in the cheers from the other navigators, who jumped up and encircled him. They shook his hand and pummelled him on the back, until Richards finally made himself heard, above the din.

"Sit down all of you," he screamed, "and you Johnson, as far as I'm concerned, you never would have had a commission."

"Oh boil it in cocky shit," an Australian voice drawled from the group clustered around Jeff.

"Who said that?" demanded Richards, his voice rising to a screech.

"Little-Bo-peep and her lamb," another navigator replied falsetto.

Amid the laughter and confusion, they began to file out of the room, leaving Richards speechless with anger.

"You'll be unpopular with one bod in your new mess tonight Jeff," a flight-sergeant said, as they left the room.

"Look for poison in your welsh rarebit."

"Not sufficiently painful, it would probably be ground-glass in the spam."

Without difficulty, Jeff managed to avoid the nav. leader for the remainder of the day. He lunched in the Sergeant's mess to the jocular protests of the crew. The squadron was not operating in the night, and the C.O. had given the crews a free afternoon and evening. With the heavy losses, he had felt that a break from the station would bolster the morale. Jean was on duty, so Jeff borrowed a cycle and rode out along the lanes in the vicinity of the 'drome. He rode haphazardly, resting often when he came to the brow of a rise. The mellow day eased the strain in him. As he lay back on a grassy bank, he thought and dreamed. He was still pessimistic of his chances of living through the two tours, but he dreamed of a life with Jean if he should. As the sun dropped and began to hide below the horizon of distant hills, he rode back to the 'drome.

Syd was seated on his bed when he entered the billet.

"Hurry up," Syd called, "you're wanted in the officers mess."

"Belt up," he replied, "I can't go up there now."

"Why not?"

"I haven't a uniform and anyway, I'd feel a gig, I'm not used to the idea yet."

Syd turned, picked up a tunic from the bed and held it out to him. It was an Australian pilot-officer's tunic with an observer's wing and the D.F.M. sewn on the breast.

"Here," he said, "I had my spare fixed up for you, don't slurp your soup on it."

"Ah heck."

"Shut up, wash up and get dressed."

Self-consciously, Jeff entered the officer's mess with Syd. He gazed round the ante-room feeling out of place. Trevor Mason turned from the bar as they came in and saw them. Quickly he wheeled back, took two mugs of beer from the flying-officer beside him, picked up his own then, carrying all three, he carefully made his way to Syd and Jeff. The flabbergasted officer watched him go, mouth agape.

"Welcome to the den of iniquity", he greeted Jeff, "may all your troubles be large ones, blonde and good-looking".

"Thanks Trev", Jeff replied, taking the beer, "for the grog if not the sentiments".

"Don't thank me for that one", Trevor said with a wave at the bar, "thank that sproggy looking clot with gob open, he paid for it".

More friends came over until the group became quite large. They drank until dinner was announced. Although many had gone into the neighbouring towns, after dinner, there was still a crowd in the mess and a party developed. By eight o'clock, tunics were off, ties were undone, and games were in progress. High cock-o-lorum, football, wall games were played until, stiff and sore, late at night, they wandered off in twos and threes to their billets. Jeff had been launched.

The following morning, operations were scheduled for the night. The crew was on the battle order as blind markers. There began the feverish rush to have everything in first class order. The gunners toiled over their guns, the ground-crew swarmed over Yorker until she glistened and there was not a wrong note in her song of power. On the night-flying test, Syd sat in the cockpit and exultantly threw her round·the sky. She responded to every pressure of his hands and feet, as though she, too, was pleased to have him back at the controls.

At the navigators' briefing, Jeff and Red stared at the wall map as Richards strung out the red wool from Base to Cromer on the coast, then to the northern tip of the island of Texel off the Dutch Coast. Richard undid more wool and walked along beside the map.

"This is a long do", Red whispered to Jeff.

Richards stopped. Deliberately and slowly he reached up, placed a pin on the outskirts of Berlin and wound the wool round it.

"The big smoke at last you beaut", Red bellowed, and slapped Jeff on the back. A shiver ran through him.

After Red's outburst, a stilled hush descended on the

room for a moment. Intent faces gazed up at the map, as Richard completed the track marking for the trip out. Silently, they copied down the latitudes and longitudes he called out for each turning point. As they pencilled them on their charts and ruled in the tracks, however, the voices rose into a babble of noise as confidence returned.

Berlin, the major city of Germany. Feared more then the Ruhr,—Happy Valley. Berlin, where the defences extended for many frightening miles, encircling the city in a belt of searchlights and guns that seemed impenetrable. Berlin, where the defences made London's, even in the height of the blitz, seem insignificant. Berlin, the most heavily defended city in all Europe and the most feared.

The squadron was operating at full strength. Twenty-one crews sat silently through the main briefing. The usual jocular banter was missing as they listened to the details. Shortly after the briefing, four airmen went sick to the disgust of the others. Each of the four had done several operations but only one was found to be legitimately ill. He was operated on for appendicitis the following morning. The other three were boarded later, as being L.M.F.—lacking in moral fibre. It took courage of a kind to go on the sick parade, knowing all their comrades would brand them as cowards. All of the remaining airmen were afraid. They were afraid, but they had the other courage, true courage, which led them out to the planes, to take off, to do their job with the hope that this time they would return. Volunteers to replace the four were quickly found in the messes and rushed through the preparations.

It was still daylight as the first plane split the silence with its warming up. One by one, the others joined in until the drome pulsated to the roar. Slowly, each Lancaster edged its way out of its dispersal onto the perimeter track. They formed a procession, one behind the other to the head of the runway in use. The green light shone from the flight van. The engines of the Lancaster first in line raised their voices, the pilot released the brakes, the great, heavily laden plane slowly eased forward, it gathered speed, the tail lifted, it bounced once, twice, as though eager to be on its way, then gracefully it rose, tucked its wheels up and steeply climbed away from the 'drome. The remainder of the first wave followed, seconds separating each take-off.

As blind-markers, Syd and the crew took off with the first wave. Jeff gave the course to be flown to Syd who set it on the two compasses.

They climbed slowly on course over the still visible countryside. England slowly slid away beneath them as they rose higher into the twilight sky. They were at eight thousand feet as they passed over Cromer and the coast fell away. The North Sea and the enemy lay ahead in the darkening east. Jeff gave the course to Texel and concentrated on his radar set to calculate fixes which would enable him to find the correct wind. The wind so essential, if they were to stay on track and not stray.

Round them were other planes, all converging into a huge gaggle miles in length. They came from all over England to concentrate at Cromer as the leaping off point. The few Pathfinder planes formed a small band in advance of the main stream. They flew on, small in numbers compared to the large host of planes a few miles behind, but upon them, the success or failure of the raid depended.

Darkness eased in shortly before they reached the enemy coast. The Gee was jammed but as they drew closer, the coast line of the island of Texel showed up on the H_2S tube.

"Texel ahead navigator," Red called from the bomb-aiming compartment.

"Thanks Red," Jeff replied, "She's coming up on the set."

Glancing at the set, Jeff saw they would cross Texel six miles south of track. Quickly he gave Syd a snap alteration of course to the correct turning-point on the Northern tip of the island. Equally hurriedly, he ruled in the track they had traversed from his last Gee fix. He measured the angle and the distance, and calculated the true ground speed. He then set down the information on his computer and worked out the latest wind. Glancing again at the H_2S, he saw that the turning point was very close. Quickly he calculated the new course from Texel to their last turning-point south of Berlin and handed it up to Syd.

"Nav to pilot," he called into the microphone, "course to turning-point before target 105 degrees, 1–0–5."

"Roger Jeff, 105," Syd replied.

"Coming up to turning point in seconds navigator," Red's voice boomed over the intercom.

"Thanks Red, tell me exactly when."

Red gazed down through the perspex bombing panel at the darkened island approaching them. He called when they crossed immediately over the northern tip. As Syd eased Yorker round onto the new course, Jeff noted time and details together with the new wind in his log.

Isolated bursts of flak studded the sky to the north and south of them, as other planes drew near the enemy coast off track. Ahead of them, searchlights beams stabbed the darkness one by one in preparation for the oncoming stream. The Zuider Zee was quickly crossed and the defences became more active. Leeuwarden, to the north, quickly claimed a plane in its searchlights, the flak poured up at the silver speck so conspicuous at the apex of the cone. The cone shifted across the sky as the bomber strove to evade the lights and continue on into Germany. Eventually it won through. The lights swung back and clutched at another bomber.

Ahead of them, the defences were alerted. Groningen and Emden, then later, Oldenburg and Wilhelmshaven, then Bremen. All threw their searchlights up as the stream approached. Bremen shot one down after a minute long battle.

From the position of the defended areas, Jeff knew he was approximately on track. However, he worked on the H_2S fixes he obtained and on Red's pinpoints, continually checking his calculations and the wind. As they passed south of Bremen, he detected a shift in the wind. It had swung further round behind them and had slightly increased in strength. This gave them a much higher ground-speed and, if they continued on the same course and speed they were on, they would be minutes ahead of time and north of their last turning point.

Jeff checked on the new wind with another fix. Then he computed the speed Syd would have to fly at and the new course to arrive on target on time. When Syd had settled Yorker on these, Jeff went forward into the cockpit for a short time and gazed out through the perspex. Above him, stars shone through the isolated cloud, their pinpoints of light giving him more confidence. The friends of the navigator, they were there if other navigational aids failed. Around the plane lay enemy Germany, its black landscape erupting with brilliance over its major towns as the lights and flak entrapped more bombers.

The premonition of trouble and the fear were still with Jeff, but with them had come a certain calmness, as though the acceptance of impending disaster had tempered his nerves. The exhilaration of the battle against the elements and the enemy was still there also. As the miles sped by, further towns lit up like eerie mile posts, Celle, Hannover, Brunswick and far to the north Hamburg added its monstrous cone.

Behind the blackout curtain in his compartment, Jeff worked continually, checking and rechecking winds and navigation as he obtained more fixes.

Eventually, the terrifying cone which pyramided over Berlin appeared ahead of them. Initially, distance made it commonplace, but as the minutes ticked away and Yorker's powerful Merlins dragged them nearer, the awful immensity of the defences became apparent. Planes ahead of time, because of faulty navigation, were caught in cones, but the lights concentrating on the three specks seemed insignificant against the remainder waiting to entrap other bombers. Flak poured up in an unbelievable curtain of steel. The bursts were pinpricks of light which seemed to pepper the entire sky above the alerted city.

As they approached the last turning point south of the city, Red came back from the bomb-aimer's compartment and sat beside Jeff. He was quiet as he plugged in his oxygen and intercomm plugs. The hugeness of the searchlight and flak belt around the city had amazed even him. It seemed unreal that they were shortly to try to pierce their way through. His thoughts flew to England, and a wry grin creased his face, as he wondered if the girls he had met on leave were sleeping peacefully.

In the turrets, Nick and Clarrie turned their guns and scanned the night sky for fighters. Each time he glanced towards Berlin Nick felt scared, however, he had come a long way from his operation on Wilhelmshaven. Even though the feeling of fear dried his mouth and made him perspire, he knew he was willing to be one of the crew in the attack even if they were shot down. He felt more grown up and mature with this knowledge, than he had ever been. Clarrie felt the same fears, but he had become fatalistic in his attitude. He revolved his turret, wondering whether he hoped to see an enemy fighter. Al remained at the wireless, seemingly oblivious to the fact that they were preparing to turn onto their bombing run.

Beside Syd, Doug unbuckled his seat and inspected all the gauges and dials. When satisfied, he returned and stood tensed, waiting. He thought of Colleen and soberly said a quiet prayer.

Syd eased his seat down and settled himself more comfortably into the cockpit. He felt tense and drained of all feeling. His hands perspired as they gripped the control column. When Jeff called for the alteration of course onto the bombing run, he slowly turned Yorker onto the new heading as though against his will. He thrust memories of the idyllic days with Paula out of his mind and strove to concentrate on the instruments before him.

As they turned, two planes were making their last fiery plunge to earth, whirling down from the apex of the cones of searchlights which had held them.

Soon they were amongst the defences. The light sought them and the flak studded the sky on all sides with the black puffs which seemed so innocent of violence yet marked the birth place of the scraps of metal which could tear through the metal skin of bombers and the flesh of airmen as though they did not exist.

The way to the aiming-point seemed endless, as Yorker edged further in towards the heart of the city. Ahead of them the first red T.I. cascaded and the first illuminating flares lit up the city for the visual markers. As Syd called out the information Jeff noted the time down in log.

"Early," he mumbled into his microphone, then turning to Red he asked, "how are we going."

"On track," Red replied, "it's coming up nicely."

He took a quick distance check on the aiming point and called it to Jeff. Jeff grasped his computer and equally speedily worked out their E.T.A.

"One and three quarter minutes," he said, "near enough to bang on."

"Good show Jeff," Syd said, "more reds and one yellow down."

"You beaut," Jeff shouted, "the visuals are on the beam even if ahead of time."

Syd added angrily with his eyes on the colourful scene ahead, "They're on the beam in spite of the bloody main force kites throwing their blasted incendiaries all over the shop ahead of time."

"The usual thing," Jeff said cynically, "they can't wait to get rid of their bloody load and ruin the chances of a really good raid. Why the hell—."

"Shut up," Red shouted, "target coming up."

His eyes never left the H2S, he gave Syd the small alterations of heading to make good the track to the aiming-point. Slowly the blips of light crept down the tube.

"Bombs gone," he called, "hold it steady for the photo."

"Roger bomb-aimer," Syd replied.

Their red T.Is. burst beside and spread into the yellow. The illuminating flares burst into their brilliance and hung suspended to add light to the scene below. Another yellow was added, then greens dropped down to complete the pattern of marking. Incendiaries spread and twinkled. Below them, the crew saw the city spread out, Templehof Aerodrome was a landmark, but as the glare of the incendiaries increased the details were lost. The flak poured up in a horrifying box barrage. Yorker kicked away from several near misses but her skin was punctured. As Jeff came forward after blacking out his compartment, a shell exploded below and to starboard. Pieces of shrapnel peppered the plane with the sound of hail, one piece grazed Jeff's wrist as it tore past to rip through the port side. Syd swung Yorker into a violent dive. The crew rose up where they sat or stood as the plane fell, then as Syd pulled back on the control column, they were thrust down by the force of gravity as though by a giant hand.

Straight through over the centre of the city they flew, harassed all the long way by search lights and flak. Round them, the other bombers were experiencing the same intense action. Slowly they approached the outskirts and the outer defences. Fighters weaved in amongst the bombers and attacked. The streams of tracer etched patterns in the sky as battle was joined. The sky was a battle field. Bombers dropped as they lost their fight and here and there, they claimed a victim.

The route home was north to a point on the German coastland east of Rostock, across Mecklenburg Bay to the east coat of Falster, turning there to cross over Falster, Lolland, the islands north of Kiel Bay, onwards over southern Jutland, to the island of Mando off Denmark, then the North Sea and Britain lay ahead.

From Berlin to the Baltic, the bombers battled the fighters. Wave after wave of German fighters attacked the homeward planes and strewed the track with their wreckage. Clarrie and Nick fought off two attacks shortly after leaving the target. They damaged one, but the other sheered away under the concentrated fire of the six browning 303s.

Rostock and Warnemunde each shot down bombers as they strayed over the cities' defences. After the two fighter attacks, the remainder of the trip was quiet for the crew. Action was round them, but they were untroubled. With the islands showing up on the H2S, navigation was easy. Jeff found winds, applied them, then sat back watching the images of the islands slide across the screen. Jutland appeared and slowly was crossed. Ahead of them to port, the defences of Sylt opened up. As usual, they quickly shot down a bomber. Even though the flaming plane, the search lights, the flak, must have been visible to them, other bombers flew into the cone of lights like moths without will.

Syd turned Yorker on track over Mando and the long flight over the North Sea began. A sigh of relief sounded over the intercomm as the enemy coast receded into the darkness. The drone of the engines was like a lullaby to Jeff, as the reaction to the intense activity and nervous tension set in. He folded his arms on the Nav table, laid his head down on them and dozed.

Syd slumped down into the cockpit, his eyes heavy, his arms and legs aching from the continual manipulating of the controls. The dreary trip back to England seemed so much longer than the trip to the target. Out of reach of the enemy defences, there was the exhilaration of having hit the target and reaching the comparative safety of the North Sea, but there was also the let down from the tension and the minutes ticked very slowly by. Syd eased Yorker into a shallow dive to build up speed.

Slowly England approached them, Jeff worked at the "Gee" getting his fixes, making occasional alterations of course as the winds changed with the descent. The English coast was crossed slightly north of track and soon afterwards the station's beacon beckoned them home with its flashing morse. The long trip ended as Yorker changed her engine song for the approach to the flare-lit runway. She dropped lower, the wheels screeched, and she ran along until turning off at the end of the runway onto the perimeter track. Mac and the ground crew waited to greet the crew and to tend to Yorker's scars.

Most of the crew had completed their thirty-fifth operation leaving ten to finish. In all, the attack on Berlin had cost forty-two bombers shot down, including one more crew from the squadron, one of the visual markers.

CHAPTER 21

While the crews still slept, or tried to sleep, in the blacked-out huts, the squadron was once again put on standby for operations. The call from group came through on the scrambler phone and was relayed to the C.O. The squadron was quickly geared into action. The leaders prepared their readiness lists. The planes were serviced. The intelligence clerks drew out the maps and charts required by the navigators and bomb-aimers. The armourers trundled out their carriages with their lethal containers, even the kitchens prepared for the operational meals.

At eleven o'clock, the tannoy blared for Syd to report to the adjutant. He did not hear it. Roberts, the small cockney batman, softly pushed open the door. Sadly, he looked round at the sleeping figures of Syd and Trevor Mason.

Syd lay unnaturally curled up, the bed-clothes twisted cocoon-like round him from the effects of a nightmare. Quietly, Roberts placed the bowl of shaving water on the dressing-table, then gently he shook Syd awake. Syd jerked up with a cry, stared round, then realising where he was, he calmed and grinned sheepishly at Roberts.

"What's up man?" he murmured sleepily; "What's the score?"

"The adjutant wants to see you immediately Sir."

"Oh hell, what for?"

"I don't know, but you was called for over the tannoy," Roberts said apologetically.

"Alright Roberts," Syd replied, as he slowly swung his legs over the side of the bed, "ring him and tell him I'm just getting up and will report as soon as possible."

"Very good Sir," Roberts said, turning to the door. "I left shaving water on the dressing-table."

"Thanks Roberts."

As the batman left the room, Syd rested his head on his hands for a moment. He still felt exhausted. His back and legs ached and his mind seemed befogged. The weariness seemed to drag on every part of his body. With an effort he stood up, he went over to the basin and douched his head with cold water. Then after a hurried wash and shave, he dressed. Trevor was still asleep, mumbling and groaning, as Syd left the room.

He rode up to the squadron office. When the adjutant saw him, he stood up with a smile.

"The C.O. wants to see you Berry," he said, "I'll let him know you're here."

He went into the C.O.'s office and quickly returned.

"Go right in."

"Thanks adj," Syd said, then warily he asked, "What's up, am I on the mat?"

"No Syd," the other replied, "it's nothing like that, the C.O. will tell you when you go in."

Somewhat reassured, Syd strode into the office. He saluted the figure bent over the table. The C.O., his face tired, his eyes blood-shot, looked up with a weary grin.

"Finally got here, eh Berry?" he said.

"Yes Sir, sorry I took so long, but I had to be woken

up."

"That's alright," the Wing-Commander replied with a wave of his arm, "suppose you're wondering what it's all about eh?"

As he spoke, he walked up and down the room, his hands clasped behind his back. Before Syd could reply, he continued.

"We lost a visual marker last night, Warrant-Officer Hudson."

"Yes I know Sir," Syd said, wondering how this affected him.

"We're also on ops tonight," the C.O. said flatly. He stopped pacing and faced Syd. He did not speak for a moment.

"Your crew replaces Hudson's as visual marker," he said, "any objections?"

For a moment, Syd stood lost for words, his mind in turmoil, then he smiled happily.

"No sir, I mean no objections Sir," he stammered, "that's wonderful news. Thanks Sir."

"Nothing to thank me for," the Wing-Commander said soberly, "it means more risks, you fly lower, you might have to make one or more dummy runs over the target if your bomb-aimer doesn't pick up the aiming-point first go spot on."

"I realise that Sir," Syd replied.

Impatiently, he waited for the interview to finish. He wanted to share the news with the crew as quickly as possible.

After gazing at the eager, young-old face before him, the C.O. turned his eyes to the table, where lay the report listing W.O. Hudson's failure to return. He turned once again and faced Syd.

"Certain you and your crew can handle the job?" he asked.

"Certain Sir," Syd replied confidently.

"Then, as soon as you've done your N.F.T. I want you, your navigator and bomb-aimer to get the full gen on the technique from the bombing-leader. At briefing, make sure you get a good picture of the run in and the aiming-point from the aerial photos. Implant the detail in your mind."

"Yes Sir."

"Well, that's all Berry," the C.O. concluded.

After saluting, Syd turned to leave. The C.O. stopped him.

"Good luck boy," he said grimly.

*   *   *

The crew cheered the news after Syd had collected them together from the billets and the mess. They had reached the pinnacle in Pathfinders and were amongst the elite. They felt proud at being chosen. Although more dangerous, there was prestige in being made visual markers and carrying the yellow target indicators. Many times previously, as the yellows had dropped on the targets, they had wished it might have been themselves dropping them. However, when Syd informed them that they were operating in the evening, their enthusiasm waned.

"Oh hell Syd," Doug complained bitterly, "the God-damned merry-go-round starts again. Last night, this night and the others to come.

"Well what's wrong with that?" Syd asked.

"What's wrong!" the flight engineer continued, "I had a date with Colleen tonight. It's always the same, every time I make a date. A man should know bloody better by now."

"Me too," Jeff joined in, "I concur and agree with word and sentiment. Jean and I were going out too, she had a night off for a change. I thought we wouldn't be flying after last night."

Nick laughed as they grumbled.

"Well Jean could easily get some other bod to take her out," he teased the tall navigator.

"If you put those ideas in her head young sproggins," Jeff snapped, "we'll be needing a new rear-gunner very quick-smart."

Red's booming laugh sounded, he slapped Jeff and Doug on the shoulders, making them lurch forward.

"Well chums," he bellowed, "forget the love lie, we'll be dicing with death dodging the old reaper with Yellow T.I.s in our belly."

*   *   *

The operation was on the industrial section of the an-

265

cient, historic town of Nuremburg. It was a town sacred to the Nazis an as such, became also a psychological target. After lunch, Syd, Red and Jeff spent an hour with the bombing leader. He explained the technique with which they were already familiar. He impressed upon them the urgency for extreme accuracy of bombing. This meant a good wind, an accurate run in on time, correct pinpointing on the run and precision dropping of the target indicators. He stressed each equally, each aspect being as important as the other. They pored over the aerial photos of the route into the city and of the aiming-point—the marshalling yards in the southern sector of the town. The sector where there was the concentration of industry which made the city such as important target.

All three memorised the detail, but on Red would fall the responsibility of actually recognising the actual target. The others could assist him on the run in by recognising detail to give Red a starting point to work from.

The operation went exactly as planned. On the route in, Jeff checked and rechecked the winds. At the French Coast, even though south of track, they struck no opposition. Across France and Southern Germany, the fighters were active round them, but they were unmolested. Scattered cloud hid the stars above them along most of the route. Saarbrucken, Karlsruhe and Mannheim became active as the bombers neared. Track indicator flares were dropped by other marker planes on the western bank of the Rhine. They served as guides to the other bombers, but acted also as lures to the enemy fighters. As they crossed the river, there were exchanges of fire between bombers and fighters and two bombers fell to explode and burn on German soil.

Clarrie and Nick in the turrets never relaxed, they worked in harmony. If one detected a plane, he called up to ensure the other kept the remainder of the sky round them under observation. Although they sighted several fighters, they evaded all without a shot being fired.

As they approached the target, the cloud thinned and finally disappeared. There was a slight mist on the ground which worried Red. The city's searchlights reached up at the sky, group after group lighting up until they formed a gigantic cone ready to clutch at the attacking force.

When they approached the final turning point before the run in to the target, Jeff was satisfied with his bombing wind. They were at 8,000 feet and from this altitude, the detail would be clearly observed. The remainder of the bombing force was flying much higher, ranging in height from 12,000 to over 20,000 feet.

They turned onto the run in. Over the target, there was only a little flak. When Syd noticed this, he called to the gunners.

"Keep your eyes peeled gunners," he said urgently, "it must be fighter night tonight."

The absence of flak continued to worry him as they penetrated the outer defences and he began to search the ground for details. His fears were justified as above them the fighters weaved in, guns tearing at the bombers.

In the navigator's compartment, Jeff concentrated on the H2S set. The layout of the city showed up on the tube, he called the mileages from the approximate position of the aiming-point as they drew closer. In the nose, Red peered through the perspex bombing panel. Quickly, he oriented himself in the light of the illuminating flares dropped with the red T.Is. of the blind markers. The reds were in a circle round the aiming-point. The bomb-doors opened and he directed Syd with brief instructions along the route they had traced out on the aerial photos. In spite of a slight haze, he saw the aiming-point coming up as the seconds ticked away towards their zero-hour. Grimly he watched it approach in the bomb-sight, when the moment came, he squeezed the bomb release button. The T.Is. and bombs fell away. An excited yell burst from Red when he saw the yellow cascade burst into brilliance over the marshalling yard.

The return trip was uneventful. Thankful and elated, they hurried to interrogation after they had landed.

Jean met them with the van.

"Thought you had the night off," Red said, as he and Clarrie threw their gear into the back of the van.

"I had," she replied, "but I swapped with another girl."

"Can't bear to see lover-boy come back without you being here eh?" he bellowed.

"You could say that," Jean said, peering into the darkness towards the plane.

"Don't worry Jeannie girl," Red laughed, "he's there and unscathed and you might have asked me how I did on our first visual."

Ashamedly, she got out of the van and went round to join Red.

"How did it go?" she asked, "bang on?"

"It was a wizard prang my girl," Red boasted, "right on the button. There we were—."

"Sorry Red," Jean laughed, skipping away, "can't wait for any more, here's Jeff."

The following day, they heard the results of the operation. Their photo showed the marshalling yards and the C.O. congratulated them. The factories in the area were heavily hit both by H.E. and incendiaries and the photo-reconnaissance planes had brought back evidence that the fires were still burning many hours after the attack. Twelve aircraft had been lost but none from the squadron.

The good weather held, but the squadron was stood down the night after Nuremburg. They had operated on the two previous nights.

At morning assembly, after they had been given the news of the stand-down, the crews, detailed for training, began to file out. Through them limped a small figure using a cane as support and a means of clearing his path. The crew were clustered together at the far end of the room, planning their day. Red glanced towards the limping airman. He broke off in his conversation, stared for a moment, then yelled.

"Tich, you old bastard!"

He rushed over, swept the little ex-member of the crew up into his arms and went back.

"Look what I've got," he called as he walked towards them cradling Tich.

"Put me down you big slob," Tich Mulgrave yelled, grinning good naturedly, "before I crown your wooden skull with me cane."

"Easy does it," Red said, letting him down with exaggerated care.

The crew clustered round the little gunner, plying him

with questions, as they shook his hand and pounded him on the back.

"Break it off," Tich said, shaking his head, "I'm only here for the day. I'm grounded permanently, worse luck, and I'm off to train more poor damn rookies up at gunnery school. I've got leave before I report, so a day here and then home."

"Attaboy," Doug said, "We've got the day off, so roll out the bomb and we'll hit Bedford."

"How do you feel Tich?" Clarrie asked seriously, looking down at the gunner's leg.

"I'm O.K.," Tich replied, "the leg isn't the best but it's still on and gets me around still."

"Good for you Tich," Jeff said.

As the rest of the crew milled round Tich, Col Nichols hung back. He had not known the ex-crew member and recalled his own first days when the contrast between himself and Tich had been so noticeable to the others. He felt self-conscious in his presence and the memory of his first trip to Wilhelmshaven came back, too vividly, to his mind.

Syd noticed him standing away from the group and called him over.

"Nick," he said, "meet Tich, the bod who's place you took."

Jeff guessed at the thoughts running through Nick's mind.

"And a better **gun**ner too," he said with a grin, "at least we can understand him when he talks."

Nick smiled as he shook hands. He felt better as the rest of the crew ragged Tich and included him in the conversation. He felt his past failure was finally wiped out in their minds.

As soon as they were able to get away unseen, after making arrangements with Paula and Jean to meet them at the Anchor in the evening, they all piled into the crew car and drove to Bedford. A noisy group, they went from bar to bar until late in the afternoon. In the early evening when they returned to the Anchor, all were feeling the effects of the **drink**ing.

Nick **and** Clarrie had fallen asleep in the back of the car. Tich sang "You are my Sunshine", from Bedford to the village, in spite of protests and the others were far from sober. However, when they arrived at the Anchor, Josh forced them to eat dinner and gave them black coffee, so that they had recovered slightly by the time the girls arrived. When they heard how the afternoon had been spent, Jean and Paula immediately fussed over Tich until he became self-consciously embarrassed.

"Ah break it up," he begged, "you're worse than my ma."

"Well you shouldn't have gone out drinking all afternoon with this crowd of no-hopers," Jean said sternly, glaring at the crew as she placed a stool and cushion under Tich's lame leg.

"You should know better you others," Paula added, "tomorrow he'll hardly be able to walk."

"Give us a go Paula," Jeff pleaded, "we had to celebrate his return to the fold, even if it is only for the night."

The three girls turned on him immediately.

"There was no need to pub-crawl," Jean said, placing her hands on her hips and leaning over Jeff as he sank into a chair, "you could have sat in one place instead of dragging him around all over the city seeing how many pubs you could visit in the afternoon."

Doug threw his arms wide and gazed towards the ceiling.

"Hell," he said, "it was the little guy's idea, he'd been cooped up in the hospital so god-damned long he wanted to keep moving."

"That's no excuse," Colleen snapped at Doug.

"You can't win fellows," Red bellowed, "I don't know why you can't control your women. I'm going to order drinks while you cop the rest of the roasting."

He walked off and Nick followed him. When they returned with trays of drinks the group was seated close together talking and laughing amicably. Red glanced round, then turned to Nick.

"I can't follow them," he said loudly, "one minute they're at one another's throats, you turn your back and they're all lovely-dovey again. Thank the gremlins I'm not tied up, I couldn't stand the strain."

"Me too," agreed Nick.

"Quiet," Jean ordered, "we're discussing a matter of

grave import.

"As you command," Red said, he bowed low then handed the drinks round.

"It must be hard," Jean continued her previous conversation, speaking to Paula and Syd, "you're married, you can't let the squadron know, you can't act married in case they find out and post Paula away, so you might just as well as not be married."

When the laughter had died down, Jeff bent over and patted her on the hand.

"That must have been an effort," he smiled at her, "now you sit back and rest."

She snatched her hand away, but her eyes twinkled as she good-naturedly joined in the laughter.

"I don't see that you've got much to worry about," Tich said ponderously, as he lolled back in an easy chair, his leg cushioned, his tunic undone and a glass of beer in his hand.

"What do you mean?" Syd asked.

"Well," their ex-gunner stated, "why don't you rent a place in Huntingdon or here, then, when you both have time off together, bingo you've got a place to go to."

Clapping her hands together excitedly, Colleen stood up abruptly.

"That's it," she said, "we've room to share over at Aunt's, I'm sure she'd be delighted when she hears the story. I'll run over and ask her if it's alright now."

"No Colleen," Paula cried, "we couldn't—."

"Don't be silly," Colleen over-rode her's and Syd's objections. "It would be perfect for you."

With that, after calling to Doug to go with her, she turned and ran out of the room, hand in hand with Doug. Within minutes, they had returned, the smile on Colleen's face was sufficient to tell them that her aunt had agreed.

"As soon as she heard it was cutting some red tape she needed no other details," Doug laughed.

"You can have half the place, Aunt said," Colleen added, "make it your own for as long as you like, use the kitchen and move in as soon as you like."

Self-consciously, Paula looked at Syd, her face reddened. She smiled at the expression of incredulity on his face.

"I don't know whether we should do it," she said, "but it would be nice to have even a night, now and then, away from the squadron, where we could change out of uniform, forget the war and live like normal human beings for a little while."

As she spoke, she became serious. Her expression changed, she looked at Syd without seeing him. He knew the threat of his being killed was in her mind, ever-present like a malignant tumour. He realised again, what a strain it was for Paula, more so than for himself, that he was still on operations. Being on the squadron with him, made it worse for her. The long hours of waiting would be horrible. The hours after watching him take-off to bomb Germany, waiting to hear the drone of the engines of the returning Lancasters, and then waiting to discover if Yorker was amongst them. He stood up, went over to her chair and sat on the arm.

"Thanks Colleen," he said quietly, putting his arm around Paula's shoulders, "that will be wonderful, we'll see your aunt as soon as possible."

"Well that's settled, bang on," Red bellowed, "now we can settle down to some steady drinking to celebrate that, as well as Tich."

The following morning after assembly, while Tich and most of the crew nursed hangovers, Paula and Syd rode over to thank Colleen's aunt and to arrange details, they insisted, over her protests, on paying rent.

While they were away, operations were scheduled for the night. The target was Hamburg.

It was a cloudless day at the drome. The sun shone and a soft breeze rustled the leaves and ruffled the W.A.A.F.s' hair. Tich, the worse for wear from the previous night, followed the crew all morning. He flew with them on the N.F.T. He helped Nick and Clarrie to clean their guns. In the afternoon despondently, he watched them go into the briefing room. He felt lonely, realising eventually, he was no longer a part of the crew, realising he would not fly on operations again. It was a sad feeling, he had been a part of them, but now he was outside.

As the crews noisily left the briefing room once again, he joined them, clinging to the last links that bound him to them in comradeship.

Red was suffering, his hang-over gave him no peace. His head felt as though it would split apart. After the operational meal, as he dressed for the operation in the locker room, he waited until the doctor made his round and asked for some caffeine tablets. Carefully he placed them in his breast pocket.

Tich jumped into the van with them when they drove out to the plane. The little ex-gunner joined in the banter, this would be the last time he would experience the ride out to the plane before the operation.

Jean stopped the van beside Yorker. The crew tumbled out, strewing their gear over the dispersal area. As she drove off, Mac and the ground crew raced over to welcome Tich back, embarrassing, but pleasing him with their good wishes. He leant on his cane. As the minutes sped by, he watched the preparations.

Red swallowed his caffeine tablets. Jeff gathered his gear on his shoulders, his sextant, navigator's bag, parachute and harness. The others struggled into their harnesses and picked up the chutes. Before they went into the plane, they came over to Tich.

"Wish you could be with us," Syd voiced the sentiments of the rest.

Slowly they filed away, climbed the metal ladder and entered the plane. A film of tears formed over Tich's eyes. He bit his lip. The separation was complete. His hand crept up to the Pathfinder badge below the ribbon on the breast of his tunic. It was his to wear permanently now, even though he had not completed the two tours, he had been grounded—wounded in action.

The door of the plane slammed. Tich moved over to the side of the dispersal as the starter motor was moved into position and plugged in. Syd called, the blades of the port inner swung slowly at first, then the engine roared into life and they raced invisibly. Engine followed engine into life, until the four made the air resound with their noise. The chocks were pulled away, Yorker lurched round and slowly edged her way forward onto the perimeter track. The crew waved to the small figure leaning on a cane, watching them as they trundled away into the dusk.

When Jean drove up minutes later, Tich was still standing there. Mac and the ground crew did not disturb him. When Jean called to him, he looked up, his reverie broken. With a look of sadness on his face he limped over to Mac and the others. He bade them good-bye, then after a long look round the dispersal he slowly limped over to the van and climbed into the seat beside Jean. As they drove back to the sergeant's mess, he was silent, his eyes watching the drome and the planes as they took off, circled and climbed.

CHAPTER 22

The good operational weather held for over a week. Night after night, the bombers roared away from the drome in the twilight, or the darkness of night, on their way to Germany. On most occasions, they returned with diminished numbers, but new crews arrived to maintain the strength of the squadron. Syd and the crew operated three times. As visual markers they went to Munich, Saarbrucken and Stuttgart.

On Munich, they took off late, with a zero hour on the target of 2356, four minutes before midnight. On the way in, they saw Amiens, Karlsruhe, Saarbrucken, Mannheim and Stuttgart lit up and active as usual. Cloud below them began to thicken when they were still far from the target. Over the city itself, there was complete cloud cover making it impossible to mark visually from above it, and too low to fly beneath. They bombed as backers-up on the concentration of red target indicators dropped by the blind markers. It was a round flight of 1400 miles and they landed at four o'clock.

Over Saarbrucken two days later, Red had difficulty picking up the aiming-point. Scattered cloud lay over the city and a haze nestled close to the ground. As they pierced the defences red T.I.s and flares went down, but no yellow followed. They flew up the leg into the city once, but could not find the aiming-point. Syd banked Yorker round inside the defended area. Even though they were ahead of the bulk of the main force, in the turn, several other Lancasters sped past, perilously close. Yorker bucked in the slipstreams. Syd turned on to course again, hoping they were in position to pick up the aiming-point. Red identified it too late to direct Syd into a bombing position. Immediately, Syd threw Yorker into a U-turn. Red again took control as they attacked down track and against the bomber stream. It was a dangerous manoeuvre with the main force arriving in strength. The crew felt the passage of plane after plane as the slipstreams slapped at Yorker. In spite of the haze, in spite of the blinding glare of the incendiaries, Red picked out the target. Calmly, he directed Syd until their yellow T.I. dropped and burst over the aiming-point.

The attack upon Stuttgart seemed anti-climactic in comparison. They made one unmolested run into the target area, Red immediately oriented himself, the run-up was perfect and he dropped the yellow on the aiming-point within seconds of their zero-hour. The run out of the target area and the trip home were equally uneventful.

Stuttgart was their thirty-ninth operation. Most of the crew had only six to finish.

In spite of the heavy losses sustained by the squadron during this period of intense operating, one incident uplifted the morale of all crews. On Saarbrucken, Joe Weldon completed his two tours. He flew his forty-fifth trip with a Canadian crew which had arrived on the squadron without a reargunner. Joe had immediately adopted them as the means of completing his tours. The long wait between his ops previously, had annoyed him and the strain was telling. He flew with them until he finished on Saarbrucken.

He became the first to finish in the months the crew had been at Battleson. A feeling of elation swept the squadron. Air and ground crew all felt that the jinx they had believed to be on the squadron had been finally beaten.

Enthusiastically, Joe volunteered to continue on with the same crew. He now felt himself to be indestructible. However, the C.O. immediately grounded him. Joe, without realising it himself, was nearly at the end of his nerves. The continual strain over the long months, the loss of his crew, the uncertainty of the "odd-bod trips", flying with any crew which was without a gunner, the long waits between operations, all these had taken their toll. As he angrily told Jeff and Al of the C.O.'s decision, they realised how correct that decision was. Joe's lips and eyes twitched with a nervous tic, the calm they had admired and marvelled at when they had first met him, was gone.

After a hectic night of celebration on the first stand-down after he had finished, Joe left on leave to await posting to a non-operational unit. When he had gone, it seemed a part of the squadron went with him. The empty bed in the billet drew the eyes of the crew and the other occupants for days. They missed Joe, but the vacant position signified hope that they too might come through. After four days, a young Welsh wireless-operator threw his gear on the bed and settled in. Within another three days he had gone missing. The spell was broken.

During this period, when they were not flying, the crew usually went together to the "Anchor". Colleen always joined them. Paula and Jean went also when they were not on duty. In spite of the continual operations of the squadron, there was a gaiety about their gathering. Beneath the gaiety however, there was serious fear of the operations to come. As they neared the seemingly unattainable forty-five, the fear deepened. Nick dreaded the day when the others reached their forty-five. It meant he would break with them and he would have to continue with another crew or finish on odd-bod trips. He felt more confident and sure of himself, but he was fearful of the future.

It was not until Paula and Syd stayed with Colleen and her Aunt during this period, that they really felt they were married. Previously, their life had seemed unnatural, as they had tried to conceal the fact of their marriage from the squadron in general. They had been able to snatch only an occasional hour alone together. When they stayed in the village however, everything was different. Paula sent home for civilian clothes and changed from her uniform as soon as they arrived at the home. There was a quietness about the place that was relaxing to their bodies and their minds.

Colleen and her Aunt rarely disturbed them and most evenings when they stayed there, they would sit side by side in front of the fire, barely speaking, just happy to be together, away from the atmosphere of the squadron. They grew more towards one another in a communion of minds as well as of bodies.

After this period of intense operating, the crew was the senior crew. The others senior to them in operations had been shot down. The weather deteriorated, both over Britain and the continent. It heralded a long period of scrubs. Each day the crews were briefed for operations only to have them cancelled, sometimes early, sometimes late. The pile of unused logs in Jeff's locker grew higher. St. Nazaire, Berlin, Stuttgart, Munich, Dortmund, Essen were some of the targets the crews worked out flight plans for, only to have the disappointment of a scrub.

The morale dropped and irritation mounted. As always, the inactivity affected the airmen much worse than the period of continual operating and the subsequent heavy losses which they had previously experienced.

During this period of inactivity Jeff was granted a forty-eight hour pass to go to London to equip himself with his officer's uniforms and clothing. On the way down in the train he looked forward to meeting friends he had trained with and friends he had made in the Air Force over the many months since he had left Australia. He booked into the "Strand Palace". After leaving his case in his room and washing, he hurried round to Australia House. As he entered the lounge he eagerly looked for a familiar face but saw none. A few he knew casually, from previous leaves, but of his own course and training flight he saw no one. Alone, he went down to lunch and quickly was drawn into conversation by the airmen at his table when they saw the ribbon of his decoration and the Pathfinder Badge. They had not been in England long and none had done more than a few operations.

After lunch, he gazed round the room once more unsuccessfully, then excused himself and climbed the stairs to the lounge again.

It was not until the afternoon of the following day that he met someone he knew well. He had been measured for his uniforms and had picked up his issue clothing. After he had taken them to his room there was nothing further he had to do. He strolled down the Strand towards Australia

House when a voice hailed him.

"Jeff, you long streak, I thought you were dead."

Eagerly he turned and saw one of those he had left Australia with. Don Charter's and his own Air Force careers had run parallel in Australia, Canada and England until Jeff and the crew had left the old squadron to go to Pathfinders.

"Don, you old so and so," Jeff shouted excitedly and stretched out his hand, "how the hell are you?"

Don had been one of the older members of the flight, a level-headed likeable Victorian with a keen mind. He had completed his tour of operations on the old squadron and was now instructing at the O.T.U. at Lichfield. He had been one of Jeff's particular friends, having certain mutual interests which had drawn them together. With genuine pleasure they went off together.

As the train trundled him back to the squadron the following morning, a feeling of despondency settled upon Jeff. He and Don had spent the previous day together. It had been a quiet time, during which they had recalled persons and incidents. They discovered when they had pooled their knowledge, that of the twenty-four in their course who had been posted to Bomber Command, only six still survived. Of that six, only three including Don had completed their tour and were no longer on ops.

As the train drew him closer to Huntingdon and the squadron, Jeff realised how his luck had been strained.

He did not believe that skill alone won a crew through, he had seen too many good crews posted missing. He believed it was luck, fate or the hand of God as well. He wondered that he had survived so long, and he feared the few remaining that he still had to fly to complete his two tours.

A premonition of disaster shook him. As he closed his eyes the feeling was so intense that he felt his hackles rise. His hands trembled as he opened his eyes and gazed out onto the hedges and fields speeding by. He dreaded his return to the squadron.

The scrubs continued. Day after day, the crews were briefed in the hope that the weather would improve sufficiently for them to operate. Each time however, the hope was in vain. Jeff became moody. Even though he feared the operations to come, he would have preferred to have flown them, rather than to sit around waiting for the break in the weather. Irritably after each scrub, he added his unused log to the pile in his locker. In the mess or the Anchor, he would mope, as the thoughts passed through his mind. Jean was the only person able to ease him.

The days dragged slowly by, days during which the C.O. tried to relieve the boredom and growing tension among the crews with films borrowed from the American dromes nearby and with other activities. They helped only a little. It was a relief therefore, when the squadron finally got away to bomb Duisberg.

Syd and the crew were not on the battle-order. The raid being to the Ruhr, within the range of Oboe, the visual markers were not required.

Despondently, the crew drove over to the Anchor. Jean and Paula were both on duty, and could not go with them. They stamped into the bar and sat on stools.

"What's up with you lads?" Josh asked looking around the group, "you look as though your cat's had pups."

"Nothing really Josh," Clarrie said leaning away from the bar "we're just sick and tired of not flying."

"You can say that again sport," Red boomed, "Hit me with a double whisky Josh. I intend to get good and blind tonight."

"Me too," Nick added.

"Well its your funeral," Josh said, reaching for the whisky bottle, "you'll be having the hang-overs, not me."

"I couldn't care less," Jeff stated flatly.

Josh poured stiff nips for all of them, except Al, who drank beer. Pouring himself a whisky, he held it up, looked through it at the light, then sniffed its aroma.

"I'd better get a couple of these into me," he said, "the way you're starting tonight, it looks as though you'll clean me out of the stuff."

After drinking his whisky, Doug placed his glass on the bar and stood up. He glanced round at the crew sitting moodily silent, staring into their drinks.

"You look like a bunch of undertakers," he laughed, "without a body to bury."

"Don't mention that word," Red admonished him, half seriously.

"Well to hell with you guys," Doug added, "I'm going over to Colleen's, she's better company than you bunch of morons."

As he walked up the path to Colleen's home, she opened the door. With a smile she ran down to him and slipped her arm into his.

"Hello honey," he whispered, as he bent his head to kiss her.

"The way you say 'honey' makes my toes curl," she whispered back, giving his arm a squeeze. "I saw the car pull up at the Anchor and I was just going over."

"Let's stay away," Doug said, "it's like a morgue."

"Why Doug?" she asked.

"Ops are on and we aren't," he stated briefly.

"What about you?" she asked "Don't you care?"

"Sure I do," he replied, "but if I can see you, bless all the scrubs and no flying, I say."

With a laugh, she turned to him, stood on tip-toes and kissed him. He put his arms round her and drew her close to him.

"Honey," he said, "I wish this god-damn war was over or we were finished, I want to marry you. Know that?"

Pushing him gently away, she gazed up gently into his face.

"Know it," she murmured, "but don't worry darling, we will, one day. I'm sure of that and I come from a long line of second-sighters."

As he put his arm round her again, the first planes started up on the drome. It was at that period between twilight and night. They sat down on the steps of the house and silently waited as the planes warmed up, taxied and took off. They roared away overhead, to be soon lost to sight in the darkness. Only their navigation lights showed their position. Colleen turned to Doug, threw her arms round him and kissed him passionately.

"Darling, darling," she cried, tears running down her face, "I'm glad you're here for a change."

"Easy does it," Doug said quietly, wiping away her tears with his handkerchief, "anybody would think you care for

280

the brute."

"I do, that's the trouble."

"Don't worry honey," he said standing up and raising her from the steps, "I'll live to present you with twins or triplets yet."

"Oh Doug," she sniffed.

In the Anchor the crew had been drinking quickly, but as the first plane started up in the distance the six heads jerked.

"There they go," Red snarled, "rubbing it in, come on Josh, hit me with a triple this time."

They drank on until closing time, when Josh helped them one by one to the car. They were all drunk, singing and happy. From Colleen's home Doug heard them. He and Colleen sat together in the darkness, their arms around each other.

"Well that's that," he said sadly.

"Do you have to go now?"

"Fraid so my sweet," he whispered, drawing her close to him and kissing her, "I'll have to drive and put them to bed for a change."

In spite of the change in the weather, the crew still did not operate often. The emphasis at the time was on the Ruhr towns with their heavy industry and armaments factories, and the French coastal ports with their U-boat bases. During this period, although the crew did not operate, Al flew as a relief wireless-operator with another crew and Nick as relief gunner four times. Each time they flew, the remainder of the crew nervously awaited their return. They could not go to their billets to sleep. They flocked together in the sergeant's mess until the time for the returning planes' arrival drew near. They then drove up to the interrogation room to greet Nick or Al as he came in.

During this period, Nick matured. Gone was the brashness, gone was the nervousness and self-consciousness which had followed. As they all had, he had aged in appearance and about him there was a quiet air of self-assuredness. He knew his job as gunner and took pride in that fact. He still felt fear but the fear now tempered him, it no longer controlled him.

Each time the crew clustered round him in the early morning after one of these raids, he felt happy. He felt one with this band of men where comradeship meant more than just friendship. There was a bond tying them together which nothing could cut. Tich was still tied to them with the same bond. It was stronger in many ways than family ties, in that they faced death together, each depending on the other to cheat death.

Once again the weather deteriorated. Fogs rolled in each afternoon, blanketing the countryside. It was impossible to operate. Once again boredom struck the squadron, the long period since the crew had operated seemed interminable.

As the fogs lessened in intensity, the briefings began again, but each operation was cancelled before take-off, due to uncertain conditions at their time of return. They were briefed for Hamburg and were eating their operational meal when the scrub signal was relayed to them. Berlin was the target shown on the briefing room wall-map for three consecutive nights. Each time the operation was cancelled before they went out to the planes. Kiel and Hannover were other targets for which the preparations were made in vain. During the day, when the fog lifted sufficiently, the planes flew on training excercises, but even these were curtailed by the uncertainty of possible operations.

When the crew did operate again, it was to Hannover and they nearly went down. Take-off was early at 1840. The crews were briefed in the afternoon, ate their operational meal and went out to the planes early. Anxiously, Syd and others watched the control-tower as the time for take-off drew near. No red verey light burst into the sky as the first planes started up. Yorker's engines opened up, were tested and Syd eased her out of the dispersal to the cheering of the crew.

On the track in from the enemy coast, they noted heavy fighter activity, but they were unmolested. They pierced the searchlight belt and Red searched the ground in the light of the illuminating flares for the aiming-point—a distinctive building near a cross-roads. A thick haze lay over the city making pin-pointing difficult. They overshot on the first run in and turned for a second. Syd banked Yorker round until they were in position.

Red T.I's were clustered ahead as Red guided Syd up to the target.

Doug, seated beside Syd, glanced above them. Although they were low, there was another bomber, a Halifax, only a hundred feet directly above, flying on the same course.

"Halliebag right over us-they're hundred feet up, Skipper," he called keeping his eyes on the other plane.

"Right Doug," Syd replied, "hope he doesn't bomb us."

"That's just what I'm afraid of," Doug said.

Red continued his directions, finally locating a landmark. From this, looking ahead, he identified the aiming-point.

Exultantly he shouted, "Target right ahead Skipper."

"Good show Red," Syd said."

As Red eagerly called the minor alterations to bring the target into the correct line and to keep it there, Doug continued to watch the Halifax. He saw the bomb-bay yawning open, the load of explosive hidden in its darkness. He heard Red's voice droning over the intercomm. The bomb-aimer in the plane above must have seen them silhouetted against the flares and incendiaries already burning. However, he gave no instructions to his pilot to direct the plane away from them, it continued at the same height above, the same speed and on the same course.

Suddenly, the incendiaries poured out of the bomb-bay, small, destructive and all consuming.

"Down port Syd," Doug screamed, "the bastards dropped on us."

"Target coming up," Red yelled, "hold it steady.".

Syd's instinctive pressure on the rudder-bar as Doug screamed was checked. He held Yorker steady as the incendiaries rained down upon her. He felt them hit. Perspiration bathed him as he followed Red's direction until seconds later, the bombing run was completed.

"Bombs gone."

As Red's voice boomed Syd saw flames licking out from the port outer engine.

"Port outer's on fire," he yelled "to hell with the

photo."

As he spoke, with his eyes on the burning engine, his hands unerringly cut the engine and pressed the fire-extinguisher button. The great blades slowly ground to a stop. The flames which had been licking out over the cowling and spreading, gradually subsided and died from view. Anxiously Syd watched, hoping they had been killed completely and were not still there beneath the metal covering.

Quickly he called up the crew on the intercomm, only Jeff, Doug and Red answered him.

"Get back quick Jeff," he ordered, trimming the plane to fly level.

In the rear of the plane, when the incendiaries struck, Al had been standing beside the flare-chute, prepared to release the photo flash when he heard Red call. Nick and Clarrie were revolving the turrets slowly, scanning the sky for fighters. The four-pound incendiaries struck the plane like hammer blows. Three crashed their way completely through the plane, leaving gaping holes in the top and sides of the fuselage. Two others broke through, cut the hydraulic lines and the intercomm wiring to the turrets and began to burn on the floor near Al. He stood stupified for a moment. Then he switched on his microphone and called Syd. There was no reply and he anxiously called again. The flames grew. He unplugged his intercomm and edged along the swaying plane towards them.

Clarrie saw the flames. He tried to call Syd also, but with the same result. He felt frightened, imagining that he would be burnt to death. His hands flew to the turret harness, be began to unbuckle it.

As Jeff opened the intercommunicating door behind the main spar, he saw the flames, their intensity magnified by their reflections in the hydraulic oil splashed on the sides and floor of the fuselage. Immediately he raced back to his position and plugged his intercomm in.

"Fire down the fuselage skipper, going back."

"Pilot to crew," Syd called, "fire in fuselage, prepare to abandon aircraft."

Only Jeff, Doug and Red heard him.

Jeff pulled his helmet off and dropped it. Grabbing the extinguisher from beside his table he hurled himself over the main spar and raced towards the burning incendiaries. He saw the last of the two disappear out through a gaping hole in the floor, through which the target showed—the searchlights, the light flak, the target indicators, the incendiaries, the mushrooming explosions of the H.E.

As Al had edged his way towards the incendiaries, he was scared. He knew the terrific heat at which they burnt, he knew they would char his gloved hands should the burning magnesium alloy touch them. Gingerly he had reached down towards the nearest. He grasped the end which was not yet flaming and worked it over towards the hole in the side of the fuselage. With a sigh of relief, he watched it drop away, then he turned towards the second. As it dropped away, Jeff appeared and shouting into his ear, told him what had happened and instructed him to tell the gunners. In the excitement of the moment, Jeff forgot to tell him of Syd's order to prepare to abandon the aircraft.

As Jeff returned to his navigator's compartment, Nick was becoming frantic. An Me 109 was closing in on them. He yelled into the intercomm but no reply came. The turret no longer worked hydraulically and he had to turn it manually. The guns could not be fired because of the broken oil lines. Each moment the Me. edged nearer, as though its pilot was aware of the damage and was closing in to make the kill. Nick had glanced back through the panel in the rear of the turret and had seen the flames. Now, although the flames were gone he could see no sign of the others. He thought he had been left, to go down with plane alone. He thought the others had bailed out, deserting him. He worked the turret round, preparing to bail out himself when suddenly, he remembered the fighter-lights buttons on the handles of his turret-control grips. The fighter had come to within fifty yards as he pressed the button for the light to flash on the instrument panel in front of Syd. In spite of the fear he felt he did not panic. The fighter was approaching from the starboard quarter, he pressed the starboard button.

Immediately, Yorker dived and banked steeply starboard. The fighter was caught unawares. Tracers poured from it shooting wide, as it endeavoured to follow Yorker into the diving turn. Disappointedly, Nick touched the guns which would not fire. He had been cheated of a kill. He followed the fighter's path and using the fighter buttons, they eluded it, losing it in the glare of the target.

They were still over the target area, the attack was continuing. Waves of bombers flew over the city dropping their loads of destruction down onto the indicator flares. Fires raged as the incendiaries burned. The block-busters and heavy explosives tore buildings apart as they erupted. The searchlights probed the skies, feeling for the bombers. The crew saw other combats take place as the German fighters fought to protect the city from the holocaust.

When Syd finally saw the signal from Nicholls flash the welcome information that the enemy plane had been eluded, he had the crew take stock of the damage.

Jeff and Al once again went down into the fuselage. In the guarded light of torches, they probed the length of the plane. The floor and sides of the fuselage were slippery from the oil which had poured from the broken hydraulic lines. Al clambered along the cat-walk to the rear-turret. When Nicholls answered his hammering on the turret, he told the rear-gunner all that had happened as briefly as he could. Jeff did the same for Clarrie. As they slithered back to their positions, the gaping holes in the fuselage drew their eyes. Through them, the target area still could be seen.

"Quite a bit of damage," Jeff reported to Syd, "but nothing that will stop us getting home. Hydraulics gone, turrets U.S., two bloody great holes in the side. An incendiary has busted the I.F.F. It is still sitting intact in the middle of it—won't go off however, so we left it alone."

"Thanks Jeff," Syd replied, "no one hurt?"

"Not a scratch, thank God," Jeff said thankfully, "incidentally, all the radar is on the blink also. From now on, it is strictly dead-reckoning navigation."

In evading the fighter, Syd had lost a great deal of height. Yorker was flying at barely 3000 feet, and still over the outskirts of the city. Slowly Syd eased the planes nose up to gain height. Yorker responded, even though flying on only three engines.

They were nearly out of the city's defended area, when the beam of a searchlight caught the starboard wing. Immediately other beams swung to it—Yorker was coned.

"Oh no," Red said unbelievingly, "this isn't our night."

As the light flak horse-piped up towards them, Syd thrust Yorker down into a sharp diving turn. With one dead engine, he had to be careful. The flak seemed to be coming directly at them only to swerve away at the last split second. It seemed to pass within inches of them on every side. When the speed had built up, Syd turned the plane and in a deep steep dive he thrust for the darkness beyond the city.

The searchlights' beams bent lower as they sought to follow the bright fleck which was Yorker. As last they were free. Although only coned for a few minutes, it had seemed an eternity after the other events of the night.

For long moments, not a word was spoken, then a babble of voices erupted over the intercomm.

"Quiet the lot of you", Jeff shouted over the voices.

"Quiet crew," Syd added.

Jeff had come forward and was plugged into the intercomm behind Doug. He gazed round trying to estimate the position of the plane in relation to Hannover.

"Skipper," he said, "do you have any idea where we are?"

"Not a clue Jeff", Syd replied, "sorry."

"Good old track and ground speed" Red laughed, "always brings you back to sanity."

"What heading are we on Syd?" Jeff asked, ignoring Red.

Making a mental note of the course, air-speed and height, Jeff looked back and estimated their distance from the center of the city. Ducking beneath the black-out curtain, he turned on his table lamp. Quickly applying the information he had, he calculated a new course to take them to the turning point at the enemy coast.

The remainder of the flight was without incident. Over enemy territory, Red was able to pick up pin points on the ground which served as checks on Jeff's navigation. Once they were over the North Sea, Jeff was able to navigate by the stars.

As they circled Battleson drome, before coming in to land, Red's voice boomed over the intercomm.

"I hope they're right."

"What do you mean?" Doug asked.

"Well they say, life begins at forty," Red replied, "that little beauty was our fortieth operation."

CHAPTER 23

As Paula waited in the operation room for the planes to return from Hannover, she wondered how she would break the news to Syd.

She was pregnant.

During the day, when she had had some hours off duty, she had gone into Huntingdon to see a doctor. He confirmed what she had already known. She was going to have Syd's baby.

Even if she had had the opportunity to do so, she had not intended telling Syd before the operation, in case it might have made him careless on the flight. She intended to tell him as soon as possible and prayed that he would not be shot down.

As the first plane returned, she went out into the interrogation room. Anxiously, she scanned the board on the wall as the planes' letters and times of return were chalked up. This was done as they returned and called up for permission to land.

Twenty planes had flown out from Battleson on the operation. The board began to fill up, but Yorker, delayed by the damage and flying on only three engines, was not amongst the first arrivals. A cold chill ran through Paula. She felt her hands tighten into fists as she watched.

Punch was about to call her to interrogate one of the crews which had returned. He saw the expression on her face as she watched the board. Going over to her, he quietly put his hand on her shoulder.

"Take it easy Paula my dear," he said, "they will be alright."

Without a word she smiled up at him and reaching up, she squeezed his hand.

"Thanks Sir," she said, "do you want me to interrogate

one of the crews?"

"If you can," Punch stated kindly, then with a twinkle in his eye, said, "you can take the table facing this way, so you can still see the board."

When only two spaces were still vacant one was Yorker. The concern Paula felt was shared by the others in the room. At long last a phone rang in the operations room. Punch answered it. It was the wireless room relaying a message from Al. Punch waved to Paula then held his hand in the "thumbs-up" sign.

Thankfully, she watched him chalk the time of return in the space for Yorker on the board. The last space was never filled, the crew had been shot down.

As Syd and the crew noisily stamped into the interrogation room, Paula could sense that they had had a bad trip. The exaggerated gestures, the jerkiness of their actions, the over shrill voices, she had been all these indications before in Syd's and other crews when they had returned from a trip on which they had nearly been shot down.

Syd walked over to her. As he winked at her with a twisted grin on his tired face, she could barely restrain herself from throwing her arms around him in relief. Instead, she quietly put out her hand and touched his briefly.

"Bad trip?" she said.

"It was," Syd replied. "I thought we'd had it this time."

"Well you're back, thank God," Paula murmured earnestly. "Are the rest of the crew alright Syd?"

"Every one of them, not a scratch."

As she interrogated them, Paula once again could sense the strain the crew had been under. The overexuberance, the laughter and the banter, as well as the tired, strained lines on their faces, testified to the tension.

As she filled in the details of their flight on the debriefing form, she realised also, how close they had come to going down. She decided to tell Syd about the baby that night. As the crew rose to leave when the interrogation was complete, she called to Syd.

"Wait for me," she said.

"I intended to," he smiled down at her.

Although the crew was the last to be interrogated, the room was still crowded with air-crew. They clustered round the pot-bellied stoves drinking cocoa and rum, recalling the details of the operation.

Gradually, they drifted away to the messes after making a last enquiry about the missing crew.

Syd waited for Paula near the doorway. He watched her as she moved round the room attending to the details necessary upon the completion of the operation. At last he saw her take a sheaf of papers to Punch and discuss them. Then she turned and walked towards him.

After the brillance of the interrogation room, the early morning seemed especially dark as they left the building hand in hand. The other squadron buildings stood as black silhouettes around them.

As they walked slowly to the mess in the distance, Paula fought for words with which to tell Syd. Eventually she found them.

"Syd," she said quietly, "I think the time has come for us to tell the C.O. that we are married."

"And get you posted," Syd replied quickly.

"Well it won't be a posting," Paula said, smiling to herself as she drew Syd closer, "I'd say that I am due for discharge."

"What do you mean?"

"Good heavens, can't you guess?" she stated shortly, "I'm going to have your baby."

"What!" Syd exclaimed, stopping abruptly and turning her to face him. Her face was barely visible in the dim light from the moon shining through the clouds.

"Well it does happen to married couples," Paula laughed, "or hadn't it occurred to you?"

With a quirk of conscience, Syd realised that it had not. He knew that he had hoped that eventually they would have a family but after he had finished flying on operations. But at the present time, when he still had operations to fly, all he could think of was Paula and what would happen to her should he be killed.

"Well aren't you pleased?" Paula asked him, an anxious tone in her voice.

"Of course I am darling," Syd reached down and holding her face between both his hands, he bent and kissed her gently and tenderly.

"You sweet adorable person," he whispered, "Of course I'm glad but all I can think of at present is you. Its going to be great telling the C.O. and the others that we are going to be parents and that that we are married. I wonder if they will believe we are."

"You have a bad mind," Paula chuckled.

Syd slid his arm round her and drew her close.

"No matter what happens my sweet," he said solemnly, "The time that we have been together has been the most wonderful part of my life. You are part of me now."

"Me too," Paula replied.

"Is everything alright?" he asked, "have you seen a doctor?"

"I have."

Then, arms round one another, they slowly walked through the darkness to the great black looming shape that was the officers' mess.

*   *   *

"Well I was wondering when you were going to tell me about you and Syd," Punch smiled at Paula the following morning, as she endeavoured to tell him of her marriage and pregnancy.

"You knew?", she asked.

"Of course, he smiled, "from a few days after you were married. You should know by now you can't get away with anything in the forces."

"But how?" Paula asked incredulously.

"Well one of your friends at the wedding," Punch said, "is a friend of mine, and my friend decided to stick her nose into the business and let me know."

With a weak smile, Paula looked up at the intelligence officer. His kindly face was beaming. She sat down in the chair in front of his desk.

"But, this latest news rather complicates things," he added, "we will be sorry to lose you. You know that you will have to be discharged?"

"I know."

"There's no hurry. When do you expect the baby?"

"In about seven and a half months."

"I'll make arrangements for your discharge and let you know."

Getting up, Punch went round his desk and took her hands. Drawing her up he said,

"Now don't worry about anything, we'll miss you but that's not important now."

"Does anyone else know?" she asked.

"Well the C.O. thought it a great joke," Punch said, "I had to tell him. He enjoys putting anything over head quarters. The Queen Bee knows also. But they are the only ones."

"Thanks again Sir," Paula said thankfully, as she went to leave. Then impulsively, she stood on tip-toes and blushingly kissed him on the cheek. As she went out, Punch watched her go, his eyes misty.

*   *   *

After nightmare filled sleeps, the crew went up to the flights the following morning before lunch. The relief at their narrow escape was still upon them.

"Indestructible that's us," Red boasted to the other airmen, "Yorker and crew—the scourge of the Nazis."

Operations were listed, but they were not on the battle-order. From the petrol load listed, they deduced that the target would be in the Ruhr.

As Jean drove them out to the plane, Jeff sat beside her.

"Narrow squeak you told me last night," Jean said as she drove along the perimeter track, "that was the understatement of the year. I saw Yorker in daylight earlier and its in a mess I can tell you. I don't know how you got back."

Jeff turned towards her, seriously he replied, "I don't either."

"Well all I can say," Jean stated, "is that your guardian angel was on overtime, thank heavens."

They had reached Yorker's dispersal, she turned the van round, stopped and switched off the engine. Then twisting in her seat to face Jeff, she smiled sadly up at him.

"You big goon," she whispered, "you worry me to death. My heart flipped over when I saw the damage to Yorker."

Lightly, Jeff touched her chin with his fist.

"You know me," he said, "the bad penny and so on. You can't get rid of me that easy."

292

"I don't want to," Jean replied.

The damage to Yorker looked startling. Gaping holes showed in the fuselage where the incendiaries had torn their way through. The port outer engine was still stained from the flames and the extinguisher. Oil smears from the burst hydraulics slashed along the fuselage skin.

"She's in a mess," Syd said to Mac as the ground crew chief came up.

"She is that Sir," he replied, "but in a day or two she will be back to her pretty self. We take her into the hanger after lunch and we'll be working on her as soon as she's in there."

As he spoke, he looked proudly at the plane which seemed to stand defiantly upon the concrete.

"She got you back in one piece," Mac added.

"She did that and more," Syd replied.

"One thing you didn't know Sir," Mac stated, "another incendiary smashed through the wing into your main starboard petrol tank. Its still there. You were lucky that it didn't go off."

A shudder ran through Syd as he realised how close they really had come to going down in flames.

* * *

With the squadron preparing for operations and their plane unserviceable the crew stayed in messes after lunch. The girls were on duty so they caught up on their letter writing.

Six hundred planes from Bomber Command took off that night and bombed Duisberg in the industrial heart of Germany—the Ruhr.

Bombing on skymarkers dropped by Pathfinder Mosquitoes fitted with Oboe, they blasted the industry of the city. They reduced to shattered ruins many of the factories which were turning out the munitions which the German armies needed on the Russian front.

The squadron was stood down from operations on the day following Duisberg. Buses were provided to take the airmen and airwomen into Bedford. Syd and the crew with Jean and Paula preferred the quiet of the Anchor, where Colleen joined them.

With the soft lighting, warm fire and comfortable chairs

in the lounge, a quiet peacefulness seemed to cloak them. They shed their worries and fears and in each other's company, found a serenity and a tranquility which seemed to transport them for that evening from the arena of war, from the world of planes, operations, flak and fighters. The couples sat side by side, hands entwined. The others sat, some on the carpet on the floor, all caught up in this brief moment of pleasurable peace. Hardly talking, they drank little, but enjoyed a communion of thought and companionship. It was such a jolt when the moment was broken when Josh called "time gentlemen please" in the bar. It disturbed them and brought them back to the world of war that for a short pleasant time had receded from them.

*　　*　　*

In the morning when the battle order was pinned to the notice board, the crew were listed on it. They drove out to Yorker for the night flying test before lunch. By working round the clock, Mac and the other ground crew had repaired the plane and put in a new port outer engine. Yorker stood, immaculate once again, awaiting the crew. The test was perfect, everything functioned as it had before the damage.

Take off was scheduled for 2000. Jeff, Syd and Red went into the navigation briefing at 1600, four o'clock in the afternoon. As they entered, their eyes instinctively went to the wall may upon which the target was marked.

Berlin again!

In spite of themselves their pulses quickened. The "big city" always was a place to be respected. A place which put fear into the veins of the flyers. Jeff and Red prepared their maps and charts. Jeff plotted the positions of the turning points listed on the board. He then calculated the tracks and distances of the various legs of the trip out to the target and return to base.

After the main briefing which followed immediately, one gunner "went sick". The Medical Officer found nothing wrong and later he was posted away—L.M.F. (lack of moral fibre). Men who had no qualms at going in against the terrifying defences of the Ruhr felt apprehension and fear at the prospect of an operation against

Berlin.

The operational meal was less noisy than it usually was, as the crews ate their "operational egg". Even in the locker room as they put on their flying kit, they were more subdued than was normal.

Yorker took off at 2005, Syd set course over the drome and steadily pushed the plane's nose up climbing as they set out on the first leg of the flight to Cromer on the east coast of England.

On the flight out across the North Sea and over Holland there was thick cloud above and below them. It began to thin as they flew into Germany. The route was South of Emden, Oldenburg and Bremen, all of which threw up their cones of searchlights and flak as aircraft strayed over them off course.

The awe-inspiring cone of Berlin loomed up ahead all too soon. The flak, even from a distance, seemed intense, as planes arrived before time and alerted the defences.

The crew were acting as visual markers and as Yorker penetrated the outer defences on the way in, the first red target indicators and illuminating flares fell ahead of them. Red quickly oriented himself and picked up a land mark. Slowly the detail leading to the aiming point drifted along the bomb sight. He called the corrections for drift to Syd.

"Bombs gone," he said, as he pressed the release button. Yorker bucked her appreciation.

When the yellow target indicators burst into life, they were directly over the aiming point. With a feeling of pride, Red reported to Syd.

"T. I's on the button Skipper."

"Good show Red," Syd replied.

He called for the bomb doors to be closed when they had flown straight and level until the photos of the target was taken. Round them other planes were in trouble. A number were glistening specks, caught in the pyramids of searchlights which followed their every turn. Bursts of flak followed the apex of the beams ripping at the caught planes. Some went down, the rest struggled through.

Once again Yorker pierced the defences unmolested and the long trip home to base began. They flew east of Rostock and then on a track to Denmark and north of

Sylt. Much of the trip over the hostile territory was again in cloud, which persisted until over the North Sea where the tops dropped to 6000 feet. The crew watched the moon rise over a bank of cloud in a truly beautiful sight. The majesty of the moment impressed them and kept them silent.

It was 6 a.m. before they finally were in their beds after interrogation and a meal.

Nine aircraft were lost on the operation but none from the squadron. Most of the crew had flown 42 operations. They had only three to fly to finish.

*   *   *

Jeff and Syd walked up to officers' mess together for lunch. Each had had a disturbed sleep full of nightmares. When they entered, Syd immediately sought Paula. She was with a small group of ground staff officers. When she saw them, she broke away and came over.

"Good sleep?" she asked, knowing from the tired lines about their eyes that they had not slept well.

"So-so," Syd replied.

"Are ops on?" Jeff asked.

"Not for you," she said, "five are listed for a short op."

"That's a break," Jeff said.

The three went into the dining room together.

During the afternoon, with other crews on operations the crew had little to do after going out to Yorker and checking their equipment.

On the drive back to the flight-office Jeff, as usual, sat beside Jean.

"When are you off duty?" he asked.

"Five o'clock," she replied, "Why?"

"Could you meet me somewhere and we'll walk over to "The Anchor" and have dinner there."

"I should be able to slip away," Jean said, "no one will miss me, so long as we aren't back late."

Jeff leaned back in his seat and closed his eyes.

"We will have a nice quiet evening," he said, "just the two of us and be back in plenty of time."

They made arrangements where to meet and when, as Jean stopped the van by the flight-office. She watched Jeff as he went off with the others to the crew room. At the door he turned and winked at her.

When they met that evening, their hands naturally entwined as they set off. It was a long walk, but neither cared. They did not talk a great deal until they reached the small bridge over the stream which flowed on the outskirts of the village.

"Let's sit here for a while," Jeff said, as he drew Jean along to a grassy bank. He placed his great-coat down upon the grass and they sat down, close together. He put his arms around her, drew her close and kissed her.

"Very nice too," Jean smiled tenderly, as they broke away.

"I love you Jean," Jeff whispered, "I love you so much."

"Me too," she replied, "but why so solemn."

"Tired I guess."

"Tired my eye," Jean said, "you've got something on your mind."

Lying back, Jeff put his hands behind his head. Jean leant over him and bending down she kissed him again, hard and longingly. Her hair fell down and brushed his cheek. Reaching up, he took her face between his hands and softly caressed it. For a long moment they were silent, then he crushed her to him and kissed her eyes, her cheeks, her nose, her lips.

"If only this damn war was over," he said at length, his arms still round her.

"There," Jean exclaimed breathlessly, "I knew you had something on your mind besides me."

With a smile, he rose and reaching down, he pulled her up. As they stood together, he put his arms round her and drew her close.

"I just wanted you to myself this evening," he said. "Just you and I. You're like a medicine and a wonderful sedative to me."

"That's lovely," Jean laughed. "I can't think of what medicine you mean."

"You know what I meant."

The levity left her.

"Of course I do Jeff," she whispered, "and I think I know what's the trouble—only three to go to finish."

Jeff picked up his great-coat, throwing it over his

shoulder,. He drew Jean's arm into his and they walked back to the lane leading to the village.

"Partly that," he said, as they walked along. "In fact that would be most of it. I want us to be married so badly it hurts."

She squeezed his arm.

"It won't be long now," she said. "I'd marry you now if we could, but I know what you would say. As soon as you finish however, we make arrangements."

Jeff stopped and turned to face her. Even in the fading light her eyes shone as she looked up at him. A feeling of peace and gentleness filled him as she put her arms around him again.

"You're sure my dear?" he said.

"As sure as I could ever be of anything in this world. I want you, you goon, now and forevermore."

Silently, once again arm in arm, they walked the remainder of the way to The Anchor.

* * *

The next time the crew flew on operations it was once again to Berlin.

This was a period of intensive bombing of the German capital, in retaliation for the bombing of British cities. Many times the bomb weight fell on the German city, compared to that which fell on Britain. The weather had deteriorated. During the afternoon, low cloud and drizzling rain enveloped the drome. As they worked on their logs and charts, the navigators anticipated that it was wasted effort. As time of take-off approached, the weather appeared even worse.

· Signals from Group Headquarters postponed take-off time first by an hour, then another hour and finally a third time.

Yorker was scheduled to be one of the first planes to take-off. As the time approached, the crew climbed into the plane, wet and cold. They settled themselves into their positions and waited. Even at that late stage, they still expected the operation to be cancelled.

Syd called for starter motor and the powerful Merlin engines shattered the quiet, as they opened up one by one. Signalling the chocks away, Syd gave a wave to Mac and the ground crew who stood huddled together in the rain on the edge of the dispersal. He eased Yorker out onto the perimeter track and along to the end of the runway. Gooseneck flares stretched along the edges of the runway, converging in the distance. Other planes were lined up ahead of them.

Over the R/T the planes were told to stand-by. Even at this late stage, there was still doubt whether the operation was to be "scrubbed" or not. At last, a green light flashed from the Flying Control Van.

The first plane revved up, slowly moved off, then gathering speed quickly, its tail lifted and it was soon airborne. They saw it finally as a black smudge in the distance, a red and a green light on its edges, as it rose up from the lights of the runway.

By the time they took off themselves, they had been at the runway's mouth nearly fifteen minutes and there was danger of the engines over-heating.

As the met officer had predicted at main briefing, they encountered even worse weather over the North Sea. Two fronts extended across their path with severe icing conditions. Syd urged Yorker up and up to clear them. As they climbed through the cloud ice formed on the wings and the air screws. The plane was buffetted round like a cork Pieces of ice, flying from the tips of the whirling blades, struck the fuselage like cannon-shells. At each fusillade the crew were startled. The tension grew. Finally at 21000 feet, Yorker drew free from the cloud. The stars shone above them, while below them the hills and valleys of the cloud stretched somberly on all sides as far as they could see.

They crossed the Danish coast without seeing it. Once again, as on previous flights, the cloud thinned as they plunged deeper into German territory.

For Jeff it was a perfect trip. At no stage was his navigation more than mile off track, North of them on the way in, they saw planes, which had strayed off track, shot down over Flensburg and Kiel. Rostock claimed another victim. The great cones of searchlights along the route were all active.   all

As they approached the defences of Berlin, they felt the usual dread at trying to penetrate them. However, they made their run in unmolested. Red picked up a landmark once again on the outskirts of the city. Quickly, he gave directions to Syd which put them on the heading to the aiming-point. As they approached, the first Red T.I's and illuminating flares exploded.

The bombs and target indicators dropped from Yorker. Red exultantly proclaimed that the yellows were cascading onto the aiming point.

The trip home across Germany and Denmark was equally uneventful. Around them other planes were attacked by fighters or caught in the searchlights and peppered by flak as they wandered off track over towns alerted by their passage.

The cloud thickened as they approached the enemy coast. Once again Syd was forced to push Yorker high to clear the fronts. The bad weather persisted as they approached England Slowly Syd eased the plane down following Jeff's directions of course to fly. Eventually though the drizzling rain, the Battleson Beacon and the Sandra lights reaching up from round the drome beckoned them home.

It had been a long, tiring trip and it was 8 o'clock before they were able to get to bed.

The squadron had lost another crew on the operation out of a total loss of 15 crews in Bomber Command.

When the crews went to the messes for lunch, they discovered that there were no operations scheduled that night, the squadron was stood down.

The afternoon was spent on training flights, Air to Sea firing, fighter affiliation and radar training.

Jean was on duty in the evening so Jeff wandered over to the sergeant's mess and joined the crew members who were there. They drank beer and played cards until the bar closed. Syd and Doug drove over with Paula to the village. As they drove up to her house, Colleen came out of the door as though she had been waiting for Doug.

"Hello there," " she called gaily, "night off?"

"Yes," Doug replied, "and welcome at that."

As they walked up the path, she slipped her arm into Doug's. When they entered the house, Paula and Syd turned into their section. Going into the bedroom, Paula changed from her uniform into a simple frock. When she returned, Syd had taken his uniform tunic and collar and tie off. Squatting in front of the fireplace, he coaxed fire from the tinder and wood already laid for them by Colleen's aunt. When it was well ablaze, he sat down in the large settee facing it. As he slipped his shoes off and wriggled his toes in front of the fireplace, Paula came and sat beside him. Syd slipped his arm around her and they sat silent, watching the flames, happy in each other's company.

When Doug followed Colleen into the house, she called to her aunt.

The elderly lady came out quickly, kissed Doug and fussed over him. The three of them sat over a cup of tea for an hour, then the aunt excused herself and retired for the night.

Colleen and Doug washed up the tea cups and plates in the kitchen, then went back to the lounge. Side by side they sat in front of a fire also.

"I only have two to finish, Colleen," Doug said slowly.

"I know," she replied, "I have been counting them too."

A feeling of apprehension came over Doug as he spoke.

"I have been worrying lately," he said, "I don't know why, but I just can't imagine that we will finish our tours."

She put her hand over his and squeezed it.

"Don't talk like that, its silly."

"I've heard about other bods and their premonitions," he continued, "well I feel like that about us."

Seeing how serious he was, Colleen made no attempt to ridicule his thoughts. Instead, she moved closer to him and drew his arm round her. She nestled her head on his shoulder.

"All I know is this Doug," she said firmly, "you and I will get married, whether you get shot down or not. Somehow, some day, you and I will be."

Then a little self-consciously, she turned and looked up into his face. He bent over and kissed her.

"I told you Doug," she said, with a smile on her lips, "I come from a long line of second sighters and I am as sure of what I said as I am that you are sitting here."

"All I hope is that you are right," Doug whispered into

her ear.

At eleven o'clock, Syd and Paula knocked on Colleen's door. They were once again dressed in their uniforms. Doug and Colleen walked out of the house after them. At the gate, Doug drew Colleen close to him and kissed her hard. She returned his kiss ardently, tightening her arms around him for a long moment. Then with tears in her eyes, she gently pushed him away.

"Be off with you," she said, "or you will be A.W.L."

She watched the car, until its rear light disappeared in the distance, then slowly turned and walked thoughtfully into her home.

CHAPTER 24

"Ops are on."

Wing-Commander Bolton-Adams had not needed to hear the Adjutant's words nor to read the slip of paper handed to him. After their long association, he could tell from the expression on the other's face whether operations were scheduled and how dangerous the target would be.

Morning assembly was nearly over. The airmen lounging drowsily about the room a moment before, became alert. A babble of sound arose as speculation upon the target began. The cigarette smoke thickened.

"The battle order will be posted on the notice board as soon as possible," the C.O. stated flatly. " Dismiss and go to your flights."

"Me for a nice easy milk-run to France," Doug said hopefully, as he and the crew filed out with the other airmen.

"No such luck this close to the finish," Clarrie replied, "It's bound to be a tough one."

"That's my boy," Red bellowed, slapping the mid-upper on the back, "always happy, carefree and gay."

"Anyway," Syd remarked dryly, "let's hope we are on, we might be left sitting on our behinds in the mess."

"Heaven forbid."

The target was Frankfurt on Main. Zero-hour was

scheduled for 2130 and the crew were visual markers, going in at zero-hour minus four minutes.

The crew were quickly caught up in the flurry of pre-operational preparations. Yorker was air-tested. Clarrie and Nick checked and cleaned their guns. Jeff and Red went over their equipment item by item. The ground crew had Yorker at the peak of performance. The four engines gave voice to a song of surging power as they hurled Yorker through the English morning sky.

After the air-test, while Syd and the others spoke with the ground crew, Jeff went over to the flight-van where Jean waited. She leant against a front mudguard of the van, her figure trim in the battle-dress of short tunic and trousers. As he approached, she winked at him.

"Hi good-looking," she smiled.

"I was thinking that about you," Jeff replied.

He threw his equipment into the back of the van, and joined her. Placing his hand over her's where it rested on the van, he leant gently against her.

"It's nice to be beside you," he said as she looked up at him.

"It's nice to be here."

"I wish this bloody war was over," Jeff erupted suddenly, his hand tightening on Jean's.

Turning abruptly, he looked at the huge bulk of the Lancaster where it seemed to rear up from the dispersal. The brown and green camouflage above and dull black below, gave it a sombre, menacing appearance.

Jean turned her hand and squeezed his.

"It won't last forever, it can't," she said, "one of these days we will wake up and suddenly, it will be all over."

"I can hardly wait," Jeff laughed mirthlessly. "Sometimes I feel so detached from any other kind of life, that I wonder if my old life was only a dream."

"You can stop that cackle right now," Jean said firmly and dug a finger into his ribs.

Jeff's mood slowly lightened, turning, he took hold of Jean and bent down to kiss her. Hastily, she broke away.

"Not here my lad," she smiled, "spies are everywhere you know, even the walls have ears and eyes. Remember my unsullied reputation."

Navigators' briefing was held after lunch. As visual markers, Jeff and Red had an additional briefing. Photographs of the aiming point in Frankfurt, and the run up to it, were examined and memorised. The responsibility for getting Yorker to the target area, in a position for Red to pick up a landmark, was Jeff's. The identification and marking of the actual point was Red's job. They worked as a team. As the navigator's briefing ended, the remainder of the crews stamped noisily in for final briefing.

The afternoon quickly passed and as take-off time approached, they and the other crews sat down to their operational meal. As they finished, the airmen drifted in groups to the flights and to the locker rooms. The usual bedlam ensued as they dressed in their flying clothing. The gunners donned their electrically heated suits and the others got into the variety of dress they wore on operations, ranging from pyjamas to civilian dress. Over these went the Mae West inflatable jackets and parachute harnesses.

As the flight-van drew up near Yorker's dispersal, Jeff leaned over and kissed Jean. They sat silently together in the cabin of the van for a moment.

"Bye darl," he whispered into her ear and kissed her again. I'll be seeing you."

"Good luck Jeff," she replied.

Slowly he got out and took his equipment from the rear of the van. She watched him as he struggled with it to the plane. At the ladder, he turned and waved. She waved back and watched until his tall, spare frame disappeared from view through the doorway in Yorker's fuselage. As always, she felt fear for him—fear that he would not return, not the vague indeterminate fear of the early days, but a deep soul-corroding fear, born of an almost superstitious dread that each additional flight was adding one more weight to the balance. A cold shudder shook her. With a sigh, she reached forward and switched on the ignition.

Inside Yorker, the crew settled into their positions and prepared for the flight. Jeff laid out his maps and charts and once again tested the angle-poise and the fixed red lights. In case it should be needed, he checked the astrograph above him. His sextant, tin of pencils, protractor and calculator were placed in their usual positions. Sitting back, he made the Sign of the Cross and prayed for a short time, seeking in prayer, assurance and acceptance of what might ensue.

In the bomb-aimer's compartment, Red sorted his maps, checking that they were in correct sequence and placed them ready for use. He inspected the bomb-sight and the bombing panel, then returned to the seat beside Syd.

Syd made himself comfortable in the cockpit, reached for the straps of the seat harness and adjusted them. He tested the controls and carried out the pre-flight cockpit drill. Doug stood by the gauges at the side of the plane behind Red. At the radio position, Al went over the set and laid his sheets of information on the small table in front of him. He inspected the remainder of his equipment to ensure that he had everything. The gunners manually operated their turrets and settled themselves as best they could in the cramped space for the long lonely trip ahead.

Syd signalled to the ground crew and Mac plugged in the starter motor. One by one, the engines started up, Doug and Syd watched the instruments for any irregularities. There were none, Yorker behaved perfectly. The engines were run up to the peak power. With a smile of satisfaction, Syd leaned out the small cockpit window, gave the thumbs up sign to Mac, then closed the window. The wheel chocks were removed by the ground crew. Gently, Syd eased the throttles forward and Yorker began to move away from the dispersal. As it trundled along the perimeter track, other planes joined in the procession to the end of the runway in use. The first planes took off into the evening sky. Syd eased Yorker forward into position.

"You've got your green Skipper," Doug called, as the green Aldis light shone from the Control Van parked to the side.

The runway stretched ahead of them, like a long road leading nowhere. In the evening twilight, it glistened wetly in the lights of the flarepath at it disappeared into the distance.

"Everything O.K.?" Syd asked.

"O.K. Syd," Doug replied.

The engines were revved up in the final check.

"Here we go crew," Syd called. Releasing the brakes, he pushed the throttles forward. As Yorker surged forward, the crew felt their bodies pressed back against their seats. The engines screamed as they reached full power, the flare-path lights sped by, the tail lifted and gracefully the powerful plane rose from the runway and began to climb.

"Undercarriage," Syd called.

"Undercarriage up," Doug replied as he retracted the wheels.

Jeff wrote the time of take-off in his log.

As Yorker took off and began to circle to gain height, Paula in the Control Tower, Colleen in the garden of her home at the village and Jean, in the seat of the flight van parked on the perimeter track, each said a silent prayer for her man in the crew.

Syd urged Yorker up into the sky to gain height over base before setting course. Finally, at the required height, he set the course Jeff had given him for Reading on the first leg of the trip to Frankfurt.

As they flew on course over England, they gained further height. The sweet metallic smell of oxygen filled their nostrils as they breathed it in from the masks clamped onto their faces. They passed over Reading and set course for Beachy Head. The English coast approached and was left behind them. The Channel and enemy territory lay ahead. Landfall was between Cayeux and Le Touquet, south of Pointe Haut Banc. Darkness settled over them, the engines pulsated and roared as they dragged them through the cold sky beneath pin points of stars which showed through the patches of high cloud. Cones of searchlights and the flashes of flak bursts indicated the French Coast. Planes, already off course, had strayed over defended areas and the enemy ack-ack and searchlights probed the sky for them.

They approached the French Coast only slightly off course. To the north and south of them, the enemy defences were active, but they saw no planes shot down.

"Course 097° Magnetic, 0-9-7 Skipper," Jeff called the alteration of course.

"Roger, 097° Magnetic," Syd replied.

The coast line showed up on the radar tube of the H^2S set. As they crossed and Syd made the alteration of course, Jeff noted the time in his log. Quickly he marked the point of crossing on his chart, ruled in the line indicating the track they had actually flown from Beachy Head and then he calculated the wind. It differed slightly from that which he had been using previously. The wind was veering as they flew east. He knew that this would continue and he would have to check constantly to stay on the required track and to arrive on time at the target.

France lay below them. Jeff turned off his lights, drew aside the blackout curtain and went forward. Red had gone below to the bomb-aimer's position shortly after they had become airborne. Doug was seated beside Syd. As Jeff stood behind the flight engineer, he looked down at the dark mass which was enemy territory. As his eyes became adjusted to the darkness after the light in the cabin, he made out some of the details of the land, a river, which would be the Authie and forests darker against the general darkness. It was a detached feeling he had, as though it was someone else standing there gazing down at this enslaved land. Ahead of them, he could see searchlights slicing across the sky like huge knives ready to cut. With a last look around, he went back to his cabin, adjusted the blackout curtain, turned on his light and prepared to take another fix on the radar. Fear gnawed at his stomach, but it was still a fear under his complete control. It was in the background, like the canvas of a painting, not seen but there.

Arras was passed on their starboard and then Douai to port. On each, Jeff checked his position and found new winds. His forecast of veering winds was confirmed and he altered his calculations accordingly. They would be ahead of time if they flew to the pre-flight plan. Jeff calculated alterations of course and estimated times of arrival forward to the target, using his calculations of what the winds would be. From this, he worked backwards from their zero-hour on target.

He passed the slight alteration of course and the new airspeed to Syd. Then, he sat back for a couple of minutes relaxing, until he began his check of all the calculations once again.

Slowly the distance was covered. Cambrai, Valenciennes and Charleroi slid by, marked in the darkness only by the searchlights and flak which rose from each. The Ardennes, dark shadows, lay beneath them for what seemed an eternity and they were flying then over Germany, closer and closer to their target.

One of the last large towns before the target was Koblenz, lying north of and close to their track. As they approached, its deadly cone of searchlights lit up and immediately a bomber was caught like a moth attracted to a flame. The flak burst round it with sharp biting flashes. Some how, the bomber evaded being shot down and passed out of range. The searchlights began probing, weaving and crossing their long fingers through the dark sky.

"Fifty miles from the turning point," Jeff called over the intercomm as Koblenz drew level with their port wing tip. As he spoke, another bright speck appeared at the apex of the cone of searchlights.

"How the hell do they get caught," Syd cried, as he watched the bomber fighting for its life. "The damn cone of lights is fully lit up and the stupid bastard flies into it."

"You'd think the sprogs were all asleep," Nick stated flatly, without looking at the lights in case it impaired his night vision.

The bomber also escaped, to the relieved sighs of the crew.

"Well, he didn't deserve to make it," Jeff remarked, as he made his way back to the navigator's compartment. He drew the blackout curtains shut, turned on the light and settled himself into his seat. After making one more check of his calculations, he passed up to Syd the E.T.A. at the turning-point before the target, together with the course and indicated air-speed to the aiming-point.

The turning point was north of Frankfurt and just outside the city's defended area. As they drew nearer, the defences of Wiesbaden, west of the city, appeared and the huge belt of searchlights which indicated Frankfurt seemed to stretch in a never-ending jungle of brightness. It seemed immense and impregnable. Syd felt his throat turn dry as he watched. Bombers ahead of time were soon trapped over both Wiesbaden and Frankfurt and were quickly shot down. As they fell, on fire, they turned and spun until they exploded on the ground, bomber and bombs combining to form a huge flashing mushroom of destruction.

When they turned onto the final leg leading up to the aiming-point, Jeff sat by the H^{2}S set and called directions to Red. On the edge of the screen Bad Homburg showed up, a bright splash of greenish yellow light. He measured the angle and distance and called out the plane's position to Red. They were on track.

Ahead of them, the city's huge defended area loomed immense and frightening. The whole sky in front seemed to be illuminated. The heavy flak burst high in a box barrage, the flashes of the exploding shells peppered the sky above the city and black balloons of their smoke appeared in the searchlight beam. Light flak began to hosepipe up in lethal technicolour display below the heavy flak. It was a formidable target.

"Red T.I's and flares ahead skipper," Red called suddenly as the first markers appeared over the city.

"We're heading straight for the aiming point on track Red," Jeff said as he worked on the H^{2}S Set. Switching over to the bombing screen, he saw the outline of the northern built up section of Frankfurt clearly defined. Setting up the bombing trace he called distances for Red to apply to his maps.

"Pilot to Navigator," Syd called, "how is E.T.A?"

"Bang on skipper," Jeff replied smugly, "the reds are down a bit early."

The aiming point was in the railway marshalling yards, crowded with wagons of supplies and amunitions for the German forces. As visual markers, the crew were to bomb at zero minus four minutes. Blind markers and illuminators were scheduled to attack on radar two minutes ahead of them, dropping red target indicators and illuminating flares in the approximate position of the aiming point. In the light of the flares, Red and the three other visual marker bomb-aimers were to identify the specific target and drop yellow target indicators. The main force then bombed on these. The reponsibility for the ultimate success of the raid lay with Red and the other visual markers. The main force crews had been instructed at their briefings not to attack until zero-hour, giving the path-finder crews time to identify and mark the aiming-point. Too often however, they ignored these instructions, especially if there had been a change of wind and they were ahead of time. If they bombed early, on the reds, the brilliant splashes of light from the incendiaries they car-ried, made it difficult, even impossible at times, to identify the aiming-point and the raid lost its maximum effect-iveness.

"Hurry it up skipper," Red called anxiously, "one load of incendiaries has gone down."

They had settled into the bombing run to the aiming-point. Red had pinpointed their position north of the city and was guiding Syd with brief calls to alter direction. The aiming-point should be to the right of a cluster of reds.

As they drew nearer, Syd hunched down into his seat, his eyes on the instruments. On all sides, the beams of the searchlights weaved and crossed. One beam scraped over their port wing-tip. Doug, standing beside Syd, felt fear tie a knot in his stomach, he waited for it to return to trap them in its light, but they went on unmolested. The box barrage over the city winked and flashed on all sides, leav-ing black puffs of smoke from their explosions to hang suspended, lit by the reflected light from the beams. The multi-coloured light flak arched and spiralled in balls of fire reaching up towards them.

"Left-left," Red called softly, "should have the aiming-point soon."

Straining his eyes ahead, he identified landmarks remembered from his study of the target photos.

"Target coming up," he cried, as he suddenly saw the marshalling yards lit dimly in the light of the flares.

"Right ------ steady."

"Steady"

"Steady"

The aiming-point slowly came down the bomb-sight. Suddenly a splash of light cut across close by it. The incen-diaries dropped by a main force plane burned brightly and in their glare, Red lost sight of the target.

"The bastards," he yelled, "Incendiaries, I lost the

aiming-point."

"Keep trying," Syd replied, "we don't want a dummy run."

"Keep on this heading," Red said, anxiously peering down through the bomb-sight, striving once again to pick up the aiming-point.

Suddenly through the glare, the marshalling yards appeared dimly. The building, which was his target, was slightly to the starboard.

"Right-right-quick," he called urgently.

As Syd responded immediately and instinctively without question, the plane yawed over.

"Steady, Syd."

As Yorker straightened, Red realised that they would overshoot the target. With a curse, he straightened up and despondently gazed down at the target area through the bombing panel.

"Dummy run skipper," he called.

"Oh lovely, lovely," Clarrie moaned.

"Turning now Red," Syd called over Clarrie's voice.

Swiftly, Syd hurled Yorker down into a 360 degree turn against the stream of the oncoming bombers. This was a dangerous manouvre, but to get back into position where Red could identify the aiming-point once again, they had to fly in a circle through the stream of bombers. They had to turn round and back onto the track they had been flying on their approach to the target. Yorker bucked in the slipstream of another plane as collision was narrowly averted. Syd felt the perspiration on his forehead as he stared into the space ahead of them. Glancing at the compass and judging time he turned Yorker until he felt that once again they were approximately in a position to run up onto the aiming-point. Before he could speak, another Lancaster loomed towards them. Quickly, Syd thrust the control column forward. Yorker's nose dipped. As they dropped, the other bomber sped over them with only feet separating them from death in a tangled mass of metal.

"Now that was close", Doug breathed softly.

Slowly, Syd felt the trembling in his limbs subside. Straightening up Yorker on course once again, he called to Red.

"On Course for target, bomb-aimer."

"O.K. Skipper, roger-dodger," Red replied, "but don't ever do that to me again please."

Settling down, he quickly picked up a pin-point on the ground.

"Left-Left ---"

"Left ---"

"Steady-Steady"

The marshalling yards appeared, partially obscured in the glare of the incendiaries, but sufficiently visible for Red to identify it and the aiming-point. He watched it creeping down the bomb sight, giving directions as he did.

Suddenly Yorker lurched violently to starboard. The flash of the exploding shell lit the plane's starboard wing and the cockpit for a brief instant. The smell of dordite pervaded the plane.

"Keep it steady," Red screamed.

"We're hit Red," Syd replied anxiously, watching the wing, the starboard wing. The starboard outer engine began to vibrate and the first tongues of fire licked the cowling. The ack ack shell had shot out the engine. Instinctively, Syd switched off the motor and feathered the air-screw. Doug, without a word, his eyes on the engine also, pressed the fire extinguisher button.

Syd straightened up Yorker.

"Can you still hit target Bomb-aimer?" he asked quickly.

"Left-left and yes skipper."

Yorker yawed to the left under the pressure of Syd's feet on the rudder bars. Red picked up the aiming-point, made a further correction then pressed the bomb release button.

"Bombs gone," he called.

"Thank God," a voice whispered over the intercomm.

Syd held the plane level until the photo had been taken as the yellow target indicators cascaded over the marshalling yards.

"Bang on target skipper," Red shouted, satisfaction evident in his voice.

"Good show Red," Syd replied.

As he spoke, his eyes were on the starboard outer engine. The air-screw was lying still, the blades unmoving.

There were no flames evident now, the extinguisher foam had done its job. Gently, Syd checked the controls for damage from the flak burst. They responded as they should. With a sigh of relief, he pushed the control column forward and Yorker went into a shallow dive over the city, building up speed to pass through the defended areas as quickly as possible.

"Skipper to crew," Syd called, "we had a near miss and are flying on three, is everyone O.K.? Doug, take a look for damage."

Their replies came back one by one. No one was hurt, but Yorker had taken other hits beside the engine. Shrapnel had torn several holes in the fuselage but had done no vital damage. Beneath them the raid on Frankfurt intensified. Seconds after their own yellow marker had burst above the aiming-point, another followed. Immediately, the whole area became a vast sea of flame as the waiting bombers dropped their loads. Their incendiaries splashed in swathes, one into the other, until they formed one mass of bright yellow twinkling light as the phosphorus bombs burned the heart out of the target. In the bright mass, sudden flashes of orange indicated the bursts of the high explosives which smashed and tore and spread the incendiaries to start other fires.

In spite of flying on only three engines, Yorker sped over Frankfurt towards the haven of darkness outside the searchlights and ack-ack. All round them, the lights still weaved and crossed. The box barrage of heavy flak slashed through the sky. Other planes were caught in cones and faced the terrific concentration of heavy ack-ack which poured up into the apex. A few were brought down, some limped on like Yorker and others evaded the flak miraculously. As they neared the outskirts of the city, a gap appeared in the searchlights as the beams in front of them turned to add their light to others which had trapped Lancasters as they tried to leave the area.

Thankfully, Syd pressed Yorker to an extra burst of speed and they were out into the darkness. Behind them the target burned, bombs and incendiaries still fell, adding to the fires already burning on the ground. Slowly, the beams of light and the ack-ack fell back behind them as they flew the course towards the French Coast on the long leg home.

As the voices rose in a babble of noise in the relief felt with their escape, Doug called urgently to Syd.

"Skipper, number three is losing power."

Without having to look at the gauges, Syd knew that it had suffered damage over the target. Damage unseen, about which they could do nothing. Anxiously he nursed it along. Yorker's speed dropped off.

"Oil pressure going down skipper," Doug called.

"Roger, Doug," Syd replied, "it looks like we'll be on two soon." As he feathered the airscrew, Syd ruefully looked out at the two sets of blades standing rigid and immobile. Carefully, he trimmed the plane to counteract the loss of power from the two starboard engines. When Yorker settled down he called the new airspeed to Jeff.

"Of course you know this will leave us miles behind the main force," Jeff stated matter-of-factly.

"Of course I do Jeff," Syd snapped, "but there's nothing I can bloody well do about it."

CHAPTER 25

All too slowly, it seemed to the crew, they flew the long miles towards home. All too slowly, the minutes ticked away to the drone of Yorker's two remaining engines. Their course was south-west from Frankfurt to a point thirty miles west of Mannheim, then nearly west, over Luxembourg and Northern France to Le Treport on the French Coast. The first leg was flown uneventfully. Mainz was passed to the north of them. Ahead, Mannheim lit up as the England-bound planes alerted the defences. At this point, the enemy fighters made their first appearance. In the vicinity of Mannheim, they saw the tracers stabbing through the sky as bombers and fighters slashed at one another. They saw three planes go down on fire, spiralling down until they crashed in flames.

"Keep your eyes peeled gunners," Syd called, as he turned onto the new course from the turning point west of

Mannheim.

Below them, Germany was dark and menacing. In the bomb-aimer's compartment, Red peered down through the perspex panel searching for landmarks. He could see none. In the navigation compartment, Jeff worked on his chart, measuring tracks and distances, applying the new, slower airspeed to his calculations to estimate their time of arrival at the enemy coast. At the radio, Al listened out to base, twisting the dials of his radio. Slowly the miles went by. In the distance eventually, Red saw the gleam of water.

"River ahead Jeff," he called. Hurriedly, both he and Jeff reached for their maps.

"It's either the Saire or the Moselle," Jeff said, as he unfolded the detailed map. In the dim light of the shaded torch which he carefully shielded, Red prepared his map for comparison with the ground detail. To the south, the defences of Saarbrucken were active. Carefully Red checked his observations against the map.

"Its the Moselle," he said finally, "we're south of track about four miles south west of Sierck."

As Jeff plotted the position on his chart, he gave a groan.

"Hell, Skipper," he stated with a troubled tone in his voice, "we're making slow going."

"I know Jeff," Syd replied, "there is nothing I can do about it—can't flog these engines any more."

They settled back into the routine of the operation.

"Bandits, port quarter up," Nick screamed the words automatically, as he saw the two black specks darker than the darkness which nearly hid them.

"Roger, rear-gunner," Syd replied, his hackles rising. All the crew momentarily stopped shock still, as they waited for the next move in the drama.

"Do you see them mid-upper?" Nick asked anxiously, "up at about 1500 yards at four o'clock."

"I spot them," Clarrie replied, his eyes had searched until he too made out the two enemy fighters. His guns were already cocked, as were the rear-gunner's. They both trained the Brownings on the approaching planes.

"Gunners," Syd called, "I'll have to turn port, its too

dangerous trying to turn sharply to starboard with both engines out on that side. Remember that."

"Roger, Skipper."

After crossing the Moselle, Yorker had slowly traversed the miles over the northern border lands of France. As the miles seemed to drag by, tension had gripped the crew. The lame duck, left behind by the main force, was an all too frequent target for enemy fighter planes. The tension stretched nerves to what seemed breaking point. Only Jeff, engrossed in his navigation seemed oblivious to the situation. He was absorbed in recalculating his flight plan for the remainder of the flight. However, when Nick yelled, even he, like the others, felt the shock of fear numb him temporarily.

"Gunner," Syd called, "I'm going into a sharp turn to port, keep your eyes on them. We'll see if we can lose them."

"Roger, skipper."

Thrusting the control column forward to gain extra speed in a dive, Syd kicked on the rudder bar and swung Yorker to port. She responded, not as quickly as she usually did, but she seemed to put out an extra effort. As she descended in the steep diving turn, the enemy fighters for a moment appeared to lose sight of her, but only momentarily.

Seeing their wing tips dip as they prepared to attack, Clarrie yelled.

"Here they come, keep turning."

The first tracers flashed past them to starboard as a Messerschmidt swooped down at them. At the speed he was flying the pilot could not tighten the turn of the plane sufficiently to hit them. The second Messerschmidt attacked quickly afterwards from the same direction, with the same result. The crew saw the enemy speed by and the gunners poured rounds from Yorker's six guns at them as they passed.

"Take it slowly Nick", Clarrie advised, "keep your sights ahead of them, allow for deflection—here they come —turn port skipper—go."

The second attack was like the first. In tandem, the German fighters attacked, pouring shells at Yorker but

316

outside her turning circle. Nick and Clarrie fought back desperately.

The crew sweated out the long minutes as they waited for each pass from the enemy planes. The gunners never lost sight of the two Messerschmidts. Co-ordinating like a team, each concentrated on one enemy until the attacks came, then both fired together as the fighters came in. In the air battle, Yorker was forced further south of track, down into France, further from the lane of the main force planes. It was impossible for Jeff to keep track of where they were. The constant manouvering followed no set pattern. He could only estimate roughly the general direction they were forced to fly.

The battle waged for long, never-ending minutes but there could be only one outcome. Hampered by the loss of two engines, Yorker's manoeuvring ability was limited. When the enemy pilots realised this, they changed their tactics and flew in from the starboard. Unable safely to turn with them, Syd made one last desperate effort to evade them. As they flew in to attack, he dragged the control column back towards him with all his strength and cut the throttles of the two remaining engines. Yorker clawed up towards the stars, gradually losing speed as she gained height. For a long moment, she hung suspended in awful stillness, then her nose dropped and she seemed to fall from the sky in a stall that lost three thousand feet in seconds. In the plane, in the seeming weight-lessness, the men felt themselves lift from their seats. Anything loose rose from where it lay. On his table, Jeff saw the sextant rise to the ceiling of his cabin, the pencils rise out of their tin and hang suspended above it. Even his maps, charts and instruments rose up from the table.

After what seemed a breathless eternity, Syd took control again, pushed the throttles forward and slowly eased Yorker out of the dive she had settled into. Slowly, the great plane responded as Syd turned the trim control at the side of his seat. As they gradually resumed level flight, he called anxiously to the gunners.

"Have we lost them gunners?"

"Can't say Skipper," Clarrie replied, "I lost them in the dive."

For minutes it appeared that the manouvre had been successful, when suddenly, Clarrie's voice broke the hushed silence on the intercomm.

"Turn port-go!" he screamed.

The two fighters sped down on them in a dual attack, again one behind the other. This time, Syd was not able to evade them.

Cannon shells and machine gun bullets tore through Yorker's skin to smash, rip and tear and burn. Incendiaries started fires in the fuselage.

In the rear-turret, Nick felt a blow like a punch in his right side. He knew he was hit and wondered why he did not feel more pain. Looking down, he could see where the bullet had torn through his flying suit, a black stain showed in the semi-darkness.

"Rear-gunner to pilot," he said softly, "I'm hit, but still serviceable."

"Radio-op," Syd called urgently, "go back and see to Nick, he's hit. Take your chute with you and plug in near the elsan. We'll have to bale out by the look of things."

Quickly, Al unhooked from his position, snatched up his chute, climbed the main spar and stumbled through the shambles which was the fuselage. As he groped his way back, the Messerschmidts attacked again.

"Starboard quarter up—here they come," Clarrie yelled, as the enemy planes swung in.

"Roger," Syd replied, swinging Yorker into a sharp futile turn to port.

"I see," Nick stated flatly. His side felt numb and his right arm seemed to have lost strength. A drowsiness was coming over him, but he lined up his sights on the leading fighter and pressed the button on the turret handle. As the fighter's guns opened up, so did his. The tracers from each crossed in a pattern of fire. Suddenly the enemy fighter appeared to explode. Flames shot from its engine, it turned abruptly onto its side and dropped away, burning and spinning.

"You beaut Nick," Clarrie yelled exultantly, as he kept firing at the second enemy fighter. It pressed home its attack in spite of it's companion being shot down. More shells burst into Yorker and it passed, over them, close and menacing, to climb quickly up to prepare for another run in.

"Got one skipper," Nick called, as he ceased firing.

"Good show Nick," Syd said earnestly, "damned good show, but how are you?"

"I'll be right for a while, but it's going numb."

"Are you plugged in Al?" he asked.

"Yes skipper, plugged in."

"Get up to Nick and bring him out."

"Roger."

"Not on your bloody life," Nick replied vehemently, "you don't get me out of this bloody turret like Wilhelmshaven."

Drawing on his remaining strength, he swung the turret, searching for the enemy fighter.

The remainder of the crew had sat tense as the battle waged until Yorker was hit. Then, Jeff groped his way back with fire extinguishers to put out the flames started in equipment by the incendiary bullets. Standing beside Syd, Doug anxiously watched the dials when he was not looking out for the fighters.

The next attack came as suddenly as the previous one. The Messerschmidt raced in from above in a steep dive. As it straightened out, its guns blazed. Clarrie and Nick fired back, the barrels of their guns were hot. Once again the streams of tracers crossed, seeming to merge in the distance. The fighter's shells ripped into the port wing. The port outer engine began to blaze, but as the fighter passed over this time, he too had been hit. Smoke was billowing back from behind him like a plume. The Messerschmidt dipped down to port and sped away towards its home drome.

After a quick look at the flames spreading over the port wing, Syd knew it was impossible to extinguish them. This was it!

"Abandon aircraft," he called, sadly, reluctantly, but urgently, as Yorker began to buck at the controls.

"Al," he added, "you and Clarrie get Nick out of his turret and see he bales out O.K."

"Navigator to crew," Jeff broke in urgently, "near as I can make it, our position is near Chalons, about 75 miles east of Paris. Good luck and I'll see you in Blighty."

"Roger," Syd replied for the crew, then he called, "can you hear me Nick?"

There was only an unintelligible mumbling from the rear-gunner. In the bomb-aimer's compartment, Red clipped on his parachute and jettisoned the forward hatch.

"Front hatch gone skipper."

"Bale out crew, get going Red, good luck and thanks."

"See you on the ground," Red whispered, then he took off his flying helmet and threw it onto the bomb sight. Crouching down at the opening he paused for a moment, swung his legs out and leaning forward, he pushed himself out.

Doug patted Syd on the shoulder, unhooked his inter-comm and oxygen, clipped on his chute and followed Red.

In the rear of the plane, Al had the rear door open. With difficulty, he and Clarrie had dragged the nearly un-conscious Nick from the rear turret. He lay at their feet on the hard, cold, duralium fuselage floor, moaning and mumbling. They clipped his chute on but knew he could not operate it himself.

Clarrie pulled Al towards him and shouted into his ear over the roar of the plane.

"I'll go out with him and pull his rip cord and then let him go."

"You'll kill yourself," Al gasped, "you won't be able to make it yourself in time."

"I'll worry about that," Clarrie replied and determined-ly bent down over Nick. He and Al lifted the wounded rear-gunner upright. Clarrie put his arms around him from behind with one hand on Nick's rip-cord. Staggering to the open door with the now unconscious gunner, he took a deep breath, vaguely remembering the bale-out drill then the two figures dropped away from the plane.

"The two gunners are out Skipper," Al called over the intercomm, "I'm going now. Best of luck skipper, see you in England."

"Thanks Al," Syd replied, "Good luck."

Yorker was becoming impossible to control. The con-trols were not responding. Syd's arms and legs ached from the exertion of the past hours, perspiration soaked his under-clothes till they stuck to his body. His feet and his head under the flying helmet felt clammy. His hands were wet on the control column. Only he and Jeff remained in the stricken plane.

"Get going Jeff," he called urgently, as he strove to keep Yorker flying.

"What about you?"

"I'll make it."

"Like hell you will."

Jeff stood behind Syd, he unbuckled the pilot's harness and moved it away to make it easier for Syd to get out of his cockpit.

"Get going Jeff, for God's sake, I can't hold it much longer."

"Start getting out, give yourself a chance."

Realising that the pilot would have little opportunity of getting to the escape hatch before Yorker fell into a spin, Jeff stood torn by emotion. He did not want to leave. He felt a great urge to stay with Syd, going down in a fiery pyre with him in the plane they had both come to love.

Wrestling with the controls, fighting them to keep Yorker level, Syd turned to Jeff.

"Thanks Jeff," he said emotionally, "I know what you think, but get going please. I'll try to make it. If I don't, you get back and tell Paula I loved her."

With a last look at his friend, sadly, Jeff unhooked his helment and went forward.

He swung his legs over the edge of the open hatch as he had done so often in bale out drills on the squadron in England. As he felt the airstream drag at him, he looked down into the darkened countryside below him. It appeared menacing in its darkness. With a momentary qualm of fear, he doubled over and pushed himself through the hatchway. Immediately, he was snatched away from the plane by the force of the slip stream. As he slowly counted to ten, as they had been taught, he seemed to twist and tumble and drop alarmingly quickly. At last he pulled his ripcord handle. The parachute pulled from its covering clipped to his chest. As it opened out above him in a silken cloud he jerked abruptly.

As he gently swayed, suspended by the silken strands of

the parachute, Jeff looked ahead to Yorker still struggling on. Vainly, he searched the sky for a parachute indicating that Syd had somehow, miraculously, managed to get out of the dying Lancaster. The sound of the two remaining engines come back to him and the flames from the port wing pinpointed its position in the sky. Finally, as though it had ceased trying, as though it had died, Yorker appeared to break up as the port wing collapsed. The flames quickly spread, it exploded and dropped like a fiery comet to the earth below, where it burned itself out.

Sadly, Jeff watched the flames flickering in the distance, knowing his friend Syd had had a viking's funeral. Involuntarily, tears came to his eyes.

"God bless you Syd," he whispered.

All too quickly, the ground seemed to be rising to meet him. In the darkness, he could only discern that he was coming down in forest country. A chill went through him as he thought of the possibility of breaking bones against the branches. As they drew closer, he drew his legs together and relaxed his body. Smashing through the outer limbs, he snapped off leaves and branches in his descent. Abruptly, he hit the ground and stumbled forward to lie full length, the breath knocked from him. For long moments, he remained there, breathing heavily. Then with an effort of will, he forced himself upright. Unbuckling his harness, he got out of it and saw that the parachute was still caught in the trees above him. It was still some time before he was able to pull it free.

Using his strong-bladed knife as a shovel after slashing his chute, he buried it and the harness in the bank of a small water channel. He covered them with leaves, making the spot as unnoticeable as possible.

Realising that the area he was in, being so close to the wreck of Yorker, would be searched intensely, Jeff sat for a moment to collect his thoughts and to think out his plan of action. The wreck was west of him, so he planned to strike due south and to gain as many miles as possible in the darkness remaining.

Reluctantly, he rose and struck out in the darkness through the trees, using the stars shining through the branches above him as his compass. As he moved away, his thoughts were on Syd and the others.

As Clarrie leapt from Yorker with Nick clutched in his arms, he feared for a time that the little gunner would be torn from him. However, he managed to keep hold. After several seconds, he pulled the rear-gunner's rip-cord and pushed him away. As the parachute opened, he seemed to speed away from Nick until he pulled his own rip-cord. As he descended, he was able to keep sight of the other. They both landed in a thinly wooded area and it took Clarrie only a short time before he was able to shrug off his chute and harness and hurry over to the little gunner.

Nick was still unconscious. He was doubled over, partly covered by the parachute which had fallen down over him. Quickly, Clarrie undid the harness and gently placed Nick on the silken chute. Opening the flying gear, he searched for the wound in Nick's side. It was a nasty slash low on the right side and was still oozing blood. Clarrie drew a battle dressing from his inside pocket and pressed it firmly onto the wound. As gently as possible, he tied the bandages round Nick to hold it in position. Covering him as well as he was able with the parachute, he ran to the edge of the clearing where he could hear the murmur of running water. Clambering down the muddy bank of the small brook, he soaked his handkerchief and some silk which he had cut from the parachute. Running back, he squeezed out drops of water onto the little gunner's lips and wiped his brow with the wet cloth.

Al jumped from Yorker's rear door shortly after Clarrie and Nick had disappeared. He was able to keep their chutes in sight until he fell into trees about three hundred yards west of them. After cutting up his parachute with a razor blade which he kept in his top pocket for the purpose, he buried the silk and the harness as best he could beneath bushes.

Immediately they were hidden, he struck out in the direction where the two gunners had fallen. Stumbling over the rough ground and through the trees took longer than he had anticipated. When he did come upon them, the little rear-gunner was conscious and Clarrie was squeezing a few drops of water onto his lips.

The noise of Al's approach startled Clarrie and Nick. The little gunner tried desperately to rise but fell back with a moan.

"You bloody great oaf", Clarrie exclaimed thankfully when Al drew close enough to be recognised, "you made enough noise for a platoon of Germans."

"How's Nick?" Al asked anxiously.

"He's bad," Clarrie replied, "if we don't get him to a doctor or something soon, he's had it. Did the others get out?"

"I don't know," Al replied, "All I know is that Yorker exploded but they had time."

"I hope so."

Squatting down beside the rear-gunner, Al put his hand out to feel his forehead. It was feverish.

"Don't worry," he reassured the gunner, "we'll get you patched up somehow."

Slowly and painfully, Nick leant up on one elbow. Through the spasms of pain, he managed to whisper.

"Look," he said, "forget about me, you two, try to get away. In the morning the Germans will be around for sure. They'll pick me up."

"Fuck that", Al stated blunty, "we'll get you out. There must be a village around here with a doctor."

Using Clarrie's and Nick's harnesses, Nick's parachute and two poles cut from the saplings around them, they fashioned a crude stretcher. Nick was placed gently onto it and tied securely with the silken strands from the chute.

"OK, here we go," Al called, as he and Clarrie raised it from the ground. Nick was unconscious once again, helped by morphine from the first aid kit which Al had carried from the plane.

Slowly, they made their way west, stumbling in the darkness through the trees, over roots and on the rough ground. They knew that eventually they must strike a road which would lead to a village, where, even at the risk of their own capture, they hoped they would be able to get medical assistance for Nick.

Red crashed through the trees, breaking branches from

them as he descended. As he hit the ground, he rolled and fell. Scratched and sore from contact with the trees, he gingerly moved his limbs to reassure himself that he had broken no bones. Slowly and painfully, he rose from the ground and undid his harness. Stepping out of it, he pulled on the chute, caught in the branches above him. He dragged it down and quickly hid it under leaves beneath a large tree.

"What I wouldn't give for a slug of whisky right now," he thought, as he painfully straightened up and prepared to move off.

He too, wondered if all the crew had managed to escape from the stricken plane. He had seen it explode and fall.

"Bloody bastards," he repeated to himself as he slowly made his way, roughly west through the trees, towards his planned destination—Paris.

Doug saw Yorker explode as he slowly drifted down, swaying under the silken canopy. In his mind, he knew that Syd would not have been able to bale out, but he clung to the hope that the pilot had somehow made it. He felt sure that Jeff would have escaped from Yorker before it crashed. A sadness came over him as he recalled some of the incidents he had shared with the crew.

The ground came up rapidly to meet him. As he saw the trees he tensed. He crashed into them and smashed his way partly through the branches before his parachute became entangled and jerked him to a sudden halt. He was swung against the rough trunk then left suspended twenty feet from the ground, swinging slowly from side to side.

Carefully, he turned the release of his harness and pressed it. He retained a firm hold on the harness and disentangled himself from it. With a silent prayer he let himself drop into the darkness below. The leafy debris of years broke his fall as he hit and stumbled upon the ground.

The stillness and the loneliness of the place enveloped him. He felt alone and lonely, wishing that others of the crew would appear, knowing however that it was improbable.

Looking up at the parachute caught in the branches above him, he knew he could not get it down to bury it.

This worried him because it gave the Germans concrete evidence that some had escaped from the crashed plane and more importantly, provided them with a starting point for their search.

"Chalons," he said to himself, recalling the position Jeff had called before they had baled out.

"Now where the hell is that," he thought, wishing either that he had studied the maps more or had sufficient light to study the escape map he carried in his escape kit.

As he came to an open space in the trees he searched the sky for Polaris, the North Star, which Jeff had pointed out to him so often in the past. He set out once more with it behind him.

The loneliness seemed to press in upon him like a dark, smothering cloak.

CHAPTER 26

The hours before dawn became a bleak, weary nightmare to Clarrie and Al, as they struggled over the rough terrain with the still unconscious body of the rear-gunner on the improvised stretcher. In the cold darkness of the forest, they could barely discern their way between the dark pillars of the trees. As they staggered along, gripping the poles tightly, they stumbled repeatedly, cursing as they did. Their only concern being for Nick, they feared lest they drop him and injure him further.

In the hilly country, as they made their way in a westerly direction, occasionally, they came upon a narrow road or a track. Each time, they carefully laid the stretcher down out of sight from the roadway, while they reconnoitred. Before they proceeded, they made sure the way was completely free from enemy troops or vehicles. When the roads or tracks led westward, they walked along them for as long as they continued in that direction through the forests, thankful for the easier going. Occasionally, they passed a small vineyard tucked away in the folds of the hills. They decided not to risk going up to any in the darkness, but to wait for daylight, so that they could inspect the surroundings of any place they approached.

The rough poles cut and blistered their hands. As the long hours of the night passed, Nick's dead weight on the stretcher dragged at them more and more, until they seemed to be moving in a half stupor themselves. In the cold air, their gasping sounded so loud, that they feared someone would hear them. Frequently they had to rest, thankfully placing the stretcher down as gently as possible on a level space. Each time they stopped, they tended to Nick, feeling grateful for the morphine which still held him insensible to the pain of his wound. Each time, they wiped his face over with a damp cloth and settled him as comfortably as possible on the stretcher. At the few small streams they encountered they each drank long draughts, sluiced the refreshing water over their faces and squeezed a few drops onto Nick's dry lips.

In their tiredness, the shadowy trunks of the trees began to take on menacing forms. They began to imagine that they saw movement of enemy soldiers everywhere. With their increasing fatigue, every noise startled them, every snapping twig, every falling branch and the noise of the birds and the small animals of the night.

It was only their determination that kept them going. More and more often, they were forced to stop as exhaustion gripped them. Several times, as one or the other stumbled, the stretcher was nearly wrenched from their sore, stiff hands. Each time, they barely managed to retain sufficient grip to prevent Nick being jolted too severely or dropped onto the ground. However, even in his unconsciousness, moans of pain were forced from him.

After one such near fall, they placed the stretcher down on a level grassy bank. Tiredly, they sat beside it, each dropping his head onto his knees, thankful for the respite.

"What I wouldn't give," Al remarked as he drew in great gulps of the cold air, "to be back in the mess quaffing a ruddy great beer in front of the fire."

"Or just tucked in nice and tight on those lovely biscuits in the billets," Clarrie replied tiredly, "I never thought I would ever see the day that I could look on that hard bed of mine with affection."

"Wonder how the others are making out," Al said, his

thoughts going to the other members of the crew.

"Yeah," Clarrie murmured in reply, "I wonder."

They lapsed into silence, feeling tired and lonely in the hostile land they had flown over so often.

When they felt the chill of early morning seep into them, they rose once again, took up the stretcher and wearily struck off into the darkness.

The long hours of the night slowly passed. As the sky lightened in the east before dawn, they stumbled down a slope onto a narrow country road. As they slithered and slid down into the muddy side drain beside it, they nearly dropped Nick again. He moaned as they desperately fought to keep their balance and their hold on the stretcher.

"That was close," Clarrie gasped as they finally managed to keep their feet.

They made their way cautiously to the other side of the road and went into a clump of trees. Gently, they laid the stretcher down and slowly straightened up.

"That's a relief," Al remarked as he stretched backwards to ease the ache in his back and shoulders.

"I never thought I could be this tired," Clarrie replied as he sank to the ground beside Nick. Gingerly he rubbed his blistered, stiff hands together.

"Well, what now?" he asked.

"I suppose this road leads somewhere," Al replied, "but if we traipse along it now, we're sure to run into a Jerry patrol."

Nodding wearily in agreement, Clarrie looked down at the wounded gunner still lying unconscious on the stretcher.

"One thing for sure," he said matter of factly, "we can't go carrying Nick through the woods any more, we'd kill him if we tried."

"If we don't get him to a doctor soon, he's a goner," Al said flatly. He leant down over the rear-gunner and wiped his forehead with the damp cloth. Nick moaned and twisted in pain.

"Well what's the score now?" Clarrie asked.

"I suppose this road leads to a village of some sort or another," Al said, gesturing towards it. "If we go down it, we might be able to hide Nick on the outskirts while you or I sneak in and try to find a doctor."

"That's a hell of a long shot," Clarrie replied, "What if a Jerry platoon drives along as we're marching down in full view?"

"We dive for the side of the road as quick as we can," Al stated, "and hope they don't spot us. We can't afford to hole up for the day as the good book says we should. Nick will peg out if he doesn't get some attention soon."

Knowing it was the only possible course of action if they were going to save Nick's life, Clarrie nodded agreement.

"O.K.," he said, "let's get on with it."

Rising, he went to the head of the stretcher. When Al was in position they bent down and gently raised it. Tiredly, aching from the exertion of the past hours, they slowly and carefully made their way out of the trees, down the bank onto the roadway.

It was easier going and soon they had developed a mechanical action which was fast, but reasonably comfortable for Nick.

At seven a.m. they rested in a clump of trees on a rise off the road. They ate a little chocolate from their escape rations and swallowed some of the malted milk tablets.

"I can just hear my mother," Clarrie laughed suddenly, "Be sure to eat a big breakfast, it will set you up for the day. I wonder what the poor dear would say if she could see me now."

"She'd faint from shock," Al replied.

Nick had become more feverish and mumbled and groaned almost continuously. They became even more concerned with his condition. When Clarrie uncovered the gaping wound to replace the dressing with a clean one, he was startled to see how inflamed it had become.

"We'll have to get him to a doctor quickly," he said as he re-dressed the wound and tied the new battle dressing firmly into place.

"Yes but how?" Al asked as he settled Nick comfortably on the stretcher. He did up his clothing and drew up the parachute silk around him and tucked it in securely.

"The only way I know for sure," Clarrie said, "is to carry this stretcher down the center of this ruddy road until a German patrol picks us up."

Al did not reply for some time. It would mean giving up all chances of attempting to escape back to England. He did not relish the thought of spending the rest of the war behind the fences of a prisoner of war camp, without at least making an attempt to avoid it. Then he looked down at the wounded gunner moaning incoherently in his pain on the stretcher. Tenderly he adjusted a fold of silk more comfortably round Nick's shoulders.

"O.K. Clarrie," he said resignedly, his eyes still on the little gunner lying so helplessly. "Here's to the bloody barbed wire. Let's go."

They got up slowly, took up the rough poles of the stretcher in their sore, blistered hands and carefully they carried it out of the trees to the roadway. Settling the stretcher as comfortably as possible in their palms, they began their last walk down the road towards captivity and medical attention for Nick.

In the hours of darkness remaining of the night after he had baled out, Red strove to put as much distance behind him as possible. In spite of the cuts and bruises he had suffered in his fall, which still stung and smarted, he set off at a fast pace, half walk, half run. As he struggled along through the trees and bushes, over the rough hilly ground, he stumbled and fell several times.

Each time he fell, he cursed as he picked himself up, finding a release in this for his tension. His determination forced him to keep moving at the fast pace, even at the risk of falling in the darkness.

The other members of the crew were constantly in his mind. As he forced himself along over the rough ground, he recalled many of the numerous incidents they had all been involved in. Fondly he recalled evenings at the Anchor with its warm atmosphere of companionship, friendliness and calm. He recalled how the crew had developed into a team on operations and the other trips they had made together.

As he pushed his way along, the hours seemed interminable. It seemed impossible that they had been shot down only a short time previously. As tiredness forced his legs into a mechanical action, he lost sense of time. He was in a vacuum of black evil. Every shadow threatened him, every noise was magnified. In his haste, he ran across the clearings he encountered, but skirted the vineyards. Like the others, he used the roads and tracks which went the way he was headed. On these he was more careful and twice he had to dash from them to take cover in grassy verges as German army trucks thundered past, shaking the ground on which he lay.

As the sky lightened in the east, Red quickened his pace even more, practically to a run. He was tired, irritable and aching over his whole body. His legs seemed numb, but kept pumping up and down propelling him along. Doggedly, he pushed on as it became brighter in the east. The trees were no longer black shadows, but took on form and substance and could be seen and avoided. The leaves above him gradually became green.

Eventually, as the sun came up above the horizon, he decided to stop. He was still too close to the scene of the crash to feel comfortable. However, at lectures on escaping given back on the squadron, they had been warned to travel only at night and to be doubly careful near where they had landed.

When he did decide to rest, he looked for a suitable hiding place and found one nearby in a clump of low bushes. A road passed within a hundred yards to the south and behind him were woods into which he could flee if he saw enemy troops approaching. Crawling into the center of the bushes, he carefully piled leaves round himself so that, from the outside, he was completely hidden from sight. Thankfully, he stretched out on the soft earth, too tired to eat even the meagre fare carried in his emergency escape rations. Closing his eyes, he tried to sleep. The tension he felt, kept him awake. At every noise he started. Thoughts whirled through his mind without substance or form like a child's kaleidoscope.

After a couple of hours, he felt he could stand the inaction no longer. He was impatient to be on his way again. Fretfully he sat up. Carefully he parted the bushes and peered out, seeking for any sign of enemy troops searching the area. He saw no one, so taking out the emergency rations he had carried inside his battle-dress, he undid the pack and ate some malted milk tablets and squeezed some of the condensed milk onto his tongue. Replacing the packet inside his tunic once again, he lay down and tried to sleep, to regain his energy for the task ahead of him.

During the morning, several German army vehicles and farmer's carts, pulled slowly by horses, passed along the road below him. He watched each from his hiding place until it had disappeared out of sight. He dozed fitfully on and off during the warmer hours of the day, but never for very long. Each time he awoke in a near panic and immediately searched the area for any sign of activity. Shortly after two o'clock in the afternoon, Red once again awoke from a short doze. A feeling of great impatience seized him. His mouth was dry, he ached from his exertions. The inaction of hiding in the bushes, waiting for darkness became unbearable. He felt caged. Slowly parting the bushes he searched the area on all sides. He saw and heard nothing. Carefully he crawled out of his hiding-place. He clambered uphill away from the road, up towards the trees covering the high ground above him.

Upon reaching the trees, he stood upright, and once again moved off at his fast gait. He felt better once he was on the move again. He was nervously cautious at first, examining the path ahead carefully as he made his way through the trees. However, as the afternoon passed he became more confident. About four o'clock he came upon a small stream which trickled along below him. Thankfully Red clambered down the slope and stretched out full length on the bank. Dipping his hands into the shallow stream, he dashed water into his face, then leant down into it and drank deeply.

As he lifted his head and straightened up, he became aware of a noise above him on the bank. A feeling of panic engulfed him.

He looked up into the faces of two German soldiers, one an officer. They were immediately above him. The officer had a Luger automatic pistol trained on him. The private carried a rifle with the bayonet fixed and it was swung towards him as he looked up.

As they began to descend the bank towards him, the officer bared his teeth in a grin of satisfaction.

"You will halt," he called out in guttural English, waving his Luger as he spoke.

"Hell, what a bastard," Red exclaimed, cursing his foolishness in leaving the morning's hiding place and trying to travel in daylight. He had no chance of evading the Germans. Desperately, he looked for a way to escape. It was futile. Before he had taken more than a few steps they would have shot him down.

He knew it was obvious to them that he was a shot down British airman. He was still in his battle-dress with the flight-sergeant insignia and his bomb-aimer's wing sewn on it.

The two Germans, with the officer leading, clambered down. Without a word, the officer gestured arrogantly downstream with his pistol. When Red gave no sign of moving he poked Red in the back with the Luger's barrel.

Angrily, Red jerked away.

"Don't do that," he exclaimed, facing the officer who simply smiled back at him.

Slowly, he turned and began to walk down beside the stream in the direction which the officer had indicated.

The two Germans followed behind him, each with his gun at the ready. As if impatient with Red's pace, the German officer barked at him.

"Move quicker."

When Red failed to respond, he poked him once again in the back with the barrel of the Luger.

Red stopped and turned angrily.

"Do that again," he snarled, "and I'll ram it right up you."

As they descended, Red vainly searched for a way to elude the two Germans, but they appeared to be too alert. Knowing that other German troops must be in the vicinity searching for him and the other members of the crew, he was angrily determined to take the first opportunity to escape from these two, before more arrived. He again cursed his foolishness. His pride rebelled at being caught on the first day of his attempted evasion.

As they followed the stream downwards, it widened slightly. Trees grew down nearly to the water's edge. At times they had to leave the bank and climb up into the trees to avoid walking in the water. Deliberately, as they neared one of these areas, Red slowed his pace. The two Germans bunched up nearly onto Red's heels. As they reached the spot where they had to climb away from the stream up the bank into the trees, Red stopped.

The two Germans were on his heels.

"Move, you dog," the officer barked.

As he once again pushed the barrel of the Luger into Red's back, the bomb-aimer's temper flamed.

Spinning round quickly, he swung his hand in a tremendous back-handed slap flush onto the German officer's jaw. He tumbled back against the private and both fell tangled together into the water. As they fell, they dropped their weapons. Swiftly Red jumped down and aimed a vicious kick to the private's head. It only partly stunned him. The officer was struggling to get to his feet. Red bent down and picked up the rifle, drawing it back he lunged forward and the bayonet stabbed down deeply into the German's chest. With a horrible scream, he fell back into the water, his hands falling, clutching at the barrel of the rifle. It was dragged from Red's grip. As his blood stained the stream crimson, the officer thrashed about, screaming, the rifle still hanging from his body. Red aimed another kick at the private's head as he stumbled onto his knees, the German sprawled once more back into the water. Quickly Red turned and raced for the bank. As he clambered up, he slipped in his haste. Behind him, the German private crawled from the stream and reached for the dying officer's Luger.

He slowly brought it up, cocked it and fired from a range of ten feet at Red's broad back as it was disappearing over the top of the bank into the trees.

The bullet smashed into Red and flung him to the ground.

"Oh God," he groaned as he died.

* * *

In contrast to Red, Doug tackled the task of evading capture calmly and deliberately. He set out at a steady, careful pace, avoiding the obstacles he encountered without falling. As he walked, he took stock of what he

334

had with him and what he had to do.

During the night, he used Polaris, while it was visible to him, as his guide for direction. He determined to strike south, making for the Spanish border, hoping, along the way, to make contact with the French underground. He knew food would be a problem and decided to eke out his emergency rations with what he could gather from farms.

Distance from the area was his only hope against early capture. He knew that in the morning the woods would be crawling with German soldiers, searching for the survivors of Yorker.

During the hours before dawn, he made ground steadily, only resting occasionally and then only for a few brief minutes while he regained his breath and rested his weary limbs. On the few occasions when he came across small streams meandering through the forest, he quickly drank a little, crossed them and kept going. He skirted round each open area, keeping to the trees until once again, he could resume his southerly direction under cover.

Carefully, he walked along the edges of any roads or tracks which went south, prepared at the slightest noise to fling himself away from the roadway into cover.

When dawn came, he had covered many miles and had come to an area where vineyards became more frequent. Small farms clung to the chalky soil of hillsides. He went on after daylight for only a short time, very carefully keeping watch for any movement around him. He went on only until he found what he considered would be good cover during the daylight hours. He found it in a wood above a small vineyard. In front of the little farm, a narrow road passed and close behind him was the cover of trees leading into rough hilly country which would provide ample cover from any enemy searching for him. There was only a small farm house and a couple of sheds on the vineyard and as he watched in the early morning, smoke began to rise from the chimney.

As he settled down in his hiding place, Doug took stock of his position once again. Turning out his pockets, he inspected the sum total of what he carried with him. It seemed very little as he laid them out, the small emergency escape rations, a battle dressing, a multi-purpose pen-

335

knife, two small bar compasses, a razor blade in a protective cardboard cover, a tobacco pouch, half full of tobacco, which contained a map of France printed on silk hidden between its inner and outer skins. Added to these were a few personal items, two handkerchiefs, a packet of cigarettes, his wristlet watch, a box of matches, the second pair of socks he had always carried on operations and half a dozen barley sugar lollies.

It did not seem an impressive array.

Intentionally, Doug did everything very slowly to make the time pass. He opened up the emergency rations and ate a little, choosing carefully so as to eke out its contents.

During the morning he cut off his chevrons and brevet using the razor blade, carefully picking out all the remaining threads and then burying the insignia deep in the soil.

Below him, the vineyard came to life. An elderly man came out from the house, gathered tools and was quickly at work hoeing weeds from between the vines. An elderly woman appeared occasionally, to feed the chickens in the yard behind the house and to do other small jobs.

To pass the time during the long day of inactivity, Doug carefully watched the work being done on the vineyard. Several vehicles passed along the road, horse-drawn farm carts, a few motor vehicles and a number of German army cars and trucks, some of which contained troops in uniform possibly setting off to search for him and the other crew members.

Lying back occasionally, he tried to sleep in an effort to prepare himself for the night ahead and to pass time. The tension within him, eating like a cancer, made it difficult. Each time he closed his eyes, thoughts tumbled one upon the other in his mind. They churned round and round, making it impossible for him to sleep for any great length of time. Constantly, the last minutes before Yorker went down a flaming wreck were recalled in detail. More pleasant thoughts of Colleen, her gentleness, her loveliness and her calm, came and went. The dangers ahead of him pressed in on his mind.

Slowly the day progressed. Thirst began to plague him during the afternoon. He slowly sucked three of the barley sugars to lessen the urge to go out to look for water.

The last hour, while he impatiently waited for the darkness to descend to cloak his movements, seemed to drag more slowly than he believed possible. When he finally judged it dark enough, he quietly slipped out of the wood, struck up higher into the denser forest and continued on his way south, using compass and the stars.

On the second night the going became easier. The terrain was not as rough, more land was cultivated and he was able to augment his small food supply with turnips from farms he passed. He gnawed at them as he walked along. Although he made a point of not travelling along any obviously busy roads, he was able to use several smaller lanes and tracks leading south. Twice during the night, he had to spring from the laneways into the cover of bushes to avoid being seen, as German army lorries thundered past.

Early in the morning, he felt completely exhausted. The strain, the lack of sleep, the constant exertion were all taking their toll. He was walking down a seemingly little used lane when as he turned a bend, a dog barked. With a start, he realised he had almost walked into a small village. The first houses were only yards from him. But for the dog barking, he would have travelled the short distance to the cluster of buildings. Hurriedly he went back round the bend, left the lane and carefully climbing up through woods and by farm fences, he skirted the small village. Dogs barking in the early morning would have alerted someone in such a place.

At dawn, he searched for and found another secure hiding place. It was on a rise above a road in a large wood. Running nearly through the wood, was a small stream where he could drink during the day completely sheltered from view on most sides.

He managed to sleep during the second day, an exhausted sleep which left him drained of energy. When he woke in the middle of the afternoon, he ate some of the turnips he had taken the previous night, some malted milk tablets and a little chocolate. To help him keep going as he started out at dark, he took one of the caffcine tablets from the emergency pack.

This became the pattern, day by day, night by night, avoiding any habitation, skirting round villages, carefully keeping to the fences of hedges between farms. Continually, he headed south, using minor roads and tracks when he could. Gradually, he began to feel weaker. His emergency rations were eaten and he was forced to forage for vegetables, digging them up from the farms he passed in the night. Thoughts of food began to intrude more frequently into his mind both day and night.

He reached the stage when he considered going to a farm house to ask for assistance. However he put the thought away and pressed on.

When eventually he came to a wide river, he felt he did not have the strength to swim across it.

Slowly he crept along the bank searching for a boat which he could use. Finding none, he climbed back up the bank and slowly continued on his way hoping to come to an unguarded bridge.

In the early hours of the morning, he saw the outline of a small town ahead of him. Skirting round it, he climbed to high wooded ground above, from which he could look down upon the town. He lay back and slept.

In the morning when he awoke, for a moment he wondered where he was. Then realisation came back to him. Moving carefully, he crawled to where he could inspect the small town. There was a bridge across the river. Fortunately also, it was towards the end of the built up area. He would not have to go through the centre of the town.

All throught the day, he watched for German soldiers and saw several, marching in pairs, quite often with rifles slung over their shoulders. The bridge did not appear to be guarded. As he watched, many vehicles, horse drawn carts and pedestrains crossed unchallenged.

Waiting until it was dark, he nervously made his way down from the hill to the outskirts of the town. Slowly and carefully, he made his way through the back streets towards the bridge.

Keeping to the shadows of the buildings beside the road, he drew nearer. When he was nearly opposite the approach to the bridge, he slid into the shadows of a doorway and watched for long minutes. There seemed to be no one about. Leaving the doorway, he crossed the road and

338

walked softly and slowly to the bridge. His heart was pounding, sweat came out on his palms. With a sigh of relief, he stepped onto the wooden footpath which ran along one side of the bridge. He could see no movement along its whole length. He was nearly over onto the other bank when only twenty yards ahead of him, two figures suddenly appeared—two German soldiers returning from duty on the other bank of the river to the village. They stepped onto the bridge and immediately saw him.

Desperately, Doug looked behind him, seeking an avenue of escape. The Germans were too close for him to run.

"Halt," he heard.

The Germans approached him.

"Votre papiers," one said in bad French.

Seven days had elapsed since Doug had baled out of Yorker.

CHAPTER 27

As Jeff moved off after burying his parachute, he considered the possibility of making contact with some of the other crew members. From discussions with escapees who had visited the squadron, he knew that loneliness in enemy occupied country, being unable to talk to anyone, would be one of the major obstacles to be overcome if he was to elude capture. He felt that if he was able to pair up with one of the others, the companionship would be the means of eliminating that hurdle for one another to a great extent.

Reluctantly at last, he reasoned that the chances of making contact with any of the crew would be too remote and would waste too much time. He had been the last to bale out of Yorker. All the others had left the plane long before he had and would have landed far from where he himself had crashed down onto the soil of France.

As he abandoned the idea of seeking out any of the others, he increased his pace. He had calculated that they would have landed somewhere east of Chalons Sur Marne.

By pushing on slightly west of a southerly direction, he would be heading for the Spanish border. This was his goal. He realised the difficulties in achieving it. His only real hope lay in making contact somehow with the French underground.

Using the stars visible through the lace-work pattern of the leaves and twigs above him as his guide, Jeff strode out with strong steady steps. Thinking of the long journey ahead of him he did not hurry.

In the darkness, he managed to avoid crashing into the trees which appeared in his path and even though he stumbled and nearly fell several times, he avoided the worst of the rough uneven ground.

The difficulty of making his way through the forest without falling was tiring. His legs began to ache, his breathing was heavier. He also was forced to rest more often, but after sitting or squatting for only a few minutes to regain his breath, he would once again resume his journey.

He encountered several small streams which he was able to wade through. Twice however, during the cold dark morning hours, he came to streams which were too deep to wade.

Each time as he came out of the trees onto the bank and looked down to see the wide stream flowing swiftly past, a feeling of depression seized him. Despondently, he watched the waters reflecting the light from the stars above. As he slowly clambered down the bank, the far side appeared to be unattainable. Each time he had the hope that the stream was fordable, but each time he was quickly disappointed, as he probed with the branch of a tree.

After walking several hundred yards up and downstream seeking shallower water he resignedly undressed. Tying all his clothing into as small a bundle as possible, he pushed out into the swiftly running water. He shivered as the cold stabbed its needles into his flesh. Striking out with a side-arm stroke, he endeavoured to hold his clothing above water with his free hand. The current took him with it as he slowly swam across. When he finally touched bottom on the far side, he found he had been carried quite some distance downstream.

He dried himself as well as possible with his singlet and quickly dressed, shivering in the cold. His clothing was only a little damp and he set out at a faster pace to warm himself through exertion.

Like the others, he used roads and lanes where possible and skirted the vineyards he encountered. During the night he also had to cross a railway line. Before crossing he reconnoitred for a distance in each direction. Quickly he slid through the fence, ran across the track and through the far fence. He was in an area of vineyards and carefully he made his way beside hedges and fences, trying to keep to shadows where he could. A few dogs barked but he made his way through undetected. At the last vineyard before the forest came to meet him, he carefully made his way towards the farmhouse. Making as little noise as possible, he searched round for a bottle or a can which he could use to carry water. Finally, beneath a tree on the hard-packed earth yard, he found a pile of used wine bottles. Feeling carefully for one which had a cork, he gently eased it out. Quietly, he made his way back to the edge of the vineyard and through its hedge into the trees beyond. As he once again moved through in the shelter of the forest, he breathed more easily. To his surprise he discovered he was perspiring. At the first stream he came to, he rinsed and filled the bottle.

By dawn he had many miles behind him. As the sun began to lighten the darkness, to which he had become accustomed, and had tinted the leaves above him with brightness, he sank tiredly down upon a soft bank. Wearily, he took out his emergency rations and ate some chocolate. After resting for ten minutes, he pushed himself up off the ground and forced his weary limbs to carry him for another hour.

He hid for the day in bushes above a small dry, eroded water channel. Trees stood close round and he was able to camouflage his hiding-place with piles of leaves so that he was completely hidden from sight.

Once he felt secure, he lay back upon the soft earth and slept. When he awoke, he was stiff and sore. His legs ached and his whole body still was tense from the nights exertion. He sat up, rubbing at his eyes. He felt he was living a dream.

Slowly he became conscious of where he was. Hurriedly he searched round for any sign of activity and slowly relaxed. Opening up the emergency pack, he ate a little, drank some water, then carefully removed his officers' bars and his navigator's wing from his battle dress tunic using the issue pocket knife. He slid out the bar compass from his collar and checked direction.

During the morning he studied the map of France which he carried as part of his escape kit. It was a small scale map which only showed main roads, the principal cities, towns and villages, the larger streams and the railway lines. From it he estimated that he was east of the Marne River somewhere in the vicinity of St. Dizier. The distance to the Spanish border seemed immense. His route would take him past Chaumont, Dijon, Lyons and he hoped eventually around the northern Mediterranean Coast to Spain.

At noon he ate a little of the contents of his emergency rations, drank sparingly of the water and again tried to sleep. He dozed fitfully during the day, tense and alert for the first signs of danger.

It came in mid-afternoon. Jeff awoke, suddenly aware of strange sounds. Carefully he parted the bushes. In the distance south of him he could discern some German soldiers slowly beating the forest towards where he lay concealed. His hackles rose as he searched for more. A line of Germans was slowly working its way to him. As they drew closer he could hear them calling to one another. Gathering his few belongings together he squeezed himself down into a small eroded water way, hurriedly scooped leaves round him and quietly broke some branches from the bushes closest to him, making certain as he did, that the bushes did not shake and betray his position. The branches he laid over himself as best he could.

With his heart-beat a drum in his ears, he peered through the foliage. The searching troops drew closer. Two gradually made their way towards his hiding place. With the bayonets fixed to their rifles ,they disinterestedly jabbed under bushes and into piles of leaves as they walked along talking to one another.

Their conversation, which he could not understand,

became louder. As they approached the bushes where he hid, he held his breath, turned his face to the ground and pushed down into the hollow. He heard the bayonets stab into the leaves around him, expecting one to strike into his back.

Then they had passed, still talking to one another. Their voices receded and became fainter. When he slowly lifted his head, he saw two sets of boots moving away from him. Jeff remained, tense, perspiring and trembling for long minutes. Straining his ears, he listened until the last vestige of sound from the German patrol came back to him, and then waited further long minutes before he sat up, thankful for what had been a narrow escape.

The tension of the period left him exhausted. Wearily he reached for the bottle of water. Tipping it up to his lips, he drank a long draught. He slept no more that day.

As evening drew in, he eased himself cautiously out of the bushes and set out once again on his journey.

The pattern of the next week was similar to the first night and day. Walking by night through woods where he was able, skirting round villages and vineyards. Where possible, he used lanes and minor roads and several times he had to quickly leave the roadway as vehicles or pedestrians approached him. The long night hours dragged as he forced himself to keep going. His whole body rebelled against the continual exertion.

During the nights as he walked, he searched for food at isolated farm-houses. In vegetable gardens he dug up turnips and potatoes which he ate raw. He made one attempt to get eggs, but the noise the hens created as he took the eggs, scared him from attempting it again. Regularly, he was able to get milk to drink from cows in fields he passed through. Squeezing the milk into the bottle he had taken on the first night, he carried some with him after drinking his fill. He forded and swam several streams and occasionally was able to use a bridge.

By day he hid, usually in woods but once, at an isolated farm, he spent the day in a haystack tucked away in a corner of the farm. He managed to sleep for part of each day but he was tense and his sleep disturbed by vivid dreams.

Slowly he got weaker. Exhaustion gripped him at all

times. The loneliness began to prey on him. Having no one to talk to, no one to confide in or to discuss the situation with, began to weigh heavily upon him. The slightest noise startled him. He was constantly on edge, nervous and jumpy. He felt dirty and cursed himself, as he felt his beard, for not bringing a razor with him. If he reached a stream towards the early morning, he rinsed out his socks and dried them during the day.

The deep feeling of exhaustion made him increasingly careless. Early on the eighth night he was wearily walking down a narrow country road. Forest was on both sides but in his tiredness he kept to the road. It appeared to be well used and Jeff was waiting until the first sign of a village or farms appeared, before seeking the protection of the woods.

Jeff did not hear the cycle, ridden by the German soldier, until it was nearly on him. The German was riding back to his billet in a village ahead of them. The tyres made little sound on the dirt road. When Jeff became aware of the danger, he sprang off the road into the water filled ditch to seek the protection of the forest.

"Halt," the German screamed when he saw Jeff move only yards ahead of him. Jumping off his cycle, he quickly unslung his rifle.

"Achtung," he called, in German, "Come back here."

When he heard the second call, Jeff paused, then began to move away again.

"I shall fire," the German warned.

Slowly, despondently, Jeff turned and walked towards the German.

"Who are you?" he was asked.

Jeff was unable to understand. When he did not reply, the German struck Jeff on the face with the flat of his hand.

"Answer Schweinhund,"

Jeff reeled back and nearly fell. Angrily, he faced the other, determined not to talk. The rifle was still trained upon him. In the darkness, the whole scene seemed unreal. It had the appearance of one of the ghastly dreams which had plagued his sleep over the preceding days.

Finally, the German soldier gestured towards the cycle

lying on its side on the roadway behind him. Slowly Jeff bent over, took hold of the handle-bars and lifted it upright.

The German gestured to go ahead.

"You will come with me," he said.

They moved off slowly, Jeff ahead pushing the cycle, the German close behind with his rifle pointed at Jeff's back. As they walked along the road, Jeff's feeling of complete exhaustion had left him. A feeling of burning anger gripped him. Anger against himself, for not being more alert, and anger against his captor, for the slap on the face and for taking him prisoner.

Determination to make an effort to get away seized Jeff. The position seemed hopeless but he did not give up hope. The opportunity arose when they had gone about a quarter of a mile. In the field beside them, an animal, startled by their movement, dashed away into the bushes. With an exclamation, the German turned towards the noise. Swiftly, Jeff flung the cycle back against him. The rifle's muzzle caught in the spokes of the rear wheel and as Jeff pushed again, the German and the cycle went down tangled together, the rifle was torn from his grip.

Desperately, Jeff flung himself upon his captor, aiming rabbit killer punches at the back of his neck.

"Gott in himmel," the soldier cried as, half-stunned, he rolled from under the cycle and tried to grapple with Jeff. They rolled off the roadway and as they struck at one another they slid down into the muddy water-logged ditch beside it.

The German, older and more solidly built than Jeff, managed to land a few hard punches to Jeff's chest, but as they came to rest in the ditch, Jeff was on top. Sitting up with his legs astride the German he drove his fist time and time again into the other's face. The German twisted, his right hand went to his belt and suddenly Jeff realised that he had drawn a long bladed knife. Before he could escape it, the knife slashed at him, he parried it with his left arm and felt the blade slice into his fore-arm. In a blinding rage, he gained renewed strength. Catching hold of the German's right wrist above the knife, Jeff stumbled up in the water and mud. With a savage twist, he forced the German over to lie face down in the muddy ditch. He wrenched the arm up between the shoulder blades in a vicious hammerlock.

Falling upon the German, he forced his face down into the mud. As the German struggled, striving desperately to raise his mouth from the suffocating mud, Jeff ground his knees into the small of his back. His right hand maintained the pressure on the hammerlock and with his slashed left arm he pushed hard down upon the German soldier's head. The blood flowed from his wound to redden the mud in which the German was drowning.

Slowly the struggles began to weaken. The German's legs and left arm slowly stopped scrabbling at the slippery mud. Then seemingly with a sigh, he was still.

As the struggles ceased, Jeff remained astride the dead German still angry and determined. When he realised that the other was dead he slowly rose. A feeling of horror overcame him. He felt cold, he shivered. As he gazed down at the dead man in the mud at his feet, nausea shook him. He turned towards the bank and vomited. The spasms wracked his body for long minutes.

When he calmed down, he again became conscious of the knife wound in his arm. It was still bleeding. He had already lost a considerable amount of blood. Taking out his handkerchief, he bound it as securely as he could, using his right hand and his teeth to tie the knot. He was covered in mud and exhausted.

When he had regained his composure and his breath, he realised that he would have to hide the dead body, the rifle and the cycle to avoid possible reprisals to the villagers nearby and to prevent an immediate search of the neighbourhood, during which he himself would probably be discovered.

Laboriously, he dragged the dead German up the bank of the road ditch into the trees. Unable to use his left hand to any great extent, he took hold of the dead man's collar in his right hand and dragged him through the trees for about forty yards and hid it in undergrowth and fallen timber. Going back for the bike and rifle, he threw them near the body and covered them with fallen branches and leaves.

Upon regaining the road, Jeff felt as though he had come to the end of his strength. He knew he could go no further without assistance. He knew he would have to seek help. Picking up his bundle and the bottle of water from where he had dropped them before attacking the German soldier, he slowly, wearily and dispiritedly, walked down the road, keeping his eyes and ears alert for the approach of any new danger.

The trees on either side of the road seemed to press in upon him. He felt that they were squeezing him into a smaller and smaller space. Unable to put his struggle against the German out of his mind, the whole episode was relived time and again in every detail. On operations, death was remote. His killing of the German was his first encounter face to face with the enemy.

Slowly, he dragged his exhausted body along the road until the trees to his right began to thin, a hedge appeared and in a break in the hedge he saw a gate. Tucked away, some distance behind it, stood the farmhouse nearly surrounded by trees. As though petrified by indecision, Jeff stood by the gate for fully ten minutes, unable to go in or to move away. He remained, his hand on the gate-latch, seemingly without the strength or the will to lift it. The decision was taken from him. From the direction he had come, he heard the sound of a motor. Quickly, he lifted the gate latch and swung the gate open only sufficiently for him to squeeze through. He eased it closed and lowered the latch. Crouching down, in the cover of the hedge to the side of the gate, he watched the lorry speed past.

He nearly collapsed as he tried to stand. His head spun, his legs felt too weak to support him. Leaning against the gate, he waited until he had recovered slightly, then he stumbled up the track leading to the farm house.

The die was cast. His freedom depended upon the loyalties of the people living there. If they were collaborators, his bid to escape capture was ended. If not, if they were loyal French, they would possibly help him. Jeff felt resigned to either fate as the dark shadows of the house and its outbuildings loomed larger and larger.

Stumbling over implements, boxes and the assorted articles lying on the ground, Jeff made his way round to the rear of the house. With hesitant step, he walked between small, well tended vegetable plots to the large door. Through chinks in the curtains drawn across the windows beside the door, he could see light shining through. He could hear voices. Uttering a prayer, he raised his hand and knocked. Nervously he waited. Perspiration wet and chilled his face. His left arm throbbed and lay practically useless by his side.

The voices were silenced. A chair scraped, heavy footsteps approached the door. As the door opened, the bearded face of the tall, heavy-set French farmer silhouetted by the light behind him was close to Jeff.

"Merde!" the farmer exclaimed as he took in Jeff's muddy, unkempt figure.

"Je suis Australien," Jeff managed to say with difficulty, "Anglais--R.A.F."

As he collapsed in a faint, the Frenchmann, moving quickly, caught him under the armpits and gently carried him into the warm kitchen.

CHAPTER 28

As his mind struggled free from the mists of unconsciousness, Jeff slowly became aware, not only of the throbbing pain of his wounded arm, but also of a feeling of comfort and relaxation. For a moment, he lay still, his eyes closed, not thinking, but enjoying for the first time in so many days, the luxurious feeling of awakening between sheets in a comfortable bed. As the events since his escape intruded upon his mind, he thrust himself up from the bed in a state of near panic.

Only vaguely could he recall arriving at the farmhouse. He had no way of knowing what had happened since his collapse at the door. He feared that he had been handed over to the German authorities. However, as he looked frantically around the room, he was re-assured. The trip-hammering of his heart calmed down.

It was a typical farmhouse bedroom. A large room, it was dominated by the huge, comfortable bed in which he lay. Solid, dark-stained furniture hugged the walls and rugs covered the floor. Through the open windows, morning sunlight filtered through lace curtains and he could hear birds singing.

He had been bathed and shaved while he had been unconscious and his wound had been attended to. Strips of white cloth bandaged it. As he reluctantly threw the bed clothes aside to get up from the bed, he saw he had been dressed in clean, if well worn pyjamas. Gazing round the room, he saw that his own clothes had been washed and ironed and were neatly folded upon a large armchair which squatted down beside a window. After the long days of having to wear dirty clothing, the scent of cleanliness permeating the room was pleasing in itself.

He felt weak and nearly stumbled, as he walked across the short space to the chair. Questions pummelled his mind, as he hurriedly undressed and washed in the large china basin which stood on a carved, wooden wash-stand in a corner. As he put on his clothing, his fingers fumbled with the clips and buttons. He felt weak and exhausted. His arm throbbed painfully, but his whole body also ached from the exertion he had demanded of it. Finally, he sank wearily into the chair and put on his shoes and socks.

As he struggled with the laces, the door quietly opened. The noise of its opening, slight as it was, startled him. Fear, momentarily, knifed into him. He half rose, then sank back with a sigh of relief when the attractive face of a teen-aged French girl appeared in the half-open doorway.

"Bon jour, Monsieur," she said brightly, "are you rested?"

Questions he needed answers for, tumbled one over another in his mind, but he could only reply briefly.

"Thank you, yes."

"C'est bon," the girl remarked as she entered the room.

"My name is Mignon, what is your's?"

When Jeff had told her his name, she chattered on gaily in a charming mixture of French and English.

"You have slept over one day," she said matter-of-factly, "you were very tired, as well as very wounded."

She led him from the bedroom and preceded him down the heavy wooden staircase leading from the upper floor where he had slept. Jeff realised that they would have carried his heavy, unconscious weight up the stairs to the bedroom. A large living room lay at the bottom of the staircase. The girl led him along a passageway beside the stairs and he found himself once again in the kitchen where he had collapsed.

The farmer and his wife were seated at the large, scrubbed, wooden table when he entered. They rose quickly and went to him. Taking him by the arms, they gently took him to a comfortable chair at the head of the table.

Grasping for the correct words in English, assisted by their daughter, they enquired how he was feeling and urged him to return to the bed for more rest.

Shaking his head, he replied.

"No I must not. I have to move on. It is dangerous for you if I stay."

Quickly, they said that he had to stay with them until he was completely well.

Jeff found that he had been fortunate in stumbling upon a passionately loyal, French family. There were only the mother, father and the daughter, Mignon, remaining on the farm. Two grown sons had fled to England after Dunkirk. They were serving with the Free French forces. Jeff introduced himself and briefly explained the circumstances of his sudden appearance at their doorway.

The farmer, Pierre Moreau and his wife Michelle, had lived in the district since their marriage nearly thirty years before. Pierre was a large man. Only of medium height, he had however, the broad shoulders, thick limbs and deep chest which denoted great strength. His mane of dark curly hair was liberally splashed with grey and two days stubble of beard darkened his chin.

His wife was a slight, fragile-seeming person, but as she quickly prepared a huge meal for him, Jeff realised that beneath the fragility lay strength of another kind. The daughter Mignon was obviously the great delight of both her parents. She was an attractive, dark-haired, slim girl, on the threshold of beautiful womanhood. As she moved around the room, her parents' eyes often followed her with loving pride.

Eventually, as he ravenously ate the meal which

Madame Moreau had placed before him, Jeff was able to explain more fully, the details of his attempt to elude capture.

He told them of his life and death struggle with the German soldier and of how he had disposed of the body. As he spoke, between mouthfuls of food, the three people were quiet, listening intently to every word. Only when he told of killing the German did they interrupt with cries of approval.

When he had finished, the farmer rose to his feet from the chair near Jeff, went to the cupboard behind and returned with a bottle of wine and glasses. Filling four glasses he handed one to each and took one himself. Gravely, he raised it to Jeff.

"Bon sante," he said, lifting it to his lips and drinking. The mother and daughter did likewise.

Self-consciously, Jeff drank down his own glass.

As he sat back in the chair, Jeff felt drowsy after the meal and wine, the gnawing hunger of the previous week was nearly forgotten. Busily, the mother and daughter cleared away the dishes and began washing them. Pierre leant towards him.

"You will want to move on?" he enquired, choosing the words slowly and deliberately.

"I must," Jeff replied.

"But first you must rest," the farmer stated firmly. "Your wound, it must be better and you must become stronger."

As though to add emphasis to the farmer's words a feeling of weakness suddenly gripped Jeff. He felt cold and faint. Only by exerting his will-power was he able to remain upright in the chair. Gripping the arms tightly, he closed his eyes, beads of perspiration appeared upon his brow.

Quickly, the farmer and his wife were beside him, fussing over him and urging him to return to bed. Gently he refused, but he allowed them to take him into the living room, where he stretched out on the large settee in front of a large open fireplace. In spite of his protests Madame Moreau soon had a fire blazing. In its warmth, Jeff began to feel stronger. The faintness left him. However, the spasm made him realise how weak he was and how unfit for further travel he had become. As these thoughts passed through his mind, he dozed off and slept for several hours.

When he awakened, late in the afternoon, he felt stronger. However, he realised that it would be several days before he would be capable of travelling any distance. This worried him. He feared for these people who had befriended him. Lying back on the settee, gazing into the flames in the fireplace, he decided to inform the Moreaus that he would leave their house and find a hiding place in the woods nearby. He would remain there until he was fit to travel.

However, before he was able to tell them of his decision, they had taken the planning away from him. While he slept, Mignon had been sent to the local village to inform the resistance contact of his presence at the farm. Preparations were already being made to assist him on his way, when he had sufficiently recovered.

Pierre explained to him during the evening over dinner, that there was no active resistance group in the area. There was little necessity for it. German troops were comparatively few, there was no industry and little other activity which could require the building up of a resistance group. However, when an emergency did arise, there were several men who could be relied upon to do what was necessary. As Jeff ate his dinner, these men were already at work, disposing of the German soldier's body, his cycle and his rifle. They would be buried where they could not be found. The farmer told Jeff that soon he would be visited by the local man, who could make contact with the resistance organisation which would help him in his bid to escape from France.

As he retired to the bedroom, which had been the eldest son's, Jeff felt even stronger. The rest, the food, the attention he had received, all had helped him to recuperate. Although still too weak to travel, he felt fit enough to insist upon hiding out at least during the day. He feared that the sudden appearance of a German patrol was still possible. It would mean death for Pierre and his family if he was captured on the farm.

In spite of their protests, the following morning after the

early breakfast, he went out with Pierre as he left the house to begin his day's work on the farm. They decided that the safest position was in a far corner of the property where a vineyard edged onto a tree clad hill. There was good cover and from the hill's slope he had a full view of the farm. He remained there throughout the day. At midday, Mignon brought some lunch and a flask of wine out to him. She sat with him, chattering gaily, while he ate.

At dusk, he carefully made his way back to the rear of the farmhouse. Thankfully, he let himself into the kitchen, closing the door behind him.

Later, as they were cleaning away the dinner dishes, a gentle double knock sounded upon the kitchen door. In spite of their expecting it, the sudden sound paralysed them, breathless with stabs of fear, for a long moment.

Opening the door, Pierre welcomed the man who entered. He was in fact, what he appeared to be, the local doctor. In his profession, he was able to travel throughout the countryside and received a petrol allowance from the authorities which enabled him to keep his ancient car on the road. It was a valuable asset in emergencies.

He was a short, slim, middle-aged man with a slight stoop and an austere manner. He was quietly spoken, had a gentleness about him, and was the exact antithesis of what Jeff had expected in a resistance leader. However, as he questioned Jeff at length, searchingly probing for proof of Jeff's claims to be a shot-down R.A.F. flyer, the quality of the man showed. When satisfied beyond all doubt, he outlined briefly what would be done to enable Jeff to continue upon his way. Firstly, contact had to be made with the resistance group in Lyons. Forged papers would be prepared and plans made to transport him initially to Lyons, then along the escape route to the Spanish border. The doctor spoke in such a calm sure way, he gave the impression that it was simply a matter of routine before Jeff was back in England. He inspected Jeff's wounded arm and cleaned, dressed and re-bandaged it.

Jeff knew that the dangers were great, not only for himself, but for every person who would help him along the way. However, the calm voice of the doctor instilled confidence into him.

As he prepared to leave, the doctor opened his black bag. Taking out his prescription pad he scribbled a formula upon it.

"Have this made up at the Chemist," he said to Pierre, "you have a slight upset in your stomach. That will cover up for my visit here tonight."

Turning to Jeff, he asked,

"Do you have any passport photographs?"

During the early weeks on the squadron, Jeff had had photos taken for this eventuality. Taking them from his battle-dress tunic pocket, he handed them to the doctor.

After inspecting them, he placed them towards the back of his pad.

"They are good," he said, returning the pad to his bag and closing it. "I shall send them off to Lyons tomorrow."

As he quietly went out through the kitchen door, he turned and gave a small salute.

"Bon sante to you," he said, "a privilege to have met you. Be careful, German patrols are still about."

"Thank you for everything," Jeff replied.

On the third day after Jeff had begun hiding in the woods, his fears were realised. The squad of German soldiers, in two open vehicles, sped along the road and turned into the farm. The cars roared up the track to the front of the house. The soldiers hurriedly got out and in two sections surrounded the farm buildings. From his distant hiding place, he saw two, who seemed to be in charge, go up to the door of the farm house and pound upon it. It opened and Pierre appeared for a moment. The Germans pushed him back into the house and all three disappeared from view.

Jeff, fearing he had been seen and betrayed to the German authorities was worried more for the Moreaus than himself. He slowly edged further up the hill where undergrowth was thick. He inched his way in, being careful not to make his track obvious. After settling in, well concealed from view, he parted the brush sufficiently to keep the farm in view.

He saw three further German soldiers enter the house. After inspecting his pockets, he felt sure that he had left

354

nothing which could betray his presence.

Others searched the outbuildings and the yard. With their rifles, they probed in the wood heap and the manure piled against the barn wall. When this proved fruitless, they spread out and beat their way through the fields.

Nearly an hour elapsed, before the German in charge emerged from the house and called the squad together. As they climbed in to the cars and roared out through the gateway of the farm, Jeff sighed his relief. He was trembling as he carefully rose from his hiding-place and watched the two vehicles out of sight.

The Moreaus came out of the house. Mignon raced across the fields towards him. Slowly he walked down through the trees to meet her.

"They are satisfied," she breathlessly said as she came up. A smile lit her face as she spoke.

"They searched and searched and found nothing. I thought ma mere would die."

Although she urged him to return with her, Jeff insisted upon remaining in the woods until darkness. When he finally did enter the kitchen, he was met by a happy babble of voices telling him of the Germans' fruitless search.

Two nights later, the doctor called again. He had heard of the Germans' visit, but was not greatly concerned. They had searched many other farms in the area as a matter of routine. The disappearance of the German soldier, whom Jeff had killed, had brought no repercussions to the local people and he had probably been listed as absent without leave.

As the doctor tended and re-bandaged Jeff's arm, he told him to be ready to move the following day. A local farmer would come to lead him to the village. He would be hidden until transport could be arranged to take him to Lyons. Contact had been made with the resistance group there and he was expected within the following seven days.

It was with a strange feeling of sadness, that Jeff sat down to dinner with the family that evening after the doctor had departed. They ate a quiet meal, hardly speaking. Jeff felt that a great bond had been tied between them. Madame Moreau fussed over him, Pierre brought out wine and they sat sipping it at the table long after they had finished their meal. Tears brought sparkle to Mignon's eyes as she sat in her chair looking at him.

After they had cleared the table and washed up the dishes, they remained in the kitchen, recalling the details of his stay until late at night. When they finally rose to retire, Madame and Mignon both came and kissed him on the cheek. Pierre took his hand and squeezed it solemnly between his own two, strong, toil-worn hands.

"It has been good for us to have you," he said hesitantly, "we feel, we have done a little for the war."

The following morning, before he had risen from the bed, Madame Moreau entered the room. In her arms she carried a complete set of clothing.

"Put these on," she said.

Then, fumbling for the correct words in English, she told Jeff that they had belonged to her second son. If he was to move about, he had to be dressed like one of the local people.

Taking Jeff's own clothing she left the room.

Jeff rose and dressed in the clothes she had given him. They were a little short for him, but he quickly saw the wisdom of her action when he looked in the mirror. In these, he would blend more easily into the local scene. When he went down to breakfast, Mignon darted over to him.

"You look splendid," she exclaimed inspecting him, "just like mon frére."

During the morning, Jeff burned his own clothing. He crushed the ashes into the ground after sifting through them for any metal clips and buttons which he buried.

An hour after lunch, an elderly farmer appeared, driving five cows through the farm gateway. He was Jeff's guide to the village. Pierre explained that the Germans would never suspect two farmers driving a herd of cows.

No time was wasted. Jeff was quickly introduced to the old man who was evidently enjoying the role he had been called upon to play. Enthusiastically, he pumped Jeff's hand.

He said his goodbyes to the Moreaus, Mignon threw her

356

arms around him in a tearful embrace. As he and the old farmer drove the cows through the gateway onto the road, he turned and waved gratefully to the three who had risked their lives to help and protect him. It seemed impossible to Jeff that only a few short days had elapsed since he had stumbled bleeding and exhausted, up to the door of the farmhouse. As they drew away from the farm, and trees began to press towards the narrow roadway on both sides, Jeff turned for one last look at the farm which had given him shelter. Pierre, his wife and Mignon still stood at the gateway. Behind them, the well-tended fields stretched away to the tree clad slopes where he had hidden from the German troops. Smoke rose from the farmhouse chimney, reaching lazily upwards in the early afternoon calm. They returned his last wave and were lost to sight as the road curved.

Using the long stick which Pierre had given him for the purpose, Jeff assisted the old man to slowly urge the cows forward. The slow pace of their progress irritated Jeff. Impatiently, he began to force the cows into a faster gait. The old farmer restrained him with a knowing smile.

"Lentement, mon ami," he spoke quietly, in a halting mixture of French and a little English, "Else the Boche will suspect we are not what we seem."

Curbing his impatience, Jeff followed his example and slowly they made their way towards the village, a total distance of nearly ten kilometres. They encountered very little traffic on the way, an occasional farm cart and military trucks. The old man acknowledged the greetings of the other farmers and ignored the trucks. However, as they neared the outskirts of the village, they saw a detachment of eight Germans soldiers marching towards them. Instinctively, Jeff searched round for cover in which to hide. Gently, the old man touched his leg with his stick.

"Attention," he said quietly, "do as I do."

As they drew near the soldiers, he adopted an obsequious air as they passed the leading file, he doffed his old cap with a slight bow.

"Bon jour messeuirs," he called, "bon jour."

They merely grunted an inaudible reply, but passed by without a second glance at them. As the sound of their marching feet receded behind them, the old man spat on the roadway.

"Cochons," he muttered to himself.

The roadway climbed a rise and from the crest, through the trees lining both sides, Jeff saw the village appear before him. It was larger than he had anticipated. In the distance, he could see the larger buildings, the stores, the hotel and others which formed its heart, but on the outskirts, small, white-walled cottages lined the roadway in two neat rows.

"Go into the third house we pass on the right." the old man said quietly, "they expect you."

His eyes twinkled as he spoke. He had enjoyed his sortie against the enemy.

"Thank you, merci, monsieur," Jeff replied gratefully.

"I thank you," the old man replied, "bonne chance."

Slowly they drew near the houses, it seemed another eternity to Jeff before he was able to slip away from the cows and the gallant old man, through the neat little wooden gateway of the third house. As he turned into it, he saluted the old farmer and received a slight wave and a beaming smile in reply.

The door of the cottage opened as he walked up the pathway. A middle-aged couple greeted him.

"Welcome", the tall, thick-set man said, holding out his hand.

As Jeff shook it, the woman closed the door behind them and also shook him by the hand. When he tried to thank them for sheltering him, they silenced him with expressive waves of their hands.

"Mais non," they exclaimed, "notre privilege."

CHAPTER 29

The sequence of events which followed over the succeeding weeks seemed to unfold like the scenario of one of the Hollywood B grade films which Punch, the Squadron Intelligence Officer, had scrounged to relieve tension in the flying crews. Although he was the principal actor in the scenario, it seemed to Jeff that he was not a part of it, that he was standing aside, remote from the actuality. It seemed more like episodes of a film acted out by others, rather than something in which he was personally involved.

The Lamys, as the couple were named, fussed over him, protected him and ensured that at all times he was safe from discovery by the Germans. They mapped out, with rough sketches, an escape route through lanes leading from behind the house should it be required. He did not have to make use of it.

On the first evening he was with them, Jeff was visited by the doctor and another man from the village. Shortly after supper, served in the large kitchen, there was a discreet knock upon the window. Carefully parting the curtains, Mr. Lamy inspected the callers. After recognising them, he opened the door and welcomed the two men who entered quickly and quietly. The doctor introduced the second man as Pierre, explaining that he was a local produce merchant who made twice weekly trips to Lyons with vegetables and other farm produce. He had an old Renault truck in which he made the journeys, but which served also as transport, when needed, for the local resistance. He also acted as the courier between the local resistance and that in Lyons. He stated that he had had few opportunities for action and it was immediately apparent to Jeff that he relished this chance to do something for France and the Allies against "les boches", as he referred to the Germans.

As Jeff's hand disappeared in the grip of Pierre's huge fist, each took his measure of the other and liked what he saw.

"Bon soir, bon soir," Pierre said, his face widening in a great grin as he pumped Jeff's hand up and down.

"It is my pleasure to meet you," he added.

The four men sat around the kitchen table. Mr. Lamy produced a bottle of red wine and four glasses. As he poured the wine, the doctor and Pierre briefly outlined the plan for Jeff's escape.

Both men spoke fair English and without any attempt to disguise the difficulties which lay ahead of him, they detailed what he could expect.

He was to remain with the Lamys for another week. On Pierre's next trip to Lyons he would contact the resistance there and make arrangements for a "safe house" where Jeff could stay. On the following trip he would take Jeff.

He would be hidden on the truck under produce and then be driven to the "safe house". There he would receive forged papers and would remain until he could be moved safely further south by train to Perpignan in southern France. This would be the jumping off point for his crossing of the Franco-Spanish border. It meant crossing over the Pyrenees. Once in Spain, he was to make his way to the British Consulate in Barcelona, avoiding the Spanish police as he would the Germans in France.

Told so briefly and matter-of-factly, it seemed it would be a purely routine operation. However, as the two men then went on to describe the difficulties he would encounter, the dangers he would face, the need for correct papers as he moved through France, the language problem, the constant possibility of being detected because of the continual spot-checks by the Germans or through some stupid slip, Jeff began to despair.

Seeing the expression on his face, Pierre leant forward across the table. With a hearty laugh he slapped Jeff on the shoulder.

"No worry, mon ami," he chuckled, "we will get you through."

The two men stayed until nearly curfew, drinking wine and plying Jeff with questions concerning the progress of the war. They were hungry for news. They both listened regularly to the broadcasts from Britain, but they sought confirmation of what they had heard and were eager for additional information.

When they had gone, once again through the rear kitchen door and the back lanes, a hushed quiet appeared to descend upon the room.

Mr. Lamy finally broke the silence.

"They are noisy those two," he said with a gentle, affectionate smile. "Sometimes I wonder how it is that the Germans do not hear them, they talk so loud."

Then quickly, thinking that Jeff may have mistaken his meaning, he added, "But they are good men and very brave."

The week passed slowly for Jeff. In the anticipation of what would be a major stage of his attempted escape, he felt cramped in the small house. He could not move outside in daylight and was also careful not to pass by open windows fronting onto the street which went to the village. His presence was concealed even from the occupants of the nearby houses, some of whom were suspected collaborators.

On his first night, Jeff slept in a small bedroom on the upper floor. It had been their daughter's room, but she had long since married and lived in Paris. Jeff spent a great deal of time in this room. Partly for reasons of security so that he remained concealed, but also because of sheer weakness. He began to feel the reaction from the tension and the long periods of exertion since he had parachuted out of Yorker. His arm had nearly healed, but a heavy lassitude had taken hold of him. He felt weak and drained of all energy. Mrs. Lamy, with a motherly solicitude, fussed over him. She brought him bowls of broth when he did not feel like eating a full meal downstairs. Jeff endeavoured to throw off this feeling of lassitude, but for the first two days he spent in the house, he slept much of the time.

Pierre made a second evening visit to the cottage. He was concerned when he saw the navigator's condition.

"Are you ill?" he asked anxiously, "you do not look well."

"Its only tiredness," Jeff replied. "Once I get moving again, I shall be all right."

On his last night with the Lamys, they made the evening meal a farewell celebration. Mrs. Lamy had gathered supplies to bake a cake for him. She placed a treasured lace cloth on the table, her husband had procured a bottle of fine wine. The meal was delicious and as he sat with Mr. Lamy at the table, smoking after the meal, sipping a glass of wine, Jeff felt content. His assurance began to return and the enervating lassitude began to lift from him.

The Doctor and Pierre came at 8.30, once again approaching from the rear of the house. They brought final instructions. However, the doctor had come mainly because of Pierre's concern for Jeff. Without making it obvious, he watched Jeff during the evening and satisfied himself that the navigator would be well enough to undertake the next stage of his journey.

It was still dark when Jeff slipped through the kitchen door the following morning. Mr. Lamy, bulky in a heavy overcoat, woolen scarf and large cloth cap, accompanied him. Before they left, Mrs. Lamy had given him a bundle which contained, as well as food, two pairs of socks, some handkerchiefs and an old razor of her husband. Before he left, she clasped him to her and, with tears in her eyes, she kissed him on the cheek.

"May le bon Dieu go with you," she whispered.

Jeff felt the tears well up in his own eyes as he kissed her in return and squeezed her two hands between his own.

"I shall never forget you," he said with emotion, "I shall always remember your kindness and courage."

In the darkness, they made their way carefully along the leafy lanes through the back areas of the village. After walking for about fifteen minutes, Mr. Lamy stopped Jeff with a gentle pressure on the arm.

"This is it," he said quietly.

Ahead of them to the side of the lane, a large barn-like building loomed up in the darkness. Mr. Lamy led Jeff to a door at the rear of the building. After giving a triple knock as a signal, he unlatched it and they went into a darkness which was complete. As they stood there, uncertain of where to move, they heard the scratch of a match, and in its light they saw Pierre's face appear eerily a few feet to their right. He lit a lamp and came over to them.

"Come with me," he said to Jeff, taking his arm and leading him to the rear of the ancient truck which stood in the centre of the building.

Working quickly for the next thirty minutes in the dim

light of the lamp, they loaded the truck with crates of poultry, boxes of eggs and vegetables, both loose and in sacks. In the centre of the load was a hollow space, the approximate shape and size of a coffin. In this space, Jeff would lie hidden during the journey. The produce completely covered it, except for the area two feet in from the tail-gate, over which Jeff would climb to enter his hiding-place, when it was time to leave.

Before first light, Mr. Lamy rose to leave. He clasped Jeff's hand.

"Bonne chance my young friend," he said gravely, "I thank you for the opportunity to do something for my poor country."

"And I thank you, mon ami," Jeff replied as he walked with Mr. Lamy to the door. They shook hands warmly. Jeff saw him out and waited until he had disappeared, merging into the protective darkness. Quietly, he closed the door and went back to the truck, to wait with Pierre until it was time to leave. The minutes dragged slowly by. Impatiently, Jeff alternately sat down and walked around the small space in the barn. Pierre showed no sign of strain or impatience. He sat quietly puffing on an old pipe.

Eventually, he rose, casually knocked out the dottle from his pipe on his boot heel and treaded it into the dirt floor until all sparks were extinguished.

"C'est l'heure de partir," he said, as he went round to the rear of the truck.

Jeff followed eagerly.

"Jump up," Pierre said briefly.

Jeff climbed up onto the edge of the truck's tray. Carefully he worked his way into the hollow space head first. It was not as cramped as he had expected. He lay face up, on a thin mattress which Pierre had placed there. When he had settled himself into the space, Pierre lifted more crates up onto the truck and stacked them against the opening. He lifted the tail-gate and secured it. Then, on top of the crates, he arranged sacks of turnips and potatoes until the truck was fully loaded and the space containing Jeff was well hidden beneath them.

The barn doors creaked open. Jeff felt Pierre's weight tip the truck slightly as he climbed into the cabin. The engine started up and, with a jerk which threw Jeff back towards the tail-gate, they moved off.

In the confined space, Jeff was thrown from side to side as Pierre drove over the rough country roads. When the truck bumped over a large hole he was thrust upwards then crashed down upon the thin mattress. His whole body was jolted. Even though the ride was so uncomfortable, Jeff was content. The fact that he was once again on his way, acted like strong medicine upon him. His thoughts, they had so often since he had been shot down, turned to Jean. He saw her vividly in his mind, her lovely features, her smiles, her gleaming blonde hair, the impish look which appeared so often on her face. The time passed quickly as he let his mind wander over many of the experiences they had shared.

The journey took slightly more than two hours. They travelled at a slow pace and were stopped at two check points. At the first, when Jeff heard the guttural tones of the German soldiers speaking bad French, fear rose like vomit in his throat. However, it was soon apparent that Pierre was well known as a regular traveller over the road. He joked with the soldiers and they made no attempt to search the truck. Jeff relaxed with a sigh of relief. He found that he had been perspiring.

The truck's engine finally roared into life and it jolted off to the sound of Pierre's shouts of "au revoir" to the soldiers.

At the second check point there occurred a repetition of what had ensued at the first.

Cramped in his hiding place, Jeff was also unable to see out. The crates and boxes creaked around him, but had been secured firmly to prevent them falling in on him. The minutes dragged and the miles slowly passed by. The roughness of the roads near the village gradually eased and Jeff realised that they had come to a major road. The wind thrusts from the passage of other vehicles became more frequent. At last, Jeff knew, from the sounds penetrating to him, that they had arrived at a large town. He hoped it was their destination—Lyons.

He felt Pierre slowly guide the truck through the streets with frequent turns. Eventually, he felt it turn another corner, slow and finally stop, its engine still running. It was reversed and carefully turned into what was obviously their destination.

Eagerly and impatiently, Jeff waited for the crates to be moved. He heard the tail-gate being lowered and the produce at his feet being moved. Light slashed into the darkened space as the crates were pulled away. His two legs were gripped at the ankles and he was dragged out. When he sat on the edge of the truck's tray, he looked down into Pierre's face, creased in a huge smile, and into the face of a short, middle-aged man with a great mane of greying black hair. The latter was clad in a blue shirt with tie and vest and wore a white apron over black trousers. He motioned Jeff into an open doorway behind him.

They were in a small enclosed yard at the rear of a three storied building. High wooden fences and an angled, galvanised iron, skillion roof, which nearly covered the whole yard, concealed them from view from nearly every angle. Empty crates, bottles and discarded tins were piled on all sides.

Quickly, Jeff slid off the truck and slipped through the doorway into a large room which was obviously a storeroom. On shelves, on the floor, a great variety of canned goods, sacks of vegetables and cases of fruit were stacked. Pierre and the storekeeper followed immediately behind Jeff and then closed the door.

Noiselessly indicating to Jeff to follow him, the storekeeper led him between the shelves and opened another door in the side wall of the storeroom. A staircase rose upwards. Quietly, Jeff followed the men up two flights of stairs then along a short passage and up another short staircase which took them into the attic of the building.

The storekeeper closed the door behind them, then turned and held his hand out to Jeff.

"Bon jour, mon ami," he said, a smile curling his large moustache.

In halting English, he introduced himself as Jean Bartolier and explained that he owned the building and conducted a grocery business on the ground floor.

"We had to be silent," he said, "there were German soldiers in the store when you arrived."

Jeff marvelled at the courage of these people who were prepared to risk their lives and the lives of their families to help men like himself to evade capture.

"Monsieur," Jeff replied as he shook Jean's hand, "I appreciate what you are doing for me very much. I will try not to endanger you in any way."

"C'est rien," the storekeeper said. "It is my privilege."

As Jeff said farewell to Pierre at the doorway of the attic room, the thought passed through his mind that his escape through France seemed to consist of a series of "hellos" and "goodbyes" as he was passed from one contact to another. The old man gravely saluted him, like the old soldier he was, then shook his hand firmly and with a quick turn was gone through the doorway.

"I will return soon," Jean said as he followed Pierre.

The room was small and the sloping ceiling followed the roof of the building. It was sparsely furnished with a single bed, a dressing table and a chair and in a corner a length of floral cloth, hung on a length of rope, partitioned off a space in which to hang clothes. Light entered the room through a small square window set in an alcove. From it, Jeff looked down from the front of the building over the old quarter of Lyons. Tall houses and buildings jammed their pointed roofs close to one another. The narrow streets climbed in steps up the steep slopes leading up from the Saone. Chimney pots erupted in their hundreds from the tiers of buildings which formed an immense canvas of red and black.

The chimney pots and the tiers of buildings of Fourviere became a familiar sight for Jeff. He spent three weeks in this room perched in the roof of the grocery store. Jean and his family, which consisted of his wife Marie, a fifteen year old son and thirteen year old daughter, did all they could to ease the tension and to relieve the boredom and frustration which settled upon him. The inaction stretched Jeff's nerves taut like violin strings. The enforced confinement in the small room during daylight hours became nearly unbearable. He improved his French by reading books and papers which Jean brought to him and by practising his vocabulary upon the family. To prepare himself for the arduous trip ahead and to remain fit, he exercised regularly morning and evening. However, as day succeeded day, he became more restless. To pass the time, he even resorted to counting the number of boards in the walls and ceiling of the room and the number of chimney pots visible from the window.

In the evening, Jeff ate supper with the family. This was the high point of the day and assumed a greater importance for him as the days became weeks. The family fussed over him, refusing even to allow him to wash up the dishes. They played cards or helped him with his French pronunication after supper, until reluctantly, he made his way back to his room. As time went by, it assumed more and more, the aspect of a prison cell.

At times, Jeff believed that it was only his thoughts and memories of blonde-haired Jean back on the squadron, which enabled him to remain sane. Several times during his stay, one of the family came to warn him of German patrols in the area. Once, the grocer, in a great state of alarm, hurried him from his room after collecting all evidence of his presence there. He led Jeff to the basement.

"The boche are searching the street," he explained. "They are going from house to house."

As he spoke, he was shovelling coal away from the basement wall. When the wall was clear, he knelt down and eased bricks out of the wall until a space, large enough for Jeff to crawl through, had been opened up.

"Climb through," Jean said, breathing heavily from the exertion. "I will replace the bricks and the coal when you are through. Remain there until I open it up again."

When Jeff had clambered through the hole in the wall, he found himself in a disused replica of the basement he had left. On the other side, Jean quickly replaced the bricks. When the last one had been put in place, Jeff was in darkness. He heard the sound of the coal being shovelled back into place for some minutes, then there was silence.

As he waited, the only sounds he could hear were the thumping of his heart, the scuffling of mice and the muffled noise of traffic, which penetrated from the street above. Sitting motionless on the cold, brick floor, Jeff waited. With nerves on edge, he started each time a mouse scurried across the basement.

367

Eventually, after what seemed hours, but which was in reality only thirty-five minutes, Jeff heard the sound of the coal being shovelled away from the other side of the wall. The bricks were again eased gently out and Jean's face appeared in the opening to Jeff's great relief.

"Vite," Jean whispered, "come through. They have searched here and will be going into that place next."

Immediately after Jeff had crawled through the hole, Jean began to replace the bricks. He was careful that no coal fell through and took pains to fit the bricks perfectly together. Jeff shovelled the coal back into place against the wall.

"Mon dieu, that was close," Jean exclaimed, as he sat down upon an upended crate and mopped the perspiration from his brow.

"That is our escape route," he added.

As they sat in the basement, settling down after the emergency, Jean explained. The whole area was connected in this manner. Fugitives from the Germans, or evaders like Jeff, were able if necessary, to travel through a warren of underground passages, through connecting basements, keeping ahead of German search parties, or backtracking, or escaping from safe exits lower down the slopes. The whole area of the old town, Fourvieres, was united in the underground struggle against the German invader. Lyons was never wholly pacified.

The Germans had searched the building giving no hint as to whether it was simply a routine check or for some other specific purpose. After inspecting every room, including the attic and the basement, they had left, apparently satisfied.

It was a subdued group which sat down to supper that evening. But for the fact that Jean had discovered that the Germans were searching the area, Jeff could have been captured. He had been with the Bartoliers for nearly three weeks.

"How much longer will I be here?" Jeff asked as they sat drinking ersatz coffee after supper.

"It should not be very much longer now," Jean replied. "I have sent word to the group that the Germans were here today."

"I don't want to put you in any more danger," Jeff said earnestly, "you have done too much for me already."

"Nonsense," Marie replied, "we are French and we must do our part."

Jeff did not have long to wait. The day following the Germans' search, two men of the local resistance group visited the store. They brought forged papers and travel documents with them. The photographs which he had given the doctor in the Moreau's farmhouse so many weeks before, were pasted on the forged papers.

He was described in the papers as an Albanian farm worker, travelling to Perpignan in Southern France to take up a job with a fictitious farmer outside the town. The men explained that posing as an Albanian, he should encounter no one who spoke the language and his bad French accent would be excused. It would also serve as sufficient reason for him to refuse to be drawn into unwanted conversations.

Because of the search by the German patrol, it had been decided to move Jeff within the week. It was possible that the Germans had received information that an evader was in the area, or that they were intensifying their campaign against the local resistance. In any case, it was considered safer for Jeff that he be moved south without delay.

Over the following two days, several people visited the store bringing gifts for Jeff. They left them with Jean. Word had spread among the local resistance members about the R.A.F. man. Eventually, Jeff had a reasonably full wardrobe of suit, overcoat, underclothing, spare shirts, socks and a suitcase.

CHAPTER 30

Three nights after their first visit, Georges and Jacques returned. They were in a state of agitation. The small group with which Jeff was to have travelled south had been captured by the Germans, together with the French family who had been sheltering them. It was feared that they had been betrayed. All were being held at Gestapo head-quarters and the French people could only expect death or the concentration camp.

The identity of the informer was not known, so to pro-'ect the grocer and his family, as well as Jeff, it had been decided to move him immediately. He was to be taken to a farm outside Annecy, which was considered safe. He would stay there until further contact was made with him by the resistance.

In the attic room as he bundled his belongings into his newly acquired suitcase, Jeff gazed around, with a strange affection, at the room which had sheltered him for three weeks. He took one last look out the small window at the vista of chimney pots and tiles leading down to the Saone which lay hidden in the misty darkness. With a last glance around, Jeff eagerly left the room and hurried down the two flights of stairs to the storeroom. The Moreaus were there waiting for him. Marie handed him a large parcel of food.

After a tearful farewell from the family, Jeff and the two resistance men made their way out through the rear of the building. They walked quietly down the back lanes and alleyways until they reached the tramway line at the bottom of the slope. The trip by tramway to the railway station was equally uneventful.

Nervously, Jeff entered the large ticket hall of the station with his two companions. It was crowded. The hackles on the back of Jeff's neck rose and his hands perspired at the sight of German soldiers who mingled in large numbers with the French people in the hall.

This was the first time since his escape that Jeff had encountered such a crowd of people. It was also the first time that he had come shoulder to shoulder with groups of Germans.

Nonchalantly, the others urged him forward.

"See the girl in the brown coat ahead of us," Georges said, "You will go up to her and kiss her as though you are old friends. She will be your guide to Annecy."

Looking ahead, Jeff saw an attractive young French woman smiling at them. She was dressed in a warm brown coat, small black felt hat, a red suitcase stood beside her. When they approached, she moved forward, lifted her face to be kissed and then tucked her arm into his.

"I'm Suzanne," she whispered with a smile, "I am to be your guide."

She had already bought tickets for Annecy and gave them to him. In soft whispers, Georges and Jacques gave him their last instructions. He was to act as though Suzanne was his girlfriend and to do everything exactly as she told him. Before leaving, Georges pressed a roll of bank notes into his hand.

"For the journey," he said simply.

Before Jeff could utter his thanks, they had gone, merging quickly into the crowd.

"Allons," Suzanne said as she took up her small case, took his arm and led him towards the barrier.

Vichy police and German soldiers were at the barrier inspecting papers. However, they appeared to be concerned only with passengers for the train going to Marseilles. Jeff showed their tickets and his forged identity card, Suzanne showed her papers and they were through the barrier.

Jeff could hardly speak. The close proximity of the German soldiers did not seem to affect Suzanne at all. She acted as though it had been a perfectly normal occurrence. For Jeff however, it had been a completely new experience. Previously, he had led a hidden existence in France. To openly mix with crowds of people, to come into such close contact with the enemy, brought spasms of fear to him. His legs trembled and he could feel himself perspiring. Suzanne sensed his feelings. She took hold of his arm more firmly. After a whispered warning to be careful and to act natural, she began to talk gaily to him of the fine time they would have in Annecy.

Quickly, they walked through the underground passage

and climbed the stairs to the platform from which their train would depart.

They selected an empty third class compartment, but before the train departed it had filled with a mixed group of French people who took little notice of the young couple sitting together in a corner, seemingly engrossed in one another's company.

It was dark and cold when they arrived at Annecy. As they alighted, Suzanne stopped him with a quiet warning. Three German soldiers stood at the exit checking the papers of everyone leaving the station.

She led him along the platform, past the exit barrier to the station buffet. They walked slowly through it and slipped out the unguarded doorway down the few stairs to the street.

As they walked through the town Suzanne pointed out items of interest including the Carlton Hotel, German headquarters. Twenty minutes after they had arrived in Annecy, they came to and entered a small cafe. They were expected.

"Suzanne, ma petite," a large plump woman, with a mass of hennaed hair piled high on her head, exclaimed fondly, as she enfolded the girl to her ample bosom.

"And this is our English friend," she added, as she inspected Jeff.

"Australien," he corrected with a smile.

They spent two hours at the cafe. While they waited, "Madame", which was the only name Jeff heard the owner of the cafe addressed by, cooked and served an enormous meal. It was followed by steaming cups of strong black coffee which could only have come from the black market. At the end of two hours, as Jeff and Suzanne sat drowsily in front of an open fireplace, a car drove up and stopped in the laneway beside the cafe. Madame motioned them to silence and left the room. She returned with two men. They stated that they would drive Jeff to the farm where he would hide out until his departure upon the next stage of his escape.

As he prepared to leave with the two newcomers, Suzanne went over to him, rose up on her toes and kissed him.

"Bonne chance," she said, "it has been nice knowing you."

"Thank you for everything, Suzanne," he replied, "take care."

He took up his suitcase and followed the others from the cafe. At the doorway, he turned and looked back at the young, seemingly fragile girl, who had so willingly risked her life to help him on his way.

They drove about six miles then turned off onto a narrow minor road leading further up into the mountains. After some time, the driver manoeuvred the car through a gateway set in a high hedge and drove up to the farmhouse nestling behind it.

The farmer and his wife, Etienne and Michelle Renaye, awaited them at the doorway at the rear of the house. They were both in their early sixties, strong and sturdy. After welcoming him, Madame Renaye, in spite of his protests that he had already eaten, set about preparing a meal on the huge black stove which dominated one side of the large kitchen.

In the two weeks he spent with the Renayes, Jeff fully recuperated from his wound and the exertions of his journey. The farm spread over both banks of a small stream on a pocket of level ground. Around the farm, thickly wooded slopes climbed on three sides. In these woods, each morning and afternoon, Jeff went for a run accompanied by the farm dogs. The only time he left the farm area during his stay, was to accompany the Renayes to Sunday Mass in the small nearby village church. They explained that is was safe to do so, because the Germans never attended and the villagers were firm supporters of the maquis.

The exercise, coupled with the good meals, soon had Jeff fit and completely well. He began to feel impatient and anxious to continue.

This was maquis country and in the mountains behind the farm, there were bands which harried the Germans over a wide area. During Jeff's stay at the farm, several members of these bands visited the Renayes for supplies and to give and receive instructions and messages. The isolated Renaye farm was a link between the maquis and the resistance movement.

On the tenth day as he was chopping wood for Madame Renaye, Jeff saw a small car travelling up the narrow road beside the stream towards the farm. Hurriedly, he returned to the house to warn the others.

"This will be news for you, I think," Madame Renaye said calmly.

The small dark blue Citroen drove into the farmyard, belching black smoke from its exhaust. A small middle-aged man, clad in a sombre dark suit, alighted. On his head, in contrast to the severity of the remainder of his garb, he wore a red beret at a rakish angle.

"Bonjour, Madame Renaye," he said warmly as he clasped her hands in his and kissed her on the cheek.

"Bonjour, Robert," she replied, "it is a real pleasure to see you again."

Robert, which was his code name in the resistance, was English. He had lived and worked in France for several years prior to the war. After the collapse, he had returned to England, had joined the Army and later had volunteered for active service in occupied France. After training in England, he had parachuted into this area, nine months previously, to direct and co-ordinate resistance to the Germans. He held the rank of Lieutenant-Colonel and was in overall charge of the resistance in the region. It was obvious that he was held in the highest regard by the Renayes.

He inspected Jeff's papers and declared them to be satisfactory. However, new travel documents would be supplied before Jeff left for the south. He was to retain his assumed identity as an Albanian farm worker, because, although by this time he could speak fluent French, he still had a prounounced accent.

Two days later, Jeff received word from a messenger who rode into the farm on an ancient cycle. He delivered the message and had departed all in a period of only five minutes. Jeff was instructed to be ready to depart that evening. During the afternoon, to curb his impatience, he went for one last run through the woods behind the farm. Upon his return, he packed his few belongings and a large food parcel, which Madame Remaye had made up for him, in the suitcase he had been given in Lyons. Then he sat in the lounge room in the front of the house, gazing expectantly out the window at the road leading up to the farm.

Eventually, in the early evening, two men of the resistance drove up in the same car which Robert had used to visit the farm. They introduced themselves as Pierre and Michel. The latter was to accompany Jeff to Perpignan and would also join him in the proposed escape to Spain. He was going to England, if they succeeded in escaping through France and Spain, with information and to receive further instructions for the local maquis and training in explosives and sabotage. He expected to be returned to the area within six or seven weeks.

After an affectionate farewell from the Renayes, they set off for Annecy.

Upon reaching the town, Pierre guided the car through the back streets to the rear of another cafe. When they entered the kitchen through the rear door, Robert greeted them. He gave Jeff his travel papers and also gave Michel the documents he would need for the journey. As they sat down, around the large kitchen table, to a meal prepared by the woman who managed the cafe, Robert gave them their instructions.

The Germans had a strong control on the station entrance. They made a strict examination of the papers of everyone who went through. To avoid this control, Robert explained, one of the local resistance men, a railway worker, would lead them onto the platform from behind the station. They would be taken there, only when the train had arrived, to prevent their having to wait on the platform.

After giving them their instructions, Robert expressed his thanks to the cafe proprietress, bade them all "au revoir", then left quietly accompanied by Pierre. The old Citroen started noisily and moved off.

Everything went as planned. Their guide, still dressed in his railwayman's clothes, arrived an hour later. He led them through the darkened streets towards the station. They saw the train standing at the platform. Their guide took them round to the rear of the station area and after a short walk beside the railway lines, they climbed up onto the platform unobserved.

"Safe journey," their guide said as he left them standing beside a third class carriage.

They went in and sat facing one another in the corner seats furthest from the doorway onto the corridor.

The journey lasted all the night. Each time the Germans made their inspections of the train, walking in twos and entering every compartment, Jeff and Michel pretended to be dozing or were busy sharing the food parcel Madame Renaye had supplied. Without a word, they handed their papers to the Germans and wordlessly they received them back.

At Narbonne, they left the train and had to wait several hours for the connection to Perpignan. The station was crowded with civilians and German soldiers. By this time, Jeff had become accustomed to the sight and proximity of the enemy troops. No longer did the hackles on his neck rise nor did his hands perspire. However, they avoided the waiting rooms and went instead into the station buffet where they sat and drank ersatz coffee until their train arrived. It was crowded to such an extent that the Germans were unable to walk along the corridors. Their papers were not inspected.

At Perpignan, they passed unchallenged through the station barrier in the midst of a large group of fellow travellers.

Michel led Jeff through the town to a large house in one of the back streets. It was the home of a city official who was also one of the leaders of the resistance. He greeted them effusively and took them to a bedroom on the second floor, on the side furthest from the street.

The official, Jacques Cartier, warned them not to be seen about the house. He explained that the Germans were very active. There was a large detachment of Gestapo in the town. He told them that the area between Perpignan and the Spanish border was a restricted area and heavily patrolled. In the town itself, many French people had been arrested and imprisoned in the Citadelle. Jeff's hopes fell, he feared that after having come so far since he had escaped from Yorker, he could still be captured when so close to freedom.

"No worry," Jacques Cartier said with a reassuring

smile. "We have our ways and means of getting people like you across the frontier."

He took their cases and placed them on the two beds which occupied the room.

"In three nights," he continued, "you will be on your way. Three American flyers will go with you. Your guide will be a Spanish smuggler who knows the area like the back of his hand."

They ventured into the town twice for meals at small cafes. Jeff paid the inflated prices from the roll of notes given him so many weeks before by Georges. They bought what food they could for the journey, using ration cards supplied by Jacques. He also gave them rucksacks in which they could carry the supplies and their belongings. He also procured from some unknown source, short warm jackets for them to wear on the cold crossing of the Pyrenees.

On their second night in Perpignan, they met the Spaniard who was to guide them into Spain. A short, stocky, strong and taciturn man, past middle-age but youthful in his actions, he immediately gave Jeff and Michel a feeling of confidence. In halting French, he calmly and dispassionately, outlined the difficulties which lay ahead of them.

They were more than forty kilometres from the frontier and would have to cross several streams, including the wide Tech River, which was the beginning of the "Zone Interdicte", the forbidden zone. Civilians were strictly forbidden from entering this area without special passes from the German authorities. Without passes, those discovered in the zone would be shot. In the mountains also, the guide said, it was still very cold and the journey would be long and arduous.

Jeff was thankful that he had exercised conscientiously and had run so frequently in the woods behind the farm at Annecy. He felt fit and ready for the long walk ahead.

Before leaving, the guide and Jacques Cartier settled upon a rendezvous point and time for the following evening. It would be on the southern outskirts of the town.

Excitement built up in Jeff and Michel from the time the guide left. This would be Michel's first trip outside France. Both found it difficult to sleep during the night. The following day, the hours seemed interminable. Restlessly, they paced around the house, still being careful however, not to be seen from outside. In the evening, when they sat down to an early dinner with Jacques Cartier and his wife, they found it impossible to eat more than a few mouthfuls each. Excitedly, they pressed Jacques for details of the trip and the difficulties they would encounter. Good naturedly, he endeavoured to answer their many queries.

When the time came for them to leave, they took up their knapsacks, put on their jackets and followed Jacques from the house and through the dark back streets of the town. Eventually, they made their way up a narrow laneway on the southern outskirts. A small group of men waited in the shadow of a building. Hurriedly, Jacques made first name introductions and shook hands with each and the guide. He wished them good luck, then turned and walked away.

When Jacques had gone, the guide motioned to them to gather round him. He gave his instructions in his halting French which Jeff translated for the Americans.

"I will lead," the guide stated, "you will follow, one after the other, behind me. Make no noise and do not smoke. If you hear me give a sharp whistle, drop to the ground and stay quiet."

He paused for a time while Jeff translated, then he continued with unconscious macabre humour.

"If we meet a German patrol, run fast after me. Do not stop, unless you are shot."

When he had completed his instructions, he took the cigarette from his mouth, threw it to the ground and crushed it beneath his espadrille.

"Come," he said, "we have far to go tonight."

The guide, whose name was Sebastian, was evidently very familiar with the route. He set out in the darkness at a fast walking pace. On his back he wore a large knapsack from which came the muffled clink of wine bottles. He apparently, was adding to his fee for leading them to Spain by smuggling in wines also.

Jeff took up the position immediately behind the guide. Michel followed him with the three Americans strung out behind.

Within a short time, it was obvious that the Americans were finding it difficult to keep up the others. It was apparent that they were not fit and their laboured breathing sounded through the still quiet of the night.

They left the roads and were soon making their way through vineyards. Although the ground was flat, it was still soft underfoot from the rain of the previous week. It caught at their feet as they walked, making the effort of walking more arduous. After an hour approximately, during which time Sebastian had paused several times to allow the Americans to catch up, he called a halt in a small clump of trees. Thankfully, the three Americans threw themselves down. Rummaging in their packs, they brought out bottles of wine and drank down large gulps. As they recovered their breath, they began to speak in such loud voices that the guide angrily told them to be quiet.

Bill, a tall, big Texan, seemed to assume leadership of the small group of Americans. From then onwards, he appeared to accept responsibility for their behaviour. He kept them quiet and ensured that the other two did not fall too far behind as they became exhausted. They had been shot down in Flying Fortresses four months previously. The French resistance had picked them up as they fled from the crash site. They had been hidden in Paris for some time before being taken in several stages through France to Perpignan.

After what seemed only a few minutes, Sebastian rose and motioned to them to follow. Slowly, they climbed to their feet and followed him out of the trees.

They went on, with only an occasional short rest, for nearly three hours, when they came to a swiftly running stream. Taking off their footwear, they rolled their trousers above their knees and waded through. The water was bitterly cold. The cold struck into the bone and numbed their muscles. On the other bank, they sat shivering as they dried off and rubbed feeling back into their legs.

As his eyes became accustomed to the darkness and the cloud thinned, Jeff could see that they were travelling through farmlands lying between two roads. Occasionally, they passed close by a farmhouse, but only twice did dogs bark. On each occasion, the guide spurted ahead with a soft Spanish curse. Stumbling in the darkness, they struggled to keep up with him.

Eventually, in the far distance ahead of them, they saw their goal, the Pyrenees. Jeff's heart sank a little. He realised that it would be impossible, at the pace they were forced to travel because of the Americans, to reach the distant rocky ridges before daylight. The Americans were tiring badly, forcing Sebastian to slow his pace and to halt more frequently to enable them to keep together.

It was well after two o'clock when Sebastian led them stumbling down a slope, through clumps of reeds to the bank of a wide river.

"Le Tech," he whispered.

Jeff felt despair drag at him as he gazed out at the swiftly running river. They had crossed a number of smaller streams previously, wading through them with the icy cold water sometimes up to their waists. The Tech however, was much wider, it ran faster and in parts, the stillness of the water indicated a depth they could not wade. It was also too cold for them to swim.

"The river is high," Sebastian said. "We cannot cross here. I will try to find another place to cross."

He took the group along the bank to a high, thick clump of reeds. In the centre, he stamped down a rough circle and told Jeff and the others to remain hidden there, resting, until he returned.

Silently, Sebastian then left them, walking carefully westward along the river bank. In the reeds, Angelo, the smallest of the Americans, a short, Italian-American waist gunner, produced a bottle of marc. The fiery spirits warmed them as they waited in the bitter cold.

They waited for more than an hour before Sebastian returned. he motioned them to silence as he rejoined them.

"Be quiet," he said softly to Jeff," tell the others to lie down and not move. A German patrol is coming this way, they must be silent."

Jeff relayed the instructions to Michel and the three Americans. They crunched down into the reed floor of their refuge. The cold, soggy soil oozed up through the reeds to make their position even more uncomfortable.

A short time later, they heard the sounds of the approaching patrol. The three Germans conversed as they walked. Lying full length on the mat of muddy reeds, they could not see the patrol as it passed their hiding place. They heard the soldiers talking as they went by and gradually, the sounds of their conversation receded as they worked their way further downstream.

In spite of the cold, Jeff was perspiring. Thankfully, he rose, stamped his feet and swung his arms to warm his aching, cold limbs. With a gesture for silence, Sebastian stood up and motioned for them to follow him. He led them out of the reeds onto higher ground up the bank. They went upstream for more than a mile, then once again he took them down to the water edge.

"We cross here," he said. "I will lead and we will clasp hands and make a chain."

Jeff glanced at the river. It was not as wide at this point. There were two fast running channels with a shallow bank separating them. On the far bank, in the darkness, he could see the line of trees indicating the bank and the edge of the "Zone Interdicte."

Following Sebastian's lead, they took off their shoes, socks, trousers and underpants and tied them in a bundle around their necks. The guide then took hold of Bill's large hand and stepped out into the stream. They formed a chain, with Michel in the middle and Jeff at the rear. Slowly, testing the depth ahead of him with a long staff, Sebastian made his way out into the stream. The icy cold water stabbed needles into their bodies. It ran so swiftly that progress was alarmingly slow. Very quickly, they were numbed from the the extreme cold but struggled on. The stony bottom cut at their feet. The first channel was negotiated with the water only slightly past their knees. Thankfully, they stumbled up onto the gravelly shoal in midstream and paused to regain their breath.

"Venez," Sebastian urged after they had clustered together on the bank, "we keep going."

He moved off into the second channel. It was about forty feet wide, but when they had inched their way forward only ten feet, the water was above their waists and deepening. Sebastian turned and led them upstream parallel to the bank. As he forced his way forward, he probed with his staff for a shallower bottom. Fifteen minutes later, after Angelo and Paul, the third American, had both lost their footing and had been soaked in the icy water, Sebastian gestured to them to return to the northern bank.

Dispiritedly, they stumbled back onto the shoal and through the shallow channel to the cover of reeds. They were shivering, their limbs were numb and they were wet. Paul and Angelo were suffering from the effects of their immersion. They sat together, heads down, their arms clasped around their legs with their wet clothing hanging limply from them. The others were more fortunate, but hurriedly they put their clothing on and endeavoured to warm themselves.

Sebastian drew a bottle of spirits from his knapsack. He handed it round and they all drank a large draught. Slowly, they felt feeling return to their limbs.

"We must work our way downstream," Sebastian said, "there is a shallower crossing where the river runs over a wide bank. The rain of the last week has brought it up. We will not be able to cross here."

"Can we reach it before daylight?" Jeff asked.

"Impossible," the guide replied. "We will go down the river bank for one hour to a place where you will stay during the day."

"Is it safe?" Jeff asked.

"As secure as anywhere else," Sebastian said with a wry smile. "Just be sure the others remain quiet and well hidden."

When Jeff repeated the guide's instructions, the Americans immediately complained about the delay. He quickly and firmly overrode their objections.

"Just shut up," he snapped angrily, "if you bastards had bothered to keep fit instead of getting fat and flabby on good French food and wine, we'd be a hell of a long further than we are now. So cut the gripes and follow the instructions."

They made their way out of the reeds, climbed the river bank and in the darkness of the early morning, they followed Sebastian downstream. It was still dark when he called a halt. They were in a small grove of trees on the bank of the river. Below them, reeds grew thickly to the water's edge.

"You will be safe here during the day if you are careful," Sebastian said. "Stay in the trees unless a patrol comes. Then you must go down and hide in the reeds."

After Jeff had translated, Sebastian stated that he would leave them during the day. He had a farmer friend nearby who would supply food and wine for the remainder of the journey. He would stay there during daylight and return at dusk to take them over the Tech and to Spain.

After Sebastian had departed, Jeff and Michel inspected their hiding place. The woods provided only limited security. They quickly realised that it would be impossible to remain undetected by a German patrol which entered the grove of trees. The reeds offered a much safer refuge. They clambered down an eroded water channel into the reeds and stamped down a long narrow line only wide enough for the five to lie head to toe. They would be unseen from the bank above.

As the day wore on, the sun came out weakly through the clouds. They were able to dry their clothes and to ease the aching numbness which had become a part of them. They ate the remainder of the food they had carried with them from Perpignan, sipped at the wine and spirits which Angelo and Paul had brought. Jeff arranged the posting of lookouts on the northern and southern edges of th wood, to give warning of any approaching patrol or French civilians. The tired Americans protested initially, but they took their turns on the one hour shifts. In the time off watch, they lay down thankfully to rest or sleep fitfully on the carpet of leaves which covered the forest floor.

Twice during the long day, German patrols passed through the grove of trees. Each time, the group had sufficient warning to make their way down the bank to the refuge in the reeds. They remained undetected.

CHAPTER 31

As the shadows lengthened in the late afternoon, the group began to worry that Sebastian would not return. Anxiously, they went to the edge of the forest to watch for him. As darkness slowly fell, they became more concerned. Eventually, to their relief, they heard a cautious whistle and the guide emerged noiselessly from the bank of the river. In the darkness three packs on his back gave him the appearence of a grotesque hunchback. He placed two packs on the ground and quietly emptied out the contents. He had brought bread, sausage, cheese and bottles of wine and spirits. The third pack remained on his back.

"For the journey to Spain," he said simply, indicating the supplies.

They divided the food and drink between them and stowed it away in their knapsacks.

"Allons," Sebastian said when the last pack had been tied, "We have far to go."

After leaving the shelter of the trees, they followed the guide downstream, some distance in from the river bank but parallel to it. He took advantage of folds and depressions in the terrain and whatever other cover appeared. After more than an hours easy walking, he led them once again to the river.

"We cross here," he said, pointing down to the river.

The Tech had widened at this point. It was two hundred and fifty yards wide and ran swiftly over a shallow, stony bar. Once again they removed their shoes and trousers and eased their way down the bank to the waters edge.

"It is dangerous here," Sebastian whispered to Jeff. "German patrols are many, especially on the other bank. Tell the others to follow me, ten paces apart and to be very quiet."

Following the guide's instructions they went, one after the other in indian file, out into the icy water. The stony bottom cut into their feet but they waded on. The water rose to their waists at the deepest part, but they struggled across without incident. When they finally reached the southern bank, they dropped exhausted to the ground under the cover of trees. After regaining their breath and wringing the water from their clothing, they dressed and once again followed Sebastian as he carefully led them along barely discernible tracks through the trees.

The hours sped by as they made their way silently through forests and fields, ever watchful for the sign of enemy patrols. They waded through more streams, carefully scouted and crossed a number of roads and followed tracks until, in the early hours of the morning, they came to olive groves. Here the land began to rise into the foothills of the mountains. Walking became more strenuous as they had to negotiate terraces and make their way over rocky stretches and through several groves of trees planted closely together.

The Americans tired badly. Jeff, Michel and Sebastian urged the other three along, but gradually, the heavy breathing and stumbling gait of the others forced them to halt more and more often.

Only once during the night did they encounter a patrol. Sebastian, in the lead, gave a soft whistle and threw himself onto the ground. Fortunately, Michel was immediately behind the guide and was able to warn the others quietly to drop down also and to lie silently until the patrol had passed. The Germans were walking along a track which meandered through the field the group was crossing. There was no cover, but in the darkness they were not seen.

The Pyrenees were now in sight, but despondently, Jeff realised that at the slow pace forced upon them by the Americans, they would not reach the frontier before morning. He began to feel angry towards them. With the frontier so close, he knew that Sebastian, Michel and he could have covered the distance from the Tech to the frontier during the night hours. He knew also, that now, another day would have to be spent on the French side of the border with the ever-present danger of detection by German or French patrols.

In his anger, he became brusque towards the three Americans, cursing them as they lagged behind or when they stumbled and fell. Continually, he walked beside each in turn, urging them to greater effort and speed.

When they left the olive groves behind, the going

became easier for some time. They trudged up tracks through trees, which, while steep, were more easily travelled over. Some time before dawn, they left the shelter of the trees and the rocky slopes of the mountains lay ahead. They passed two shepherds' huts as they climbed. Sebastian left them hidden in bushes beside the track for a short time, while he carefully visited one of the huts.

On his return, he told Jeff that a German patrol had passed only thirty minutes previously. Another patrol would not go through for some time. They would be able to climb higher safely for some hours without the constant fear of stumbling onto a patrol. Each of the Americans was in a distressed state. Tex, who had assumed leadership of the three, although physically in worse condition than the other two, did not complain and endeavoured to encourage his companions to greater efforts. He struggled along with the aid of a stick, his large chest heaving, perspiration dropping from his face, in spite of the cold wind which lashed at them whenever they crossed an unsheltered area. In spite of himself, Jeff grudingly admired the large man. Angelo, the small waist-gunner complained continually, pleading to be allowed to rest. Paul, the third member of their group, stumbled along as though in a coma. His breathing came in gasps, his shoulders hunched forward and he dragged his feet leadenly, one slowly after the other.

After hours of climbing, when the eastern sky began to lighten, Sebastian called a halt. He pointed ahead of them to the distant peaks.

"Tomorrow you will be in Spain," he said, "but there is still much more climbing and much danger ahead."

He allowed them three minutes rest, then told them to move on.

"We will continue for thirty minutes," he said, "then you will remain hidden during the day and we will go on later when it is dark again."

Drawing Jeff aside, he spat out a Spanish curse and blamed the Americans for their slow progress.

"With Michel and you," he said, "we would be in Spain now. I do not like this slow pace, we are in danger all the time we are in France."

In the remnant remaining of the night's darkness, he led them up a narrow animal track beside a rocky cliff-face. Thorn bushes clawed at their clothing and exposed skin. After half an hour, Sebastian led them down, off the track, through thorn bushes to the shelter of a grove of pine trees.

"You can remain here safely," he said, "but be quiet, do not smoke and do not light a fire. There are German frontier posts nearby."

He then stated that he was returning to one of the shepherds' huts, where a friend lived. He would sleep there during the day and promised to return shortly after nightfall.

During the morning, while the others fell into exhausted sleep, stretched out on the soft, leafy ground, Jeff and Michel were unable to sleep. The knowledge that they were so close to the frontier excited them to wakefulness. The sun came out but did not penetrate through the trees. They shared the food and wine which Sebastian had provided and conversed quietly and hopefully of the future. Through the trees, they saw, spread out below them like a map, the area of France over which they had travelled during the previous days. Perpignan and the River Tech lay in the distance. The coast and the blue waters of the Mediterranean were bathed in sunlight. Here and there, tendrils of smoke reached up thin fingers from farmhouses. Otherwise, the whole region seemed without life. As they watched, it seemed incredible that only such a short time before, they had had to inch their way through it in darkness, in danger, and at the risk of their lives.

Jeff felt a feeling of exultation sweep over him. His thoughts returned, as they had so often during the many weeks of his escape, to Jean. He lay back on the leafy floor of the wood, closed his eyes and mentally recalled the beauty of her face and the trimness of her figure. He recalled many of the incidents they had experienced together. When the memory of Paula and Syd's wedding came to his mind, he felt a moment of great sadness. The vivid recollections of the last minutes when Yorker died, with Syd still at the controls of the great plane, brought a spasm of pain which shook through him. He wondered again how the other members of the crew had fared and was thankful that he had come as far as he had. He reached into his pocket, took out his rosary and quietly prayed.

Taking turns at keeping watch, both he and Michel were finally able to sleep for short periods during the afternoon. Throughout the day, the three Americans rested and slept most of the time. They ate and drank water and wine, but were too exhausted to talk, even amongst themselves. After a seemingly endless day, darkness slowly settled over them. As they were becoming anxious that Sebastian would not return, they heard his soft whistle. He slithered down the slope and joined them.

"Bon soir," he called, "how are our invalids?"

Tex, with Jeff's and Michel's assistance, had already forced Paul and Angelo to pack their knapsacks and to prepare for the night's journey. The three of them were stiff and sore and their feet were in bad condition. Tex was in a worse state than the others. Large blisters had burst on his feet and he had torn strips from a singlet to bind them before replacing his socks and boots. In spite of the pain and difficulty he found in walking, he remained the most cheerful of the three and uncomplainingly, he urged the others along the way.

Walking became more difficult. They followed rocky tracks, climbed and slid over bare rock ridges and stumbled through streams which splashed along stony beds. Gradually, as they made their way over the inhospitable terrain, the pace of their progress became slower. Angelo and Paul began to stumble and fall more frequently. Even Tex, who had difficulty walking himself and was in constant pain, failed in his attempts to urge them to greater speed.

They came to a series of ridges which ran at right angles to their path. Sebastian, Jeff and Michel had to assist Angelo and Paul to climb over and down the steep slopes. When Tex could not walk, he crawled on hands and knees, refusing help. A cold wind made conditions even worse, so that, in spite of the exertion, they were all chilled to the bone.

Occasionally, Sebastian called a halt in the shelter of pines or in the lee of a rock face. He passed round a bottle of spirits at each stop, giving all a mouthful to counteract the extreme cold. After a rest of only two or three minutes, he urged them on again, before their muscles stiffened up.

Jeff lost all sense of time as they struggled up the rocky ridges which appeared to become progressively steeper.

In the early hours of the morning, Sebastian called another halt. Once again he passed around the bottle of spirits. After they had all taken a mouthful, he pointed upwards.

"The last ridge," he said rather dramatically, indicating with some satisfaction a steep, bare, rocky slope which loomed above them in the darkness.

He allowed them five minutes respite, then he began the climb up the steep ridge, walking upright with ease. Jeff and Michel had tired, their legs ached from the long hours of climbing. The cold bit into them, their whole bodies seemed masses of pain. The three Americans appeared to have reached the end of their endurance. Even Tex complained that he could go no further, stating flatly that his legs would no longer carry him. Angelo lay crying that it was impossible for him to go on. Paul lay on his back on the cold, rocky ledge, seemingly·oblivious to everything about him.

The guide returned when he realised that no one had followed him. For the first time he became angry. He went from one American to the other in turn, cursing them and kicking them to their feet.

"Pigs," he snarled vehemently, "sons of pigs. Get on your feet. After this ridge there is only twenty minutes walk down to the Spanish frontier. Get on your feet."

Slowly and painfully, they stumbled to their feet, groaning with the effort. Jeff and Michel took their packs from them and added them to their own. Equally painfully and slowly, sometimes upright, sometimes crawling, they climbed the steep slope to the summit of the ridge. It was a bare, rocky, narrow plateau. When they reached the top, they thankfully threw themselves down and gasped the breath back into their lungs.

From this point, to their relief, they found the way to the frontier much easier to travel over. After crossing the bare, rocky plateau, they walked down a narrow track into the cover of dense woods. Even Angelo ceased his complaining. They waded through a shallow stream and made their way along its bank until they came to a long cleared area.

"This is the frontier," Sebastian declared to Jeff. "We have to cross this clearing to the trees on the other side and we are in Spain. Tell the others that they must be very careful here. They must hurry, run across. It is under constant watch by the Germans and Spaniards. There are frontier posts and many patrols."

As he spoke, concealed in bushes on the edge of the clearing, Sebastian carefully scrutinised the open area. Eventually, when apparently satisfied that it was safe to attempt crossing, he stood up.

"Allons," he said, "we cross now. Follow me quickly."

When he finished speaking, he turned and with a long, loping stride, ran across the open space to the distant trees. Jeff repeated the guide's instructions and told the Americans to cross. Angelo went first, followed by Paul. They tried to run, but each stumbled and fell his way to the woods. Tex had fallen down. He sat, propped up against a tree. A tired, wry grimace creased his face.

"I can't do it guys," he whispered. "I just can't. My feet have given out."

With an effort, Jeff and Michel lifted him up onto his feet. They stood one on each side of him, placed his arms over their shoulders and, half-lifting, half-assisting, they struggled and stumbled their way across the clearing to the shelter of the trees.

Once in the forest, they collapsed and lay on the ground, panting for breath for long minutes, before they realised that finally, they had reached their objective—Spain. They had escaped.

Jeff felt a tremendous feeling of relief, of exultation. Although his chest heaved from the exertion, he felt like yelling his joy. He turned to Michel, whose face was split in a wide grin. The French youth crawled over to him and clasped him in his arms.

"We have done it," he laughed, "we have done it."

Sebastian stood above them, breathing evenly, showing no signs of tiredness. He allowed them a short time to recover, then beckoned to Jeff.

"There is still much danger," he said. "You must not be caught by the Spanish police or you will spend months in

Miranda prison. We still have far to go before we are out of danger."

Now that they were over the frontier, they were all in better spirits. Even Angelo ceased his complaining. They were stiff and sore, aching and tired, but eagerly they climbed to their feet to continue on their way. Tex stumbled along on feet which were raw and bleeding. Sebastian led them by narrow tracks and paths down into the foothills below the mountains and onto the plain. Once on the plain, he worked eastward towards the sea. They travelled over narrow roads and paths until they reached the outskirts of a small village.

"We are here," Sebastian said dramatically, as he called a halt in a clump of trees. "Wait here while I arrange for you."

The sun was tinting the eastern sky when he returned. He stated that Tex, Paul and Angelo would be billeted in a farmhouse visible in the distance, where relatives of his lived. Jeff and Michel would be taken to a house on the edge of the village and would wait there until contacted.

At the farmhouse, Sebastian's relatives made them welcome. The farmer's wife, Sebastian's sister, had a warm meal ready for them, a thick broth, which they ate ravenously and they ended the meal with thick slabs of bread and butter and hot, strong coffee.

As they said their goodbyes to the three Americans, Tex placed his large hands on their shoulders.

"Thanks," he said simply, "without you guys, we would never have made it. Vaya con dios."

After leaving the farmhouse, Sebastian led them through tracks and paths around vineyards until they came to a large white-painted house which stood on the outskirts of the small village. He walked up to the front door and knocked. Immediately, the door opened and he ushered them in. After introducing Jeff and Michel to the middle-aged couple who lived there and who obviously shared in his smuggling operations, he gave them his final instructions.

"You will stay here for a day or two," he said. "Be careful not to be seen from outside. You are still not out of danger. The Spanish police, if they find you, could be worse than the French or Germans. Someone from the British consulate in Barcelona will come to organise the remainder of your journey."

He paused and smiled at them warmly.

"It has been good with you," he said, "but I could have done without the other three."

As he shook hands with both of them, Jeff gave him what remained of the money, which he had received, so long ago it seemed, from Georges.

"No, no," he protested, "I have been paid."

"Please take it," Jeff insisted, "It is a small token of our thanks."

Sebastian finally placed the money in his pocket, clasped each of them roughly against his chest, then quietly, as always, he slipped through the door and closed it behind them.

After a long hot bath and soak, they dressed in Spanish styled clothing supplied by the farmer's wife. It was apparent to Jeff and Michel, that the farm was a regular staging post for escapers and others coming from France. When they had dressed, they sat down to a huge meal of highly spiced mutton stew. While they ate, the woman fussed over them until they had eaten everything on their plates. After the meal, they all sat drowsily in front of an open fireplace, sipping a sweet red wine. They were unable to converse, the farmer and his wife only spoke Spanish.

Over the following two days, they recovered from the strain of the journey from France. They lay on their beds, sleeping most of the time. The farmer's wife called them for meals, but otherwise did not disturb them. Early on the second evening, a short, young well-dressed Spaniard came to the house.

Stating that he was an official from the Britich consulate in Barcelona, he interrogated them about their escape. He took down details of Jeff's rank and Air Force number and squadron. He questioned Michel about his activities in the maquis for nearly an hour before he appeared to be satisfied. Eventually, he stood up and prepared to leave.

"I will return tomorrow night," he said in French. "Be ready to leave by 7 p.m. We will walk to an automobile and we will be driven to a railway station near Figueras.

We will board a train there for Barcelona."

Noticing the eagerness on their faces, the Spaniard paused.

"There is still much danger," he said. "In the prison at Figueras at this time, there are ten like you, Johnson. They were arrested by the police. We can do nothing to help them but protest and wait. They are crowded into one cell, they have lice, cannot wash properly or shave and are nearly starved."

Eager to be on their way, Jeff and Michel impatiently waited out the following day. They had recovered from their exertions and to relieve their pent up energy, they walked aimlessly around the farmhouse. Punctually at 7 p.m. the Spaniard returned.

Patiently, he detailed the plan to get them to Barcelona. They would be driven to a railway station beyond Figueras where the three would board a train. They would travel for several hours and leave the train at a small station before it reached Barcelona. They would then be driven by car to the city and would be dropped some distance from the consulate. They would separate and make their way there individually. The Spaniard again impressed upon them the need for caution. They would board and leave the train as it slowed before pulling up to a halt at the stations. Jeff found himself recalling the trip to and from Annecy. He wondered if Suzanne and all the other gallant French people who had helped him were still free.

Everything went as planned. They were driven to the station beyond Figueras by a thin Spanish youth in an old sedan. Huddled together, beside the railway line close to the station building, they waited while their companion allowed three trains to go by. When the fourth appeared, he stood up, quickly gave them each their ticket, which he had bought previously, waited until the engine drew level with them, then moved out.

"This is it," he said, "follow me and watch for when I leave the train at the other end."

As the train slowed down, he ran beside it and climbed up onto the rear platform of a passenger carriage. They followed him in quick succession, onto the platform and into the carriage, where they sat, separated, feigning sleep to avoid conversation with the passengers who came on board at the station.

The journey took several hours. Each time the train slowed down, they watched to see if their guide moved. Eventually, as the train once again slowed, they saw him rise from his seat. As he passed each, he gave them a slight nod of his head. He walked to the rear of the carriage, paused for a moment at the door to check that they were following, then he went out onto the rear platform. They jumped one by one from the train as it slowed in its approach to the station, which they could see lit up ahead of them. Quickly, they grouped together and their guide led them back along the railway track for a short distance, then through a wire fence into a narrow lane. Fifty yards up the lane, they saw a large black sedan.

"We will be in Barcelona in the morning," he said, as he walked with them to the car.

On the way, as they lolled in unaccustomed luxury in the large car, he explained that they would leave it some distance from the consulate. They would then walk there, fifty metres apart. In case they lost sight of him, he gave them detailed instructions of the route to the consulate.

Again they experienced no difficulty. They left the car and with the guide leading, they walked, fifty metres apart, through the streets which were already becoming crowded in the early morning. One by one they came to and entered the building which housed the British consulate. They passed the Spanish policeman on duty in the hallway and climbed the stairs to the consulate.

A pretty young English girl greeted Jeff with a smile.

"Welcome to Barcelona and congratulations on your escape," she said.

They spent three days in Barcelona. They were housed in a nearby hotel, were fitted out with new clothes, were given the necessary papers and were able to get their hair cut. They were then driven to Madrid, to the British Embassy, where Sir Samuel Hoare presided as Ambassador.

Jeff was able to send word to Jean and his parents that he was alive and safe, messages which were brief, without details, but which brought great relief to those who loved him.

After a week in Madrid, they boarded the night train for Gibraltar and England.

EPILOGUE

As he descended from the train onto the platform of Huntingdon station, Jeff saw that nothing had changed there during the months he had been away. The weather worn posters were unchanged, the station buildings still needed painting and the platform and the waiting rooms still appeared to be in need of a good sweeping.

He phoned the Adjutant at Battleson to inform him of his arrival and to request transport. The delight expressed by the Adjutant, when he phoned, brought a feeling of great pleasure and comradeship to Jeff. He asked him to send a message to Jean that he was back, then he went into the bar and ordered a whisky and water.

He sat on the high stool at the bar, hardly touching his drink.

After Michel and he had arrived in the Sunderland flying-boat at Poole in Southern England, after the long flight from Gibraltar, they had been quickly caught up in the clutches of officialdom. They had had to pass through a customs check and had to pay duty on the presents which they had bought in Madrid. It was only through the generosity of the flying-boat pilot that they were able to pay the duty.

An Army captain appeared, obviously informed of their arrival, who took control of them and their meagre baggage. He took them to a waiting car and they were driven to London.

Eventually, they drew up outside a large dark-coloured building.

"Johnson, you get out here," the Captain said, "you are expected. Michel, you stay in the car, I am to take you to your people right away."

The realisation that they were to be separated so quickly,

after all the experiences they had shared together came as a surprise and a shock.

"Can't we stay together?" Jeff asked.

"I'm afraid that's impossible," the Captain replied disinterestedly.

It was evident that argument would be useless. Michel leaned forward and placed his hands on Jeff's arms.

"Au revoir, mon ami," he said, as tears welled up in his eyes. "Thank you for all you did. I will never forget our journey together. We did good, you and me, eh?"

"We surely did, Michel, we surely did," Jeff replied. He was saddened by the thought of losing the companion with whom he had shared so much and with whom, he had faced so much danger.

They shook hands warmly for long moments, then Jeff slowly got out of the car, shut the door and stood there, his suitcase beside him, until they turned a corner. He gave a last wave as the car disappeared. Then, wondering what to expect, he took up his suitcase and went into the gloomy, grey building. It was an old hotel which had been taken over by the Army and which now housed a section of the Intelligence Service. Immediately he had given his name to the Sergeant on duty, he was ushered into a large lounge room. An army major stood in front of a marble fireplace, from which a log fire gave warmth to the room.

With what appeared to Jeff to be an expression of regret, the Major left the fireplace, went over to Jeff and extended his hand.

"Well done, Johnson," he said, "jolly good show."

* * *

The following two weeks were weeks of interviews and interrogations, during which he told and retold the story of his escape to several officers from different branches of the services. He was able to phone Jean once and the sound of her voice brought all the memories of her, back vividly to him. As she whispered her love for him and her relief that he was back and safe in England, he cursed the restrictions imposed upon him, which prevented him from going to her at that very moment. He was permitted to speak to the Commanding Officer of the squadron, Wing-Commander Bolton-Adams and the Intell. Offr. Punch. He was able to phone Paula also, to tell how gallantly Syd had died. He was relieved that Paula had had time to accept the fact that Syd had died. He also cabled and wrote to his parents.

He learned the fate of the other members of the crew. Red's death came as a deep blow. The huge bomb-aimer had always given the impression of being indestructible. Nick was still recovering from his wounds in a German military hospital and Al, Clarrie and Doug were prisoners in a Stalag Luft in Germany. The information had been channelled through the Red Cross only a short time previous to his own return.

Eventually, after more than two weeks, the restrictions were lifted and he was permitted to leave. He caught the first train to Huntingdon, to return to Battleson and Jean.

* * *

Slowly, he raised the glass to his lips and savoured the taste of the whisky. His mind wandered back to the long weeks he had spent in France. Vividly, he recalled the last fight Yorker and the crew had fought before the great plane had plunged on fire, to crash and die on the French countryside. Fond memories of each of the crew came and went.

The stark memory of his fight to the death with the German soldier in the dark lane returned also. He shuddered at the recollection. His arm, which had been cut during the struggle, twitched involuntarily. Fondly, he recalled the happy circumstance which had sent him stumbling and fainting to the Moreau's farm. Through them, he had been put in contact with the resistance who had made his escape possible. He thought with pleasure of the others who had helped on his way through France, Pierre, the courier, the doctor, the elderly couple, the Lamys, Jean the grocer and his family, who had sheltered him for so long, at great peril to themselves, Suzanne and Georges, the Renayes and their farm outside Annecy and Jacques Cartier and his wife at Perpignan, who had made the final stage of his escape possible. He marvelled again at the courage they had and prayed that they would continue to live in "safe houses."

Into his musings as he sat at the bar, there intruded the sound of a motor engine approaching at high speed. It neared the station, then, as the driver apparently endeavoured to change down gears prior to stopping, there was a crashing and clashing of the gears. The engine stopped abruptly.

"Jean," Jeff said to himself, a smile curving his lips. Eagerly, he stood up. He had only taken one step towards the door, when a trim, blond-headed girl clad in W.A.A.F.'s uniform hurtled through the doorway. Glancing quickly round the bar, Jean saw him. Racing over to him, she threw herself into his arms, tears streaming down her lovely face.

"Jeff, Jeff, you great goon," she cried as his arms went round her and he squeezed her closer to him. She raised her face to his.

"You've lost weight," she whispered.

She placed a finger on his face and ran it down the lines etched in beside his mouth.

As he bent down and kissed her, his arms tightened around her and his tears mingled with her's.

A great feeling of peace, happiness and contentment swept over him.

· He was home.